SOMEHOW, SOME WAY,
HE WAS GOING TO SAVE HER

Stuart pushed the door open a crack and squeezed through. "Claire?" he whispered, stepping into the inky blackness of the unlit cell.

She was there, huddled on a mattress, staring at him with huge, terrified eyes.

"You shouldn't be here," she croaked. "It's not good for your chest for you to be moving around so much."

Stuart closed his eyes, knowing that he'd never cared more for anyone on earth than he did for this woman who, despite her terror, was worried about his wound. "My chest is fine. I had a good nurse."

A sound somewhere between a chuckle and a sob escaped her, and Stuart squeezed her hand reassuringly. "Don't cry, Claire. I'm going to get you out of here."

As he reached out, his hand brushed her waist, and with an abrupt movement he circled its small circumference and pulled her up against him. "I'm not going to let them kill you!"

"But why? I'm a Confederate patriot, and you're a Yankee officer."

"That's true," he conceded, his lips hovering a breath above hers, "but what's more important is that you're a woman and I'm a man." Lifting his hand to her cheek, Stuart guided her mouth toward his, lowering his lips to hers and kissing her with a desperate passion.

JANE KIDDER

PASSION'S CAPTIVE

ZEBRA BOOKS
KENSINGTON PUBLISHING CORP.

ZEBRA BOOKS are published by

Kensington Publishing Corp.
475 Park Avenue South
New York, NY 10016

Zebra, the Z logo, Heartfire Romance, and the Heartfire Romance logo are trademarks of Kensington Publishing Corp.

First Printing: October, 1993

Printed in the United States of America

To Manos and Ann Fourakis,
who showed me where
Louisa May Alcott lived.

And to
Bill and Stella Pence,
who showed me
the real way to eat lobster.

Thanks, guys!

Chapter One

"What's that?"

"What's what?"

"*That.*"

The bedraggled soldier clad in the tattered remnants of a Confederate private's uniform pointed down the road. "That there."

"I don't know," his companion said, shielding his eyes against the bright Georgia sun. "Looks like a pile of rags."

"Yeah, a pile of *blue* rags." Drawing his gun, the first soldier slowly advanced.

"What are you doin', Jim?"

"I'm gonna investigate."

"Investigate? Are you nuts? It could be a trap."

"Ain't no trap, Clyde. Ain't nobody around for miles, Yank or Reb."

Clyde squinted hard at the object lying in the road ahead of them. "Looks like a Yank to me," he noted. "Hell, Jim, we're desertin'! What business is it of ours?"

Jim had walked far enough down the road by now that he could clearly make out a man's form. "It *is* a Yank," he agreed. "But, I think it's a dead

Yank, and if he's got his rucksack with him, there may be somethin' in it we can use."

A dawning of understanding crossed Clyde's coarse features, and he hurried to catch up with his friend. "Maybe he's got money," he enthused. "Real money. Not our stuff."

"Exactly," Jim agreed. "And food, too."

The two men continued their wary approach, guns drawn and senses alert. Reaching the prostrate man, Jim nudged the body with his foot. It didn't move.

Squatting down, he grabbed the man's shoulder, rolling him over. The front of the soldier's blue uniform was soaked with blood. "He's sure enough been shot, but whoever did it musta took his rucksack."

"Damn!" Clyde swore, still standing a few paces back. "Is he dead?"

Jim looked at the Yankee's ashen face and nodded. "'Pears to be."

"Let's check his pockets," Clyde suggested. "Maybe whoever got him missed somethin'."

Setting down his gun, Jim began patting the soldier's pockets, smiling with satisfaction when he felt a flat object inside his shirt. He unbuttoned the placket and gingerly lifted out a bloody wallet, flipping it open and checking it for money. Digging into one of the compartments, he lifted out several gold pieces, holding them aloft and grinning up at Clyde. "By God, you're right! The bastard's carrying a small fortune in gold."

"Hallelujah!" Clyde crowed, squatting down next to his friend and grabbing the gold pieces out of his hand. "Check and see if there's any more."

Jim eagerly searched the wallet, but to his disappointment, the only items left inside were a crumpled letter and the man's identification papers. These he unfolded, quickly scanning them and then whistling softly through his teeth.

"What is it?" Clyde questioned.

"Do you know who we got here?"

"Yeah, a very rich, very dead Yankee."

"You're almost right," Jim agreed. "A very rich, very dead, very *famous* Yankee."

"Famous? What'd ya mean?"

"This here is Captain Stuart Wellesley of the Fourth Massachusetts."

Clyde shrugged. "So?"

"So?" Jim snorted. "You mean you ain't never heard of Stuart Wellesley?"

"Well, pardon me all to hell, but no, I ain't never heard of no Stuart Wellesley of the Fourth Massachusetts."

Jim shook his head. "Sometimes you're so ignorant I can't believe you're my best friend."

Clyde's eyebrows snapped together with offense. "I ain't neither ignorant, and I'm real sick of you sayin' that just 'cause I can't read and you can. But, okay, Mister Know-It-All, since I know you're dyin' to, why don't you tell me who Stuart Wellesley is?"

"He owns Wellesley Shipping," Jim said knowingly. "It was in all the newspapers. This here fella is the one that designed part of that *Monitor* ship the Yankees used in that big battle with our *Merrimac*. The newspaper said it was his idea to use revolvin' turrets for the guns. He *gave* the design to the Federals—wouldn't even take money for it. Then, to top it all off, he turned around and enlisted, 'stead of stayin' safe up north. Yup, Clyde, this here is a genu-ine Yankee hero."

Clyde grinned. "Well, now, he's a *dead* Yankee

hero, and we got his money. Should get us back to Tennessee in real nice style."

At that moment, the *dead* Yankee hero emitted a long groan, causing both men to jump back and yelp in startled terror.

"Jesus Christ, Jim, he ain't dead!"

Snatching up his gun from where he had set it on the ground, Jim again trained it on Stuart Wellesley while bending over to lay an ear on his bloody chest. "Damned right he's not," he said excitedly. "The bastard's still breathing!"

"Well, let's finish him off!" Clyde suggested, cocking his pistol and pointing it at Stuart's head.

"Hell, no, Clyde! We don't want to kill him."

"Why not?"

"'Cause he'll be worth a fortune if we take him back to Fort McAllister and turn him over to the commander. I just told you, he's a hero, and the Yanks will probably pay big money to get him back."

"Why the hell should we take him back to the fort?" Clyde whined. "We just lifted a fortune off him, and there likely wouldn't be nothin' in it for us even if we did take him back. Besides, if they find out we robbed him, they might make us give the money back."

"They ain't gonna find out we robbed him, 'less you go braggin' to somebody about it, and you never know, there might be a reward in it for us if we turn him in."

"There ain't gonna be no reward for turnin' in a shot-up Yankee," Clyde argued. "The commander will just say it's our patriotic duty and our reward is knowin' we aided the Cause. I say, forget it. We've waited a long time for the chance to desert, and we finally got it. So let's just leave him here and get on with our desertin'. He'll be dead soon enough anyway."

"No," Jim said stubbornly. "We're takin' him back."

"Jim, we ain't even got a horse, and the fort's five, maybe six miles back! How do you think we're gonna get him back there? And look at him. He's gut shot. He won't live long enough for us to make it. Let's just go!"

"We're takin' him back," Jim insisted. "We'll take turns carryin' him, and if he dies 'fore we get there, then he dies. But I still think there might be some sort of reward for bringin' in somebody this important, and if there is, I aim to get it." Rising to his feet, Jim holstered his gun, then bent over and hoisted the unconscious man onto his shoulders. "Come on."

Clyde snorted with annoyance but nodded, knowing he was too much of a coward to make the trek all the way back to the Tennessee hills without his sharper-witted friend. If Jim was determined to make this crazy journey back to Fort McAllister, he'd just have to accompany him. But for the life of him, he couldn't see why they were going to risk their lives to retrace their steps with a half-dead Yankee in tow. It made no sense. No sense at all.

Fort McAllister, located near the mouth of the Ogeechee River, just a few miles south of Savannah, had long been a formidable Confederate stronghold. Even now, in the late autumn of 1864, the fort still housed over two hundred gunners and was securely held by Southern forces.

But despite the seeming security of the fort,

Commander Major George Anderson knew that his outpost was one of the few remaining impediments to William Sherman reaching his ultimate goal of conquering Savannah. It was only a matter of time before Sherman's massive forces traversed Georgia and attempted to lay waste to the fort.

It was this knowledge, coupled with numerous intelligence reports involving Captain Stuart Wellesley's contributions to the Union's military efforts, that made Clyde and Jim's arrival at the fort that evening such a propitious occasion.

Major Anderson was seated at the cluttered desk in his office when one of his aides, Sergeant Joshua Tucker, arrived to tell him about their newest prisoner.

"You're sure it's Stuart Wellesley?" Anderson asked excitedly.

"Yes, sir," Tucker answered.

"And he's not dead?"

"No, sir, but he's badly wounded. One of our medics had a quick look at him and said he's amazed the man is still alive."

"Who brought him in?"

"Two of our men. Privates from a Tennessee regiment that's bivouacked here at the fort."

"Where did these men find him?"

"Out on the north road."

"What were they doing out there?"

"I don't know, sir. Actually, I think they may have been deserting and had a change of heart."

"Did he have any documents on him when he arrived? Dispatches, maybe?"

"No, sir. The men said that when they found him lying along the side of the road, he had no rucksack. The only thing we found on him were his identification papers."

Major Anderson digested this information thoughtfully. "You don't think the men would have stolen any papers Captain Wellesley might have been carrying, do you?"

"No, sir. I think if the captain had money on him, they may have taken that, but I don't think they would have had any interest in anything else. In fact, the only thing that seems to interest them now is whether or not they'll get a reward for bringing him in."

Major Anderson snorted. "Reward! Their reward is having the opportunity to serve our Cause. That's reward enough."

"Yes, sir." Sergeant Tucker smiled wryly.

"So, Sergeant, what condition is Captain Wellesley in now?"

"Grave, sir. It appears the two soldiers took turns carrying him on their shoulders to bring him here. Being jostled that much certainly didn't help his wound."

"Where is he wounded?"

"Shot near the stomach, sir. We'll know more once the doctors have a chance to conduct a more thorough examination."

"I want this man given the utmost care," Anderson directed, scraping his chair back and rising to his feet. "He must not be allowed to die. It is vital we have the opportunity to interrogate him."

"Sir," the sergeant hedged, "our medical supplies are very limited, as you know. I am confident the doctors are doing everything possible to save Captain Wellesley, but it will be a long time before the man is well enough to interrogate, even if he does survive."

"He *must* survive!" Anderson said vehemently.

"And we must do everything in our power to make sure he does. I want you to go find Lieutenant Emery and send him to me. I will put him personally in charge of the prisoner's care. Is Wellesley currently in a ward?"

"Yes, sir."

"Then after you find the lieutenant, notify the physician in charge that Captain Wellesley is to be removed immediately to a private room."

"But, sir! We don't have any private rooms anymore. All of them have been converted into wards."

"Well, unconvert one, Sergeant! Captain Wellesley is to be put in a private room and assigned a round-the-clock nurse."

"A nurse, sir?" the sergeant asked disbelievingly.

"Yes, Sergeant, a nurse. But you needn't worry about that. I will have Lieutenant Emery arrange it. Now, go. And, don't dally, Tucker. Time is of the essence."

"Yes, sir," the sergeant nodded, backing toward the door. "If I might ask one question, sir?"

"What is it?" Anderson responded, his voice impatient.

"We have many wounded prisoners in the hospital who are higher ranking officers than this Captain Wellesley. What is it about this man that makes him so important?"

"Stuart Wellesley happens to come from one of the most wealthy and influential families in the United States. He also is responsible for the design of several very successful gunboats. I have heard that he is in the confidence of both Grant and Sherman. If that is the case, it makes him one of the most valuable prisoners we have, regardless of his rank. Does that answer your question, Sergeant?"

14

"Yes, sir," the sergeant answered, saluting smartly. "I will find Lieutenant Emery and deliver your message immediately."

"I told you, Tucker, we pulled the ball out of him. That's all we can do. You know the blockade has exhausted our medical supplies. Why, our own boys are dying by the hundreds right under our noses. Why should we worry about one Yankee prisoner?"

Sergeant Tucker sighed. The last thing he needed was an argument from Dr. Marks.

It had taken him the better part of a half hour to finally find Lieutenant Emery. Who would have thought the man would be taking a bath? Another five minutes had been spent trying to convey to Emery the urgency of Anderson's summons and to persuade the man to give up his turn in the tub.

After that, he had headed directly over to the hospital, and now this damn sawbones was wasting more time arguing with him!

"I'm telling you, Doctor, my orders come directly from the commander. Captain Wellesley is to be put in a private room and no effort is to be spared to save him."

"A private room," Marks grumbled. "Where does Anderson think we are, for God's sake? We've got men stacked up like cord wood in here and he wants to give some damn Yankee a private room? Well, it can't be done."

Tucker's lips thinned. "Should I tell the commander that you are refusing to obey his direct order, Doctor?"

Marks expelled a long, irritated breath. "No, I

15

guess not. Just find a couple of men to come over here and help me clean out this storeroom." The doctor jabbed his thumb in the direction of a door behind them. "I suppose there aren't really enough supplies left to warrant taking up a whole room anyway. We'll put Wellesley in there."

"Good," Tucker responded, breathing a sigh of relief. "I'll go muster some men to help you."

Dr. Marks nodded and turned away. "One goddamn Yankee prisoner," he muttered. "It's going to take half the night to rearrange all this stuff—and for one goddamn Yankee who probably isn't even going to live till morning. God, how I hate the military!"

Lieutenant John Emery stood in front of his commanding officer's desk, his hair still damp from his unfinished bath. "You sent for me, sir?"

"Yes," Major Anderson replied. "As I'm sure you know by now, two of our men brought in a very important Union officer tonight."

"Yes, sir. Sergeant Tucker told me. Is it really Stuart Wellesley?"

"Apparently, although I've not seen him myself."

"I've seen a picture of the man," Emery supplied. "I'll be happy to go over to the hospital and verify that it's really him."

"Good. I know you understand how vital he could be to us, so I am putting the responsibility of his care into your hands."

"My hands, sir?"

"Well, not directly," Anderson chuckled, "but you know how overworked the doctors are, and I can't be sure they'll devote the attention to Captain

16

Wellesley that he's going to need. I'm looking to you to make sure that happens."

Emery nodded, not quite sure how the commander expected him to care for the prisoner. Anderson's next comment answered the question.

"Your first order of business will be to engage a full-time nurse to care for him."

Emery's eyebrows rose. The commander really was serious about saving this Yankee. "Do you have someone specific in mind, sir?"

"Yes. Tomorrow morning I want you to ride into Savannah and deliver this letter." Pausing, Anderson held out a sealed envelope.

Major Emery glanced down at the name scrawled on the front of the envelope, his eyes widening in surprise. "Archibald Boudreau, sir? Claire Boudreau's father?"

"None other," Anderson smiled. "He is an old friend of mine. I'm sure after he reads this letter, he'll convince his daughter of the importance of her cooperation."

"Claire Boudreau," Emery murmured, "the Angel of Atlanta." Looking skeptically at the major, he asked, "Do you really think she'll agree to take care of a Yankee? She's well known to be one of the South's staunchest daughters."

Anderson shrugged. "That's what the letter is for. But if my personal plea doesn't work, then it's up to you to convince Miss Boudreau that it's her duty as a Confederate patriot to aid us in this endeavor. It's well known that she distinguished herself last summer in Atlanta as one of the finest nurses ever to assist at the receiving hospital, so she's definitely my first choice to nurse Captain Wellesley back to health."

17

"I'll try my best, sir," Emery promised. "Between the two of us, we will convince Miss Boudreau to assist us."

Major Anderson crossed two fingers and held them up. "Let's hope so, Lieutenant. Let's hope so."

Chapter Two

"No. I absolutely refuse."

Claire Boudreau shook her head vehemently and sat down on the edge of a delicate tapestried chair in the parlor of her Savannah home. "I'm sorry that you wasted your morning riding all the way here, Lieutenant Emery, and I assure you, I'm not trying to be difficult, but I'd sooner die than spend one minute nursing a Yankee officer."

Lieutenant John Emery gazed mournfully at the woman seated across from him and fidgeted with his hat, trying desperately to think of another argument that might sway her. "Miss Boudreau," he began, his voice conciliatory, "I understand your feelings, really I do, but Major Anderson himself is making this request."

"I realize that," Claire nodded, "and I appreciate the major's predicament, but what he is asking is impossible. I simply cannot do it."

For a long moment, she looked away, gazing out the front window of her home and unknowingly presenting Lieutenant Emery with a heart-stopping view of her perfect profile.

In a city renowned for its beautiful women,

Claire Boudreau was one of Savannah's greatest sources of pride. At twenty-two, she was in the full bloom of young womanhood. She was tall and slender, with a bosom that was surprisingly full and a grace and bearing about her that could only be termed regal. Her skin had the golden cast to it that only true redheads can boast, and her emerald green eyes sparkled with mischievous spirit and a *joie de vivre* seldom still seen in southern women after four years of hardship, worry, and deprivation.

Enchanting, thought John Emery, gazing at her in unabashed appreciation. Enchanting, intriguing, and impossibly stubborn. His breath caught in his throat as Claire again turned toward him, her full, expressive mouth set in a determined line.

"Please extend my apologies to your commander," she murmured, her soft voice with its well-modulated southern lilt flowing over him like warm honey, "but I simply cannot fulfill his request."

Emery sighed wearily and rose to his feet, casting a pleading look in the direction of Claire's father.

Archibald Boudreau drew on his pipe and returned the soldier's gaze solemnly. "Claire," he boomed, hefting his generous bulk out of his chair, "perhaps I might have a word with you before the lieutenant leaves."

"Certainly, Papa," Claire nodded, knowing what her father was going to say, but far too well bred to argue with him in front of a stranger. Together, father and daughter left the parlor and stepped into Archibald's library, closing the double doors behind them.

"Papa," Claire began, before Archibald could say a word, "please don't ask me to do this. I know that's what you're intending, but I cannot nurse a Union officer."

Archibald looked at his willful daughter pensively, knowing from long experience that arguing with her would net him nothing. "I'm not going to try to talk you into doing something your conscience tells you is wrong, daughter. I just want to be sure that that same conscience of yours won't be pricking you in the future when you think about the fact that you've refused to aid the Cause in these days of our greatest need."

"Papa, that's not fair. Why, I stayed at the hospital in Atlanta until Sherman was practically on the courthouse steps. I changed bandages, cleaned bedpans, mopped brows, and listened to hundreds of those poor men whisper their last words into my ear until I was so sick and tired I just wanted to lie down on a cot and die with them."

"No one knows better than I what a contribution you made in Atlanta," Archibald agreed. "But the Confederacy needs you again, Claire. You're a good nurse and a better confidante. You just said yourself that the dying boys often whispered their final secrets into your ears. According to Major Anderson's note, the government thinks this Captain Wesley—or whatever his name is—"

"Wellesley," Claire corrected.

"All right, *Wellesley*, then. As I was saying, if the government thinks this Captain Wellesley is carrying information vital to the safety of Savannah, and that of all the women in this county, you are the most suitable to extract that information from him, then I don't see how you can refuse."

"What they are asking me to do is spy!" Claire cried.

"What they're asking you to do is your patriotic duty!" her father shot back. "And these days, many of us are being asked to do things that do not come easily to us."

"But, Papa, he's a Yankee! I don't think I could stand to be around a Yankee all day, much less care for one. Certainly you should understand! The Yankees killed your son!"

"I'm perfectly aware of that, Claire. But your brother died in the line of duty standing up for what he believed was right. A father learns to accept the loss of a son when his death is for a cause as sacred as ours."

"There's David, too," Claire persisted. "Have you forgotten him?"

"No, and I know you haven't, either. But, like it or not, Claire, your fiancé has been missing for nearly two years now, and you have to face that fact and get on with your life."

"And you think taking care of an enemy officer is 'getting on with my life'?"

"I think extracting vital military secrets from an enemy officer is a step in the right direction to help bring this conflict to an end. And bringing it to an end is the only way David will ever be released, if he is indeed still alive and being held in some Northern prison."

"Oh, Papa, I just don't know," Claire moaned, covering her face with her hands and shaking her head miserably. "I'd have to . . . to *touch* him!"

Archibald laughed, a deep rumbling sound that trailed off into a wheezing cough. "Claire, Yankees don't feel any different than Confederates do. Men are men. They're all the same under their uniforms."

Claire exhaled a long, shuddering sigh and slowly raised her head. "I can't do it, Papa. I'm sorry, but I just can't."

Archibald shrugged in resignation. "All right, dear. I'll go tell the lieutenant that your decision hasn't changed."

"Thank you," Claire whispered, sinking down onto a plush sofa as her father left the room.

She couldn't do this. As much as she wanted to please her father and help her country, she just couldn't! Why, every southern lady knew that Yankee soldiers were hardly more than animals. The stories of their brutal atrocities toward the citizens of the Confederacy were legion, and the whispered rumors about what Sherman's soldiers had done to innocent women who had protested the pillaging of their homes were enough to send most maidens into a swoon.

Although Claire was not the swooning type, and despite the fact that for months in Atlanta she had assisted in sewing up parts of men's bodies that even long-married women of her mother's generation had probably never seen, she still recoiled from the thought of actually touching a Yankee. How could Major Anderson request this of her and, even more shocking, how could her father agree? It was unthinkable.

Archibald walked slowly into the foyer where Lieutenant Emery still stood. "I'm sorry, Lieutenant," he began, then paused as he heard the library door open behind him. Turning, he saw Claire hurrying toward him, chin thrust out, mouth set.

"All right, Lieutenant," she announced, "you win. You can tell Major Anderson that I will be at Fort McAllister first thing tomorrow morning. Please ask him to have some sort of quarters set up for me. If Captain Wellesley's condition is as grave as you say, I will plan to stay at the fort until he either improves or dies."

John Emery was so relieved that he wasn't going to have to take a negative answer back to Major Anderson that he hardly noticed the hard edge that had crept into Claire's voice when she said the word "die."

"Yes, ma'am," he beamed. "I'll make sure everything is ready for you by tomorrow morning. And, Miss Boudreau?"

"Yes?"

"On behalf of the commander, thank you."

For the first time, Claire's beautiful face relaxed into a smile. "You're welcome, Lieutenant. I'll see you tomorrow—unless, of course, Captain Wellesley succumbs during the night. If that happens, please send me a message so that I don't drive all the way out to the fort for nothing."

Emery nodded uncertainly, not quite knowing how to react to Claire's unfeeling attitude toward the Yankee officer. "Of course, Miss Boudreau," he said, backing out the front door onto the portico. "If that unfortunate turn of events occurs, I'll be sure to let you know."

Claire looked at John Emery quizzically. "Unfortunate, Lieutenant? The man's a Yankee hero. For all I know, he might be the one responsible for the death of my brother or the imprisonment of my fiancé. I'd hardly call his death 'unfortunate,' sir. I'd call it a blessing."

And, turning away, she headed up the staircase, calling to her maid to find her satchel.

"Miss Boudreau," Commander Anderson smiled, "thank you so much for coming."

Claire nodded graciously, her thick auburn hair gleaming in the morning sunlight. "I am always willing to help our Cause, Major, no matter how odious the task."

Lieutenant Emery had advised his commanding officer of Claire's initial abhorrence when asked to nurse Stuart Wellesley, so the major was not surprised by her callous statement. "I understand your reluctance to care for this man, Miss Boudreau, and believe me, your sacrifice will not go unrewarded."

"I'm not looking for a reward," Claire smiled, immediately regretting that she had obviously made the major feel guilty. "If I can assist in Captain Wellesley's recovery so that you can interrogate him and, hopefully, find out information that will aid the South, that is reward enough."

Major Anderson smiled back at her, relieved that the beautiful woman appeared to be coming around. He had heard much about Miss Boudreau. Many of the soldiers bivouacked at Fort McAllister were natives of Savannah, and the stories they told over the lonely campfires of Claire's beauty, elegance, and charm were legendary.

In fact, so renowned was she that Anderson had felt compelled the previous night to gather his troops and inform them of her imminent arrival, warning them in the strongest possible terms that any ungentlemanly behavior toward her would result in swift and severe punishment.

Now, as he stood outside his office, beholding Claire Boudreau's beauty for himself, he was glad he had issued the warning. She was indeed one of the most striking women he had ever seen, and there was no doubt that she could cause trouble among the soldiers just by her very presence.

But Anderson's smile betrayed none of the concern he was feeling as he himself picked up Claire's satchel and politely offered his arm. "If you will come with me, Miss Boudreau, I will show you to your quarters."

"Thank you, Major. It will just take me a moment to change my clothes and then I'll be ready to attend my patient."

Anderson escorted Claire over to the hospital building, leading her down a long, narrow hall to where an office had hurriedly, the previous night, been emptied of its furniture and turned into a makeshift bedroom for her. The tiny room was spartan, its only accoutrements being a cot, a small table and chair, and a wooden stand upon which sat a basin and pitcher for washing. A pole had been hung in one corner to hold her clothes, and it was beneath this that Major Anderson set her satchel. "I'm sorry your accommodations aren't more luxurious," he apologized, "but I'm afraid this is the best we could do on short notice."

Claire laughed, a soft melodic sound with just a trace of huskiness to it, guaranteed to make a man's blood race. "This is fine, Major," she assured him. "I don't require much in the way of luxuries anymore, and I doubt I'll be here long enough for the size of the room to bother me."

Anderson relaxed, liking the woman more with every passing moment. "Whenever you're ready, ma'am, Lieutenant Emery will escort you to where we're housing Captain Wellesley." With a final nod, he backed out of the room, closing the door softly behind him. Enchanting, he thought as he strolled back toward his office. Just like everyone says. Absolutely enchanting.

"He's right in here, Miss Boudreau." Lieutenant Emery opened the door to Stuart Wellesley's room and stepped aside, allowing Claire to pass.

She walked into the room, sweeping the small cubicle with a cursory glance. There was nothing in it except a bed, a hard chair, and a small table upon which sat a washing basin and a brown bottle.

Stepping forward, Claire reluctantly looked down at her charge, but nothing she had ever heard or read about him could have prepared her for what she saw.

Perfection. Absolute masculine perfection.

Captain Stuart Wellesley was the most handsome man Claire had ever laid eyes on, and for a moment, all she could do was stand and stare at him.

His hair was inky black, and even though it was dirty and unkempt, she could see that it was thick and soft. Under his matted black beard, his face was pale, its chiseled planes ashen, with an unhealthy gray pallor alleviated only by two bright fever spots high on his cheekbones. His nose was straight and narrow, and his lips, though cracked and dry from his illness, were full and so perfectly formed that they looked like they had been shaped by a sculptor's blade.

As she stood looking down at him, Stuart drew a strangled breath, his chest shuddering with the effort. Claire's eyes widened at the monumental effort the unconscious man was making to continue to live. Peering more closely at him, she saw his lips tighten as he again struggled to inhale and, for a moment she forgot he was the enemy. With a sharp jolt of surprise, she realized that Stuart Wellesley wasn't just one of the faceless blue invaders from the north. Rather, he was simply a man—a man who was, despite all odds, somehow finding the strength to stave off death's beckoning finger, a man who was in grave need of her help.

"Has he regained consciousness at all?" she asked, turning toward Lieutenant Emery who stood near the door.

"Not that I know of. Dr. Marks is in surgery, but he should be here soon. I'm sure he'll be able to answer any questions you might have."

Claire nodded and turned back to Stuart, folding back his blanket and deftly unbuttoning the top of his longjohns. What she saw made her draw in her breath in alarm. Although his chest was covered with a large bandage, angry red streaks spread out past its edges, betraying the fact that his wound was badly infected. The bandage itself was bloody and in dire need of changing.

"Hasn't anyone done anything for this man since yesterday?" she gasped.

"I'm sorry, ma'am, I don't know. The hospital is not among my responsibilities. In fact, this is the first time I've been here, except to direct the men in cleaning out this room for Captain Wellesley."

"We have to change this bandage immediately," Claire announced. "Will you bring me some of that rolled linen from over on that table, and some fresh water, too?"

Emery swallowed hard. Did Miss Boudreau expect him to assist her in bathing and changing Wellesley's bandages? The mere thought made his stomach roll sickeningly. But before he could open his mouth to protest, Claire whirled around and gave him a hard look, causing him to swallow his words and hurry over to the little table where the clean bandages were piled.

"What's in that bottle, Lieutenant?"

Emery picked up the brown bottle, glancing at the small amount of liquid inside and then reading the front label. "Laudanum," he answered.

Claire snorted. "No wonder he's unconscious, although it's probably for the best. He wouldn't be able to stand the pain if he was awake."

Carefully, she peeled back the edge of the blood-soaked cotton, grimacing at Stuart's moan of pain as the grimy bandage ripped open a newly formed scab.

Claire had spent weeks working in one of the huge receiving hospitals in Atlanta, and she knew a mortal wound when she saw one. Now, looking down at Stuart Wellesley's chest, she was sure there was no hope for him. She could see where the surgeon had probed to remove the bullet from where it had lodged against Stuart's breastbone but, far from helping to save the man, the doctor's ineptitude may have cost him his life. The wound was jagged and torn, and it was obvious

29

that no care had been taken when Stuart had been crudely stitched back together.

"Dear God, Lieutenant!" Claire cried. "This man needs a doctor's attention right now. Please go get him."

"I just told you, Miss Boudreau," Emery said placatingly, "he's in surgery, and he said he'd come as soon as he could."

Claire looked up into the lieutenant's troubled eyes and immediately felt chagrined that she had taken him to task over a situation he'd not been part of. "I'm sorry," she muttered, "but there is just no excuse for the lack of care Captain Wellesley has received. This bandage looks like it hasn't been changed since he was operated on, and an infection is setting in that is probably going to kill him. Considering how important the commander seems to think this man is, it's hard to believe no one has shown any concern for his well-being."

"Miss Boudreau," Emery sighed, "please try to understand. We are terribly understaffed, and we have almost no medications left. I'm sure Dr. Marks did the best he could under the circumstances. There are many, many Confederate soldiers housed here at the fort's hospital, and I think they are the doctor's first concern."

"I do understand," Claire relented, "but Captain Wellesley is going to die unless he gets some serious attention fast. Yankee or Confederate, he deserves better than to lie here and suffer from sheer neglect."

Emery's eyebrows rose in surprise at Claire's impassioned defense of the man who, twenty-four hours ago, she had sworn she wouldn't lower herself to touch.

"I'll see if I can find the doctor."

"Thank you," Claire nodded, again leaning over Stuart's chest. "While you're about it, see if you can find any antiseptic that I could use to clean this wound. If nothing else, bring me a bottle of whiskey."

"Yes, ma'am," Emery responded, then turned on his heel and tore out of the little room, breathing a long sigh of relief as he left the cloying confines of the hospital and stepped out into the fresh morning air. Hurrying down the steps, he nearly ran down the hapless Dr. Marks, who was on his way into the building.

"Is the nurse in there with Wellesley?" Marks asked.

"Yes," Emery affirmed, "and if I was you, I'd be very, very careful."

"What d'ya mean?"

"She's very upset about the condition of her patient, and I think she holds you responsible."

"Me? What have I done?"

"I think it's more what *hasn't* been done that's bothering her."

"Jesus Christ," Marks grumbled, "this is just what I need. Some damn woman lecturing me about some damn Yankee officer who should by rights be dead anyway. What'd you say her name was?"

"I didn't, but it's Boudreau. Claire Boudreau."

"Claire Boudreau?" the doctor gasped, his eyes widening. "Oh, no! I heard about her from the doctors in Atlanta. She nearly drove them crazy with her demands. Now, why the hell did Anderson foist a virago like that off on me?"

"Because," Emery chuckled, "she's the best nurse in the state of Georgia, and the major does *not* want Stuart Wellesley to die!"

"Well, shit," Marks swore, slapping his hat on his leg in frustration and continuing up the stairs. "I have the worst damn luck of any man in creation. Claire Boudreau. Claire Boudreau! Of all the women in the Confederacy who could have come here and nursed this damn Yankee, I have to get her. Why me? Now, I ask you, why me?"

As Dr, Marks disappeared through the hospital doors, Lieutenant Emery stood for a long time looking after him and laughing. Then, loath to bring the beautiful Miss Boudreau's wrath down on his head again, he hurried across the parade grounds, wondering where in hell he was going to find a bottle of whiskey.

Chapter Three

"Where am I?"

Claire jerked awake, her heart pounding in reaction to the unexpected sound of her patient's voice. Hurriedly rising, she stepped up to the side of Stuart's bed, unconsciously straightening her rumpled dress and patting her thick hair into place.

"Well, Captain Wellesley," she said, careful to keep her voice impersonal, "you're finally awake."

"Where am I?" he repeated, his gray eyes glazed with pain and confusion as he stared up at her. "Who are you?"

"I am Miss Boudreau," she answered coolly, "and, you're in the Fort McAllister hospital."

He's a Yankee, she told herself sternly, tamping down the inexplicable gladness she felt that he had revived from his stupor. He might have killed your brother!

"Fort McAllister?" he mumbled, looking groggily around the small room.

"Yes," Claire affirmed, keeping her back to him as she fumbled with the laudanum bottle and a spoon. "You are a prisoner of the Confederate

States of America.''

She sneaked a covert look over her shoulder to see what his reaction would be to this piece of news, but his eyes were again closed and she wasn't sure he'd heard her.

Walking back to the bed, she said sharply, "Captain? Did you hear what I just said? You're a prisoner.''

Slowly he reopened his eyes, blinking several times as he tried to focus on her. "My chest . . .''

"You've been shot,'' Claire explained, her voice gentling. "I know you're in terrible pain.''

Weakly he nodded.

"Here. Take some of this. It will make you feel better.'' Pulling the stopper out of the bottle, she poured a liberal dose of laudanum into a large spoon and held it out to him. For a moment, Stuart stared at the spoon, then shook his head and closed his eyes again.

"Captain Wellesley, open your eyes and take this medicine.''

Again Stuart's eyelids fluttered. "What is it?'' he croaked.

"It's not poison, if that's what you're worried about. Just take it.''

"What is it?''

"It's laudanum. Now, please open your mouth.''

"No. No laudanum.''

"Well, fine!'' Claire snapped, turning away to return the bottle to the small table by the bed. "Have it your way.''

"Laudanum's bad,'' Stuart added vaguely, then his eyes closed, and with a ragged sigh, he again lapsed into unconsciousness.

"Stubborn fool,'' Claire muttered, angrily trying to pour the laudanum back into the bottle, then snorting with annoyance when her shaking hands caused her to spill the precious liquid all over the table.

What was it about this man that upset her so? she wondered. Why, she was shaking like a debutante at her first cotillion! "It's just because he's a stupid, stubborn Yankee," she told herself. But as she again glanced over her shoulder at him, she knew it was more than that.

In the two days she'd been at the fort, she'd heard a great deal about Captain Stuart Wellesley from the officers stationed there. Apparently the man was a bona fide hero of the Union, decorated again and again for bravery and highly regarded by top officials of the Yankee government. The northern newspapers exploited his deeds until tales of his heroic triumphs, as well as his personal charm and intelligence, had made him an almost legendary character. But Claire knew that this information, even when coupled with repeated visits from Major Anderson to check on the progress of his star prisoner, was not what was causing her such unease. Rather, it was Stuart Wellesley himself.

She had spent the last forty-eight hours at his bedside, straightening his blankets, sponging him off, and trying to think of a way to force some liquid through his parched lips. But even these back-breaking tasks had not filled all the hours, and much of her time had been spent simply sitting and staring at him while he lay unconscious. As hard as she'd searched his face for some imperfection she could gloat over, there simply wasn't one. Nor could she find a flaw on his sun-bronzed body. It was downright infuriating that every time she tended his wound, she was struck anew by the beauty of the smooth, taut skin on his chest and the corded perfection of the rippling muscles which covered his stomach and continued down into the shadowy area below his waist. That part of his anatomy she refused to look at—even though she was shockingly curious to know just how far his physical perfection extended.

But even the beauty of his body was not all that was holding her in thrall, and though she would have sooner died than admit it, she found herself harboring a growing respect for the Yankee's spirit and will to live.

From the moment she had first seen him, Claire had been convinced that Stuart's wounds were mortal, that it was only a matter of time till he finally gave up the torturous battle to continue breathing. But each time he appeared to be beaten, each time his breathing slowed to the point that she was sure she had lost him, he would suddenly draw another rasping breath, filling his wounded lungs with air and defying the hand of death that hovered so near.

After two days of watching his struggle, Claire had to admit that if sheer dint of will could keep a man alive, Stuart Wellesley was not going to die.

Her grudging respect for her patient confused and frightened her. This man was not at all what she had expected. Yankees weren't supposed to be handsome and brave. Yankees were devils incarnate—ugly, brutal beasts who had gleefully invaded a land to which they had no claim, raping and killing innocent women and children for the sheer delight of it. Could this one be so different? Of course not, she told herself sternly. Handsome and brave he might be, but Stuart Wellesley was still a Yankee.

And despite his good looks and valiant struggle

for life, she had been convinced that when he finally regained consciousness, he would live up to her biased expectations and be stupid or rude or crass. But he hadn't displayed any of those characteristics, either. Despite the fact that his clipped northern accent had grated on her ears, his questions had been softly voiced and even his refusal of the laudanum reasonable and polite.

In actuality, Claire didn't believe in laudanum, either, having witnessed, firsthand, its stultifying narcotic effects and frightening addictive powers. Obviously, Captain Wellesley was also aware of the drug's dangers, so she couldn't really fault him for refusing it.

Throwing down the dirty medicine spoon, Claire returned to her hard chair, frowning at her charge. "You may be right not to want to take the opiate, Captain, but the next time I pour whiskey into that wound of yours, you'll wish you had. You're going to feel like all the fires of hell are licking at you."

The thought that her next ministration would cause her patient excruciating pain should have given her a feeling of smug satisfaction. It didn't. In fact, instead of looking forward to seeing Captain Wellesley pay for his stubborn refusal of the narcotic, her mind was busily trying to think of some way to dull the pain she knew he was going to suffer.

"The message . . . got to get it to Sherman."

Claire's eyes snapped open as the sound of Stuart's hoarse cries roused her from a deep sleep. Shaking her head in an attempt to clear her foggy mind, she rose groggily from her chair and staggered over to the bed. Looking up at the small window near the ceiling, she realized it was late. The moon was already high in the black sky, and the single candle she had lit earlier had guttered and gone out.

Quickly, she struck a match and relit the candle, then gasped in alarm as she looked down at Stuart. His eyes were open, but he stared up at her unseeingly. His hands moved restlessly, flexing and closing as he clutched at the edge of his pillow. He had kicked his blankets off in a vain attempt to cool his scorching body, but even from where she stood, Claire could feel the heat emanating from him.

Suddenly, he raised himself on an elbow and clutched at her skirt with such force that he almost pulled her down on top of him. "The message!" he cried, his eyes wild with delirium. "Can't fall. Can't!"

"Captain Wellesley," she said, desperately trying to pry his fingers loose from her skirt. "Captain Wellesley, let go. I'll get some water for you."

Despite her words, Stuart just held on tighter, staring up at her with a look so fierce that she feared he was going to lunge for her throat.

"Captain, please lie back and relax. Everything is all right. You needn't worry."

"The message!"

"Shh," Claire soothed, "the message has been delivered."

"To Sherman? He knows?"

"Yes," she nodded, reaching out to run gentle fingers through his tangled hair. "The general got your message. Everything is fine."

For a moment, Stuart looked up at her, his eyes

seeming to clear as he searched her face for the truth. Then, his hand suddenly dropped away and he fell back against the pillows. "Hot," he moaned. "My chest . . ."

"I know. I'll get some water and sponge you off."

"No!" he cried, again latching on to her skirt. "Don't go. Don't go!"

"I won't go," she promised. "I'm just getting some water. Relax, Captain. Everything is going to be all right."

Again he released her, seeming once more to lose consciousness. Claire seized upon her freedom to dash over to the table and pour some fresh, cool water into the basin. Racing back to the bed, she perched on the edge and, dipping a clean cloth into the water, began to stroke his fiery body. She dabbed the water against his forehead, then moved the cloth down to his mouth, running it against his parched lips and squeezing it slightly in an effort to force some water into his mouth. He lay still as death.

"Don't you die on me, you damn Yankee," Claire ordered frantically, as if her warning could force him to keep struggling. But as she flipped open the two top buttons of his longjohns, she knew she was fighting a losing battle. Despite hot compresses and whiskey, the infection was worsening—the flesh near the wound taking on a grayish color and putrid smell—the first warning signs of the dreaded gangrene.

"Oh God," she wailed, biting her lip hard to keep from screaming with panic, "I'm going to lose him."

Again Stuart's eyes jerked open, startling Claire so much she let out a shrill little cry.

"The message. I can't fall!"

"You won't fall," she promised, running her fingers lightly over his temples. "I won't let you fall. Just relax. Sleep."

With a swift, harsh movement, he reached up and grabbed one of her hands, pulling it down to his mouth and feverishly kissing her fingers. "Don't go," he pleaded, his eyes beseeching. "Please, don't go."

The sensation of Stuart's hot mouth against her fingers made a tremor run all the way up Claire's arm, and with a little shriek of alarm, she yanked her hand out of his. "Don't do that, Captain."

"Stay with me," he croaked, heedlessly grasping her hand again and pressing it against his bearded cheek. "So sweet . . . so sweet. Sweet little Paula. So soft. You smell so good."

Claire stared down at him in astonishment, oblivious to the fact that he was again holding her hand. Paula. Who was Paula? She knew from what the soldiers at the fort had told her that Captain Wellesley wasn't married, but could it be that he had a sweetheart safely tucked away somewhere up north, waiting for him to return to her? Somehow this thought made him seem a little more human, and Claire, to her great surprise, felt a wave of sympathy for this unknown girl who was most likely never going to see her beau again.

Stuart's hand dropped away as he again closed his eyes, but without even realizing it, Claire continued to stroke his flaming cheek. "If only I had some quinine," she sighed, then looked around guiltily, as if worried that she might be caught caressing the enemy's cheek. With a snort of self-derision, she jerked her hand back, saying fiercely, "If you're going to die, why don't you just get it over with, so I can go home?"

But uttering these hateful words, far from assuaging her guilt, pricked her conscience like a spear, and she quickly grabbed the cloth from the basin and trickled some more cool water over Stuart's lips. "Don't die, Captain Wellesley," she begged, "please don't die!"

From far away, Stuart heard her. That voice. That soft, lilting woman's voice coaxing him to breathe, to drink, to open his eyes. He wanted so badly to please her, but it was just too much effort. It would be so much easier just to let go. Just to drift and let the pain slip away. But her voice wouldn't let him. Every time he thought he wouldn't bother taking another breath, she was there, whispering to him from out of the mists, encouraging him to inhale just one more time.

He wanted to touch her, wanted to feel her skin next to his, but he didn't know where she was. He had reached for her . . . many times . . . but he could never seem to find her. He could hear her, he could even smell her. She smelled like roses and talc and a unique spicy scent he couldn't identify. He loved the smell of her. It reminded him of Colorado springtimes and his baby sister, Paula. Her scent made him want to touch her . . . kiss her. It had been a long time since he'd kissed anyone. If he asked her, might she let him? He opened his mouth, trying to speak, but nothing came out.

But it didn't matter, because she was touching him now. He could feel her hand on his cheek. If he turned his head a little, he could kiss her palm. With herculean effort, he turned his mouth toward her hand, but before he could make his lips form the kiss, she pulled her hand away.

41

Don't. Don't pull away! Please! Just one kiss. Why did she always pull away?

The night wore on endlessly as Stuart lapsed in and out of consciousness, rambling on about a message and begging Claire not to leave him. Hour after hour she bathed his dry, hot body until, by dawn, she was so exhausted she could hardly hold her head up and her back felt like it might snap in two from the exertion of fighting off his fearsome grip when the delirium sent him into a frenzy.

The sun had barely risen when Major Anderson walked into the small room and looked from the exhausted Claire to the thrashing Stuart. "Miss Boudreau! Why is there no one here assisting you?"

"Major Anderson!" Claire gasped, clamping her hand against her chest in surprise, "I didn't hear you come in! You gave me a terrible start."

"I'm sorry, Miss, I didn't mean to scare you. I was just shocked to find you here alone. Didn't Dr. Marks come by to spell you?"

"No. I think there were some wounded soldiers brought in last night that he was tending."

"Then he should have sent someone else. How long has it been since you've slept?"

"I don't know," Claire answered truthfully. "A while."

"This is appalling," the major blustered. "I will have someone sent immediately to relieve you."

"That's not necessary."

Anderson looked at her in surprise. "Miss Boudreau, you need rest."

"I know, but my patient . . ."

"How is Captain Wellesley?" Anderson interrupted.

"Not good, I'm afraid. An infection has set in, and nothing I do seems to help. He needs medicine."

"I know," the major nodded dismally. "They all do, but the Yankee blockade is so tight now that there is no hope of getting anything through."

Anderson's face betrayed his sense of futility and anger, and Claire felt a surge of anguish. The damn Yankees. The damn Yankees! Then she turned back toward Stuart, too exhausted and overwrought to think about the fact that he was one of the group she was cursing.

"Has he said . . . anything?" Major Anderson asked from behind her.

Claire turned back to the officer. "As a matter of fact," she responded, her voice low, "he has."

"Really?" Anderson's face brightened. "Come over here and tell me." Leading Claire over to a corner of the room, he whispered, "What has he said?"

"He keeps mumbling about a message."

"A message? What kind of message?"

"I don't know," Claire admitted, "but I think he was carrying a message to Sherman when he was ambushed."

"Sherman! But, the men who found him said he had no papers on him except his identification."

"I don't know about that," Claire shrugged, "but in his delirium he keeps talking about how he has to deliver his message and that he can't fall. I think he believes he's still on his horse."

Anderson glanced toward Stuart, respect evident on his face. "He's a brave soldier. I wish we had more like him on our side." Turning back to

Claire, he added, "Do you think you could entice him to tell you what the contents of his message were?"

"I don't know. He's out of his head with the fever. I doubt that he would even hear me if I asked."

Anderson frowned. "Then we must do everything possible to bring him through this crisis. I'm positive that he has information that would be invaluable to the future of this fort and to Savannah. You *must* try to get it out of him."

Claire nodded, but her expression remained skeptical.

"What's the matter, Miss Boudreau?"

"It's just that right now he's so ill . . ."

"I understand that, but surely there's some way to get him to answer a simple question!"

"I don't think so, sir," she responded, unconsciously rubbing at the persistent ache at the base of her spine.

Anderson gazed at her for a moment, feeling guilty for pressuring her as he noticed the weary stoop of her shoulders and the dark smudges of exhaustion beneath her eyes. "All right, Miss Boudreau," he relented. "You're the nurse. Since you say Captain Wellesley is in no condition to be interrogated yet, why don't you go get something to eat and perhaps take a little nap? I will send one of our orderlies to spell you."

"But, Major . . ."

"Don't argue with me, Miss," Anderson interrupted, holding up a staying hand. "I insist. I appreciate your loyalty to your duty, but you'll be no good to us if you collapse from exhaustion, and God knows, we don't need you in the hospital, too."

Claire smiled, a weary grimace that didn't reach her eyes before it faded. "You have a point. All right. As soon as you can find someone to sit with the captain, I'll do as you say."

"Thank you. I'll have someone sent immediately."

It was hours later when Claire awoke. Glancing out the small window of her cubicle, she was amazed to see the sun setting. Springing up from the bed, she quickly ran a comb through her hair, twisting it into a semblance of a chignon, then tied a clean apron over her rumpled dress and hurried back down the hall to Stuart's room.

One glance at her patient lying so still and pale against the sheets and she knew it was over. The fever had finally broken.

"How is he?" she whispered to the young orderly sitting in the hard chair next to the bed.

"Better, ma'am," he answered, quickly rising. "The fever broke about two hours ago, and he's been sleepin' since. I know you told me to call you if there was any change, but since it was a *good* change, I didn't want to bother you."

"Has he said anything? Asked any questions?"

"No, ma'am. Not a word. Rambled on some before the fever broke. Somethin' about some message. I really couldn't make out much of what he was sayin'. But ever since, he's just been sleepin' like a babe. Hardly's moved at all, as a matter of fact."

Claire smiled at the eager young man, making his heart leap into his throat. He'd heard a lot about the beautiful Miss Boudreau in the last few days, and he knew it would do much to raise his stature with his fellow soldiers when he went back to his tent and told them he'd actually talked to her.

Quietly approaching the bed, Claire bent over, placing her ear close to Stuart's face. His breathing was deep and even, and when she lightly touched his forehead, it was cool and damp. With a smile of satisfaction, she turned back to the beaming soldier. "I don't know what you did, Private . . ."

"Buckman, ma'am, Jonas Buckman."

"Private Buckman," Claire acknowledged, "but whatever it was, you saved his life."

"I didn't really do nothin', ma'am. Just sponged him off like you told me and dribbled water against his lips."

"Well, it worked," Claire praised. "He's past the crisis."

"I know it's probably none of my business, ma'am, but I don't understand why we're all workin' so hard to keep this Yankee alive. I thought the point of this war was for us to kill 'em, not break our backs savin' 'em."

Claire smiled, having had much the same thought during the past few days. "We're all just following orders, Private. Captain Wellesley is an extremely valuable prisoner to our Cause, and Major Anderson wanted everything possible done to save him."

"Well, ma'am," Buckman grinned, "I guess we did that."

"Yes, Private, I guess we did."

For a long moment, the young man continued to stand and smile at Claire, until finally she cleared her throat and said, "I wonder if you would deliver a message to the major for me?"

"Yes ma'am, I'll be happy to."

"Tell him that Captain Wellesley has come through the crisis and that hopefully by tomorrow morning, I should be able to have a . . . a conversation with him."

"A conversation, ma'am? Why in the world would you want to have a conversation with a Yankee?"

Claire frowned, having no intention of telling this young man of her agreement with the major to interrogate Stuart. "Just please deliver my message, Private," she said quietly.

"Yes, ma'am," he responded, blushing with embarrassed chagrin at her gentle rebuke. "Right away. You can count on it, ma'am." Bowing profusely, he backed out of the room, then turned on his heel and raced down the hospital corridor, hell bent on finding his commanding officer and delivering the beautiful lady's strange message.

Chapter Four

Stuart opened his eyes and stared in bewilderment at the dingy gray wall in front of him. Where was he? Shifting slightly on the hard bed in which he lay, he emitted a sharp gasp of pain. Why did he hurt so much? Every bone in his body ached, and his chest felt like he had been shot.

Shot! Suddenly it all came back to him. Riding toward Savannah to bring Grant's message to Sherman, the Confederate guerrillas leaping out of the bushes along the side of the deserted road, the fiery explosion of pain when one soldier fired a bullet into his chest at nearly point-blank range, and then the struggle to try to stay on his horse until he reached his destination. Finally, he remembered falling, and the world turning gray, then red, then ultimately black as he embraced the welcoming oblivion that reached out for him.

He could recall nothing after that—except a vague memory of a beautiful woman's soothing voice and soft, cool hands on his body. But that must have been a hallucination, for certainly no such creature would reside in this small, dank place where he was now housed.

He shifted again on the uncomfortable bed as another vague memory pricked at his brain. Someone had told him that he was a prisoner—but who? He seemed to remember that same woman's voice, but she had to be a hallucination, so perhaps he was wrong.

Then, what *was* his situation? Where *was* he and how long had he been here? Most important, how was he going to find Sherman in time to deliver his message, now that he was wounded? And where was the message? In his boot—his left boot. But where were his boots? Vaguely he looked around, hoping to spot them somewhere in the room, but to his disappointment, they were nowhere to be seen. If only someone would come to him, maybe he could find out where they'd been put.

He looked to his left, noticing a small chair pulled up next to the bed, a book lying open, face down on the seat.

The woman had red hair—no, not red. Copper. And her hands were gentle . . . so gentle when she touched him. He had wanted to kiss her, but he'd never gotten the chance. Or had he?

Stuart shook his head, trying desperately to clear the mist from his brain. Why was everything so unclear? His mind was so foggy, it was almost like he was drugged.

Drugged. That was it! Laudanum. He remembered arguing with the beautiful red-haired woman that he didn't want any laudanum—and she had gotten angry. So she *was* real. He was sure of it. But where was she now? Why was he alone in this strange place? Slowly he closed his eyes, too tired to think anymore . . .

*   *   *

"Captain Wellesley, wake up. You must try to eat something."

There it was again. That voice. That soft, drawling voice telling him to open his eyes. Willing himself to obey the command, Stuart opened his eyes, blinking several times as he tried to bring his surroundings into focus.

"I've brought you some broth."

He turned his head in the direction of the voice. It was her. She was standing next to his bed, looking just as beautiful as in his dreams.

"Good morning," he croaked, surprised at how hoarse he sounded.

"Good morning," she answered, unsmiling. "Can you sit up?"

"I . . . don't know."

"Well, you must try. You need to eat, and I can't feed you if you're lying flat."

Why was the beautiful woman angry? He remembered her being so sweet, so kind. What had he done to make her mad?

With a great effort, he braced his elbow behind him and tried to raise himself up on the pillows. The pain that immediately shot through his chest and shoulders was overwhelming, and with a moan he sank back against the pillow. "I can't," he whispered.

"Captain Wellesley," the woman snapped, obviously annoyed by his refusal to comply with her command, "you must sit up. Here, I'll help you."

"Who are you?" he asked, trying hard not to yelp with pain as she dragged him up into a half-seated position. "How do you know my name? Where am I, and how long have I been here. Where are my boots?"

"See if you can eat some of this," she responded, ignoring his stream of questions.

He clamped his jaws firmly together. "No. Not until you answer me."

She frowned and set the cup of broth down. "You don't seem to understand, Captain. I don't care whether you eat or not. As far as I'm concerned, you can lie here and starve to death. But Major Anderson seems to feel differently. Now, please, open your mouth."

"Who is Major Anderson? Where am I? Where are my boots?"

"Open your mouth!"

"All right! This wide enough for you?" Stuart opened his mouth, displaying all thirty-two of his perfect white teeth.

Claire was furious. To think that two days ago she had practically been in tears, thinking this damn Yankee was going to die on her, and now here he was, demanding she answer stupid questions about his boots and making fun of her attempts to feed him. Well, she'd feed him, all right! Whirling away, she grabbed the cup of broth, then turned back and poured most of it into his open mouth.

Stuart immediately started to choke, and his harsh, wracking coughs brought such a searing pain to his wounded chest that he doubled over, screaming with agony.

Realizing what she had done, Claire gasped in horror, throwing the cup on the floor and pounding him on the back.

"Don't do that!" he yelled, coughing and groaning as he clutched his chest and fell back into the pillows. "You vicious little bitch! My God, are you trying to kill me?"

"No! I mean, I'm sorry! I didn't mean to . . ."

"Sure you didn't," he gasped, closing his eyes and trying to draw a breath. "Get out of here!"

"But Captain . . ."

"Get out!"

Her hands clapped to her mouth in genuine terror, Claire turned away and fled the room. She ran headlong down the hallway until she reached her tiny quarters. Slamming the door behind her, she leaned against the wall, closing her eyes and willing herself not to cry. What would Major Anderson do to her when he heard about this? She had no doubt he'd send her home in disgrace and her father would never forgive her.

Although she believed Captain Wellesley had deserved a setting-down for his obnoxious behavior toward her, even she had to admit that throwing soup in his face was a little extreme. If he told Dr. Marks what she'd done, she'd never be able to defend her actions. Still, if the man hadn't been so presumptuous in demanding answers from her and refusing to eat, she'd never have been provoked into such an unladylike act! What right did he have to question her? He was nothing more than a dirty Yankee prisoner, and now that he was fully conscious, she could see that he was just as crass and boorish as she'd first suspected he'd be. It was obscene that she was going to be forced to apologize to him, but how else could she keep him from reporting her? And even though she'd be delighted to be released from this intolerable assignment, she'd never be able to explain her outrageous actions to her father.

Taking several calming breaths, she patted her hair and straightened her apron. Then, with shaking hands, she opened the door to her room and retraced her steps down the hall. Coming to a halt in front of Stuart's room, she stood for a long moment, trying to shore up her courage enough to face him again. Finally, she lifted her chin in a gesture of defiant hauteur and reentered the room.

Her willful expression quickly faded to one of genuine regret, however, as her eyes lit on him. He was lying just as she'd left him, his eyes closed, his mouth white with pain. His previously clean longjohns were now discolored from the spilled chicken broth, and she could see greasy splotches on his neck where he'd tried to wipe it off and missed.

She cleared her throat nervously and walked over to the bed. "Captain Wellesley?"

"Go away," he groaned, not opening his eyes.

"I'm truly sorry. I shouldn't have done what I did."

"You're right. Now go away." Still his eyes remained closed.

"Let me clean you up."

"No."

"Please, Captain . . ."

"I'll take care of myself."

"But, you can't! You're hurt and . . . and you can't even see where the soup spilled."

"I can *feel* where the soup spilled."

Walking over to the small table, she poured some fresh water in the basin, then returned to the bed and perched on the edge. "Let me do it."

This time he didn't argue. Encouraged, she wrung out a clean cloth and began gingerly dabbing at his greasy neck.

"You're never going to get me clean by patting me," he said irritably, his eyes still closed.

"I'm sorry," she murmured, nearly choking on

the apology. "I just didn't want to hurt you."

Slowly, he opened one eye and looked up at her. "Lady, nothing you could do at this point could hurt me more than that little stunt you just pulled."

Claire paused in her ministrations, her lips thinning in annoyance as she threw the cloth back into the water and planted her hands on her hips. "Captain Wellesley, I've tried to apologize for my behavior—and that's more than I can say for you."

"Me?" he barked, both eyes suddenly snapping open. "What the hell do I have to apologize for?"

"Well," Claire blustered, completely disconcerted by his clear gaze, "if you hadn't been so rude and obnoxious, you wouldn't have angered me."

"Rude and obnoxious? You think it's rude and obnoxious for a man to ask where he is? All you would have had to do is give me a straight answer and all of this could have been avoided." With a feeble gesture, he indicated the greasy mess covering him and his bed.

"May I remind you, Captain, that I already answered your questions—several days ago. And may I also remind you that you are a prisoner here and you have no right to ask anything."

"A prisoner," Stuart repeated, turning his head away and staring at the wall. "So I *was* captured."

"I told you all this before!"

"Pardon me, Miss, if I don't remember," he retorted sarcastically, again training his cool gray eyes on her. "It appears I've been a little under the weather, and perhaps it temporarily affected my mind."

"You're right," Claire conceded. "You've been very ill."

Stuart continued to look up at her, but when it

became clear she was not going to offer any more information, he sighed wearily and tried again. "Will you please tell me where I am and how long I've been here?" he asked simply.

"You're at Fort McAllister, outside of Savannah. It's my understanding that two of our Confederate soldiers found you unconscious by the side of the road and brought you here almost a week ago."

"Why didn't they just leave me to die?"

"Because you're Stuart Wellesley!" she blurted, then instantly regretted her words as she saw a small smile tip the corners of his mouth.

"You're right about that," he nodded, surprised to find how pleased he was that she seemed to know of him. "But I still don't understand why they didn't leave me to die."

"Because everyone in the South has heard of you," Claire admitted, infuriated that she couldn't seem to pull her eyes away from his. "They probably intend to use you in a prisoner exchange."

"Maybe, but it's my guess that they are more interested in interrogating me than trading me."

Quickly Claire turned away, again wringing out the cloth and vigorously scrubbing at his neck. Stuart gently grasped her wrist, staying her hand. "I'm right, aren't I?"

"I'm sure I don't know," Claire answered evasively. "Is there some reason they'd want to interrogate you?"

"I'm sure I don't know," Stuart parroted just as evasively. "Is there?"

"Captain Wellesley," she murmured with an innocent smile, "I'm just a nurse. I don't know about these things." Rising from the side of his bed, she picked up the basin and returned it to the table.

Stuart's eyes followed her as she walked across the small room, his attention divided between unbidden masculine appreciation of her beauty and concern about his situation.

"I'll leave you to sleep now," she said lightly, heading toward the door. "I'll check in on you later."

"Miss?"

"Yes?"

"What is your name?"

"Boudreau. Claire Boudreau."

"Ah, of course," Stuart nodded. "The famous Miss Boudreau."

"You've heard of me?" she asked, genuinely surprised.

"Everyone in the North has heard of you," Stuart smiled, throwing her own words back at her. "I'm flattered that the Confederacy considers me important enough to assign the Angel of Atlanta to see to my care."

"Don't overestimate your importance, Captain," Claire retorted dryly. "I was close at hand and available. That's all."

"You really know how to wound a man, Miss Boudreau."

"No, Captain, you men take care of that. Y'all need no help from me in that respect."

Stuart chuckled. "How little you know about wounds, Miss Boudreau. There isn't a gun in the world that can tear a man up as much as a woman's tongue can."

"Oh? And have you had a lot of experience with women's tongues, Captain Wellesley?" The words were out of her mouth before she could stop them, and Stuart's immediate burst of laughter left no doubt that he'd interpreted her inadvertently provocative comment exactly as she feared he would.

"Some," he rasped, torn between laughing and grimacing as another pain tore through his chest. "And I'm usually quite adept at handling them, too. But I don't know about yours, Miss Boudreau. Yours might be too much for me."

"That's something you'll never find out," she snapped, incensed that he was baiting her. With a flurry of skirts, she swept out the door, slamming it loudly behind her. But still she could hear his infuriating laughter all the way back to her room.

Stuart's laughter faded as soon as he heard the door to Claire's room close. He was exhausted from their verbal sparring, but he couldn't let himself go to sleep. Not yet. He had to try to sort out his situation and figure out what to do next.

His undelivered message was his biggest concern. Had the Confederates found it? If he could just get Miss Boudreau to give him his boots, at least he'd know whether it was still safe. He didn't think the Reb who had shot him had taken his boots. As near as he could remember, they'd merely stolen his rucksack, which had contained nothing but dispatches of minor importance, and plans for a new ship he was designing. A groan of frustration escaped him as he thought of the loss of those plans. He'd worked on them for weeks and now, obviously, they were gone.

"That'll teach you not to make a copy for safekeeping," he muttered, annoyed with his own negligence.

His mind swung back to the message. Closing his eyes, he tried again to remember those foggy moments after he'd been shot. Had he still had his boots on? He must have. He'd crawled back into the saddle after his attackers had ridden off and, even in his shocked and weakened state, if he hadn't had his boots on, he certainly would have noticed it as he mounted. So, where were they now, and how could he convince someone to find them for him?

"Damn!" he cursed. The information contained in that message was so vital to Union troop movements that if the Confederates actually had it, it could change the whole tide of the winter campaign.

He had to get his boots back and assure himself that the secret was still safe. Barring that, his only other recourse was to try to escape. Then, he could at least deliver the message to General Sherman verbally, provided, of course, that he could find him. But, how could he get out of here undetected? It was obvious that he was being closely guarded. He could hear soldiers in the hall outside his room at all times.

Claire Boudreau had said that he would probably be exchanged, but that could take months. He had to get away long before that. Could he somehow woo Miss Boudreau into helping him? He pondered this possibility for a moment, then shook his head wryly. He doubted it.

Stuart knew that his charm with women was considerable, and never in his twenty-five years had he lacked for female companionship. But this little red-haired witch didn't seem to have any interest in him as a man. It was just his luck that he would be assigned a nurse who was a well-known breast-beating Confederate patriot. Why couldn't he have gotten some sweet, simpering belle who would be swept away by his astonishing good looks and deep, velvety voice? Then he might have had a chance of effecting an escape.

Stuart sighed and wearily rubbed his fingers against his forehead. If he was going to attempt an escape, then he must concentrate his efforts on healing and getting his strength back. Since he was already a week late in delivering his message, a few more days probably wouldn't make any difference, and there was nothing he could do anyway until he was strong enough to travel.

"I'll just sleep a little, and when I wake up, I'll think of something," he muttered, closing his eyes. "If only I could charm Miss Boudreau into falling for me, maybe she'd tell me where my boots are . . ."

Chapter Five

"Major Anderson will see you now."

Claire rose from the hard chair on which she was sitting and followed the young corporal into Major Anderson's office.

"Ah, Miss Boudreau," Anderson said, a smile gracing his distinguished features as he rose to greet his visitor. "How is our patient?"

"I'm happy to report that he's making good progress, Major. He survived the infection and is getting stronger every day."

"Excellent! We owe you a great deal, Miss Boudreau."

"Thank you, sir." Claire hesitated a moment, not quite sure how to proceed. For a long moment she toyed with the handkerchief she was holding. Then, clearing her throat, she plunged ahead. "Major, I was wondering if, since Captain Wellesley is now past his crisis, I might be relieved of my duties and allowed to return to my home?"

Anderson frowned. "Is something the matter, Miss Boudreau? Have we not made you comfortable here, or has one of my men, perhaps, made improper advances toward you?"

"Oh, no," Claire said quickly. "It's nothing like that. Everyone has been very accommodating, and my quarters are fine. It's just that I find Captain Wellesley . . . difficult, and I'd prefer not to tend him any longer."

"Difficult?" Anderson's eyebrows rose in surprise. He knew from the many newspaper articles he had read that in addition to Stuart Wellesley's renown as a soldier, he was also reputed to be quite a ladies' man. In fact, it was well known that the foremost hostesses in Boston considered it quite a coup to have the illustrious captain in attendance at their social functions.

"Yes, sir," Claire murmured, embarrassed to have to admit how much Stuart Wellesley disconcerted her. "He's . . . well . . . arrogant in the extreme."

To Claire's astonishment, Anderson began to chuckle. She immediately felt a flush creep up her neck. "Excuse me, Major," she bristled, "but I fail to see what you find so amusing in that."

"Forgive me, Miss Boudreau, I'm not laughing at you. It's just that at Captain Wellesley's tender age and considering his unprecedented success in both business and the military, I'd be astounded if he weren't a bit arrogant."

"But, Major," Claire protested, "he's nothing more than a prisoner here, and he acts as though he should be treated like an honored guest!"

"Oh? In what way?"

"In every way! First of all, he's impossibly demanding. He constantly asks me questions and then demands I give him answers."

"What kind of questions, Miss Boudreau?"

"All kinds. He wants to know where he is. He wants to know how he got here and what your plans are for him. More than anything else, he wants to know where his boots are."

"His boots?"

"Yes."

"Why does he want his boots?"

"I have no idea, except that he keeps saying that a soldier always dies with his boots on and he wants his."

"Have you assured him he's not going to die?"

"Yes, I've told him that, but he still insists he wants his boots."

"I don't think that's such an unreasonable request, unless he wants them because he's going to attempt an escape."

"Even he's not foolish enough to try something like that," Claire snorted. "Right now he's so weak he can barely get out of bed to relieve himself."

"Well, then," Major Anderson shrugged, "I see no reason why we shouldn't humor the man in this small way. Many soldiers are superstitious about always having their boots nearby, and perhaps Captain Wellesley is one of them. Do you know where they might be?"

"Yes," Claire admitted. "They're with the rest of his uniform in a closet in the surgery."

"And have you told Captain Wellesley that?"

"No! I told him in no uncertain terms that he has no right to ask me anything, and I categorically refused to answer his questions. Actually, Major, I try to talk to him as little as possible— except, of course, as it relates to his recovery, or to the message he mentioned while he was delirious."

Major Anderson's frown deepened, and rising, he walked around his desk to the window, staring out pensively at the bleak November afternoon.

He had always heard that Claire Boudreau was one of the most sophisticated young women in Savannah, well able to handle herself in trying situations, but apparently she had met her match in Stuart Wellesley.

"Miss Boudreau," he said slowly, choosing his next words with care as he turned back to face her, "if you truly do not feel that you can care for Captain Wellesley any longer, then, of course, you are free to return to your home. You, unlike him, are not a prisoner here. However, I wish you would reconsider."

"But why do you want me to stay?" Claire asked. "I assure you, Captain Wellesley is on the mend and no longer needs round-the-clock nursing. I'm convinced that any member of the hospital's medical staff could attend him satisfactorily at this point."

"I'm equally sure we could handle that aspect of Captain Wellesley's care," Anderson agreed, "but as we've discussed before, there is more at stake here than just his physical well-being."

"Do you mean the message?"

"Yes."

"Major, I have tried to get him to talk about it, but he won't. He plays word games with me every time I bring it up."

"What kind of word games?"

"Oh, you know. I ask him a question and he answers me with one of his own. That type of thing. He . . . toys with me."

Anderson sighed and perched on the edge of his desk, somewhat at a loss as to how to broach his next question. "I understand how unpleasant this must be for you, Miss Boudreau, but we really do need your continued assistance. You see, we feel

64

that you are probably the only person who can gain the information we so desperately need."

Claire's eyes widened with astonishment. "You mean *you're* not going to interrogate him?"

"Not unless we have no other recourse. Frankly, I don't think it would do any good. Since his capture, I have been intently studying everything I can find on Captain Wellesley, and I have come to the conclusion that he is of a character that nothing short of physical torture would make him betray his mission. Even though such methods have been successfully utilized in the past on officers from both sides, I do not sanction them. I do not want to submit a man who has been as ill as the captain has to that type of interrogation unless it's absolutely necessary."

"But you can't count on me to get the information, Major! I've tried to get him to tell me something . . . anything . . . and he won't."

Anderson drew a deep breath, hating the desperate situation that was forcing him to ask this lovely woman what he knew he must. "I think he might . . . given the right impetus."

Claire's mouth dropped open in shock, then snapped closed as outrage flared in her emerald eyes. "Exactly what are you suggesting?"

"Only that you might consider using your, ah, feminine wiles to coerce the information out of him."

Claire jumped up from her chair, her face a mask of disbelief and anger. "Are you saying that you want me to seduce the man? Major Anderson, I am appalled that you would ask me such a thing! Are you unaware that I have a fiancé out in the field who has been fighting since the first shot at Fort Sumter was fired? How could you ask me to betray him in such a way?"

Anderson was aware that Claire was indeed betrothed, but he also knew that her fiancé, David Henry, had been missing in action since the battle of Gettysburg, a year and a half earlier. "I know of your betrothal, Miss Boudreau, and of course, I wouldn't dream of asking you to betray your fiancé. Please don't think that."

"Then what exactly *are* you asking?"

"I'm simply asking you to be friendly to Captain Wellesley. Make the man like you . . . trust you. I know it is not an easy task, particularly if he is being unpleasant, but if you can just see your way clear to stay on a few more days—long enough to gain his confidence . . ."

"His confidence, or his affection?" Claire snorted.

"Miss Boudreau, I'm going to be perfectly blunt. These are desperate times. We know that General Sherman's forces are not far from Savannah, and we are convinced an assault on the city is imminent. If Captain Wellesley is indeed in possession of information regarding Sherman's plans for that assault, then, is asking you to charm the man into confiding that information too great a request?"

Claire sighed with resignation. "I suppose not," she admitted. "But let us be clear on one thing, Major. I will not compromise my virtue. I know there are women in the south who have done that for the Cause, but I will not."

Anderson inclined his head in agreement. "Nor would I expect you to."

"All right then," Claire nodded, heading for the door. "I'll stay on a few more days and I'll try, within reason, to 'charm' Captain Wellesley out of any information he might have."

66

"Thank you, Miss Boudreau," Major Anderson said genuinely. "You are a brave and patriotic woman."

Claire smiled wryly. "I'm afraid 'brave and patriotic' are not the words I'd use to describe me."

"Oh? What words would you use, Miss Boudreau?"

"Foolish, Major. Just plain foolish."

"Good day to you, Captain Wellesley," Claire said brightly, walking into Stuart's room carrying a tray of food. "You're looking much better this morning."

Stuart pushed himself up into a sitting position and smiled. "Thanks to you, I'm feeling much better, too."

Claire blinked in surprise at Stuart's flattering words. "Thanks to me?"

"Yes," Stuart nodded. "I know you nursed me through my infection."

"It's my job, Captain," she responded, setting the tray down on the small table next to the bed.

"I owe you my life," he countered, reaching out and lightly touching her hand. "Thank you for saving me."

Claire jerked her hand away and quickly turned back to the tray. "I brought you your breakfast. Do you feel up to eating?"

"If you're going to feed me."

Good Lord, Claire thought, her heart pounding, what was going on here?

In the past few days, she had become accustomed to dealing with the demanding, cynical Captain Wellesley, and although she didn't like him, she at least felt that she knew what to expect from him.

But this morning, it was as if a different person was waiting for her. She could hardly believe this handsome, charming man, with his cool gray eyes and blinding smile, could be the same difficult and acerbic Yankee she'd come to know. The change in his mien was so unnerving that Claire hesitated a moment, trying to compose her features before she turned back toward him. "I'll be happy to feed you your breakfast."

Stuart's eyebrows rose imperceptibly. The last thing he'd expected from the prickly Miss Boudreau was her immediate, smiling agreement. "And you promise you won't throw anything at me?" he asked, feigning a look of fear.

Claire smiled despite her trepidation. "I promise." Perching on the side of Stuart's bed, she picked up a bowl of grits and offered him a spoonful. "This should make you feel better."

Stuart obediently took a bite of the tasteless cereal, forcing himself not to grimace as he slowly chewed the pasty, tepid mush. "What would really make me feel better," he commented, swallowing with distaste, "would be a shave and a haircut."

"That can probably be arranged," Claire said smoothly, spooning up some more cereal. "I could check with the commander and find out if there's a barber at the fort."

"No, thank you," Stuart negated, holding up a hand. "If the fort barber is as adept as the soldier who just bathed me, I'll just keep my hair till I get out of here."

The spoon clanked against the bowl clumsily as Claire realized what Stuart was hinting at. "Would you like me to do it?" she asked shakily, hating the fact that the mere thought made a queer thrill course through her. What would he look like without that thick, black beard and dirty, shoulder-length hair? she wondered.

"*Would* you do it?" he countered, his voice low.

"If you like," she agreed, hurriedly retrieving the spoon as she tried to pull her eyes away from his.

Stuart slowly reached up a hand and stroked his bearded cheek. "Have you ever done it before, Miss Boudreau?"

Claire's eyes widened. "Done what?"

Stuart grinned, realizing what Claire had read into his innocent question. "Why, shaved a man, of course," he drawled, unable to keep himself from teasing her. "What did you think I meant?"

Claire bit back a sharp retort and ignored his question. "I shaved many men in Atlanta, Captain."

"Ah, yes, Atlanta. Well, Miss Boudreau, since you got so much experience doing it in Atlanta, I'm sure I can trust you to do it to me properly."

Once again the spoon clattered against the bowl, but this time Claire didn't even try to cover her clumsiness. Jumping up from the side of the bed, she hurriedly picked up the tray and started for the door. "I'm leaving now, Captain. I'll be back in a few minutes."

She was already out the door and halfway down the hall when she heard Stuart call after her. "Hey, Miss Boudreau, come back! I wasn't finished with that great cereal."

It was a half hour before Claire could compose herself enough to return to Stuart's room. During that time, many a soldier's eye followed her speculatively as she raced in and out of rooms, gathering up supplies and muttering to herself.

"Damn Yankee boor! It isn't enough that I have to take care of him. Oh, no! Now I have to be nice to him, too. So, what happens when I offer to shave his ugly face and cut his dirty hair? He makes lecherous comments about my experience! Well, Captain Stuart Wellesley of the Fourth Massachusetts, you're in *my* hands now, and if you don't start acting like a gentleman, you may find yourself with your throat slit!"

The very thought of wielding a razor in the vicinity of Stuart's throat made Claire chuckle. Although she'd never dream of actually hurting him, it certainly would do wonders to her offended sensibilities to scare him a bit!

Loaded down with a fresh pitcher of water, soap, shaving mug and brush, razor, and scissors, she returned to his room, proceeding directly over to the little table by the bed, where she unceremoniously dumped the implements onto its surface. Picking up the large pair of scissors she had commandeered, she turned toward her waiting patient. "All right, Captain," she said, brandishing them, "let's cut your hair first."

"No."

Claire lowered the scissors. "What do you mean, 'No'?"

"I mean 'No.'"

"I don't understand. Not a half hour ago, you asked me to cut your hair."

"I've changed my mind."

"But, why?"

"Because."

"Because why?"

"Just because."

"Captain," Claire snapped, "you sound like a

70

child. Now, do you want your hair cut or not?"

"No."

"All right," she shrugged, "have it your way. But, you'd feel a lot better if you'd get rid of the filthy stuff."

"That's why I don't want you to cut it," Stuart muttered.

For a moment Claire just stared at him, then a small smile quirked the corners of her mouth. "You don't want me to cut it because it's dirty?"

Stuart nodded, looking away. "I don't want you to touch it until someone washes it. It's probably crawling with lice, and I don't want you to catch them."

Claire felt an unexpected twinge of sympathy for the man. It was obvious he was not used to being dirty. It also somehow pleased her that he was considerate enough to want to spare her having to touch him. "Captain Wellesley," she said softly, laying down the scissors and gazing at him earnestly, "I'll wash your hair for you. That's why I brought in fresh water and soap. But I thought I'd cut it first. There's no sense in washing what I'm going to cut off."

"No. I don't want you to touch it until it's clean. Call one of the guards in and let him wash it."

"Don't be silly," Claire placated. "I washed many a dirty head of hair when I was nursing in Atlanta."

"Well, you didn't wash mine, and you're not going to," Stuart said adamantly. "You can go ahead and shave me, but then I want you to get one of the staff to come in and wash my hair."

With a sigh, Claire nodded, then reached over and picked up the shaving mug, adding water and a bit of soap to whip up a lather. Picking up the scissors again, she turned toward Stuart and said, "Your beard is too long to shave. I'll cut some of it off first."

He nodded.

Claire wrapped a clean towel around his neck, then paused. "How do you normally wear your beard? Short, like Mr. Lincoln, or long, like General Sherman?"

Stuart shot her a jaundiced glance, loath to be compared to the two high-ranking Northerners. Although both were men to be respected, neither of them was known for his good looks. "Normally, Miss Boudreau, I don't wear any beard at all."

"Really?" Claire responded, her eyebrows rising in genuine surprise. "How unusual. Just a moustache, then?"

"No. No moustache, either. I prefer to be clean-shaven."

"Clean-shaven, Captain? Why I can't think of a single man I know who likes to be clean-shaven."

"Well, this man does. It's a lot cleaner."

Claire nodded her agreement. "It is that. All right, Captain Wellesley, clean-shaven it is." Leaning forward, she energetically began cutting the bushy dark hair of his beard. When she had it cut back to a length that could be shaved, she set down the scissors and picked up the razor and shaving mug. "Now lie perfectly still," she ordered, hardly able to contain her mirth when she saw his eyebrows rise with alarm.

"Are you sure you know what you're doing?" he asked, barely moving his lips.

"Absolutely—as long as you lie perfectly still."

Stuart immediately clamped his lips shut, and with deft strokes Claire began to shave him. When his beard was completely gone, she leaned back and looked at him with satisfaction. "There, not a single nick."

Stuart reached up to touch his smooth cheeks, looking at her with a smile. "You're very adept, Miss Boudreau."

The blaze of his smile, coupled with her first clear look at his lean jaw and sculptured lips, almost rendered Claire speechless. She had always thought him to be remarkably handsome, but until now, she'd had no idea how truly incredible looking he actually was. She could see why he wore no facial hair. Why would anyone want to cover up even an inch of that perfect face?

"Do I look all right?" he asked.

"Yes . . . you look fine," she stammered, busying herself with the shaving apparatus. "I'll go find someone to wash your hair now." And bolting toward the door, she raced out of the room.

I can't charm him, she thought desperately, leaning against the wall outside his door. How am I supposed to inveigle him into telling me anything when I can't even put three coherent words together if he's looking at me? Oh, why does he have to be so good-looking? *Why?*

For a solid hour, Claire tried to find someone who could wash Stuart's hair for him, but it was hopeless. The hospital staff was frantically working on a large group of Confederate soldiers who had been wounded during a skirmish near the river. There was no one who had the time or inclination to worry about whether the Yankee prisoner's hair was dirty. Finally, Claire gave up her futile quest and returned to Stuart.

"There's no one who can wash your hair," she

73

said bluntly, walking into the room and pointedly avoiding looking at him. "I'm going to have to do it, and I'll have no argument from you. I have other things to tend to today, and I don't have time to waste while you worry about whether you have lice or not. I have some strong pine tar soap here, and if there's anything living on your scalp now, it'll be gone when I'm finished."

"Nice to see you again, Miss Boudreau," Stuart commented wryly, secretly amused by her tirade and the fact that she wouldn't look at him. "Okay, you win. And since I don't want to take up any more of your valuable time than necessary, just tell me where you want me to put my head and we'll get on with this."

Claire shoved the small table up to the head of Stuart's bed. "Just move up in the bed and lean your head over here," she directed, pointing to the basin atop the table.

Stuart did as she bade, and when he was in the position she'd indicated, she walked over to the side of his bed. Standing near his head, she leaned forward and picked up the pitcher of water, pouring a small amount over his hair, then following it with a liberal dose of the strong-smelling soap which she energetically began working into his scalp.

Stuart emitted a sharp gasp of shocked pleasure as he suddenly found his face buried in the lush softness of Claire's bosom. His nostrils filled with the scent of her and his mind swam with erotic thoughts of what would happen if he opened his mouth. He felt his manhood surge to lusty life beneath the sheet and with a strangled sound, turned his head aside and quickly raised his knees.

Hearing his muffled cry, Claire straightened,

looking at him in consternation. "Captain Wellesley, are you all right?"

"Fine," Stuart choked. "Best I've been in ages."

"Feels good, doesn't it?" Claire smiled.

"Better than you can imagine."

"I always think it feels wonderful to have someone else wash your hair," Claire commented, again bending forward and unwittingly treating him to another dose of her feminine charms.

Stuart's erection swelled, causing him to shift his hips uncomfortably and bite down hard on his lip.

"Captain, are you sure you're all right?" Claire asked again.

"Fine. Just please finish."

"Oh, I'm sorry," she apologized, truly chagrined as she noticed how red his face was becoming. "I bet all the blood is rushing to your head, isn't it?"

That's not the only place it's rushing, Stuart thought irreverently, but he remained silent, fearful that if he spoke, he might betray his condition.

"There," Claire murmured, pouring the remainder of the water through his clean hair and reaching for a towel. "All done."

Wrapping the towel around Stuart's head, she put her arm around his shoulders, helping him to move back down into the depths of the bed.

"Do you think you can sit up so I can dry your hair?" she asked.

Stuart cast a wary glance downward in the direction of his midsection, wondering if he could manage to sit up without straightening his legs. Brace yourself on your elbows and dig in with your heels, he silently directed. You drop those knees and this sheet is going to look like a pup tent!

75

With tremendous effort, he sat up, then turned to look at Claire. "I can dry my hair myself. You've done enough."

"Nonsense," she protested, frowning with concern at how breathless he suddenly sounded. "You just sit here and relax. I'll do it."

Relax? he thought. Lady, unless you get out of here quick, you may find yourself doing something that's going to relax both of us more than you can imagine!

Willing himself to think of anything other than the sensation of Claire's soft hands in his hair, Stuart sat staring straight ahead, barely able to contain the agony of desire he was suffering as she finished drying and combing his hair.

Finally she laid down the comb and took a step backward, drinking in the beauty of the man sitting so rigidly in the bed. "All finished," she smiled. "Now all we have left to do is cut it."

"Oh, God," Stuart moaned.

"Captain?" Claire asked sharply. "Are you in pain? Did I somehow hurt you, washing your hair?"

"Oh, God," Stuart repeated.

"Maybe you'd better lie down a minute."

As she moved toward him, his eyes flared with alarm, knowing that if she touched him one more time, he was lost. "I'm okay!" he barked, holding up a hand. "I just want to be left alone now."

An expression of bewildered offense flashed across Claire's face. "Don't you want your hair cut?"

"No," he answered, "not now. Please, just leave."

"Well, fine," she huffed, gathering up her supplies and heading for the door. "I'll check on you later."

"Miss Boudreau?" Stuart croaked.

"Yes?"

"Thank you."

"You're welcome," she snapped, yanking open the door and slamming it hard after her.

Gingerly, Stuart raised the sheet and peeked under it, frowning down at his fully aroused manhood. With a sigh, he dropped the sheet and leaned back against the pillows, his mouth suddenly twitching with amusement. "Guess I'm going to live, after all . . ."

Chapter Six

A week passed, and Stuart recovered with amazing speed. By the time he'd been at the fort for two weeks, he knew he was well enough to be transferred to the prison barracks and was surprised that no such move had been implemented. It further surprised him that Claire seemed oblivious to his remarkable progress and continued to treat him as if he were gravely ill. Although his every instinct warned him that she was no fool and that she must have an ulterior motive for continuing to coddle him, he was careful not to let on how much better he was feeling. He was still intent on trying to find some means of escape, and if Claire really was being duped by his playacting, then he would stretch his days of freedom out as long as possible. But every day, when he was sure she was nowhere around, he got out of bed and walked the length and breadth of his small room, knowing that exercising his unused muscles would help him regain his strength.

Deep down, Stuart knew there was another reason he was in no hurry to be transferred to the prison barracks. During the past week, he and Claire had spent many hours together, and although he suspected that her friendly demeanor was a ploy to lull him into betraying Union information, he was so entranced by her breathtaking beauty and sparkling wit that he was loath to see their relationship end.

Stuart's suspicions were correct. Claire knew exactly how well he was progressing, but at Major Anderson's request, she kept her knowledge to herself in the hopes that her continued involvement with Stuart would cause him to relax his guard.

"He must think I'm an idiot," she had commented to Lieutenant Emery one morning. "He'll be sitting up in bed looking perfectly fine, and then, as soon as I come through the door, he sinks down under the covers and closes his eyes."

She decided that Stuart's transparent behavior was simply a cowardly way of avoiding the prison barracks and clung to that disparaging thought tenaciously as the days passed and she realized, with horror, that she was actually beginning to enjoy the hours they spent together. She was furious with herself when, night after night, she lay on her hard little cot with thoughts of him filling her head. She stubbornly told herself that her fascination with the handsome Yankee was caused only by the challenge he presented, since regardless of how subtle and nonchalant her questions were, she could not seem to trip him into revealing any of the information she so desperately sought.

He's a dirty, lying, deceiving Yankee, she told herself over and over, and he'd kill you just as quick as look at you if he thought it would do him any good!

But as the days slipped by and she spent more time in Stuart's company, her words rang increasingly hollow in her ears. As much as she hated to admit it, even to herself, the man's charm was undeniable, and his wit and intelligence were so natural and spontaneous that even she could understand why he had become such an object of admiration among the northerners.

If only he wasn't so handsome, so witty, so smart, she mourned one night as she lay, sleepless, in her tiny cubicle. . . . If only he was ugly and mean and stupid—like Yankees are supposed to be. But he wasn't, and her growing realization that a member of the hated enemy's forces could be intelligent and charming bothered her greatly. It went against everything she had ever been taught, forcing her to reexamine beliefs long held and closely guarded. It was very troubling.

One morning, after Stuart had been at the fort nearly three weeks, he was sitting up in bed, eating his breakfast, when Claire nonchalantly asked him if he had family in Boston.

"Not in Boston," he confided, between mouthfuls of the tasteless gruel. "My family is in Colorado."

"Really?" Claire responded, surprise evident on her face. "But if your family is in Colorado, why do you live in Massachusetts?"

"Went to school there."

"Oh, Harvard, I suppose?" she asked sarcastically.

Ignoring her gibe, Stuart nodded. "Yes. Thought I wanted to be an attorney, but I had a friend whose father was a shipbuilder. I spent Christmas at his home a few years ago, and after that, I was hooked. After I graduated, I realized that I really had no interest in practicing law, but I was fascinated with designing ships. So, I just never went back to Durango."

"Durango," Claire repeated slowly. "Is that your home town?"

"Yes," Stuart affirmed. "It's just a little place way up in the mountains. I think it's probably the prettiest little town on earth, but the western slope of the Rockies is hardly the place to pursue a career in shipbuilding."

Claire smiled and nodded her agreement. "Do you come from a big family?"

"Yeah. I have six brothers and one sister."

"Eight children?" Claire gasped. "My word! Where do you fit in?"

"I'm second. I have an older brother, Miles, who lives in England."

"What's he doing there? Trying to convince the British to support the Northern cause?"

Stuart set his spoon down and looked at her quizzically, surprised by the sudden bitterness in her voice. "Miles doesn't have anything to do with this war. My parents are British, so as the eldest son, he went to college in England. While he was there, he met a girl and married her. Now he lives south of London, on a farm where he breeds horses."

"Oh," Claire said, looking quickly down at her lap to cover her embarrassment. "So, you're the only Yankee in the family?"

"We're all Yankees," Stuart said quietly, "but I'm the only soldier in the family. The rest of my brothers are younger—kids, mostly—although my brother Eric is old enough to join up if he wants to."

"But he hasn't so far?" she queried.

"No, and I don't think he will. He's an artist and doesn't have the temperament to be a soldier— unless the war threatens a lot closer to home. But that won't happen. It's all going to be over soon."

Claire's mouth hardened. It was the first time Stuart had ever mentioned just how close the South was to losing the war, and the quiet assurance in his tone infuriated her.

Glaring, she rose quickly from her chair. "I beg to remind you, Captain Wellesley, that this war is not over yet, and you, sir, are still very much a prisoner of the Confederate States of America."

Stuart frowned, angry with himself for letting the conversation take such an adversarial turn. The last thing he wanted to do was debate politics with Claire. The more time he spent with her, the more he realized how much he was coming to care for her, and he studiously avoided any mention of the political chasm that separated them. He wanted her to think of him as a man—not a Yankee.

"Do you have any brothers and sisters?" he asked, trying to steer the conversation back to a more personal subject.

"I had an older brother," Claire answered tightly. "He was killed at Gettysburg."

Stuart sighed, again reminded that no matter how hard he tried, there was no way to keep the war from coming between them. "I'm sorry," he said, his tone genuinely sympathetic. "It's such a waste. All those men . . ."

"How would you know?" Claire demanded bitterly. "You just said all your brothers are safe in your little mountain town in Colorado."

"I've lost friends," Stuart answered softly, his

expression taking on a faraway look. "So many, many friends—including the one I told you about whose father is the shipbuilder. He was my roommate in college and my closest friend. He's been gone two years now."

"Oh, God!" Claire moaned, covering her face with her hands as tears welled in her eyes. "When will it ever end?"

Stuart reached out and clasped her hand in his, gently pulled her toward the bed until she sat down next to him. "It can't go on much longer, Claire," he whispered. "It has to end soon."

For a long moment, she allowed him to hold her hand, taking comfort in the warm strength of his fingers wrapped around hers. Finally, she pulled away and stood up, wiping her eyes with the hem of her apron. "So," she said, her voice still shaking with emotion, "tell me about your sister. Does she have a beau fighting in the war?"

"Hardly," Stuart chuckled. "Paula's only four years old."

"Paula! Your sister's name is Paula?"

"Yes," Stuart answered, looking at her in bewilderment. "Do you find that odd?"

"No! It's just that . . ." She paused, not knowing how to tell him that she had assumed the "Paula" he had rambled about in his delirium was his sweetheart.

"What?" he questioned.

"When you were delirious, you talked about a Paula."

"I did? What did I say?"

"You said you loved her. You said she was precious and sweet . . . and soft."

"She is—and I *do* love her very much." Then, suddenly noticing Claire's embarrassed blush, he

84

grinned. "You thought Paula was my girl, didn't you?"

"Of course not!" Claire blustered, making a great pretense of straightening his covers. "I didn't care who she was."

"Oh, come on, Miss Boudreau," Stuart teased, reaching for her hand and dropping a quick, impetuous kiss on her fingertips. "Admit it. You thought Paula was my sweetheart and you were just a little bit jealous, now, weren't you?"

Claire yanked her hand away, horrified by the tingling sensation that had streaked up her arm when his lips touched her. "Jealous!" she blurted, rubbing her arm energetically. "Why would I be jealous?"

"I don't know," Stuart shrugged, barely able to contain the excitement that coursed through him as he watched her reaction to his impulsive kiss. "Why would you?"

"Well, I'm not! I couldn't care less if you have a thousand sweethearts in Boston. To me, you're just a tiresome, demanding, arrogant Yankee who has caused me no end of work. In fact, I'm going to go right now and tell Major Anderson that you're fit enough to be transferred to the prison barracks." Wheeling around, she stalked quickly toward the door.

"Oh, Miss Boudreau?"

Halting, she turned back toward him, furious to see that he was grinning at her with unrepentant glee. "What do you want now, Captain?"

"Do you suppose I could have my boots?"

"Oh, you and those boots!"

"Well, I can't very well go to prison in my stocking feet, now can I?"

"I don't care if you go barefoot!" she announced, again turning toward the door. "But I'll find your boots," she added softly, and disappeared into the hall.

"Private, I know Captain Wellesley's boots were in this closet. They didn't just get up and walk away by themselves, so where could they have been put?"

"Everything was cleaned out of there last week, ma'am," the young soldier stammered, "and I think all the clothes and other Yankee belongings were throwed over there for our soldiers to pick from." Turning, he pointed to a corner of the room where a huge pile of clothes and boots lay heaped together.

"Do you mean that one of our soldiers could have confiscated Captain Wellesley's boots for his own use?"

"It's possible, ma'am, but not likely, since I don't think nobody told our men the clothes were there for the takin'. They probably haven't been touched since they got throwed there."

"Good," Claire nodded. "Then, I guess I'll just have to rummage through and see if I can find them."

"But, ma'am, most of them boots are dirty and bloody. You don't want to go through that pile."

Claire turned a blinding smile on the young boy. "You're right, Private, I *don't* want to go through that pile, but how else will I find them?"

The naive soldier was instantly smitten and happily fell into her trap. "Well, ma'am, I'd be obliged to look for you, but most of them Yankee boots all look the same. How'll I know when I find the right ones?"

"Oh, Private, how gracious of you," Claire beamed. "Captain Wellesley told me his boots were custom made for him and that they have the initials SJW tooled into the leather near the tops. I'm sure you'll have no trouble locating the right ones."

"Okay." The boy nodded, gingerly picking his way through the mire of filthy, blood-soaked clothing and boots. After several minutes of choosing and discarding various items, he let out a whoop of triumph. "Found one of them, Miss Boudreau! The left one!"

"Wonderful!" Claire praised. "Now, just find the mate and his uniform and we'll be done."

"His uniform, ma'am?" the private asked, straightening.

"Yes, he needs that, too."

"But, there are hundreds of them here! Does it have his name in it also?"

"I don't know," Claire admitted. "Here, let me look at some of them. I can probably find one that looks to be about the right size. It doesn't actually have to be his."

Together, the two of them sorted through the reeking pile until finally the private found the mate to Stuart's boot and Claire picked out a Yankee uniform shirt and pants that looked to be the right size and still in reasonably good condition.

"Here are the boots, ma'am," the private said, holding them out to her.

"Lord, but they smell!" Claire said, turning her nose up in disgust. "So do these clothes. How can you men stand to wear such filthy clothing?"

The private looked down at his own ragged, dirty uniform and blushed with embarrassment.

"Sometimes, a fellow don't got no choice, ma'am," he said apologetically.

"I understand, Private," Claire said quickly, upset that she had embarrassed the kindly boy. "I'll tell you what—I'll take the captain's boots and clean them up if you'll see if you can do something with this uniform."

"Surely, ma'am, I'll be happy to. And you don't have to clean them boots. I can take care of those for you, too."

"No," Claire said, clutching the boots protectively. "I'll clean these myself."

"Okay, ma'am, whatever you say. I'll see if I can find you some saddle soap."

"Fine. Thank you, Private."

Walking over to a bench near the hospital's front door, Claire sat down, smiling down at Stuart's dirty boots. She really didn't know why she had insisted on cleaning them herself, but somehow she wanted to. "It's just because I've taken care of him for so long now," she told herself quickly. "And since today is probably the last time I'll see him, and knowing how important these stupid boots are to him, I guess it's the least I can do."

The private appeared with the saddle soap and a cloth and Claire started energetically working the gooey substance into the first boot. Her efforts were immediately rewarded as the dry, clinging dirt and manure fell away to reveal beautiful, soft leather. The boots were an inky black color—just like his hair, she thought wistfully—and were designed to cover the leg all the way to the knee. The leather was as soft as a pair of fine gloves, and Claire couldn't help but marvel at the obvious quality. These must have cost a fortune, she mused. Maybe he really is as rich as everyone says . . .

She found it intriguing that Stuart had never made any mention of his money, and further, that he was fighting in the war at all. Many men of substantial means paid others less well off to serve in their place.

No, he wouldn't do that. He's far too honorable, she decided.

With a small smile, she set down the second boot and sat for a moment admiring the gleaming pair. Then, on a whim, she leaned forward and folded back the top of one so she could see his initials. There they were—SJW. I wonder what the "J" stands for—John, James, Joseph? she thought. Mentally, she tried each possibility with his first name, then shook her head, annoyed with herself that she cared.

Picking up her cloth, she reached down inside the boot, wiping away the last traces of dirt, then picked up the other and did the same. But as she reached inside this one, she met with an obstacle. Curious, she pulled her hand out and held open the top of the boot, peering down inside. She couldn't see anything. She reached inside again, this time feeling something that definitely resembled paper, wedged along the inside of the back of the boot.

"He must have torn the lining and tried to patch it," she murmured. "I wonder if I can find any cloth to fix it properly."

Standing, she carried the boot out of the building and into the sun, again holding open the top and peering inside. This time she could see that there was definitely a piece of paper shoved against the heel. Reaching into the boot, she tugged at it, surprised to find that it lifted out easily. She turned the paper over in her hand, her brows puckering with bewilderment as she peered at row upon row of nonsensical symbols which covered the sheet.

For a long moment she just stared; then, suddenly, the symbols' meaning became clear. It was some sort of code—which meant that what she was holding must be the desperately sought-after message!

"Lord in heaven!" she gasped. "No wonder he wanted his boots so badly!"

A surge of victory washed over her, followed almost immediately by a rush of anger. Stuart didn't care about dying with his boots on, she thought angrily, he just wanted that message back before someone found it. Enraged that she had been so duped by what she had thought to be a soldier's last wish, she flung the offending boot down and stamped on it, grinding dirt and dust into the leather until it was nearly as dirty as it had been before she'd cleaned it.

Furious tears of betrayal sprang to her eyes. She'd believed him—believed him when he'd thanked her for saving his life, believed him when he'd told her how much he appreciated the care she'd given him, believed every pretty phrase that had passed through his handsome, lying lips.

As she glanced down at the message she still held, her mouth hardened with determination. She had promised Major Anderson that she'd try to coerce Captain Wellesley into confiding the contents of the message he'd carried. Well, now she could do better than that. She could deliver the message straight into the major's hands—and deliver it she would.

With angry resolve, she shoved the paper inside the bodice of her well-worn brown day dress and started across the compound toward the commander's headquarters.

She hadn't taken ten steps before she stopped short, jumping with fear at the sharp, staccato report of a rifle. She looked around in confusion, trying to determine where the shot had come from, when suddenly all hell seemed to break loose around her. Soldiers appeared from everywhere, running, shouting, pulling on boots, grabbing weapons, and scrambling toward the fort's high walls.

Whirling around, open-mouthed and wide eyed with terror, Claire spotted Lieutenant Emery tearing across the parade field toward her. "Lieutenant!" she screamed, surprised to find that her voice was hardly more than a squeak, "Lieutenant Emery!"

Turning, he spotted her and raced over, roughly grabbing her arm and dragging her unceremoniously back toward the hospital. "Get inside and take cover!" he ordered.

"But why?" she protested, stumbling in her efforts to keep up with the galloping man. "What's going on?"

"What's going on?" he yelled, nearly throwing her through the hospital's front door. "It's the Yankees, Miss Boudreau. We're being attacked!"

Chapter Seven

The battle was over before it really began. Fourteen minutes after the first shot sounded, Major Anderson surrendered the fort, and for the first time in almost four years, the Stars and Stripes again flew over Fort McAllister.

The few minutes of chaos seemed like years to Claire. Terrified that the Yankees would overrun the hospital, she locked herself in a small storage cabinet where she sat huddled and sobbing as the battle raged.

Stuart, hearing the first warning cries of the impending attack, leaped from his bed, oblivious to the pain which ripped through his chest at his abrupt movements. Running into the hall, he grabbed a young orderly who was racing toward the hospital's front door. "Is the fort under attack?" he demanded.

"Yes!" the boy answered, looking at the northern officer with sudden fear in his eyes.

"Where is Miss Boudreau?"

"I don't know . . . sir."

Stuart glared at the boy, annoyed that he was suddenly acting like he expected Stuart to lunge at him. "Good God, man, have you seen her this morning? Is she in the hospital?"

"I don't know!"

Stuart turned away from the frightened private with a grunt of disgust and looked around frantically for some article of clothing to put on over his longjohns. There was nothing. The sound of a cannon being fired sent him racing for the door. He looked out at the chaos on the parade field and again cursed with frustration at his state of undress. As he stepped outside, his gaze swept the area, coming to light on his boots, which were still lying on the ground near the door. He picked them up and hurried back into the building, heading for his room and bellowing Claire's name.

Claire could hear him frantically calling her, but she didn't answer, so overcome by fear that she couldn't make a sound. She peeked through a crack in the door and saw him running down the hall, boots in hand. She almost opened the cabinet door to let him know where she was, but quickly changed her mind, reminding herself that he was, after all, a Yankee officer, and if the battle went badly, he could very easily turn her over to the Northern command.

Suddenly, the noise stopped. The gunfire died away, the shouting ceased, and an eerie quiet overtook the fort. Unable to control her curiosity, Claire opened the cabinet door a crack and peered out. No one was in sight. Silently, she crawled out of her hiding place and crept toward the hospital door, gasping with horror at the sight which met her.

There were Yankees everywhere. As she gazed across the parade field, all she could see was blue,

blue, blue. There must be thousands of them, she thought, clutching her throat as she tried to draw a breath.

Where were the Confederates? Had the Yankees killed every man in the fort? No, that wasn't possible, she silently assured herself. The southern troops must be hiding somewhere, readying themselves to make another stand.

Suddenly, she saw Major Anderson step out of his office door and walk slowly across the parade field, carrying his saber tip-down. With great dignity, he approached a Yankee officer who was seated on a horse. The Yankee dismounted and Major Anderson held out his sword in a time-honored tradition of surrender.

"Oh, my God," Claire whispered, the full import of what she was witnessing finally sinking in. "It's over."

The Northern officer accepted the major's saber with a grave inclination of his head, then signaled two of his men to take the distinguished man into custody.

There was a commotion somewhere to her left. Gazing around, she saw that up on the ramparts, the Yankees were rounding up the fort's soldiers, prodding them with the butts of their guns as they herded them toward a fenced compound.

So engrossed was she in watching the little piece of history unfolding before her that she was completely unaware of the two Yankee officers who were quietly approaching her. They were nearly upon her before she saw them and with a startled shriek of fear tried to duck back into the building. But they were too fast for her. With lightning speed, one of the men grabbed her arm, halting her flight and whirling her around to face him.

"Excuse me, ma'am, but what are you doing here?" Despite his polite words, the man's nasal Yankee twang sent a tremor of fear coursing through her.

"I'm a . . . a nurse," Claire stammered, her heart beating so hard she was afraid it would jump out of her chest.

"I'm sorry, ma'am, but you'll have to come with us."

To her mortification, tears sprang to Claire's eyes. "Where are you taking me?"

"To the general's office."

"General? What general?"

"General Hazen, ma'am. He is now commander of this fort."

For a moment, Claire thought she might faint, but then she thought of the bravery of her brother and her fiancé, and with a great show of dignity, she blinked back her tears and nodded to the Yankee soldier. "Very well, sir. I will consent to speak to your general."

Rebelliously jerking her arm away from the soldier's light hold, she picked up her skirts and marched down the hospital steps, leaving her captors to stare after her in stunned surprise.

General Hazen stood behind Major Anderson's gleaming mahogany desk and beamed. "Captain Wellesley! It is truly a great pleasure to see you. Many people in very high places have feared for your safety during the past weeks."

Stuart, dressed in an immaculate officer's uniform, nodded graciously. "Thank you, sir. I regret causing anyone undue worry."

"I have sent General Sherman a message that you have been located," Hazen continued. "I know he will be gratified to learn of your safety. But, tell me, Captain, how did you come to be held here?"

"I was carrying a message from General Grant to General Sherman when I was ambushed by a Confederate patrol," Stuart explained. "They left me for dead on the road just north of here. Apparently, two Rebel deserters found me and, hoping for a reward, brought me to the fort."

"Ah, yes," the general nodded, "I expected it was something like that. You can put your mind at rest about your message, Captain. We have found it, and it never reached Confederate hands."

"Found it?" Stuart asked, startled. "Found it where? I had it hidden in one of my boots, but by the time I finally recovered them, it was gone."

"A nurse here at the fort had it," Hazen confided. "A Miss Boudreau. She was taken into custody yesterday, after the battle, and when we searched her, we found it on her person."

"Claire had it?" Stuart gasped, his voice betraying his shocked astonishment.

Hazen's eyebrows rose at Stuart's use of the woman's first name. "Yes. It was tucked inside her bodice."

A million thoughts assailed Stuart. How long had Claire had the message? Why hadn't she taken it to Major Anderson? How had Hazen's men found it if it was inside her bodice? *Had they stripped her?* By God, if anyone had hurt her . . .

"Where is Miss Boudreau now?" he questioned, his voice tight.

"We're holding her in a small office in this building, pending further orders. She will, of course, be brought up on charges of treason. We are not sure at this point, however, whether her trial will be conducted here, or in Savannah."

"You're going to try her for treason?" Stuart asked incredulously, his heart leaping into his throat.

"Of course, Captain."

"But, General, she's a nurse!"

"She's also a Confederate spy, Captain Wellesley. No doubt she'll be hanged."

"Hanged!" Stuart barked, his jaw clenching. "You can't do that . . . sir!"

General Hazen threw down the pen he was toying with and riveted Stuart with a hard look. "Captain, is there something personal between you and Miss Boudreau?"

"No," Stuart answered quickly, trying hard to rein in his rampaging emotions. "It's just that . . . well, she saved my life when she didn't have to. Naturally, I feel a sense of obligation to her for that."

"She was under orders to save your life," Hazen retorted. "Major Anderson knew you were carrying a message, and he wanted you recovered enough to interrogate you about its contents."

"But, General," Stuart protested, desperately trying to think of anything that would soften the man's attitude, "you just said that Miss Boudreau had the message in her possession and she hadn't turned it over to Major Anderson. Isn't it possible that she might have had a change of heart?"

"Absolutely not. After questioning her, we learned that she had only found the message minutes before our attack—apparently while cleaning your boots. We have every reason to believe that she was planning to turn it over to Major Anderson and simply did not have the opportunity before the battle started."

Stuart drew a deep breath, telling himself he must present a calm, professional demeanor in front of his commanding officer. "May I see her?" he asked quietly.

"Why?"

"Just to reassure her that she has nothing to fear from us. As I said, Miss Boudreau took excellent care of me during my convalescence. I don't want her to be . . . unduly frightened."

General Hazen looked at Stuart for a long moment, then shook his head. "I don't think it's a good idea at this time, Captain. Knowing General Sherman's feelings about spies, the very worst thing we could do to Miss Boudreau would be to give her false hope. But I will mention your concern for the lady to the general and see if he wishes to speak to you about her before making a decision as to her fate."

Stuart's heart sank. It was well known that Sherman showed no leniency toward spies—regardless of their age or sex— and Stuart doubted whether General Hazen would put up much of an argument to save Claire from the gallows. Somehow, he had to make sure that he was given the chance to talk to Sherman himself. "Where is General Sherman now?" he asked.

"On his way to Savannah," Hazen smiled. "He plans to make the city his Christmas present to President Lincoln."

It was well after midnight when Stuart crept down a narrow hall in the headquarters building, headed for a door in front of which a guard sat snoring noisily. After his futile conversation with

General Hazen, he had spent the rest of the day trying to determine exactly where Claire was being held and then lay his hands on a key that would gain him access to her.

He was exhausted, having had no rest since early that morning, and the wound in his chest burned like someone had imbedded a torch in it. But he paid his discomfort and fatigue no heed, so intent was he on gaining entrance to Claire's small prison.

Several times during the long day, he had asked himself why he was risking so much for a woman whom he now knew never really cared for him at all. The hours she had spent with him these past weeks—reading to him, talking with him, sharing confidences and memories about their families—had been only a ruse to attempt to pry information from him.

He should have been more wary then—and more angry now. She had cared nothing for him, save for the information she was trying to extract from him. So, why was he still determined to find a way to help her out of her dangerous predicament? And, why, even now, did his heart pound with fear just thinking about her being executed for her crimes? It was exactly what she deserved. Hazen was right. She was a spy, and spies deserved to die.

But although Stuart could understand the Union's reaction to Claire's possession of his message, his stomach still turned sickeningly when he thought of her actually being hanged. After all, he reasoned, she was actually only doing her patriotic duty for the South, just as he had for the North. How could she be hanged for that?

She deserved a champion, and he had decided to be that man. He owed her. After all, she had, for

100

whatever reason, saved his life. But deep down, Stuart knew his feelings for Claire went much further than simple gratitude. Although he refused to allow himself to put a name to his real feelings for her, he was determined that somehow, some way, he was going to save her.

It was appallingly simple to get past the guard. The man's snoring never abated, even when Stuart inserted a key in the door lock not six inches from his ear.

Quickly, Stuart pushed the door open a crack and squeezed through. "Claire?" he whispered, stepping into the inky blackness of the unlit cell and silently closing the door behind him. "Are you in here?"

His question was met by silence.

"Claire?" he tried again. "It's Stuart Wellesley. Please answer me."

Again there was only silence. Cursing the total lack of light, Stuart dug in his pocket until he found the match and candle stub he had shoved in it earlier. Lighting the candle, he held it up, peering anxiously into the corners of the room.

She was there, huddled on a mattress, staring at him with huge, terrified eyes.

His face suffused with anger as he gazed at her. She looked so small, so helpless, and they hadn't even given her a blanket. "Claire," he repeated, as he took a step toward her, "don't be scared. It's just me."

"What do you want?" she asked fearfully.

"I came to see if you were all right," he answered, easing himself down on the mattress next to her and blowing out the candle.

101

"You shouldn't be here," she croaked. "It's not good for your chest for you to be moving around so much."

Stuart closed his eyes, knowing that he'd never cared more for anyone on earth than he did for this woman who, despite her terror, was worried about his wound. Groping around in the darkness, he found her cold, clenched hand and covered it with his own. "My chest is fine. I had a good nurse."

A sound somewhere between a chuckle and a sob escaped her, and Stuart squeezed her hand reassuringly. "Don't cry, Claire, I'm going to get you out of here."

A long silence ensued as Claire tried to digest this possibility. "Can you do that?" she finally whispered.

"I *will* do it," he answered positively.

"But why would you? I had your message."

"I know. Were you going to give it to Major Anderson?"

She couldn't lie to him. "Yes."

Stuart sighed, a long, disillusioned sound that twisted Claire's heart.

"I'm a Confederate patriot, Captain," she said, by way of explanation, "and you're a Yankee officer."

"The war is almost over, Claire. We'll work something out."

Slowly, she withdrew her hand from his and he heard her get up and walk to the far side of the small room. "No, we won't. We both had our duty. I have done mine, now you must do yours. But please don't come here again. I really don't want to see you anymore. Just put that salve I mixed up on your chest and you should be completely healed in another week or so."

"Claire, I'm not going to let them kill you!"

"Just go. Please. I don't want you here. Besides, you might get caught, and then how would you explain yourself?"

"I don't care," Stuart growled, struggling to his feet and making his way across the dark room. As he reached out, his hand brushed Claire's waist, and with an abrupt movement, he circled its small circumference and pulled her up against him. "Nothing is going to happen to you, sweetheart," he whispered, his mouth next to her ear. "I'll see to it."

"Oh, God, Stuart," Claire wailed suddenly, her composure breaking as she leaned against him and circled his neck with her arms. "I'm so frightened!"

Lifting his hand to her cheek, Stuart guided her mouth toward his, lowering his lips to hers and kissing her with a desperate passion.

To his utter surprise, Claire returned his kiss, her lips melting against his and her mouth opening under the gentle pressure.

He held her tighter, burying his hand in her thick hair as he deepened the kiss. When he finally raised his head, she continued to cling to him and he could feel her tears wetting the front of his tunic.

Nuzzling her cheek, he kissed the side of her nose, then trailed his lips across to her temple. "Trust me," he breathed, kissing the soft skin by her ear, "I'll figure something out."

"There's nothing that can be done," she responded, her voice shaking with fear and the first awakenings of desire.

"Yes, there is. Whatever it takes, I'll get you out of here. But I've got to go now, so kiss me and promise you'll trust me."

"We shouldn't be kissing."

"What?"

Claire raised her head from where it lay against his chest. "I said, we shouldn't be kissing."

"Why not?" he whispered, kissing her eyes.

"Because you're a Yankee and I'm a Confederate."

"That's true," he conceded, his lips hovering a breath above hers, "but what's more important is that you're a woman and I'm a man." And before she could protest further, he lowered his lips and kissed her with a passion that sucked the very breath from her.

The sensation of his soft mouth on hers made Claire's head start to spin and a small moan of pleasure escaped her. The heady sound caused Stuart to hold her even tighter, crushing her breasts against his chest. Just as Claire thought she might actually faint, he released her, slipping out the door before she even realized he was gone.

For a long time after he left, Claire stood in the darkness, brushing her lips with her fingers and smiling as she realized she no longer felt quite so afraid.

Chapter Eight

"This is never going to work."

Stuart drew a nervous breath as he stood and gazed at the imposing structure in front of him. The Georgian-style house was considered one of the most beautiful in Savannah and was now the temporary headquarters of General William Tecumseh Sherman.

On December 21, the Union had taken control of Savannah without a single shot being fired. In an unprecedented move, the town's citizens, fearing that the dreaded general would lay waste to their city, as he had Atlanta, had laid down their arms and surrendered without so much as a skirmish. Some society matrons had even gone so far as to invite high-ranking Northern officers into their homes for Christmas dinner.

Now, on the first day of 1865, the city was quiet and peaceful, its streets nearly deserted and its houses closed against the brisk wind that whipped off the Savannah River, chilling the air with a biting cold.

"This is never going to work," Stuart repeated, then tightened his lips, annoyed with himself.

"Don't say that, Wellesley," he chastised, "it *has* to work. It's all you've got." With a look of grim determination, he clapped his hat on his head and strode up to the door, knocking once before turning the handle and entering.

A young lieutenant sat at an exquisite Queen Anne desk in the foyer of the beautiful house. As Stuart entered, he rose and saluted sharply. Stuart returned the salute and pulled off his hat and gloves. "Captain Stuart Wellesley to see General Sherman," he announced.

"Do you have an appointment, sir?" the lieutenant barked, still standing rigidly at attention.

"Yes. At two o'clock."

"I will check and see if the general is ready to see you. Please have a chair."

"Thank you," Stuart responded, trying hard to hide the smile that threatened. Obviously, the lad was taking his assignment as one of Sherman's staff very seriously.

The man disappeared across the foyer, knocking on a set of carved double doors, then disappearing through them when a voice summoned him from the other side.

Stuart sat on the edge of a hard chair, impatiently slapping his gloves against his knee. He was vaguely aware of the beauty and elegance of the room in which he sat, but was too preoccupied and nervous about his upcoming interview to pay it much heed.

Only a moment passed before the lieutenant reappeared, marching forward and saying stiffly, "If you will follow me, Captain Wellesley, General Sherman will see you now."

With a nod, Stuart rose and followed the soldier

106

as he retraced his steps across the foyer and again opened the double doors, ushering Stuart through with a wave of his hand.

Stuart stepped into the handsome room which was obviously a well endowed library, but now was strewn with maps, battle plan sketches, and messages.

Behind a massive oak desk stood William Sherman. At forty-five years of age, he was rail-thin, with cold, piercing eyes and a wild shock of unkempt red hair. A melancholy man, Sherman was as prone to fits of despair as he was to his well-touted fits of temper. It was whispered that more than once he had attempted suicide and that it was only the constant vigilance of his wife at home and his closest aides in the field that kept him from succumbing to the melancholy that so often afflicted him.

But today, Sherman's thoughts were far from suicide. Savannah was his, and his promise to Lincoln that he would march through Georgia all the way to the sea, crippling the Confederacy by cutting it in half, was a reality.

As Stuart approached the wiry little man behind the desk, Sherman's pleasure was obvious. "Major Wellesley," he boomed, holding out his hand and shaking Stuart's warmly, "it is indeed good to see you up and looking so well."

"Thank you, General," Stuart responded. "I'm very pleased to be here. But it's 'Captain' Wellesley, sir, not 'Major.'"

"Not for long," Sherman responded slyly, then turned away and splashed a liberal amount of brandy into two elegant crystal glasses. Thrusting one into Stuart's hand, he continued, "Come, *Major*, let us drink to our triumph. Georgia is finally ours, and with the help of God, by the time those peach trees out there blossom, this war will be over."

"Here, here!" Stuart answered, lifting his glass and clinking the cut crystal against Sherman's. "To the end of this long, terrible conflict."

Sherman took a huge swallow of the mellow liquid, then wiped his mouth on the back of his sleeve. "Conflict, Major? This hasn't been a 'conflict.' This has been hell on earth."

Stuart nodded.

"But the end is in sight, thank God," Sherman continued, "so let us speak of happier things. What is it you wanted to see me about?"

Stuart set his glass down on the edge of Sherman's desk and cleared his throat. "I've come to ask a favor, sir. A very large favor."

Sherman's eyebrows rose with interest. "Name it. With the outstanding services you have rendered your country, no one could be more deserving of a boon. If it's in my power to grant your request, I will happily do so."

Stuart expelled a long, relieved sigh. Perhaps this wasn't going to be as difficult as he'd anticipated. "As you know, sir, because of my recent injury, I am being relieved of active duty and am returning home to Boston next week."

"Yes, I had heard that," Sherman acknowledged.

"There is a woman . . ."

"Miss Boudreau?" Sherman interrupted.

Stuart blinked with surprise. How had Sherman heard about Claire?

"I know most everything that goes on around me, Major," the general chuckled, answering Stuart's unasked question. "I understand that Miss Boudreau cared for you during your convalescence and that at the time the fort was taken, she was found to be in possession of the message you were carrying to me."

"That's correct," Stuart admitted, his throat tight with fear.

"I also know that she is currently in custody at Fort McAllister, awaiting trial for espionage."

"That's correct also."

"And you are here today to beg clemency for her?"

Stuart swallowed hard and, gathering all his courage, said, "I am here to ask for more than that, General. I would like Miss Boudreau released to my custody."

Sherman's mouth dropped open. After General Hazen had told him of Stuart's feelings of gratitude toward his nurse, he had expected him to intervene on her behalf, but even in his wildest dreams he'd never anticipated the young officer making such an outrageous request as to have the woman released!

"Oh, you would, would you?" Sherman countered.

"Yes, sir."

"And, what do you plan to do with her if I release her to you?"

"Take her to Boston with me, sir."

Again Sherman's eyes widened. "Have you taken leave of your senses, man? You can't take a known spy to Boston. It would never be allowed."

Stuart drew a deep breath. "It would be if I married her first, sir."

"Marry her?" Sherman exploded. "Are you telling me that you have fallen in love with a Confederate spy, Captain?"

Stuart winced as Sherman verbally demoted him

back to his present rank. It was a sure sign that the general was not pleased. "Let's just say I'm beholden to her, sir."

"Beholden?" Sherman sputtered, "Beholden! Captain Wellesley, this is preposterous."

"General, if you would just allow me to explain . . ."

"By all means," Sherman snorted, pouring another draught of brandy into his glass, "please do."

"Miss Boudreau is not a spy . . . not in the technical sense of the word, anyway."

"Oh?"

"She's a nurse, General. She was asked by General Anderson to care for me and try to extract whatever information she could regarding my mission at the time of my capture."

"General Anderson told you this?"

"Yes, sir. I spoke to him this morning. He also told me that Miss Boudreau was very reluctant to accept the assignment, and that it was only after heavy coaxing by her father that she finally agreed."

Sherman pursed his lips thoughtfully, staring out the window as he mulled over all he'd just heard. He had to admit that Captain Wellesley's plea was certainly heartfelt, and even if Anderson's explanation of Claire's actions was a cock-and-bull story, it was obvious that Stuart believed it to the very depths of his soul.

"Let me get this straight. What you're telling me is that you think Miss Boudreau is nothing more than a patriotic victim of circumstance?"

"Something like that," Stuart muttered, clamping down hard on his temper in the face of Sherman's obvious sarcasm.

"Then I ask you again, Captain—do you love this woman, or are you, as you just said, merely beholden to her?"

Stuart hesitated a moment, looking down as he pondered Sherman's question. Did he love Claire? A sudden vision of her as she had looked that night in her cell flashed before him. His silence lengthened as he remembered the moment—the fear in her eyes, the iciness of her hands, the feeling of her lips clinging to his. He raised his eyes and looked at Sherman squarely. "I love her, General."

"And are these tender feelings reciprocated?"

"I doubt it."

This frank admission took Sherman back for a moment. "Have you broached the subject of marriage with Miss Boudreau?"

"No, sir."

"So, you don't know if she'd even agree to this plan."

"No, I don't."

"Yet you were still willing to tempt my wrath, and God knows it's legendary, by coming here and asking me to grant you this favor."

"Yes, sir, I was."

Sherman stared at Stuart speculatively for a moment. Then, to Stuart's complete astonishment, he chuckled. "Well, Captain, I'm going to let you in on a little secret—I am a great believer in marriage. I've been married myself for a long time and consider it a fine institution."

Stuart's heart began to pound as hope flared.

"So," Sherman continued, "I'm going to grant you your boon. I will order the young lady released . . . but only under the provision that she agrees to marry you and leave the South. I will further demand that she sign a sworn statement that she will not attempt to return or have any contact with her family or friends until after the war is over. Is that understood?"

"Yes, sir," Stuart responded, barely able to contain his excitement.

"If Miss Boudreau declines to marry you, she will remain incarcerated and will stand trial for her crimes, as originally planned."

"Yes, sir."

"So, Captain, it is now up to you to convince the lady that marriage to you is a better fate than hanging."

"I understand."

"Think you can do it?"

"I hope so, General."

"So do I, Captain. I'll be anxiously following the outcome of your campaign."

"Thank you, sir."

Sherman's fierce little face split into a reluctant grin. "You're dismissed, Captain. Go see the lady while I write the appropriate pardons."

Stuart slapped his hat on his head and quickly saluted, backing toward the door. He had just turned to open the carved portal when the general's voice stopped him.

"Captain?"

"Yes, sir?"

"Good luck."

"I'd rather hang."

"What?"

"You heard me. I'd rather hang."

Stuart's jaw clenched with a combination of anger and hurt at Claire's devastating response to his proposal. He glared at her from across the small

112

table where they sat in the prison commandant's office. How *dare* she turn him down? He had run all the way back to the jail from Sherman's headquarters, so excited was he by the prospect of proposing marriage to her. His admission to Sherman that he was in love with Claire had been a revelation, and the more he thought about her, the more he realized he really did want to marry her—more than anything he'd ever wanted in his life.

And even though the general had warned him that he might meet with resistance from the stubborn little Rebel, he'd never expected that she would turn him down flat—and in such incredibly insulting terms as to state that she'd prefer death over marriage to him!

"You're being a fool," he gritted, his temper roiling just below the surface.

"Maybe," Claire replied, with a defiant toss of her head, "but it's my life to save or sacrifice, and I'd choose death a thousand times over before I'd marry a Yankee."

"Claire," Stuart began, deciding to take another tack, "the war is going to be over soon, and then there'll be no more Yankees or Confederates. We'll all just be Americans."

"No," she said, "we'll never be that again. Maybe sometime in the far future, but not in our lifetime."

Stuart slammed his fist on the table in total exasperation. "Maybe you're right. God knows, we'll never again be one nation if people like you persist in regarding all northerners as your enemies!"

"You *are* our enemies!" Claire shot back. "And no peace treaty or surrender agreement will ever change that. You and your generals marched down here, killed our men, raped our women, burned our houses, and laid waste to our homeland. You expect us to forgive that?"

Stuart bolted out of his chair, his fists clenched with frustration at her unrelenting stubbornness. "We all have to forgive each other," he insisted, "and there's much on both sides to get past. You seem to forget that it was the South that fired the first shot, the South that refused to compromise, the gallant lads of the South who shouted that they wanted this war. Well, they got it, lady, and in spades!"

Taking a step closer, he riveted her with a hard look, his eyes stormy. "And now, whether you and your compatriots want to believe it or not, the South has lost. The 'Glorious Cause' is dead, and all of us, *all of us*, must try to forgive each other and put this country back together!"

"Fine," Claire flashed, rising also, "you go right ahead and put it back together, my high-minded Captain, but you won't do it with me by your side!"

Adroitly sidestepping him, she raced over to the door and beat on it frantically. "Guard! Guard! Take me back to my cell, please."

Promptly the door opened and a nervous-looking young corporal poked his head in, glancing warily from Claire's stony face to Stuart's furious one. "Are you finished in here, Captain?" he asked hesitantly.

"Yes!" Claire responded before Stuart could answer. "We are finished."

"No, we're not!" Stuart thundered. "Leave us, Corporal, and don't open that door again until *I* call you. Is that clear?"

"Yes, sir!" the shaken soldier responded, his

114

head bobbing so hard it looked like it might snap off his neck. "Just call when you're ready."

"Go!" Stuart shouted, slamming the door rudely behind the fleeing man and turning again toward Claire.

"We are done, Miss, when *I* say we're done, and you might as well resign yourself to talking this out, because you're not leaving this room until we do."

With great dignity, Claire sat back down at the table. "I hate you," she said quietly.

"I know you do," Stuart sighed, "but I also know that only a week ago, you stood in this very building and kissed me."

Claire's head jerked up. "Is that what this is all about, Captain? Did you interpret my hysteria that night as passion? Well, I'm sorry to disappoint you, but it wasn't. I kissed you because I was terrified and you told me you'd help me get out of here. That was all there was to it."

Stuart's eyes narrowed. "You're lying, Claire. That was no kiss of gratitude."

"You're flattering yourself, Captain."

Stuart shook his head. "No, I don't think so. I've kissed enough women to know passion when I see it."

Claire's chuckle was mirthless. "Oh, yes, of course, I forget. The great Stuart Wellesley—the most eligible bachelor in Boston. What a blow it must be to your pride to find out that there's at least one woman on earth who isn't dying of love for you."

"Stop it!" Stuart commanded. "Pride has nothing to do with this, and you damn well know it!"

"Do I?" Claire countered. "Why *do* you want me to marry you? I'm sure there are lots of women who would be thrilled to receive your proposal. Why would you want to marry one who doesn't want you?"

"Because," Stuart stammered, knowing that the way this conversation was progressing, he couldn't possibly tell her how he really felt about her. "Because I'm beholden to you for saving my life, and because now I feel I can repay you by saving yours."

"Don't bother," Claire said wearily. "You don't owe me anything. I took the assignment to care for you only because I was told about the message you were carrying and I thought I might be able to aid the Southern Cause by coercing you to divulge its contents. If it hadn't been for that, I would have let you die."

Stuart drew in a sharp breath, his expression anguished. "I don't believe you."

Claire closed her eyes against his look, her heart breaking. If only things could have been different between them. If only the times had been different, she might have met him while vacationing in Saratoga. They might have danced, taken long walks under the stars, had picnics on a lazy summer afternoon. They might even have fallen in love and decided to spend the rest of their lives together.

But, times were what they were and she couldn't marry him, even if she wanted to. With her southern voice, her southern manners, her southern upbringing, it would never work. She was a daughter of the Confederacy, and regardless of how foolishly optimistic Stuart was about the United States again becoming one unified nation once the war was over, she'd never be accepted by Boston society. The chasm between them was just too deep, and in the end, Stuart would come to hate her. Although she was loath to admit it, even to herself, Claire knew she could not bear to see the look in his eyes change from one of desire and affection to one of contempt and regret. She cared too much for him to see that happen.

With a tremulous smile, she walked over and placed a light kiss on his cheek. "You're right, Captain Wellesley, I wouldn't have let you die."

As she started to step back, Stuart grabbed her shoulders and pulled her hard against him. "Claire . . ." he rasped, burying his hands in her hair and reaching for her mouth. "Claire, please. *Please* marry me. I can't see you die!"

Claire allowed him to kiss her, but was careful not to return the caress. When he finally lifted his lips from hers, she quickly stepped out of his embrace. "You won't," she smiled, trying desperately to make light of this impossible situation. "You'll be back home in Boston long before they hang me."

"Claire, for God's sake!"

"No, Stuart, don't say anything else. I won't marry you, no matter how long you keep me locked in this room, so please let me go back to my cell. I'm very . . . tired."

With an agonized nod, Stuart moved to the door and signaled the guard. Then, turning back to her, he said, "This isn't over, Claire. Not by a long shot."

Before she could argue further, he jerked open the door and walked out, not hearing her soft voice as she murmured, "Goodbye, Captain Stuart Wellesley of the Fourth Massachusetts. God speed."

Chapter Nine

"Papa!"

Claire's cry of delight resounded through the small office as her eyes lit upon the unexpected sight of her father. The guard who had escorted her from her cell smiled and said quietly, "You have fifteen minutes, Mr. Boudreau."

Claire cast the man a frowning glance as he departed, then hurried forward, throwing her arms around her father's neck. "Oh, Papa," she whispered, "it's so wonderful to see you. But, however did you get permission to visit?"

Archibald Boudreau closed his eyes for a moment, clasping his daughter to him and willing himself not to cry. "Your young man arranged it," he said gruffly.

Claire stepped back and looked at her father quizzically. "My young . . ." she started, then frowned and said tonelessly, "Oh, you must mean Captain Wellesley."

"It's *Major* Wellesley now," her father informed her. "He's been promoted."

A spark of interest momentarily flared in Claire's eyes, then was quickly masked. "He's

119

hardly my 'young man,' Papa. Please don't call him that."

Archibald grunted and gestured toward the small table where Claire and Stuart had sat two days before. "That's exactly what I want to talk to you about. Let's sit down."

Before Claire could protest, Archibald lowered himself heavily into a chair and said, "How are you, daughter? You look thin. Are you being treated well?"

Claire glanced down at her drab gray dress, realizing for the first time that it did hang more loosely on her than it had a few weeks before. "I'm fine, Papa, really," she assured him, lowering herself into a chair opposite his. "Now, what's this about *Major* Wellesley?"

"He came to see me yesterday."

"He did?"

"Yes, and I must admit, I have to admire him for having the courage to do so."

"What did he want?" Claire asked, unable to contain her curiosity.

"He wants to marry you," Archibald answered bluntly.

"It's out of the question, Papa."

"Don't be a fool, Claire! The man is willing to save you from hanging, and you are not going to let some misguided sense of patriotism prevent him from doing exactly that."

Claire's lips thinned. "I won't marry him, Papa. I already told him that, and I haven't changed my mind. I'll hang first."

"Over my dead body!" Archibald bellowed. "I've lost one child to this war, but that couldn't be helped. But know this now, girl: I'm not about to lose you when I can prevent it. You'll marry

120

the major and you'll move to Boston, where you'll be safe."

"Don't do this to me, Papa!" Claire cried. "I'm a grown woman, well able to make my own decisions, and I won't be dictated to by some . . . some Yankee!"

"That Yankee, as you call him, is your salvation, Missy! Can't you see that?"

"I don't believe that he had the audacity to ask you to intervene," Claire huffed. "He had no right!"

"Well, thank God he did. Did you know he also went to General Sherman himself and begged him to pardon you?"

"He did?" Claire gasped. Quickly she rose from the table and turned her back on her father, unwilling to let him see how shaken she was by this astonishing news. "I can't imagine why he would do that."

"Well," Archibald replied, hefting himself out of his chair and coming to stand behind her, "according to him, he feels beholden to you for saving his life, and now he wants to save yours."

"I've already talked to him about that. I explained that I was merely doing my duty and that the only reason I saved him was because I hoped to aid the Cause by doing so. He doesn't owe me a thing. If it hadn't been for the message I knew he was carrying, I'd have let him die."

"No, you wouldn't have," Archibald said positively. "And I don't believe you're as immune to the man as you say you are."

Claire whirled around and gaped at her father in astonishment. "Papa, how can you say that? He's a Yankee!"

"He's a damn fine Yankee," Archibald shot

back, "and when this war is finally over and there aren't any more Yankees or Confederates, he'll simply be a damn fine man."

"You sound just like him," Claire muttered bitterly. "He talked about that when he was here—that after the war we'd all just be Americans again."

Archibald nodded. "Well, then, since we're both saying the same thing, maybe you should quit being so stubborn and listen to us."

"You sound like you *want* me to marry him," she accused.

"Of course I want you to marry him! Do you think I want you to die?"

Claire threw out her hands in supplication. "Papa, I don't want to die, either. Please believe that. But I truly think I'd prefer death to being married to a Yankee officer and living the rest of my life in Boston. Can't you understand?"

"What I understand is that nothing in life is permanent," Archibald said slowly. "Not if you don't want it to be. As long as you're alive, situations can be changed. Only death is final."

Claire raised her eyes to his, trying hard to glean the true meaning behind his words. "Are you saying that I should marry Major Wellesley to save myself and then, after the war, have the marriage annulled?"

Archibald smiled slyly. "All I'm saying is that as long as there is life, there are options."

Claire returned to the table, sinking into a chair and staring at her father incredulously. "That *is* what you're saying . . ." she murmured.

"Interpret it any way you like, Claire. Right now, the important thing is to do whatever is necessary to save your life."

Claire nodded distractedly, and for a brief moment, her father thought he had won her over. Then her eyes clouded again. "But what about David?" she asked quietly.

Archibald joined her at the table, taking her hand and squeezing it reassuringly. "Claire, darling, David is dead."

"Don't say that!" she hissed, yanking her hand out of his. "We don't know that for sure!"

"Yes, we do, child. Major Wellesley checked into it."

"No!" she cried, jumping up and pacing the small room in agitation. "No, he didn't! He's just telling you that to bring you over to his way of thinking!"

"Claire," Archibald said calmly, "listen to me. The major contacted every northern prison in the vicinity of Gettysburg. There is no David Henry listed on any of their rolls. He's dead, Claire. You must face it."

Just then, the young guard who had escorted Claire to meet her father opened the door. "Time is up, sir. I'll have to ask you to leave now."

Claire threw the man a wild-eyed glance and raced over to where her father still sat. "Get out!" she cried, her eyes streaming tears. "It can't have been fifteen minutes yet!"

"Please," Archibald entreated, "leave us alone for just a moment to say goodbye."

With a curt nod the private disappeared, softly closing the door.

Archibald rose and pulled Claire into his embrace, holding her close. "Promise me, my dear, that you'll think about what we've said today. There's very little time left. You must give Major Wellesley your answer by noon tomorrow. Otherwise, the Yankees will proceed with your trial."

Claire clutched her father around his thick waist, burying her head against his worn brown jacket. "I promise, Papa."

Unclasping her arms, Archibald took a step back, placing his hands on her cheeks and raising her face till she was looking at him. "Please, Claire. Marry this man. Do it for me, if not for yourself. I don't think I could stand to lose you."

"I'll think about it, Papa," Claire nodded, then whirled away just as the guard again opened the door. Covering her mouth with shaking fingers, she pushed past him, fleeing down the hall toward her cell.

With heavy steps, Archibald walked back to the outer office, his tired gaze lighting on Stuart, who was sitting tensely on the edge of a chair.

"Well?" Stuart demanded, jumping to his feet. "Did she say 'yes'?"

"No," Archibald shook his head, "she didn't." Seeing Stuart's devastated look, he quickly added, "but she didn't say 'no,' either. She said she'd think about it."

"Well, at least that's something," Stuart said, seizing on this slim hope.

"Yes, son," Archibald nodded, "at least it's something." Then, with a weary sigh, the old man put his hat on his head and trudged slowly out of the building.

"Major Wellesley, General Hazen sent me to fetch you. Miss Boudreau has asked to see you, and the general has granted permission."

The private who stood at the door to Stuart's small office had never seen a man move so fast.

After spending a sleepless night, Stuart had risen, washed, shaved, and dressed in a clean uniform which now sported the bars of a major's rank. After that, the morning had dragged on endlessly as he tried to busy himself with paperwork. Now it was nearly noon—the deadline which General Hazen had set for Claire to make her decision about marrying him. As the clock had crept closer to midday, Stuart had become more and more despondent, sure that Claire had not changed her mind. He had just about decided that he was going to ask Hazen's permission to see her one more time, regardless of whether she wanted to see him, when the private had appeared at his door.

Without so much as a word to the smiling soldier, Stuart grabbed his hat, clapped it on his head, and tore out of his office, nearly running the poor man down. He raced across the parade field, taking the prison's steps two at a time and bursting into the foyer of the small building with such eagerness that several attendants looked up at him in amazement.

"Major Stuart Wellesley to see Miss Boudreau," he announced to a corporal seated at the receiving desk.

"Yes, sir," the attendant answered, scraping his chair back and rising. "If you'll follow me."

"That won't be necessary, Corporal," Stuart announced, "I know my way." Hurrying past the gaping man, Stuart strode down the hall to the now familiar little office and pushed the door open.

Claire was already there, standing near the small window. She started as the door slammed open, whirling around to face Stuart, her eyes wide and her hands clasped nervously in front of her.

"Well?" Stuart demanded, "what is your answer?"

Claire let out a long breath and swallowed. He was so big, he seemed to completely fill the little room. "Good morning, Major Wellesley," she said, her voice quaking with nerves.

"Good morning," Stuart acknowledged, closing the door behind him and pulling off his hat. "You have something to tell me?"

"Congratulations on your promotion."

"Damn my promotion!" he thundered, completely exasperated by her evasiveness. "Are you going to marry me or not?"

Claire opened and closed her mouth twice, trying to find voice for her answer, but no sound would come. She, too, had spent a sleepless night, pondering everything her father had said and finally making her decision just before dawn.

"Quit gasping like a beached fish," Stuart ordered. In two long strides, he closed the distance between them. "Are you going to marry me? Yes or no."

"Yes," Claire breathed, nearly undone by his huge presence and the enormity of what she was agreeing to. "I will accept your offer of marriage, Major."

Stuart closed his eyes and blew out a long, relieved breath. "Good," he nodded. "Good. We'll do it this afternoon. I'll have your father here at three. He can bring you an appropriate dress." Then, to Claire's complete amazement, he turned to leave.

"Major!"

"Yes?" he asked, turning back expectantly.

"You can't go yet. There are . . . things we need to discuss."

126

"What things?"

"If we could sit down a moment, I'll tell you."

Stuart's expression grew wary, but he did as she bade. When they were both seated at the table, he waited impatiently for a moment, then said, "Okay, we're sitting down. What things?"

Claire drew a deep breath, praying her courage would not fail her. All morning she had mentally rehearsed what she wanted to say, but now that the moment was at hand, she was nearly tongue-tied. "Before I marry you, I have a few terms you must agree to," she whispered.

A frown settled over Stuart's handsome features. "There aren't going to be any terms, Claire. This is going to be a marriage just like any other."

"Well, not quite," she responded, her resolve suddenly returning and her voice gaining strength as she spoke. "Marriages generally begin with love. When they don't, things are bound to be a little different."

Stuart's face darkened even more. "What are you saying?"

With a jerky little movement, Claire rose from the table and walked back to the window, unable to face him while she stated the obvious. "I won't sleep with you."

"Yes, you will."

"No, I won't," she repeated, turning around and looking at him squarely.

Stuart bit down hard on the inside of his lower lip, telling himself this was no time to lose his damnable Wellesley temper. After all, he should have expected something like this. Should have known that she'd never willingly climb into a Yankee's bed.

"Claire, I will not agree to a titular marriage. I

expect you to be my wife . . . in every way. Starting tonight."

"The only way that will happen is rape, Major, but then, you Yankees are good at that, aren't you?"

A flush of anger crept up Stuart's neck, but he managed to keep his voice calm. "It won't be rape, lady. I guarantee you that."

Claire could feel herself begin to shake. He was so *sure* of himself! So confident that she wouldn't be able to resist him. "I told you once before, Stuart, that although I might be the only woman in existence who feels this way, I am not dying of love for you—nor am I in the least infatuated with your masculine charms."

Her insulting words hit him like a blow, but he refused to let her see how she had hurt him. "You'll change your mind," he said quietly.

"You couldn't live long enough to see that happen," she returned.

For a long moment, the two combatants stared at each other, both of them breathing hard. Finally, Stuart broke the silence. "Okay," he sighed. "You want to talk terms, then here are mine. You will marry me, return to Boston with me, and live with me as my wife. That includes sleeping in my bed. But I promise, you have nothing to fear from me. I'm not a rapist, regardless of what you might think."

"You couldn't sleep in the same bed with me every night without touching me!" Claire said, her voice tinged with disbelief.

"Couldn't I?" Stuart asked, his gaze raking her insolently. "You think an awful lot of yourself, don't you, Miss Boudreau?"

Claire blushed crimson, outrage warring with

embarrassment at his mocking words.

"Or maybe it's just that you're not *really* sure that *you* could sleep in my bed without touching *me*," he continued. "Maybe you're just a little more infatuated with my—what did you call them?—my 'masculine charms' than you care to admit."

"You're disgusting," Claire hissed. "You're acting like a . . . a dirty Yankee!"

Suddenly, Stuart shot out of his seat and grabbed Claire by her shoulders, whirling her around to face him and tilting her chin back with an insistent finger until she was forced to meet his blazing eyes.

"A dirty Yankee, Miss? You think that only a dirty Yankee would expect his wife to be a wife? Well, I beg to differ. From what I've seen of the size of most families in this area, I'd say that a great many Southern gentlemen have the very same expectation. No, Claire, I'm not acting like a Yankee *or* a Confederate. I'm acting like a man— with a man's desires and a man's expectations. Maybe it's just that you're not woman enough to handle them."

"Let go of me!" Claire shrieked, wrenching away from his grasp. To her great surprise, he immediately released her. She backed up several steps, trying desperately to put some space between her and his overwhelming masculinity. "How dare you say such things to me?"

"How dare you set terms for a marriage that is going to save your life?"

The air fairly crackled between them as they stood on opposite sides of the small room, glaring at each other. The silence lengthened and lengthened until Claire could stand it no longer. "All right," she said suddenly, "I will not demand separate bedrooms."

"You're damn right you won't," Stuart muttered.

"But you must promise not to force me to accept your, ah, attentions."

"Force you?" Stuart repeated, smiling slightly. "Absolutely, I will agree to that. In fact, if you like, I'll sign a sworn statement that I will never, ever, 'force' you into any intimacy you do not desire."

"You will?" Claire's eyebrows rose with genuine surprise.

"Yes. In fact, I'll sign it today, before we're married."

Claire looked at him thoughtfully for a moment. "That won't be necessary."

"It won't?"

"No. Your word is good enough."

"Very well," he smiled, secretly pleased that she trusted him at least that much. Rising from his chair, he walked over to her, his eyes holding a peculiarly soft expression. Taking her hand, he raised it to his lips and softly kissed her knuckles. "Everything will work out, Claire. All you have to do is let it." And leaning forward, he brushed her lips with his. "I'll see you about four."

He turned and walked out of the small room, leaving his much bemused fiancée to stare after him and wonder just what he had really agreed to.

Chapter Ten

Claire looked down at the dull gleam of the gold band on her finger. She was married. To a Yankee. A Yankee she hated. Well, maybe not *hated*, exactly, but certainly one with whom she had no desire to spend the rest of her life.

Feeling a slight pressure at her elbow, she pulled herself from her reverie and looked up into the soft gray eyes of her new husband. "General Sherman would like to offer his congratulations," Stuart said softly.

"General Sherman!" Claire gasped. "Is he here?"

"Right over there," Stuart acknowledged with a slight tilt of his head.

"But why?"

"I think he wanted to make sure we actually got married before he signed your pardon."

"My pardon," Claire muttered sarcastically. "My pardon for being a Southern patriot."

Stuart's expression hardened. "Don't start, Claire. Not here. Now, come on. We're keeping the general waiting, and he has more important things to attend to."

With lagging footsteps, Claire allowed herself to be propelled across the room to where the small, fierce figure of William Sherman stood. She cast a furtive glance at her father, who had insisted on attending her brief wedding ceremony, even though it had been held in a small anteroom of the fort's headquarters building. He now stood hovering near the door, obviously uncomfortable at being surrounded by so many blue-clad soldiers, but stoically refusing to leave before he had a chance to kiss his daughter and whisper a few words of encouragement.

"Will I be allowed to speak to my father before we leave?" Claire asked.

"Of course," Stuart smiled. "You're not a prisoner any longer. You're a major's wife. You can speak with anyone you please."

"As long as you are near enough to hear the conversation, and make sure I'm not talking sedition, right?" Claire added sarcastically.

Stuart ignored her bitter words, and as they approached Sherman, he gently squeezed her hand. "General, sir, may I present my wife, Claire."

Sherman's steely little eyes raked Claire as if assessing whether she was worth all the trouble she'd caused.

Claire drew in a startled breath, sure the horrid man was going to say something insulting, but when he spoke, his words were polite and his voice was surprisingly soft and cultured. "Mrs. Wellesley, may I be the first to offer my felicitations. I'm sure you and Major Wellesley will be very happy."

Claire could not speak, her emotions were so conflicted. Here she was, face to face with the

Yankee devil who had laid waste to her homeland, and yet he was speaking to her in a most civilized manner and actually seemed to be genuine in his good wishes.

"I hope you will find Boston to your liking," Sherman continued, seeming not to notice Claire's discomfiture. "It's a lovely city, and one that I've always enjoyed."

Swallowing hard, Claire looked the hated man squarely in the eye and responded in a deceptively light tone, "I'm sure one Yankee city is as good as another." She heard Stuart's swift intake of breath and winced slightly as his hand tightened on her arm.

General Sherman did not miss the mutinous challenge in Claire's eyes as she stared at him, but he did not respond to her verbal volley. Rather, he swung his gaze over to Stuart, his eyes sparking with amusement at the other man's frozen smile. Major Wellesley had his work cut out for him if he hoped to have any domestic harmony in his home. Well, he'd been adamant in his desire to marry the feisty little Rebel, so good luck to him! With a wry twist to his lips, Sherman pulled a packet of papers out of his uniform blouse and held them out to Stuart. "Here are the documents you need to make the trip north."

"Thank you, sir," Stuart nodded, accepting the papers.

"I must return to my duties," Sherman continued. "Have a safe journey, Major, and, again, my congratulations."

With one last cursory glance at Claire, the general turned away and walked out of the room.

Stuart turned on Claire, his eyes blazing. "Don't

133

you ever do that again," he hissed, his voice low despite his anger.

"If you think I'm going to exchange pleasantries with that murdering devil, you're very wrong, Major! Now, let go of me. I want to talk to my father."

Hurrying over to where Archibald Boudreau still stood near the door, she stepped gratefully into his embrace, dropping her forehead to his shoulder and whispering, "Oh, Papa, I don't think I can go through with this."

To her surprise, Archibald stiffened and grasping her arms, held her away from him. "Don't talk nonsense, Claire. It's done. You're married, and you must come to terms with it."

Claire stared at her father, her eyes filled with hurt and bewilderment at his curtness.

"It's only a temporary situation, daughter," Archibald reminded her, his voice cajoling. "And just remember, you had no alternative."

"But you're sure I can have the marriage annulled once the war is over?"

Archibald hesitated. "I'm not sure of anything right now," he said carefully. "And at least until the war is over, you must keep Major Wellesley happy."

Claire's eyes widened as she realized what her father was really saying. "I can't be a true wife to him, Papa. I just can't!"

"Hush," Archibald admonished, looking around nervously to see if any of the soldiers present had heard her outburst. "You do what you must to stay in the man's good graces."

"But, Papa, you can't expect me to . . ."

"Claire, what *I* expect isn't important. But you

must remember that you are still in a very tenuous situation. The only thing keeping you from the hangman's noose is Stuart Wellesley's largesse."

"But I've been pardoned! I saw General Sherman hand the papers to Stuart myself."

Archibald snorted. "And how fast do you think those papers could be lost or destroyed if Major Wellesley decided to rid himself of you? Claire, use your head! Until relations between the North and South normalize enough that you can return home, you have to be the wife he expects."

"I can't, Papa. I'd rather die than have him touch me."

Archibald sighed. "Then do it for me, daughter. It would kill me if anything happened to you."

At that moment, Stuart sauntered up to them. "Do what?" he asked nonchalantly, holding out a fresh glass of champagne to Claire.

She ignored his question and the proffered glass, instead, turning back to her father and hugging him warmly. "I'll try, Papa," she whispered. "For you."

"Thank you," Archibald whispered back. Then, straightening, he looked at Stuart and said, "What time does your train leave?"

"Six," Stuart responded, reaching for his watch. When his fingers touched his flat pocket, he frowned. "Forgot it got stolen."

Archibald threw him a sympathetic look and reached for his own timepiece. "It's four-thirty."

Stuart nodded. "We have to leave," he said, turning toward Claire. "Are your trunks ready?"

"They're outside," Archibald responded, "such as they are. I had Valencia pack everything she thought appropriate, but I'm afraid that after four years of blockade, there's not as much as there should be."

"Don't concern yourself, Mr. Boudreau," Stuart interjected smoothly, "I'll buy Claire anything she's lacking once we get to Boston."

"I'm sure that what I already have will be perfectly satisfactory," Claire rejoined, loath to let Stuart think she'd accept gifts from him.

"As you wish," he shrugged. "Now, if you'll both excuse me, I'll see to the loading."

Archibald looked assessingly at Stuart's retreating back. "You shouldn't be so hard on him, Claire. He's a good man, and I think he truly cares for you. You could have done much worse."

"And I could have done much better," Claire snapped, "so I wish you'd quit saying how wonderful you think he is. He's a Yankee, Papa—a dirty, murdering Yankee officer, and there is nothing wonderful about him!"

Archibald shook his head sadly. "Just don't make things worse on yourself than they have to be," he advised, wrapping his arms around her and pulling her close.

Suddenly, all the bizarre events of the last few days seemed to press down on her, and despite her earlier vow not to cry, tears sprang to her eyes. "Oh, Papa," she sobbed, throwing herself against him, "I'm going to miss you so much."

"I'll miss you, too," Archibald responded, his voice suddenly gruff, "but it won't be long till we'll see each other again. Just promise me you'll take care of yourself."

Slowly, she raised tear-glazed eyes to her father and nodded. "I will, Papa. I promise. But you must promise that the minute this hateful war is over, you'll do everything in your power to help me get an annulment.''

"Claire,'' Archibald said quietly, ''I don't know if an annulment will be possible.'' For a moment, he looked at her as if he wanted to say something further but didn't quite know how to begin.

"What do you mean, Papa?'' Claire asked, her voice suddenly wary. ''Why wouldn't it be?''

"Well, it's just that . . .'' He shuffled his feet, cleared his throat, and looked down at his boots.

"Papa! You're acting like a schoolboy! What is it you want to say?''

Archibald blew out a long breath, muttering, ''Why is it that there's never a woman around when you need one?'' Then, looking up at Claire, he blurted, ''In order for a marriage to be annulled, it must remain unconsummated, and if you are going to keep Major Wellesley happy, I don't think that's going to be possible.''

Claire blushed crimson, but she raised her chin defiantly and demanded, ''What exactly are you trying to say, Papa?''

"I'm saying that it may take a divorce to end your marriage.''

"A divorce!'' Claire gasped. ''Why, I could never disgrace the family with a divorce.''

"You may have no other choice. Besides, there are worse things than divorce.''

"Well, I can't think what!'' she huffed. ''I'll just have to think of some way to prevent him from . . . from . . .''

She groped around mentally, trying to think of a delicate word to describe what she wanted to prevent Stuart from doing, but before she could seize upon one, he suddenly reappeared.

"Come on, Claire, it's time," he said gently, as he reached her side.

Claire made one more lunge toward her father, squeezing him around his corpulent waist until the old man grunted from the pressure. "Goodbye, dearest," he whispered, hugging her back. "Write to me often . . . and please be careful."

"I will," Claire promised, then, taking a deep breath, she turned toward Stuart. "I'm ready."

Stuart shook hands with Archibald, promising that he'd send a wire when they arrived in Boston, then placed his hand on the small of Claire's back and ushered her toward the door.

After they'd disappeared out of the room, Archibald hurried over to a window and watched Stuart hand Claire up onto the seat of the wagon he'd commandeered to take them to the train station. Even after she was settled and had given Stuart a curt nod of thanks, Archibald noticed that Stuart's hand lingered at her elbow. When he finally released her, he gave her hand a light caress before walking around the wagon and climbing in.

Despite himself, Archibald chuckled, a low, resonant sound that rumbled up from deep in his chest. "There's never going to be an annulment," he predicted softly. "It's going to have to be a divorce."

The train was slow, crowded, dirty—and full of Yankees.

"I'm in hell," Claire muttered, looking around at the packed car. "Yankee hell."

"What did you say?" Stuart asked, leaning

toward her.

"Nothing."

"I'm sorry I couldn't get us better accommodations," he apologized, "but on such short notice, there was no way to engage a sleeper."

"It doesn't matter," Claire answered, silently thanking God that no sleepers had been available. She didn't think she could have lived through three days locked up with him in a tiny room whose only accoutrement was a bed!

"I thought that maybe when we stop in Washington tomorrow, enough people will get off that I'll be able to book one there."

"It's really not necessary," Claire said quickly. "I don't mind sitting up."

Stuart looked at her a moment, then sighed. "Yeah, I bet you don't."

Turning away, he stared glumly out at the passing countryside. Perhaps he *had* made a grave mistake with this marriage he'd insisted upon. Since they'd boarded the train the previous day, Claire had hardly said ten words to him, except to comment occasionally on the tragedy and waste of the burned-out plantations they passed.

She had been particularly morose over one large house, telling Stuart in a voice laced with sadness that it had belonged to a friend of her family's and that she'd spent many an enchanting spring evening dancing in the magnificent ballroom, which had now been reduced to charred rubble. "And to think, the demon responsible for all this was at *my* wedding!" she'd gritted.

After that, she'd become even more withdrawn, concentrating on the knitting she'd brought with her and responding to his struggling attempts at conversation with curt one-word answers.

Now, after twenty-four exhausting hours aboard the crowded, dirty train, Stuart had finally given up trying to be sociable.

"We'll be getting off at Washington for a couple of days," he announced suddenly.

Claire turned toward him in surprise. "Why?"

"Because there is some business I need to attend to—and because I know an excellent seamstress there." In actuality, Stuart had no business in Washington, but the thought of remaining on this stinking train for another two days was more than he could bear. Perhaps if they cut the trip in half and spent some time enjoying the capital, with its many amusements, they would again find something to talk about. He almost wished they were back at Fort McAllister, closeted in his dingy little room. During those long days of his convalescence, they had spent many an hour together talking about books, music, and art, and reminiscing about life before the war.

"I don't need any clothes, Major," Claire announced, her soft voice breaking into his reverie.

Stuart frowned. "Please stop calling me 'Major.' My name is Stuart, or Stu, if you prefer, and I would very much like you to call me by one or the other."

"I don't need any new clothes, *Stuart,*" Claire repeated. "What I have is perfectly adequate."

"Well, your father seems to disagree. He told me yesterday that most of your clothes were purchased before the war and that even your newest dresses are more than two years old."

"They're fine."

140

"Damn it, Claire! They're *not* fine! What do you have against me buying you some new clothes?"

"It's too . . . husbandly!" she blurted.

"I'm your husband!"

"Don't say that!"

"Why not? Do you think if I don't say it, you can pretend it's not true? Well, think again, lady. We are well and truly married, and I *will* buy you new clothes—and anything else I feel is fitting for my *wife*. Do you understand?"

Claire sat frozen on the hard train seat, staring down at her clenched hands. She knew that every passenger within twenty feet must be listening to their angry exchange, and she couldn't bring herself to look up and face their Yankee smirks.

"Do you understand me?" Stuart repeated, his voice cracking like a whip as he demanded she answer him.

"Yes! Yes, I understand you! Now, leave me alone!"

"Fine," he nodded, crossing his arms over his chest and compressing his lips in frustration. "I'll leave you alone. But you give me one more word of argument about this when we reach Washington and I'll throw your damn valises in the Potomac. Then you'll have to accept some new clothes from me or run around naked!"

Claire buried her head in her hands in utter mortification as a burst of laughter arose from the soldiers surrounding them. "Thataway, Major," a fat sergeant chortled. "Only way to keep 'em in line is to show 'em who's boss."

"Oh, yeah, right!" interrupted a private seated across from them. "And forcing your wife to accept a new wardrobe is some tough punishment!"

Again, raucous laughter pealed through the train car.

"All right, soldiers, that's enough," Stuart growled.

The men sobered, their guffaws quickly reduced to lingering smiles as they attempted to quell their amusement. After all, the man was a high-ranking officer and they shouldn't be laughing at him. But, damn, it sure did a man's heart good to know that even a major could have trouble with his woman!

Chapter Eleven

The train pulled into Washington shortly after noon. The day was bright and sun-drenched, and the light dusting of snow that covered the ground sparkled under a cerulean sky.

But to Claire, she was truly entering the gates of hell. Everywhere she looked were Yankee soldiers —thousands of them packing the station or lounging on the sidewalks surrounding the building. She had thought nothing could be worse than the last two days on the train, but looking out the dingy coach window, she was overcome by a fear so profound she felt paralyzed.

Stuart waited until most of the soldiers crowding the train's aisles disembarked, then rose from his seat, picking up a suitcase and turning toward Claire expectantly. "Are you ready?"

She didn't answer.

"Claire?" he repeated, his brow furrowing with concern as he noticed her ashen face. "Are you all right?"

"No," she croaked, her voice nearly inaudible.

Stuart sat back down, picking up her icy hand. "What's wrong?"

Claire turned toward him with stricken eyes. "I can't get off."

"What do you mean, you can't get off? We have to get off now. We're in Washington."

"I know, but I can't get off."

Stuart's unease was increasing with every second. "Are you ill?"

"No."

"Then why can't you get off the train?"

Claire closed her eyes and pulled her hand out of her husband's warm grip. Drawing a deep, shuddering breath, she whispered, "All those Yankee soldiers. I can't go out there with them."

Stuart gazed out the window, trying to figure out what was scaring her so badly, but all he saw was typical train station activity—throngs of soldiers milling around, some celebrating joyous reunions with their families, some waiting with bored patience to depart for a new tour of duty, some just sitting and staring at nothing. It looked no different than the Washington train station had looked at any time during the last four years, but then he suddenly saw it as Claire must, and immediately he realized how terrifying the scene must be to a young Southern woman.

"Sweetheart," he said gently, again covering her cold, clenched hand with his own, "no one is going to hurt you."

"I just can't go out there! Please don't make me, Stuart. Please!"

For a long moment, Stuart simply stared at her, then nodding slowly, he said, "Would you rather go straight on to Boston?"

Claire bit her lip in an attempt to quell her panic enough to answer. "Boston won't be like this, will it?"

"You mean, will there be this many soldiers there? No."

"Then, yes, I'd like to go straight there."

Stuart sighed. So much for a romantic interlude. "All right. If it would please you to continue on to Boston directly, then that's what we'll do."

"What about your business here?"

It took Stuart a moment to remember that he'd used the excuse of having business in Washington as a reason to spend a few days there. "It can wait," he said quietly.

"Do we have to change trains here?"

"No. This one goes to Boston, but it will probably be an hour or so before it departs again. Wouldn't you like to get off and stretch your legs for just a bit?"

Fear again flared in Claire's eyes. "No," she answered tremulously, "I'd rather just stay here. But feel free to get off for a while if you want to."

Stuart frowned. He couldn't think of anything he'd rather do than get off this damn train, but he couldn't leave Claire sitting in the coach alone. No telling what rowdy might approach her. "No, that's okay," he said. "I'll stay here with you. But I really think you'd be more comfortable if we engaged a sleeping compartment. Don't you want to come into the station with me just for a minute while I see if there's one available?"

"No," Claire answered hurriedly. "There's no reason to spend the extra money for that. I'm fine."

"Money isn't a problem," Stuart commented wryly. "Is there some other reason why you don't want me to get a sleeper?"

Claire blushed and quickly turned away. "I just don't think it's necessary," she murmured. "It's

145

only one more day until we get to Boston, isn't it?"

Stuart shot her a meaningful look. "One more day *and* night."

"I'll be fine," Claire assured him, still refusing to meet his eyes. "We Southerners are used to hardship."

"You're in the North now," Stuart reminded her. "And, as my wife, there's no reason why you need to endure any hardships ever again."

Claire's lips thinned with annoyance at Stuart's pointed reminder of their marital status, but she remained silent, pretending to have a sudden great interest in what was going on outside the window.

"It's cold here," she said, in a desperate attempt to turn the conversation away from the personal turn it had taken.

"It will be colder in Boston," Stuart warned. "That's one of the reasons I wanted to stop here and get you some new clothes. Your wardrobe isn't going to be suitable for a Massachusetts winter."

"I'll be fine."

"Claire, if you say, 'I'll be fine' one more time . . ."

"What are you going to do?" she flared, abruptly turning toward him. "Beat me? I always heard that Yankee men beat their women if they disagreed with them."

Stuart's mouth dropped open. "Beat you? Of course I'm not going to beat you. Who told you all Yankee men beat their wives? That's the craziest thing I ever heard!"

"I don't think it's crazy at all, especially after what you just threatened."

"Threatened! I haven't threatened you."

"Well, what *are* you going to do to me if I say 'I'll be fine' one more time?"

146

To Claire's astonishment, Stuart started to laugh. "Nothing," he answered, his shoulders shaking with disbelieving mirth, "I'm not going to do anything to you. I know this trip is difficult for you, and I'm just trying to make you more comfortable. I thought a sleeping room and a warm coat might help, that's all. You're my wife, Claire, and I just want you to quit denying me the pleasure of taking care of you a little."

His tone was so sincere and the expression in his eyes so honest that Claire felt like a fool. "I'm sorry," she mumbled, looking down at her hands in chagrined embarrassment, "I'm not trying to be difficult. I just don't want to feel beholden to you."

"How can you be beholden to your own husband?"

Claire sighed, not knowing how to make it more clear to him that she didn't want him to act like a husband. During their entire trip north, she had mentally rehearsed ways of telling him she was planning to have their marriage annulled as soon as the war was over, but she couldn't seem to come up with a decent way to broach the subject. And it didn't help that he was being so solicitous . . .

Then, too, her father's warning kept drumming through her brain. Would Stuart really destroy her pardon and turn her over to the authorities if she denied him his conjugal rights? She stole a quick look over at him. He was so handsome with his dark hair, clear gray eyes, and proud military bearing. She couldn't imagine him doing anything as despicable as purposely sending her to the gallows, but then again, he *was* a high-ranking Yankee officer, so how could she be sure?

The one thing she *was* sure of was that there was bound to be a confrontation between them, and soon. Although he had said no more about his expectations regarding the marital bed, Claire knew that his repeated suggestion that he engage a sleeping compartment for them was meant to give her a clear indication of his intentions.

Tomorrow night. We'll be in Boston by tomorrow night. I have to say something before that, she reasoned.

She shot him another cursory glance. It wasn't going to be easy. As little as she really knew about her husband, she was sure he wasn't used to being denied what he wanted. And she knew he wanted her. As her eyes glided over his features, she was again struck by his physical perfection. Why did he have to be so good-looking? And, why did he have to be a Yankee?

It was early the next evening when they finally arrived in Boston. The street lamps were lit, but heavy fog enshrouded the city and Claire wasn't able to get a clear look at her new home as they slowly chugged into the station.

Stuart had been smiling for the past hour, and this time, when the train finally pulled to a screeching, blowing halt, he did not wait for the other passengers to disembark. He leapt up from his seat and eagerly reached for Claire's arm. "Come on, we're home!" he said excitedly.

No, *you're* home, Claire thought sullenly. This will never be my home.

But her bitterness soon passed as, much to her surprise, she found herself getting caught up in Stuart's excitement. He ushered her quickly off the train and into the station. As she looked around, she felt a tremendous sense of relief that there wasn't a single Yankee soldier in sight. The station was nearly deserted, but the people who were there appeared to be well-dressed gentry who looked like they might be on their way to visit relatives or conduct business in another town.

Stuart found a porter who gathered up their luggage and escorted them to the front of the station, where he hailed a hansom cab.

"Number Twelve Louisburg Square," he directed, then helped her into the cab.

"Is anyone expecting you?" Claire asked, as they clattered noisily down the cobblestone street.

"No," he answered, peering eagerly out the windows into the foggy night, "but I retained most of my staff to see to the townhouse while I was away, so it won't be deserted."

Claire's eyebrows rose in surprise at Stuart's mention of servants. "How many people work in your house?"

"Usually four, but right now there's only my valet, the coachman, and a maid who does the cleaning. Now that we're home permanently, though, I'll engage a new cook and a maid for you."

"I don't need a maid," Claire protested.

Stuart looked at her dubiously. "Didn't you have a personal servant at your home in Savannah?"

"Well, yes," Claire admitted, "but that was different."

"Oh? How so?"

"Well, she was the daughter of one of my mother's servants. She was born in our house."

"Why don't you just say it, Claire? She was a slave."

"All right," Claire snapped. "Yes, she was. But,

after Mr. Lincoln freed the slaves, she stayed on with me.''

''Where is she now?''

''I'm sure she's still there. My father would hardly throw her out.''

''Why didn't you tell me?'' Stuart questioned. ''She could have come with us, had I known about her.''

Claire peered closely at him in the dim light of the coach. ''You'd have done that?''

''Of course,'' he snorted. ''I'm really not the ogre you try to make me out to be. All you would have had to do is ask. In fact, if you still want her to join you, I'll send some money to your father and ask him to send her along.''

Claire was so taken aback by Stuart's unexpected generosity that for a moment she didn't even answer him. *Please stop being so nice to me,* she thought—*you're just making everything harder!*

''Do you want her to come?'' he prodded.

''No,'' she stammered, shaking her head, ''that . . . won't be necessary.''

If only she could tell him she would not be staying long enough for it to make any difference! But somehow she couldn't bring herself to ruin her husband's happy mood, and she remained silent.

''Whatever you say,'' he shrugged, ''but if you want her to come, I'll arrange it.''

''Thank you,'' Claire murmured, then hurriedly turned back to look out the window.

''Too bad it's so foggy tonight,'' Stuart remarked. ''It's pretty hard to see anything. But tomorrow we'll go out for a drive and I'll show you some of the sights.''

Before Claire could think of a reasonable excuse to prevent her from having to spend the next afternoon cloistered in a coach with her suddenly all-too-attentive husband, they made a sharp right turn.

"Home," Stuart murmured.

"We're here?"

"Yes."

The coach came to a lurching halt as the coachman's voice boomed, "Number twelve, sir."

Stuart flung open the coach door and leaped down. "Wait a minute," he said, looking back at Claire. "I'll come round and help you."

He quickly rounded the back of the coach, then opened Claire's door and held up his hand. As she reluctantly placed her fingers into his palm, he flashed her a dazzling smile and said, "Welcome to Louisburg Square, Mrs. Wellesley."

Claire winced at his use of her married name, but rose and gracefully descended the carriage steps. Before them stood a four-story brick townhouse, one of a row of immaculately tended structures which looked like they might all be joined by common walls. The front door was flanked by two large windows from which streamed welcoming shafts of light. Each of the three stories above contained identical windows and, with the exception of the top floor, all were brightly lit.

"Now, why in hell would the servants have every light in the place lit?" Stuart muttered, as they walked up to the front door. Just as he raised his hand to knock, the door flew open to reveal a tall, handsome man in his fifties, wearing a grin that greatly resembled the one Stuart had been sporting all evening.

Stuart let out a gasp and, much to Claire's

151

astonishment, released her arm and hurtled himself against the man. The older man enthusiastically returned Stuart's bone-crushing embrace, his eyes filling with tears as he bellowed, "Mary! Mary, come quick! It's Stu!"

From the back of the house, Claire heard a sharp scream, then the sound of running feet. Looking into the front hall in confusion, she saw a tall, slender woman of about forty-five come tearing around the corner and launch herself against the two men.

Claire's eyes widened in disbelief. Never in her life had she seen such a display of affection between an employer and his servants.

Stuart stepped away from the man and folded the woman into his embrace, hugging her tightly against him and burying his face in her neck. "Mother, my God, I can't believe it. What in the world are you and Father doing here?"

It was Claire's turn to gasp. These people weren't Stuart's servants. *They were his parents!* With a look of horror etching her features, she took a startled step backward and raised shaking fingers to her lips.

Please, God, she prayed, let me have heard wrong! These people can't be his parents. He said his parents live in Colorado. Please, please, don't let them be his parents!

Suddenly, everyone seemed to notice her at once. The older man took a step toward her at the same moment that Stuart and his mother released each other, and Stuart reached to pull her up against his side. "Mother, Father, this is my wife, Claire. Claire, these are my parents, James and Mary Wellesley."

James and Mary both began talking at once,

welcoming Claire to the family and telling her how delighted they had been to hear of Stuart's unexpected marriage.

For once, Claire was grateful that Stuart was holding on to her, for without him, she was positive she'd have collapsed in a swoon.

"We know it's positively atrocious for us to just appear uninvited," Mary Wellesley laughed, "but we haven't seen Stuart in almost two years, and we were so excited when we got his wire that we just grabbed the first train east before we really stopped to think about it. I hope you don't mind the imposition, dear."

"No," Claire choked, "of course not."

"Why don't we all go inside?" James suggested, stepping aside to allow the couple through the door.

Suddenly, to Claire's absolute horror, she found herself being swept up in Stuart's arms. "Have to carry my bride across the threshold," he whispered.

Stuart's mother let out a little giggle of delight and hurried in behind them, closing the door. "Stu," she said, her smile knowing, "why don't you and Claire go upstairs and freshen up a bit while your father and I see to some refreshments."

"Sounds like a good idea," Stuart nodded, setting the mortified Claire on her feet. "Pa, could you ask Samuel to bring a pitcher of water and some clean towels up to the master bedroom?"

Then, turning toward Claire, he took her hand and led her through the marble foyer toward a beautiful oak staircase. "Are you hungry?" he asked, as they started up the steps.

"Not really," she murmured, trying desperately to disentangle her fingers from his. But Stuart was having none of it, and there was no way short of peeling his hand off hers and making a scene in front of his parents that Claire could break the contact.

After what seemed an eternity, they finally reached the first landing. They turned to take the next flight, and knowing that his parents could no longer see them, Claire angrily shook his hand off.

"What's wrong?" he asked innocently.

"Stop it!" she hissed. "There's no reason for you to keep touching me!"

Stuart's eyes narrowed and, in a move that brooked no refusal, he clamped his fingers onto her elbow and propelled her up the rest of the stairs. They walked down a long hall, then turned left, entering one of the most elegant bedchambers she'd ever seen.

The room faced the front of the house and one wall was flanked by the large windows she'd noticed from outside. Cream-colored velvet drapes with voile sheers beneath graced the windows, and the floor was covered with a thick forest-green carpet. A large mahogany armoire stood against one wall. There was a fireplace nestled into a corner of the room in front of which sat two cream-colored chairs with a small table between them. On top of the table was a beautiful crystal brandy decanter with four matching glasses set artfully around it.

Claire's eyes drank in the beauty of the room until suddenly they came to rest on the bed set against the far wall. It was unlike anything she had ever seen and the very sight of it set her heart to pounding. It wasn't just a bed—it was a retreat: huge, sumptuous and inviting. For a long moment Claire just stared at it, until suddenly Stuart grasped her shoulders and turned her toward him.

"Now, you listen to me," he ordered, the steely quality of his tone instantly commanding her attention, "those people down there think we're wildly in love, and you will do nothing, I repeat, *nothing*, to disabuse them of that notion."

"Why would they think that? Simply because we're married?"

"No, because I told them we were. I sent them a wire before we left Savannah and told them I had fallen madly in love with my nurse and was marrying her and bringing her home with me. Granted, I didn't expect them to be here when we arrived, but they are, and I'm not going to upset them by having them think there's something wrong between us."

"I understand," Claire nodded, "and I won't do anything to raise their suspicions. But newly married or not, you don't have to paw me every time they're in the same room with us."

"Claire," Stuart gritted, clamping down hard on his fast-rising temper, "we are newlyweds, and whether you are aware of it or not, newlyweds usually can't keep their hands off each other."

"Well, that's hardly the situation between us."

"The situation between us is that you're my wife and I expect you to act like it. You owe me that."

"We've had this conversation before, Major, and you've made your expectations very clear."

"Yeah, well, they're going to be even clearer when we climb into that bed tonight."

With a gasp, Claire wheeled around and looked again at the huge bed. "You promised me you wouldn't force me," she whispered.

"I know what I promised and, I will tell you again, I have no intention of forcing you. But I

155

will make love to you. Never doubt it. And you will want me to."

"Oh, you're disgusting!" Claire raged. "I wouldn't want you if you were the last man on earth and it was the last day of my life!"

Stuart smiled and threw her a look so full of challenge that she wanted to slap him. "Disgusting, Mrs. Wellesley?" he said smoothly, running a tantalizing finger down her cheek and across her bottom lip. "You think I'm disgusting? Let's see if you're still saying that tomorrow morning."

Claire raised her hand to brush his away, but he caught it in midair, holding it firmly against his chest and bending his head to give her a quick kiss on her lips. "When you come downstairs, I expect you to return this kiss," he whispered, "for my parents' sake, of course."

He had barely closed the door behind him before he heard his hairbrush hit the portal from the other side. Chuckling, he shook his head and walked down the stairs to join his family, wondering what surprises the rest of the evening was going to bring.

Chapter Twelve

The evening went much better than Claire expected.

After Stuart joined his parents downstairs, Claire dallied in the bedroom as long as she dared. Finally, after washing, repinning her hair, and changing into a fresh yellow silk dress, she knew she dared tarry no longer and so proceeded to make her way slowly down the splendid staircase. She could hear the deep voices of Stuart and his father coming from what she guessed must be the main parlor. Walking quietly across the foyer, she stopped just short of the parlor doorway, careful to remain out of sight as she peeked inside. She wasn't sure what she expected to see, but the scene before her made her jaw drop in surprise.

Mary and James Wellesley were seated side by side on a beautiful rose settee. Stuart was seated opposite them on a matching sofa, grinning broadly and holding a beautiful little blond-haired girl on his lap.

Claire took a quiet step forward as she tried to get a better look at her husband and the child, but Mary saw her. "Claire!" she called. "Here you are.

Come in and join us, dear."

Claire forced a smile and walked into the room, careful to keep her eyes averted from her husband's.

"Did you have a nice rest?" James asked, rising.

"Yes, thank you." Despite her resolve, her eyes flicked over to Stuart, who was now standing, holding the child.

He took a step forward, catching her hand in his and pulling her gently down on the couch. "Claire," he said, his eyes dancing with merriment, "I'd like you to meet my baby sister, Paula. This is the same Paula you asked me about one day at the hospital. Do you remember?"

Claire blushed crimson. "Yes," she answered shortly, furious that Stuart would remind her of that embarrassing conversation when she'd thought Paula was his sweetheart. "I remember."

"Paula, baby," he continued, barely able to keep his laughter in check as he turned back to the exquisite child, "this is your new Auntie Claire. Can you say 'hello'?"

"Hello," Paula answered, promptly hopping off Stuart's lap and executing a perfect curtsy for Claire.

Claire was instantly enchanted. "Hello," she answered, her face relaxing into the first genuine smile Stuart had seen in days. "I'm very pleased to meet you, Paula."

Paula grinned and climbed back into her brother's lap, her china-blue eyes bright with curiosity as she sized up her new aunt.

"She's lovely," Claire remarked, turning to look at Mary.

"And very, very spoiled," Mary chuckled. "She just turned four years old, so her father felt she was old enough to take her first train journey and insisted we bring her along.

"I'm very glad he did," Stuart laughed, hugging Paula to him and affectionately tousling her golden curls.

"Is Paula your youngest child?" Claire asked.

"Yes, and our last," Mary laughed. "We were both delighted after seven sons to finally have a daughter."

"I'm sure you were," Claire murmured.

"We feel like we've done our part populating the country with Wellesleys," James enjoined with a hearty chuckle. "From now on, we'll leave that task to the boys."

"James!" Mary scolded, seeing the color rise in Claire's cheeks. "You're embarrassing poor Claire. After all, she and Stuart have been married for only a few days."

Stuart, who was greatly enjoying the exchange between his parents and his new wife, jumped in. "We'll be happy to do our part, won't we, Claire?"

If possible, Claire's color rose even higher. With a reproving glance at her husband and her son, Mary reached across the tea table and picked up Claire's hand. "You'll have to excuse these Wellesley men, Claire. They're absolutely shameless. Now, stop it, both of you," she ordered, trying her best to look stern. "Claire's going to think she's married into a family of absolute boors."

"I understand you and Mr. Wellesley are from England," Claire commented, saying the first thing she could think of that would turn the conversation away from herself.

"Yes," Mary nodded, "I'm afraid we both still have a bit of an accent which gives us away, but we have lived in America for such a long time now that we truly think of it as our home."

"What made you decide to immigrate?"

"Opportunity . . . and a bit of the wanderlust," Mary smiled.

"Opportunity?"

"Yes," Stuart interjected, "Father was the seventh son in his family, and in England, inheritances tend not to extend quite that far. So Father and Mother decided to strike out for the New World after they married."

"And this country has been very good to us," James added. "It was the best decision we ever made, even though it was difficult to leave family and friends behind."

"Did you know," Stuart asked, turning to smile at Claire, "that in ancient folklore, seventh sons are supposed to possess magical powers?"

"No, I'd never heard that."

"Well, they are, and what's more, seventh sons of seventh sons are even more magical, so we're expecting my youngest brother, Adam, to be truly remarkable."

"How old is he?" Claire asked.

"Only five," Mary chuckled, "and at this point, there's absolutely nothing magical about him, except maybe his ability to get dirtier than any child God ever created. Besides, all those superstitions about seventh sons are just nonsense."

"We'll see," Stuart grinned. "Father certainly has seemed to live a charmed life. No telling what fate has in store for little Adam."

"Well," Mary said, rising and plucking Paula off Stuart's lap, "I don't know what the future holds for Adam, but the future holds bedtime for this little girl."

"Oh, Mother, does she have to go already?" Stuart asked, reluctant to relinquish his cherished little sister. "Can't she stay up just a little longer? Please?"

Mary laughed. "Why, Stu, you sound just like a whiny little boy."

"No, he doesn't," James laughed. "He sounds like a man who's eager to be a father. And high time, too, I say. You need to talk to your wife, Stu. With a little bit of luck, you two will have a Paula of your own in no time at all."

"We'll discuss it, Pa," Stuart promised. Then, leaning toward Claire, he whispered, "I'm going to kiss you and you're going to kiss me back."

Before she could protest, he lowered his lips to hers. They were soft and warm, and, much to Claire's astonishment, something stirred deep inside her—something she had never even dreamt existed. Goosebumps rose all over her body, and before she could stop herself, she *was* kissing him back.

Stuart held the kiss for several long seconds, and when he finally did break the embrace, his eyes were full of unasked questions. Hurriedly, Claire turned away, mortified by her behavior in front of Stuart's parents. What must they think? What must *he* think? Sitting up very straight, she made a great pretense of smoothing down her skirt, consciously avoiding having to make eye contact with anyone in the room.

But she needn't have worried. When she finally found the courage to raise her eyes, Mary had departed with Paula, and James was pouring another brandy over at a sideboard against the east wall. Claire flicked her gaze over to Stuart, but he just smiled and toyed lightly with her hand, which he still held.

What an odd family, she thought in wonderment. At home, a man would never be so bold as to embrace his wife in public, yet here, no one had seemed to think there was anything strange in Stuart's kissing her for no other reason than that he'd wanted to. Lord, but Northerners were strange!

The rest of the evening passed uneventfully. The four of them ate a light dinner and sat for a long time at the table, talking of inconsequential things. To Claire's great relief, no one mentioned the war or the unusual circumstances of Stuart's sudden marriage. Claire knew the elder Wellesleys must wonder why their son had abruptly chosen to marry a Confederate nurse, but neither of them had asked any questions that might prove embarrassing for her to answer. As the evening wore on, she found herself relaxing in the Wellesleys' warm company and she actually enjoyed participating in the easy conversation flowing around her.

Still, she knew they must be intensely curious about her. *They're probably just waiting till I go to bed so they can talk to Stuart alone,* she thought. And so she stifled a delicate yawn and said, "If you all would excuse me, I believe I'll retire. It's been a very long day."

"Of course, dear," Mary said sympathetically. "I'm afraid we've kept you up far too late, considering that terrible train ride you've just endured. Please forgive us."

Claire smiled gratefully. "I've enjoyed the evening very much. Thank you for your hospitality."

"Actually, we should be thanking you for *your* hospitality," James chuckled. "It's your home."

A look of surprise crossed Claire's face as she realized he was right. This *was* her home—at least, for the time being. Suddenly she found herself looking around the beautiful dining room with a new, more proprietary eye.

"I'll come up with you, Claire," Stuart announced suddenly, rising from his chair and tossing his napkin on the table.

"Oh, no," she protested, trying hard not to show the panic she immediately felt, "that's not necessary, Stuart. You haven't seen your parents in such a long time, I'm sure you'd like to spend some time alone with them."

"Nonsense," James chuckled. "Go with your wife, Stu. You and your mother and I can breakfast together in the morning. We'll talk then."

Stuart threw his father a look of thanks and walked briskly across the elegant dining room to join his wife. "To bed, sweetheart," he whispered, leaning close and wrapping her arm securely in his.

Claire turned angry eyes to him, but there was nothing she could say with his parents sitting there. Reluctantly, she allowed him to escort her out of the dining room and up the stairs.

"Did you really think you were going to bed alone tonight?" Stuart asked pleasantly, as they reached the landing and made the turn.

"I am forever hopeful," she retorted coolly, wrenching her arm out of his and hastening her stride down the hall.

"Not a chance, lady," he growled, taking three long strides and catching up with her just as she rounded the corner into the bedroom.

Claire took a couple of steps into the room, then stopped short as her eyes fell on the massive bed.

163

The sight was even more daunting than it had been earlier, since someone had turned down the covers and carefully laid a sheer white nightgown across the sheets.

"Whose is this?" she whispered, picking up the gown and turning toward Stuart.

"It's yours," he returned quietly. "A gift from my mother, I would imagine."

"Well, I won't wear it!"

Stuart shrugged and started unbuttoning his uniform blouse. "Suit yourself, but it's that or nothing."

Angrily, Claire threw the delicate gown back on the bed and marched over to where her valise was sitting on the floor. For several seconds she rummaged through it, then rose and threw Stuart a withering glare. "Where are *my* nightgowns?"

"I have no idea," he lied, tugging his shirt out of his pants and shrugging it off his wide shoulders.

"You took them, didn't you?"

With studied nonchalance, Stuart continued to undress, unbuttoning his trousers. "Lower your voice, Claire, or everyone in the house is going to hear you."

"I don't care," she retorted defensively, her eyes widening as she realized that he was going to pull his trousers off right in front of her, "and don't you *dare* take those pants off! Have you no modesty at all?"

"In front of my wife?" he asked, sitting down on the bed to pull off his boots. "Why would I?"

"Oh, God," Claire moaned, pressing the heels of her hands against her eyes, "why are you doing this to me?"

The agony in her voice made Stuart pause, one boot half off. "You really think I'm a monster,

164

don't you?" he asked quietly.

"Yes," she blurted, her shoulders shaking with fear and the tears she could no longer hold back. "What you're doing is unconscionable!"

"And just exactly what is it that you think I'm doing?"

"You're making me stand here and watch you prepare to rape me," she choked. "Why don't you just throw me down, toss my skirt over my head, and get it over with?"

For a long moment, Stuart stared at her in disbelief. Then, with a weary sigh, he rose and walked over to the armoire, opening one of the carved doors and reaching inside. Pulling out a high-necked, long-sleeved nightgown, he tossed it to her. "Here. Here's your nightrail. That door over there is the bathing chamber. You can go in there and change."

"Th . . . thank you," she stammered, clutching the nightgown to her as she raced over to the door he'd indicated.

After Claire had disappeared into the bathing room, Stuart pulled off the rest of his clothes, then looked down at himself, frowning at the swelling erection which jutted out in front of him. "Not tonight, Major," he muttered, shaking his head.

With slow, disappointed steps, he walked over to his bureau and extracted a pair of light, linen underwear, pulling them on and carefully adjusting his swollen shaft. Then he extinguished the lamp and climbed into the sumptuous bed.

He was barely settled back into the pillows when the bathing room door opened with a soft click and Claire tiptoed silently back into the room. Although the heavy gown concealed any trace of her womanly curves, she had taken her hair down and its coppery brilliance, highlighted by the firelight, made Stuart catch his breath in awe. Just looking at her made his erection strengthen, and with a groan, he squeezed his eyes shut.

He could hear her padding across the carpet toward the bed, could smell the heady fragrance of her hair as she neared him. For a moment, he wondered if he really *could* control himself with her, as he'd promised.

The other side of the bed dipped as she slowly, tentatively, climbed in next to him. The tension radiating from her ramrod-stiff body was so palpable that Stuart could actually feel it through the mattress. To his profound relief, her overwhelming fear did much to cool his flaming senses. "Claire," he whispered, "relax. I'm not going to hurt you."

"Yes, you are," she whispered back, her voice shaking. "I know you are, but . . . I'm ready now, so please, just get it over with."

Stuart sighed, a long, dejected sound that made Claire glance over at him in bewilderment. She had always heard that men turned into animals when they did what he was going to do to her, but, for some reason, he seemed almost reluctant.

Claire had enough married friends to know that the act of procreation was unpleasant, messy, and painful—at least for the woman. However, according to her friends, men loved it—thrashing around and working themselves into a frenzy not unlike a half-crazed stud horse, then lunging over and over into their wives' bodies until they nearly rent them in two. She'd always heard that the only thing that made this horrible ordeal bearable was the prospect of begetting a child. She'd also been told that once a woman was pregnant, her husband usually left her alone and sated his lust on other, more unsavory women—some of whom, it was whispered, actually found perverse enjoyment in the whole process.

Several long moments passed as Claire waited for Stuart to hurl himself on top of her. What was taking him so long? Why didn't he just do it? When he finally did move, she was wound up so tight with fear that she nearly crawled up the headboard.

"Claire," he whispered, raising himself on an elbow and leaning over her, "slide over here next to me."

Biting down hard on her lower lip to keep from screaming, Claire turned slowly toward him. Stuart slipped one arm beneath her shoulder and gently pulled her against his side until her head lay on his shoulder. "There," he murmured, running his hand over her hair in a soothing, repetitive motion, "now, just relax."

Claire swallowed hard and her voice came out in a frightened squeak. "When are you going to do it?"

"Sweetheart," his voice was soft, "I'm not going to *do* anything."

"You're . . . you're not?"

"No. I told you I wouldn't force you, and I won't."

"So, when *are* you going to do it? Tomorrow? The next day?"

Stuart chuckled. "We'll do it when you're ready."

"I'll never be ready," she assured him. "I know how horrible what you're going to do is for women—even when they love their husbands."

Stuart frowned into the darkness. "Claire, what

167

nonsense have you been told about this whole thing?"

"It's not nonsense," she bristled. "I have married friends, and they've all said the same thing."

"Oh? And what's that?"

"That making love is awful—and that it has nothing whatsoever to do with love. That men like it, but for women, it . . . oh, I can't talk about this. It's not proper for us to discuss such things."

"No, you're wrong," Stuart countered. "It's absolutely proper for us to talk about this. Maybe, if more men would talk to their wives, women might feel differently about lovemaking."

"What good does talking do?"

"Well, for one thing, men would find out what their wives like or don't like."

Claire snorted. "From what I've heard, there's no part of it that women like."

"Really? Don't you like what we're doing now?"

"We're not doing anything."

"Sure we are. You're lying with your head on my shoulder and I'm stroking your hair. Don't you like that?"

"Well, yes."

"And if I move my hand down and rub your back . . . like this . . ." For a moment, Stuart's hand drew light swirls across Claire's shoulder blades, then dipped lower to gently knead the tight muscles at the base of her spine. "Do you like that?"

"Yes," she murmured, the soothing pressure of his fingers on her spine making her feel slightly light-headed. "I do."

Slowly Stuart drew his hand forward, running it up her side until his thumb lightly brushed her breast. "What about this?"

"Oh . . ." Claire sighed, her body feeling more and more languid. "That's nice, too."

Raising himself above her, Stuart slowly dipped his head, barely touching his lips to hers as he continued to feather his fingers against her breast, his thumb swirling ever closer to her nipple. But to his keen disappointment, she jerked away when his thumb finally touched the excited little nub. "Don't do that."

"Okay," he soothed, "so, I've found something you don't like."

"It's not really that I don't like it . . ." she admitted, "it's just that . . ."

"Shh," he whispered, stilling his hand on her breast and running the tip of his tongue slowly across her lips. "You don't have to explain. I understand. Now, kiss me—like you did downstairs."

He covered her mouth gently with his, and just as she had in the parlor, Claire found herself responding. She really did love the sensation of his mouth on hers. It was so warm . . . so soft . . . so gentle. Suddenly, she wanted to tell him. "I like it when you kiss me . . ."

"Good," he smiled, a shiver of pleasure rippling through him that she'd admitted at least that much. "Open your mouth a little and you'll like it even more."

Almost without realizing it, Claire obeyed, parting her lips and then gasping with delight as Stuart's silky tongue invaded her mouth. Her senses reeled as he swept it against the sensitive insides of her cheeks, and instinctively she wrapped her arms around him, threading her fingers through his soft, thick hair and pressing her breasts against his chest.

He continued to kiss her, slowly lowering his hand until once again his thumb brushed over her nipple. This time she didn't jerk away. Instead, he felt her breath rush into his mouth as a little sigh of blossoming ecstasy escaped her.

The sensation of Claire pressing against him was almost more than Stuart could bear. It had been so long . . . so incredibly long since he'd even kissed a woman, much less made love. And even though he had considerable experience with women, never had lovemaking been like this. He felt like his entire body was on fire and the erection he had fought so hard to control had long since won its battle. It now pressed insistently against his underwear; hot, pulsing, and demanding release.

Pulling his lips away, he buried his head in Claire's neck and released a shuddering sigh. "Do you like this?" he questioned softly, placing nibbling little kisses against the sensitive skin by her ear.

"Yes," she sighed. "It's very nice . . ."

"Do you know what would make it nicer?"

"What?"

"If we both took our clothes off."

He winced as he felt her stiffen. "I won't hurt you, sweetheart. I just want to feel your skin against mine."

Claire was shocked to realize that she wanted the same thing. Without allowing herself to think about what she was doing, she slid out from beneath him and sat up, pulling her heavy gown over her head and flinging it away.

For one brief moment before she slid back under the covers, Stuart was treated to a view of her full, lush breasts reflected in the firelight. The sight was so arousing that his whole body began to shake, his hands trembling so badly that he couldn't find the button to release his underwear. After several moments of acute frustration, he gave up the struggle and with a softly muttered oath, grabbed the waistband and ripped the soft linen, kicking the torn garment off without another thought.

Taking a deep, shuddering breath, he turned back to Claire, gathering her in his arms and burying his head in the exquisite softness of her bare breasts.

A wave of ecstasy washed over Claire as she felt Stuart's tongue sweep erotically over her nipple and somewhere, deep inside, she felt something warm and liquidy spread through her. "What are you doing to me?" she moaned, reaching down to again bury her fingers in his hair.

"Making love to you," he answered hoarsely, raising his head and looking up at her, "and if we go on much longer, I'm not going to be able to stop. So I'm going to ask you now, Claire. Do you want me to continue?"

Claire swallowed and closed her eyes as somewhere, deep in her brain, a warning bell went off. She shouldn't be doing this. He was a Yankee . . . the enemy . . . one of the blue-clad devils who had shattered her world. She should leap out of this bed and run away from him as fast as she could. But somehow she just didn't have the will to do it. And what he was doing to her felt so good . . .

"I . . . you . . . you don't have to stop, Stuart."

But he did stop, moving up in the bed until he loomed over her, his face dark and intense. "Tell me you want me to make love to you, Claire. Tell me, so we're both sure."

Claire turned her head away, unable to look into his probing, gray eyes. "Don't make me say it, Stuart. Just do it."

"No. I want you to say it. I want to hear you say you want me."

"Why?"

"Because I don't want you crying rape in the morning. And, because, if we do this, there will be no annulment when the war is over, and I know that's what you've been secretly planning."

Claire's eyes widened. He'd known her plans all along! My God, how could he have known? And why hadn't he said anything before this? Why now, when she wanted him so badly she couldn't think?

You can't let him do this, a voice deep inside her warned. If you do, there's no chance for an annulment. No chance to go home. As much as you want him, you can't do this!

The silence yawned between them, until finally Stuart flopped onto his back and released a long, pent-up breath. "You don't need to say anything, Claire. Silence says it all."

"I can't say it, Stuart," she whispered, reaching over the side of the bed and feeling around for her nightgown. Finding it, she hurriedly pulled it over her head, then lay back down. "Even if I did want you," she continued softly, "I couldn't say it. I'll never be able to say it."

"Why not?" Stuart rasped, his voice hoarse with need and disappointment. "I want you, and I know you want me. Damn it, Claire, it could be so good between us if you'd just let it. Why can't you say it?"

"Because," she whispered, "because you're a Yankee."

"Of course," he responded, his shoulders shaking with mirthless laughter, "Of course that's it. And yes, I am a Yankee. One of those dirty, murdering, raping Yankees. Go to sleep, Claire. I won't bother you again."

Chapter Thirteen

Claire woke up slowly and looked around with unfocused eyes at the strange room. Where was she?

Suddenly, the events of the last day came rushing back, and with a little gasp, she turned to see if Stuart was in bed with her. He wasn't. For a moment she didn't know whether she was relieved or disappointed.

Her mind spun back to the previous night's intimacies and a small shiver of remembrance rippled through her. She stared at Stuart's rumpled pillow, the imprint of his head the only evidence that he'd spent the night beside her. But in her mind, she could again see that dark head bent over her as he kissed and caressed her. Her fingers tingled just remembering the texture of his hair, and she raised a hand to gently run a finger along her lips, closing her eyes as she relived the sensation of his soft mouth on hers.

Stop it! she told herself firmly. You're acting like a lovesick school girl! He's a Yankee! A Yankee who almost ruined any chance you'll ever have of disentangling yourself from this misbegotten marriage and returning to Savannah where you belong. And you very nearly let him do it! Why, you're no different from those women you've read about in the newpapers—totally swept away with the dashing Major Wellesley's charms.

But, a little voice asked slyly, how many of the women quoted in the newspaper as having had the honor of Major Wellesley attending one of their soirées had ever been in bed with him? How many of them had ever seen him naked above them, passionately kissing and stroking them? And how many of them had felt his hot, hard shaft pressed against them, as she had last night?

Claire felt herself blush just thinking about that moment when she'd felt Stuart's manhood pressed so intimately against her inner thigh. If she'd shifted her position, even an inch or two, what would have happened? There had been something undeniable in her body's reaction to that pulsing erection—something that had made her want to reach down and touch it. Something primitive and female that had made her want to feel it slip deep inside her, filling her with its heat and fulfilling some strange need within her that she didn't even understand.

"My God!" she gasped out loud, sitting upright in bed and clapping her hand over her racing heart. Her breath was coming so fast that she felt like she'd just run a race, and her entire body seemed to be throbbing. "What's happening to me?" she cried, her cheeks flaming. "I'm acting like some . . . some harlot, lusting for a man's touch!"

With great effort, she forced her thoughts away from the provocative moments she'd spent in her husband's virile embrace and made herself think instead of how disastrous it would have been if she'd actually succumbed to his masculine charms and allowed him to make love to her.

You couldn't go home again . . . ever! she realized. You'd be tied to him for the rest of your life. Even if you could somehow escape him, you'd be a tainted woman and no gentleman would want you—at least, no Southern gentleman. And what if Stuart liked making love to you so much that he wanted to do it again and again and again?

That thought made her heart start to race again, so she didn't allow herself to dwell on it.

Worst of all, she continued sternly, you'd end up pregnant—with a Yankee's baby—and you'd have to kill yourself!

Well, maybe not actually kill herself, but her life would certainly be ruined forever. No self-respecting Southerner would even speak to a girl who had willingly allowed a Northern officer to father her child.

It was far better that she had made the decision she had last night and stopped Stuart before things had gotten out of hand. But what about tonight, and all the other nights to come until the war ended and she could get away from him? Would he put her through that exquisite torture every night? And could she continue to resist him if he did?

No, she assured herself as another little shudder of remembered pleasure shook her—Stuart had promised her. "Go to sleep. I won't bother you again," he had said. Those words must mean that since she had rejected him last night, he realized she wanted no part of him and so would not seduce her again.

Claire sighed, gazing blankly at the far wall. She should be happy that he had promised not to make any further demands on her. After all, it's what she'd wanted all along—what she'd prayed for all the way north on that hideous train. So, why did she feel so bereft? What was wrong with her?

He's a Yankee! her mind screamed. A Yankee, a Yankee, a *Yankee!*

Why didn't that seem as important as it once had?

"Because," whispered the devilish little voice she couldn't seem to quell, "he's also your husband . . . and right or wrong, you want him."

It was nearly ten by the time Claire finally came downstairs. She had fallen asleep again after fighting her little moral battle with herself and hadn't awakened again until the sun was high in the sky.

Appalled by what the elder Wellesleys would think of her, lying about on her first day as mistress of her new home, she bolted out of bed, quickly washing and dressing. Then taking a deep breath, she walked calmly down the stairs to join the family.

But when she reached the dining room, most of the family was gone. Only Mary Wellesley and a young woman she'd never seen before were seated at the table.

"Good morning, dear," Mary beamed as Claire hesitantly entered the room. "Did you sleep well?"

"Yes, thank you," Claire replied, blushing as she realized to what Mary was probably attributing her late rising. She forced a smile to cover her embarrassment and glanced surreptitiously around for some sign of her husband.

"I'd like you to meet Grenita Forten," Mary continued, gesturing to the other woman. "Grenita's parents are old friends of our family.''

"It's very nice to meet you, Miss Forten,'' Claire acknowledged. Grenita was about twenty-five, tall, and slender, with angular features and brown corkscrew curls. She was far from pretty, but there was a warmth and sincerity in her brown eyes that immediately set Claire at ease.

"It's Mrs. Forten,'' Grenita corrected, smiling, "or, to be perfectly correct, Widow Forten.''

"Grenita's husband was killed at Gettysburg,'' Mary supplied quietly.

"I'm so sorry,'' Claire murmured. "My brother was killed in the same battle.''

"So am I,'' Grenita said wistfully, "for all of us. But, I certainly did not call to talk about the war. I heard that Stuart had returned home with a bride, and I wanted to be the first to congratulate you. You must excuse me for arriving at such an unholy hour and catching you by surprise, but I was so excited that I just couldn't wait.''

"Grenita's mother and I have been friends for many years,'' Mary remarked, "and since Stuart and Grenita are the same age, they've known each other all their lives. In fact, Grenita spent many summers with us on our ranch in Colorado.''

"That's right,'' Grenita giggled, "and with all Stuart's wild younger brothers, it's a wonder I'm still here to talk about it!''

Mary laughed out loud, shaking her head in remembrance and reaching for a silver coffeepot to pour Claire a cup. "Now, Grenita, don't frighten Claire. She hasn't met any of the boys yet and you'll make her think they're savages.''

Grenita turned to Claire and in an exaggerated stage whisper, hissed, "They are! One time Geoffrey locked me in a woodshed and set it on

179

fire! Lord knows what would have happened if Eric hadn't come along."

"Grenita!" Mary gasped, her face scarlet with embarrassment. "Do you always have to tell that story?"

"Who is Geoffrey?" Claire asked, taking a sip from the cup Mary had handed her.

Both women turned toward her, their expressions registering their surprise. "He's my fourth son," Mary explained. "Hasn't Stu told you anything about his brothers?"

"Yes, of course he has," Claire said hurriedly. "It's just that I'm afraid I don't have them all quite straight in my mind yet."

"There are a lot of them," Grenita laughed.

"Stuart is the second to the oldest, right?" Claire asked.

Again, Mary looked at her new daughter-in-law quizzically. "I guess Stu *hasn't* told you much about his family," she murmured. "Yes, Stuart is the second to the oldest. Miles is a year older. He's twenty-six. Then there's Eric, who is nineteen, Geoffrey is sixteen, Nathan is twelve, Seth is eleven, Adam is five, and of course, you've met Paula."

"Paula!" Grenita squealed. "Is she here with you?"

Mary nodded. "I'm afraid so. Her father is so dotty over her, he wouldn't leave her at home, even to make this quick trip. In fact, I'd better go upstairs right now and check on her. You two girls stay here and chat. It will give you a chance to get acquainted." With a rustling of skirts, Mary rose from the table and glided out of the room.

Grenita plucked a scone off a platter in the center of the table, then leaned back in her chair and smiled at Claire. "I'm sure you know that you're the envy of every unmarried girl in Boston."

"I beg your pardon?"

Grenita's smile widened. "Oh, yes. Why, half the girls in town, not to mention their mothers, have been on absolute tenterhooks waiting for Stuart to come home."

"Really? Why?"

"Why?" Grenita laughed. "Have you looked at your husband recently? He was the most eligible bachelor in town! Surely you must have known that."

"Not really," Claire lied. "In Savannah, he was just a Union army captain."

"Well, my dear," Grenita confided, leaning forward and placing her hand over Claire's, "in Boston, he was the man everyone wanted." She smiled conspiratorially and leaned even closer. "I must confess, even I was smitten. At one time, I hoped he might turn his eye toward me, but I think we'd known each other too long and too well for that to happen. Anyway, I'm hardly Stuart's type."

"Oh?" Claire asked, her curiosity acute. "And just who *is* Stuart's type?"

"Why, you are, of course."

"And what type do you think I am?"

"Beautiful, intelligent, sophisticated . . ."

Claire blushed becomingly. "Thank you very much for the lovely compliment, Mrs. Forten, but I'm afraid I really don't fit into any of those categories."

"Oh, but you do," Grenita protested, "or Stuart would never have married you."

If you only knew, Claire thought, but she remained silent.

"Anyway," Grenita continued, "I'm just telling you this so you'll be ready . . ."

"Ready for what?"

"For the onslaught."

Claire looked completely blank.

"You know—parties, teas, balls. Everyone who's anyone in Boston is going to want to throw some sort of celebration for you two—if for no other reason than to get a look at the girl who caught Stuart Wellesley!"

"Oh, how terrible," Claire moaned.

"Terrible?" Grenita gasped, astounded by Claire's distressed look. "For all those other girls, maybe. They lost him. But you're the winner, Claire. You got him. You and you alone are Mrs. Stuart Wellesley. For you, it'll be wonderful."

"What will be wonderful?" Mary asked, reentering the room.

"All the parties that are sure to be given in Stuart's and Claire's honor."

"Oh, yes, those will be fun, won't they? There probably won't be very many though, what with the war and everything."

"Nonsense," Grenita smiled, rising and picking up her reticule. "War or no war, all those mothers who were counting on marrying their daughters off to Stuart are going to throw a party just to get a look at Claire."

Mary nodded and turned bright eyes on her new daughter-in-law. "Grenita's right, my dear. They *will* all want to get a look at you. And I can't wait to show you off!"

Show me off, Claire thought dismally. Show me off! At that moment, Claire Boudreau Wellesley wished she were anyone in the world other than who she was.

*   *   *

It was about noon when the invitations started arriving. Claire and Mary were still sitting in the dining room when Samuel, Stuart's valet, appeared for the fourth time, carrying a small silver tray bearing yet another cream-colored vellum envelope.

"Oh, dear," Mary fretted, plucking the envelope off the tray and ripping it open. "I hope this one isn't for this week, too. You and Stu will have such a full schedule, you won't have a single moment to yourselves. I really think the two of you should take a short wedding trip. You'll have no peace as long as you're in Boston."

"Oh, a wedding trip isn't necessary," Claire quickly assured her. "I know how eager Maj . . . Stuart was to get home. By the way, do you know where he is this morning?"

Mary's eyebrows rose imperceptibly, but her voice betrayed none of her surprise. "He and his father rode up to Marblehead."

"Oh?" Claire asked, trying desperately to sound nonchalant. "Did they say what time they planned to return? Stuart said something about us driving out to tour Boston this afternoon."

Mary frowned. What was going on between these two? "From what I understand," she said placidly, "they won't be back until tomorrow."

"Tomorrow?" Claire blurted, unable to hide her astonishment. "Are you sure?" How dared Stuart leave without even having the courtesy of telling her where he was going and when he planned to return!

"That's what James said. Of course, Marblehead is only about twenty miles away, so it's

183

possible they might be back this evening."

"It doesn't matter," Claire said quietly. "I must have been confused. Would you excuse me, please? I . . . I feel a bit weary. I guess that train trip was more taxing than I realized."

"Of course, dear," Mary said graciously. "Take a little nap, and when you come back down, we'll have some tea and a light lunch. Maybe then you can tell me about your family."

With a curt nod, Claire fled the room, running up the wide staircase till she reached the sanctuary of the bedroom. "Wait till I get my hands on him!" she muttered angrily, closing the bedroom door behind her and leaning heavily against it. "Embarrassing me like that in front of his mother. I suppose he's 'punishing' me for not letting him make love to me last night. As if his absence were punishment!"

Angrily she flounced across the room and threw herself into a chair in front of the fireplace. What was she going to do with herself all afternoon? She wasn't the least bit tired, but after telling Stuart's mother she wanted to take a nap, she couldn't very well go back downstairs.

As much as she hated to admit it, she had been looking forward to driving out with Stuart to see the sights. Of course, she told herself, she hated spending time with him, but she was curious to see what Boston looked like, since she was going to be forced to live here for a while.

Damn him anyway, she thought, moodily staring into the fire's dancing flames. Damn him for the rude, uncaring scoundrel that he is. Just wait till he gets home. Then wouldn't she give him a piece of her mind!

*　　　*　　　*

Downstairs, Mary's thoughts about her son were much the same. Something was wrong between the newlyweds, and whatever it was, Mary was sure it was Stuart's fault.

"Just like his father," she mused aloud, then smiled. Maybe that was why she loved Stu so much. Of all her sons, Stuart was the one Mary found most fascinating. His intelligence and uncanny business sense, coupled with his extraordinary good looks and teasing charm, all conspired to make him a man any woman would be proud to call her son.

But at the same time, Mary knew he could be difficult. Headstrong, temperamental, and stubborn, Stuart was a force to be reckoned with, and from what she had seen so far, it appeared that Claire was not reckoning very well.

Mary couldn't put her finger on it, but there was a tension between her son and his new wife that didn't sit right with her. They were too polite . . . too *careful* with each other. There were none of the "I just can't wait to be alone with you" looks that she'd have expected, and not once had she seen them touch each other.

Why *had* Stuart insisted on going to Marblehead today? He had told his father he wanted to buy some property in the pretty little coastal town, but surely that could have waited a few days. It was almost as if he'd wanted to get away. And although James had seemed oblivious to the tension radiating between the newlyweds, even his eyebrows had risen when Stuart had told him to pack a valise, since he planned to stay overnight.

Mary sighed. More than anything else, she wanted her son to be happy in his new marriage. It was going to be enough of a problem to launch a Southern wife into Boston society without the two

185

of them having trouble between them. Or could it be that Claire's Southern roots were the cause of the tension?

Whatever it was, Mary was worried, and she hoped that Stuart would take advantage of the time alone with his father to confide in him.

Rising from the dining room table, she walked over to the bay window and looked out at the dreary January afternoon. What was she going to do with herself the rest of the day except sit and wait for James to return and, hopefully, enlighten her? "One thing is for sure," she murmured, turning away from the window and idly pouring herself another cup of coffee, "if James hasn't gotten to the bottom of this by the time they get home, I will."

Chapter Fourteen

Stuart returned home late that night.

Claire was just starting to doze off when she heard the soft creak of the bedroom door. She opened her eyes a slit, saw Stuart's face eerily reflected by the candle he carried, and quickly closed them again. She didn't think he had noticed she was awake until he lay down next to her and said quietly, "Goodnight, Claire."

She didn't answer, but her breath caught in her throat as she waited to see if he would touch her. He didn't. Finally, she relaxed and fell into a light sleep.

Stuart lay awake long after he heard Claire's breathing become slow and regular, thinking about the past twenty-four hours.

He had slept poorly after their brief, passionate interlude, and had risen feeling tired and frustrated. He needed to get away—to put some space between himself and his maddening wife, so he coerced his father into traveling to Marblehead with him. There was a house there he had considered buying before he'd left for the war, and now that he was married, he was anxious to see if it was still available. But even more, he wanted a chance to talk to James alone—to explain his situation and ask his advice.

They talked of inconsequential things during the ride up the coast. It wasn't until they stopped for lunch at a small inn outside Marblehead that Stuart actually brought up the subject of his marriage.

His father listened intently as Stuart recounted the events of the last two months. When he finally finished his story, James's only comment was, "Do you love her?"

"That's the question everyone asks me," Stuart sighed, raking his hands through his hair. "Even General Sherman. And it's the same question I keep asking myself—over and over."

"And have you come up with an answer?"

"Yes," Stuart nodded slowly. "I do love her. She's everything I ever wanted. But, Pa, she makes it so hard. She won't relinquish her damn Confederate pride for a minute, and every time I think I might be making some progress with her, she pushes me away and reminds me I'm a Yankee."

"You *are* a Yankee," James noted.

"I know. God, do I know! But I'm also her husband."

"And have you reminded her of that?"

"She doesn't want to be reminded. She married me only because her father coerced her into it, and I know that as soon as the war is over, she plans to seek an annulment."

"An annulment! Haven't you explained to her that an annulment isn't possible—that it would have to be a divorce?"

Stuart threw his father an embarrassed look.

"An annulment *is* possible, Pa."

James's mouth dropped open in surprise. Stuart? Married for over a week, and an annulment was still possible? Obviously, the problems between his son and his new wife were far more serious than he'd first thought.

"What do you think I should do, Pa?"

James leaned back in his seat and thoughtfully sipped his brandy. "I know what you *shouldn't* do. You shouldn't run away from her like you have today. And what is this nonsense about us spending the night here in Marblehead? We've looked at the property you want, made an offer on it, and had lunch, and there's still enough daylight left to get home."

"I just felt like I couldn't face her this morning."

"Why? Because you tried to make love to her last night? What's wrong with that? You said it yourself, Stu, you're her husband. Making love to your wife is a perfectly normal thing for a husband to do. In fact, I don't know why you're not back in that big bed of yours doing it right now."

"I guess I just don't know quite how to approach her."

"Well, you have to do it sometime, and there's no time like the present. Now, finish your drink and let's head back to Boston. You can think about what you're going to say, or do, while we ride."

"You're not going to tell me what *you* think I should do?"

James shook his head. "No. You're a grown man, Stu, and a damn fine one at that. You'll figure it out for yourself. But tell me this—what do you *want* to do?"

"Want to do?" Stuart chuckled. "What I *want* to do is crawl into bed with my bride and not get out

189

for about a week."

"Sounds like a capital idea to me," James approved. "Let's go."

So, here he was—home, bathed, and in bed with his bride. Now what?

When he'd first opened the bedroom door, he'd noticed Claire's eyes were open, and for a moment, he'd hoped she might be waiting for him. But then he'd seen her quickly close them again and feign sleep, and her obvious dismissal of him had the same effect as a bucket full of cold water being thrown over his head.

So much for warm and willing, he'd thought dismally as he'd climbed into bed. He could feel the tension radiating from her where she lay next to him and he just couldn't resist slinging a little barb by saying goodnight and letting her know that she wasn't fooling him one bit with her possum act.

But still, she had ignored him, and then, she had actually gone to sleep!

At that moment, Claire turned over so that she was facing him, her head so close to his that he could feel her warm, soft breath against his cheek.

"You, lady, are going to be the end of me," he mumbled irritably, moving away from her in the big bed and adjusting himself uncomfortably as yet another unwanted erection swelled.

With a little mewl of protest, Claire unconsciously moved closer again, sighing with contentment as she cuddled up next to his big, warm body.

Stuart was lost. Even though he knew it was going to make him even more uncomfortable, he slipped an arm beneath her and pulled her closer until her head rested on his shoulder and her glorious auburn hair fanned across his chest. Even through the heavy material of her nightgown he could feel her breasts pressed intimately against his bare side, and the sensation caused such exquisite torture that he thought he might burst. He wanted nothing more than to turn her on to her back, kiss her into insensibility, and then bury himself deep within her, releasing all the pent-up passion and love he felt for her.

"You can't take advantage of her like that," he told himself through clenched teeth. "Not when she's asleep, for Christ's sake!"

Tomorrow . . . tomorrow, they'd spend the whole day together. Alone. Just the two of them. No well-meaning parents, no curious friends, no one. He'd take her out in his carriage and seduce her with the beauty of Boston. Then, he'd seduce her with food—he'd feed her lobster and wine until she was giddy and sated. Finally, he'd bring her home and truly seduce her—kissing and caressing every inch of her body until she couldn't find the will or desire to say no to him. And then he'd make her his.

"Please, God," he moaned, placing a cool hand over his hot, throbbing shaft, "make tomorrow come soon. Please . . ."

It was barely eight o'clock when Stuart bent over Claire and gently shook her awake. "Get up, sleepyhead," he coaxed. "It's a beautiful day, and I thought we'd go out and see the sights."

Claire opened one eye and peered up at her husband. "What time is it?" she mumbled.

"Time for you to get up. We have lots of things to do today, including buying you some new clothes."

"Oh, don't start that," Claire groaned.

"Stop arguing and get out of this bed before I pull you out myself."

"You wouldn't."

"Oh, wouldn't I?" Grinning like a naughty boy, he yanked the covers off and scooped her up into his arms.

"Stuart! Put me down. Stuart, I mean it. Put me down!"

"Do you promise to get dressed and come straight downstairs if I do?" he bargained, still holding her tightly against him.

"Yes, yes, I'll get dressed," she giggled, smacking ineffectually at his chest. "Now, put me down!"

Stuart promptly set her on her feet and walked over to the door. "God, you're a lazy wench in the morning!"

Claire threw him a jaundiced look, but before she could think of a suitably stinging rejoinder, he was gone.

It occurred to her as she hurriedly dressed that Stuart was acting very odd this morning. She had expected him to be angry with her after she'd feigned sleep when he'd arrived home last night. So, why was he being so . . . playful?

"Don't fight it," she told herself, as she pinned up her hair. "He's in a good mood, and you're going to get to see Boston. Enjoy it."

When she got downstairs, she found Stuart sitting alone in the dining room, dressed in a pair of buff-colored trousers and a dark brown serge coat. It was the first time Claire had ever seen him wear anything except his military uniform, and the sight of him in the perfectly tailored clothes was so arresting that she stopped dead in her tracks and gaped at him.

Stuart noticed her startled gaze and with a small smile he rose and walked toward her. "What are you looking at?" he asked, taking her hand and leading her over to the table.

"You," she admitted. "You're not wearing your uniform."

He poured a cup of coffee for her. "I'm not a soldier anymore," he said softly.

"You look very . . . nice," she stammered.

"I thought you might approve."

Claire felt much more than just approval. Many women thought that men looked most handsome dressed in military garb, but right now, she didn't agree. It was as if the daunting, dangerous figure of Major Stuart Wellesley of the Fourth Massachusetts had disappeared, and in his place stood the most urbane, sophisticated man she had ever seen. No wonder the women of Boston made such fools of themselves over him. He was magnificent.

They set out directly after breakfast. "Samuel has pulled the carriage round," Stuart informed her as he helped her on with her coat, "so we'll go out the front."

As they stepped out the door on to Louisburg Square, Claire drew in her breath in pleased delight. "What?" Stuart queried, turning curious eyes to her.

"Your street is absolutely lovely in the daytime," Claire smiled, looking up and down at the row of immaculate townhouses surrounding a small, fenced park set in the middle of the wide, oval avenue.

"Didn't you go out at all yesterday?"

"No. I spent most of the day in my . . . our . . . the bedroom."

Stuart felt a sharp stab of guilt at his abandonment of her the previous day. "I'm sorry," he said genuinely. "I shouldn't have gone to Marblehead."

"That's all right. I spent the day resting. I was tired . . . from the trip."

From the trip, hell! More likely from fighting me off the night before, he thought.

The silence between them grew until Claire said, "Is that little park open to anyone who wants to walk there?"

"No. It's private."

"Oh," she murmured, disappointed.

"Claire, it's there for the people who live on the square. *You* can walk there anytime you please."

Her eyes brightened. "Wonderful! How do I get in?"

"I'll give you a key for the gate," he promised with a smile. "If you go out for a stroll in the morning, you might run into some of our more interesting neighbors."

"Do we have interesting neighbors?"

"As a matter of fact, we do. The Mayor of Boston lives four houses down, and right next to us, in Number Ten, is a fascinating woman who writes books."

"Really?" Claire said, looking with interest at the bow-fronted building directly next to theirs. "What kinds of books does she write?"

"I'm not really sure. Mostly children's stories, I think. Her name is Alcott, and she lives there with her father."

"I hope I'll have a chance to meet her."

"I'm sure you will. Before I left, I used to see her taking a turn around the square almost every morning." He paused, chuckling as if at a private joke.

Claire looked at him curiously. "What is so funny?"

"Miss Alcott."

"What about her?"

"She talks to herself while she walks. Talks and gestures, as if she's carrying on a conversation with someone—except that she's always alone."

"I bet she's mentally working on her books," Claire conjectured. "I've heard there are writers who plot out their dialogue that way. They talk to themselves and then answer, like they're two people carrying on a conversation."

Stuart grinned. "That's probably exactly what she's doing. Anyway, she's a lovely, friendly lady, and if you get a chance to introduce yourself, do so. You'll enjoy her."

They settled into the small carriage and Stuart picked up the reins, flicking them gently over the horse's back and heading off down the cobblestone street. "Isn't someone driving us?" Claire asked, surprised that Stuart was assuming that task himself.

"No. I thought I'd do the driving today. I want us to spend some time alone."

"Why?"

"Why?" he asked, looking at her in astonishment. "Why not? We're married. Don't you think it's time we got to know each other a little?"

"I suppose so."

"Claire, quit looking at me like you expect me to eat you, for God's sake. I just thought it might be nice to have a day to ourselves."

Claire nodded, but remained silent. Her mood soon lightened, though, as they turned the corner and headed down Mount Vernon Street toward the state house.

"That park is called the Boston Commons," Stuart said, pointing. "It's been there since well before the Revolution. In the early days, Boston's citizens used to graze their cattle there."

"It's lovely," Claire nodded, craning her neck to look down the hill.

"Actually it's much prettier in the spring and summer. We'll have a picnic there when the weather gets warmer."

Claire shot Stuart a curious sidelong glance. He was making plans like he expected them to be married forever, yet he had admitted that night in bed that he knew she was planning to seek an annulment once the war was over.

They drove on for a few moments, continuing down Beacon Street, which flanked the park.

"Do you truly think the war will be over soon?" Claire asked suddenly.

Stuart's eyes narrowed as he tried to guess what had brought on this question. "Why do you ask?"

"Well," she hedged, wishing she hadn't, "you keep saying that it's bound to be over soon, and I just wondered when you think it might be."

"I don't think anyone knows for sure," Stuart said quietly, "but the Rebs can't last through another winter, so I expect it will be sometime in the next few months."

"Don't call them Rebs," Claire snapped. "I hate that!"

"Sorry," Stuart amended quickly. "The *Confederates.*"

"Thank you."

Suddenly, Stuart pulled the carriage to a halt and turned toward her. "Look, sweetheart, let's make a pact. Let's not talk about the war at all today. Let's just enjoy the sunshine and the city and the sea and each other.''

"All right," she nodded. "But not talking about it doesn't make it go away, Stuart. It's still there between us. You know it is."

"Not today, it's not," he said firmly, and with a snap of the reins, headed the horse on down the avenue.

Leaving Beacon Hill, they moved toward the center of the city. Stuart again pulled the horse to a halt and pointed to a large building on their left. "See that? That's Faneuil Hall. It's a building that was given to the city for the purpose of providing the citizens with a public meeting place. It also served as the town hall for many years."

"Really?" Claire asked, fascinated. "It looks very old."

"It is. It's been here since the 1740s. Old Sam Adams and his cronies incited the good Colonial citizens of Boston to revolt against their King in that building."

"What's it used for now?"

"Same thing," Stuart smiled. "It's still a public speaking forum where people can gather and share their views on politics or religion or city laws or anything else that might be on their minds."

"Only now they probably talk about the South revolting against them instead of them revolting against the King, right?"

Stuart frowned. "Claire, you promised."

"I'm sorry," she murmured, dropping her eyes to her lap. "It just slipped out."

"Would you like to go down to the waterfront?" Stuart suggested quickly, desperate to change the subject. "It's not especially pretty, but it offers a

197

great view of Boston Harbor."

"Where the tea party took place?"

"That's the one."

"I'd love to see it."

As they passed through the business district, Stuart again pulled back on the reins. "Isn't that a beautiful church?" he asked, pointing to a large stone Gothic structure.

"Yes. Is that where you go to church?"

Stuart nodded. "Trinity Episcopal. That's where I wish you and I had gotten married."

Claire's eyes widened at this unexpected statement, and not knowing how to respond, she said simply, "It's a lovely church, Stuart. Perhaps we can attend services some Sunday."

They could begin to smell the salty, fresh scent of the sea, and a few minutes later, Stuart pulled the carriage to a halt near a large, busy pier. "Want to get out and walk a little?" he asked.

"Oh, yes," Claire said, excitedly hopping down from the carriage's high seat.

They strolled along the boardwalk for a few minutes, then stopped to gaze out at the ocean.

"Are those islands out there?" Claire asked.

"Yes," Stuart responded, "there's a whole chain of them."

"Are they inhabited?"

"Some are. Georges Island houses Fort Warren. There's a lot of activity there now, because it's being used as a Confederate pris . . ." He stopped short, wanting to bite off his tongue, but his unthinking words were already out and there was no way to take them back.

"What?" Claire gasped, whirling on him. "There's a Confederate prison out there?"

"Claire . . ."

"Oh, my God!" she cried. "You see, Stuart? This is exactly what I mean. We can pretend we're a happily married couple enjoying a day's outing, but there's no way to block out reality. My countrymen are being held prisoner on that island. My fiancé may even be out there somewhere . . ."

"You don't have a fiancé," Stuart rasped, angry at both himself and her. "You have a husband, and he's standing right here."

"You don't understand," Claire moaned, burying her head in her hands, "you just don't. Take me back to the house, please. I don't want to see anymore."

"Claire, please," Stuart entreated, reaching to put his arm around her.

"No!" she snapped, shrugging him off. "Don't touch me. Just, *please,* take me back to the house. I have . . . I have a headache."

With a look of utter dejection, Stuart nodded, and silently they walked back to the carriage.

The ride home seemed interminable. Claire stared straight ahead, completely oblivious to the same landmarks she'd found so fascinating just a few hours before.

"Would you like to stop and get something to eat?" Stuart asked, finally breaking the long silence. "It's at least two o'clock and we haven't had anything since breakfast."

"No, thank you," Claire answered quietly. "I'm not hungry."

Suddenly, something deep inside Stuart snapped. "I'm sure you're not," he growled, "and even if you were, you'd probably rather starve than suffer another moment of my stinking Yankee company, wouldn't you?"

199

As much as Claire wanted to agree with him, she said nothing, sitting instead in tight-lipped silence until they again turned on to Louisburg Square. Stuart had barely pulled the horse to a halt before she sprang out of the carriage and ran up the front walk.

With a curse, Stuart jumped down also, throwing the reins at a surprised Samuel, who came hurrying out of the house. "Put the horse up. I'm done with the carriage for the day." Without another word, he turned and strode into the house after his wife.

He took the stairs two at a time and headed down the hallway just as he saw the hem of Claire's skirt disappear through the bedroom door. "You lock that door on me, lady, and I'll kick the goddamned thing in," he shouted, guessing her intent.

Claire paused, her shoulders slumping. Locking the door was exactly what she had been planning to do, but she knew from Stuart's tone that he wouldn't hesitate to do exactly what he'd threatened. Before she could decide whether to defy him, he strode into the room, kicking the door shut behind him.

Claire had seen Stuart angry before, but never anything like this. "What's the matter with you?" she asked fearfully.

"I've had it," he retorted, his gray eyes the same flinty color as the sea they'd just left, "with you, with the bloody war, and, most of all, with this goddamned situation between us."

"Stop swearing."

"I'll swear if I damn well feel like it!" he thundered. "This is my house, you're my wife, and we're going to get things straight between us."

"There's nothing to get straight," Claire said haughtily, determined to brazen out the sudden storm of his temper.

"Oh, yes there is, Mrs. Wellesley. And we're not leaving this room until we do. Now, you can either sit down in this chair of your own free will, or I can tie you into it, but one way or the other, you're going to listen to me."

Claire sat down.

Chapter Fifteen

For Claire, the next few minutes were torture as Stuart paced the length and breadth of their beautiful bedroom, carefully formulating what he was going to say.

Finally, he turned toward her, his expression somber. "I can't help that I'm a Yankee, Claire, and I can't help that Fort Warren is being used as a Confederate prison. You have an uncanny knack of making me feel like I'm responsible for this whole bloody war, and I'm not. I'm just a man who went to fight for what he believed was right—just as your brother and your fiancé did. I realize that my believing in the Northern Cause and you believing in the Southern one has created some unusual problems in our marriage, but . . ."

"Our marriage is unusual enough all by itself," Claire interrupted softly.

Stuart frowned, but ignored her comment. "As I was saying, we have been faced with some unusual problems, but regardless of what you think, none of them are insurmountable—if you'd just give us a chance."

Tears welled in Claire's eyes and she quickly

looked down at her clenched hands. "I can't do that," she murmured.

"Why not?"

Taking a deep breath, she looked up again, meeting Stuart's gaze steadily. "I just can't. Not as long as there is a chance that David might still be alive."

"Jesus Christ," Stuart gritted, spinning away from her and raking his hands through his hair in utter frustration. "Are you going to start that again? David is dead, Claire. *Dead!* How many times do I have to tell you?"

"You don't know that for sure," she argued, jumping up from the chair. "You *don't!*"

"You're right," he admitted with a tired sigh. "But, I've told you before, I conducted as extensive an investigation as I possibly could before we left Savannah. From every report I had, the man is dead."

"He could be in a Yankee prison somewhere," Claire said stubbornly.

"I contacted the prisons. He's not in any of them, Claire, and no one has seen him or heard from him since Sharpsburg. No one—including you."

Claire squeezed her eyes shut, allowing the tears to course unchecked down her cheeks. "You're right," she choked. "I know you are, but I just can't let him go. I loved him so much. I'd loved him since we were children. We'd always planned to marry, but then the war came and he went away. But he promised me, *he promised me* he'd come back—and I believed him."

Stuart turned away, not wanting her to see how much her declaration of love for another man hurt him. But when he looked back at her, she was staring at him, wearing a look so plaintive and beseeching that a wave of compassion washed over him. Walking quickly to where she stood, he gathered her into his arms. "Claire, David would have come back if he could have. But, sweetheart, he can't. He'll never be able to. He's gone, Claire, and you have to face it."

"I can't!" she sobbed, her face pressed against his jacket.

"You have to," Stuart repeated, taking her by her upper arms and holding her away from him, "or there's no hope for us."

"Us!" she exclaimed, wrenching out of his grasp. "There is no 'us,' Stuart."

"There could be if you'd quit fighting it," he insisted, his gray eyes darkening with anger.

"You expect too much."

"I expect you to be my wife. Is that too much?"

"Yes!" she blurted, spinning away. "I don't want to be your wife. Can't you understand that?"

"You *are* my wife!"

"No, I'm not. Not really."

"That can change."

"But it won't. I won't let it."

Suddenly, all the anger and hurt Stuart had harbored for so long erupted, and in a strangled voice, he shouted, "Why not? Do you know how you make me feel every time you reject me? Every time you shrug me off? Well, I'll tell you. I feel like a leper, Claire . . . like something unclean that you'd sooner die than touch."

Claire's eyes widened at this startling revelation and she sank slowly into the chair. "I don't mean to make you feel that way," she said quietly. "I'm very grateful for the sacrifice you made by marrying me. I truly am."

"It was no sacrifice, and I don't want your

goddamned gratitude!" Stuart bellowed.

"Then what do you want?"

"I want you to love me!"

There, it was said. And now that he'd admitted that much, the rest followed in a torrent. "I want you to want me, Claire. I want you to get into bed with me and let me make love to you. I want to kiss you and caress you and hold you in my arms when we go to sleep at night—and I want you to want me to do it!"

"I *do* want you to," Claire whispered. "And I hate myself for it."

For the rest of her life, when Claire would think back on this moment, she could never believe how fast Stuart had moved. One second he was standing across the room, and the next, he was pulling her out of the chair and kissing her.

His hands and lips seemed to be everywhere. He was like a beggar at a feast, his hands running down her back, then up her sides, pausing to hungrily cup her breasts before he threaded his fingers into her flaming hair. He bent her back over his arm, kissing her neck and muttering unintelligible words against her soft skin. His lips moved up toward her ear, his hot, rasping breath leaving a fiery trail as his passion quickly mounted.

"Come to bed with me," he panted, his tongue swirling around her ear, until she was shivering all over.

"But," she gasped, feeling like she couldn't draw an even breath, "it's the middle of the afternoon."

"I don't care. Please, Claire, don't say 'no' again."

Claire was of no mind to say "no," and with a

little cry of surrender, she abandoned herself to him, throwing her head back and offering him greater access to her throat and the upper swells of her breasts.

Stuart fumbled with the tiny buttons running down the front of her bodice, but he was shaking so badly he could make no progress. Finally, with a frustrated curse, he curled his fingers inside the neckline, intending to tear it.

Feeling his fingers against her throat, Claire wrested her lips away from his. "Don't rip my dress. It's one of my good ones."

"I'll buy you ten more tomorrow," he promised, and with a quick jerk, he ripped the bodice from collar to waistline. Jet buttons flew everywhere, skittering across the floor.

Claire looked at the bouncing buttons in disbelief. "I don't *believe* you just did that."

Stuart ignored her. "Why the hell do you have so many clothes on?" he demanded heatedly, his fingers now working at the tie to her petticoat.

"Wait a minute," she pleaded. "I'll do it."

"Hurry," he ordered and started pulling pins out of her hair, dropping them carelessly on the floor to join the buttons.

"Are you always like this?"

"I don't remember," he rasped, burying his face in her breasts as she shimmied out of her chemise.

Suddenly, she was naked, and for a long moment, he just stood in front of her, drinking in her beauty.

Claire could feel a blush creep up her entire length at her husband's hot-eyed perusal, and with a nervous little giggle, she attempted to cover herself.

"Don't," he said softly, shaking his head. "Let

me look at you."

"You're embarrassing me."

"Don't be embarrassed," he whispered, reaching out and running a gentle finger over her nipple. The little peak immediately tightened, making him catch his breath.

Claire glanced down, and seeing how her body was betraying her escalating desire, she again clapped her arm over her breasts.

Stuart wrapped his hand around her wrist and gently pulled her arm away. "Do you know how long I've dreamed of seeing you like this?" he whispered, raising his eyes to gaze into hers.

His look was so honest, his question so straightforward, that despite her embarrassment, Claire couldn't deny him. Dropping her arm to her side, she swung her hair behind her shoulders, letting him see every inch of her.

Stuart's lips parted and he sucked air through his teeth, struggling mightily not to succumb to his basest instincts and take her right there on the floor.

"Get in bed," he commanded softly, his fingers flying down the placard of his trousers as he unbuttoned them.

Claire walked over to the bed and lay down.

Never in his life had Stuart shed his clothes so quickly. When he was as naked as she, he walked over to the side of the bed and gazed down at his waiting wife.

"Claire, look at me," he said quietly.

Claire turned her eyes on him, careful to keep them focused above his shoulders.

"What do you see?"

"My husband," she said tentatively.

"What else?"

"A man come to make love to me."

Stuart smiled at the slight tremor that shook her voice when she said that.

"Anything else?"

Claire hesitated. "No. Should there be?"

"You don't see a Yankee come to rape you?"

Claire searched his tense face for a moment, then lowered her eyes to gaze at his jutting erection. "No," she said slowly, surprised to find that she meant it. "I don't see a Yankee. And I know it's not going to be rape."

Stuart felt like he was about to burst into flames. "You know that if we do this, there'll be no annulment."

"Yes," she whispered, unconsciously running her tongue across her lips as she continued to stare in fascination at his throbbing arousal.

Her provocative gesture brought him close to the edge of his control, but he was determined to ask one more question. "And knowing that, you still want me to make love to you?"

"Yes. God help me, but I do."

With a moan, Stuart bent a knee to the bed and scooped her up in his arms, falling on his back into the soft mattress and taking her down with him.

"Kiss me," he whispered as she stretched out full length on top of him.

Claire's eyes closed, and with a sigh, she offered her lips to him. Stuart eagerly took them, plunging his tongue into her warm, welcoming mouth. He moved his hands down the length of her back, pressing her against him so she would feel his desire.

Claire shivered as she felt Stuart's hot, hard shaft against the inside of her thigh. She rubbed against it, then smiled with pure, feminine satisfaction as he answered her sensual call with a low moan.

Placing his hands against her ribs, he pulled her up his body, lifting her above him until her lush breasts brushed his mouth. "You smell so good," he groaned, inhaling deeply of her spicy, feminine scent.

"So do you," she returned softly, burying her lips in his hair. And he did. He had a scent about him she had never noticed before—an intoxicating aroma that was rich and musky and excited.

Slowly, very slowly, Stuart lowered her upper body, opening his mouth until her left breast completely filled it.

Claire gasped as he sucked on her breast, his soft, warm tongue swirling round and round her nipple, his teeth nibbling the soft flesh. Her body stiffened against him, and without even realizing it, she began to rotate her hips against his stomach, squirming to move back down so she could again rub herself against his pulsing erection.

Without even realizing that he had turned her over, Claire suddenly found herself on her back. Opening her eyes, she treated herself to the erotic sight of him crouched above her, his breath coming in harsh little spurts, his entire body shaking with his need for her. "I can't wait any longer," he panted, his face dark with desire.

His rasping words triggered a ripple of fear in her and in a small voice, she said, "You're going to hurt me now, aren't you?"

Stuart winced, hating the terror he saw in her eyes. "A little," he nodded, unwilling to lie to her. "But only this time. I promise you, sweetheart, it will never hurt again after this."

Every sexual horror story that Claire's friends

had ever told her flooded her mind, and in a voice laced with trepidation she said, "Couldn't we just stop now?"

"Stop?" Stuart repeated in disbelief, his throat so dry he could hardly form the question. "Oh, God, Claire . . ." Taking a deep, shuddering breath, he lowered himself to lie on top of her, his manhood nestling intimately between her parted thighs. "You want me to *stop?*"

Claire could feel the pulsing tip of his shaft pressing with heated demand against the threshold of her womanhood, and suddenly, she knew that despite her maidenly fears, she didn't. "No," she whispered. "Don't stop."

Stuart's heart slammed against his ribs, and lifting his head, he kissed her—a slow, sensual blending of mouths and tongues that made Claire feel like she was melting. Instinctively, she wrapped her legs around his lean hips, extending love's ultimate invitation.

With as much care as his starved, lusting body would permit, Stuart entered her, forcing himself to pause when he confronted the tiny barrier. "This is the part that hurts," he murmured apologetically, "but then we'll be done with it."

The quick, hard thrust that followed *did* hurt, and for a moment, Claire stiffened, trying to draw away. But, just as quickly, the pain ebbed. She stopped struggling, sighing with pleased surprise as the pain was replaced with a delicious feeling of fullness.

"Are you all right?" Stuart murmured.

"Yes, I'm fine. Is there more, or is it over?"

"Oh, sweetheart, it's barely begun." He smiled, his hips flexing as he set a gentle, rocking rhythm.

"Mmm, that's nice," Claire moaned, her body matching his ebb and flow.

Succumbing to his own body's screaming demands, Stuart increased his pace, trying desperately to hold himself in check long enough to give Claire satisfaction. A sheen of sweat broke out over his body as he fought for control, but after only a few seconds, he could hold back no longer. With one last hard thrust, he poured himself into her.

An exquisite pressure was building within Claire and, instinctively, she knew something was about to happen to her. She felt as if she were reaching for something—something wonderful that was just beyond her grasp—but before she could claim it, Stuart ceased his erotic dance and, after several wrenching shudders, collapsed on top of her.

Claire's elusive quarry fluttered away—leaving her feeling slightly bereft. She felt Stuart gently kiss her temple, and as he did so, the strange feelings of frustration faded, replaced by a sense of satisfaction that she had obviously pleased him.

Her friends had warned her that men enjoyed lovemaking far more than women did, and now she knew that that was true. But, they had been wrong when they had told her that the encounter was horribly unpleasant. She had actually enjoyed Stuart's attentions, and if she still felt somehow unsatisfied, then that must just be a woman's plight.

She smiled as Stuart turned on to his side and pulled her into his arms, but her expression turned to one of genuine bewilderment at his next words.

"I'm sorry, sweetheart. I promise it will be better next time."

"It didn't hurt that much," she whispered, not wanting him to feel guilty for her brief pain. "It really didn't."

"That's not what I meant. I knew I was going to have to hurt you, but that's over now and it'll never hurt like that again. What I'm talking about was my rather, ah, poor performance."

Claire raised herself on an elbow and looked down at her husband curiously. "I didn't see anything wrong with your . . . performance."

"Of course you didn't," he chuckled. "You have no basis for comparison."

Claire blushed furiously. "But, Stuart, I sort of enjoyed it."

With a laugh, Stuart pulled her back down on top of him, kissing her lustily. "You're easy, aren't you?"

Claire ducked her head in embarrassment, causing him to laugh harder. "Look, baby, I appreciate your words of praise, no matter how unfounded they might be, but I can assure you that the next time we do this, I'll do my best to see to it that you more than 'sort of' enjoy it."

Claire felt a tremor of excitement course through her. "Can we do it again now?" she asked, her eyes widening in disbelief at her own boldness.

Stuart was entranced by this new, provocative side of his wife. "Oho, so you like it *that* much, do you? Well, I would love to accommodate you, my randy little temptress, but don't you think we better start getting ready for the Hilliards' ball?"

Claire shot upright in the bed. "Oh, Stuart, the Hilliards' ball! I forgot all about that! What time is it?"

Stuart leaned over and looked at the small clock sitting on the night table. "Nearly five."

"Five!" Claire shrieked, bolting out of bed like someone had set her on fire, "I'll never be ready in time!"

"Yes, you will." Throwing back the covers, he got up and walked over to where she stood in front of her armoire. "I'll help you." He reached out and pulled her hard against him, cupping her breasts in his hands as he bent to kiss her. His tongue plundered the sweetness of her open mouth and Claire felt him immediately start to harden again. With a startled little yelp, she pushed him away.

"We'll never be ready on time if you start this again," she reproved.

"Me?" Stuart countered, his tone innocent, "you're the one who just asked if we could do it again."

"That was before I remembered the Hilliards' ball."

Stuart pulled her back into his embrace and playfully rubbed his lengthening erection against her belly. "So we'll be a little late. Let's go back to bed."

"But Stuart," she protested faintly, her voice losing much of its conviction as she parted her thighs, "we're the guests of honor."

"You're right," he sighed, and reluctantly took a step backward, breaking their intimate embrace. "And I don't want the next time to be hurried. We'll just have to wait till we get home."

Claire looked at him groggily and nodded. "Till we get home," she repeated dumbly.

Stepping forward, Stuart planted a quick kiss on her passion-swollen lips. "Right after the ball," he affirmed, then moved off toward the bathing chamber.

Claire stood where she was for a long moment,

214

trying to right her reeling senses. When she finally felt like she could again walk without her knees buckling, she headed over to the bathing chamber. "Stuart?" she called through the door.

"Yes?"

"How late do balls in Boston usually last?"

Chapter Sixteen

"Why aren't we riding to the ball with your parents?" Claire settled her wide skirts on the plush leather seat of Stuart's luxurious coach and looked at him curiously.

"We don't often ride together," he answered, stepping into the coach after her and closing the door. "They usually want to leave these functions much earlier than I do, and although that may not be the case tonight," he paused, looking at her meaningfully, "I didn't want to tell *them* that."

Claire blushed at his suggestive words, causing him to grin and move a little closer to her on the seat. "Besides," he continued, "the Hilliards are their oldest friends in Boston, so Mother thought she'd go a little early and help Margaret with last-minute details."

"How do your parents know the Hilliards?"

"When my folks first came to America, they lived in Boston for several years before Pa got the itch to move west. That's when they met the Hilliards. I'm surprised Grenita didn't tell you that."

"Grenita Forten?"

"Yeah, she's their daughter. We've known each other all our lives."

"She mentioned that," Claire remarked. "But how could you have when you were born in Colorado?"

"I wasn't. I was born here."

"You were?"

"Yes. Miles and I both were, and since Grenita and I are the same age, we played together when we were babies. But I was only four when Pa bought Well Springs and we moved to Durango. I really don't remember much about living in Boston."

"What's Well Springs?"

Stuart looked over at her, realizing again how little they actually knew about each other. "Well Springs is my family's ranch."

"What a pretty name."

Stuart's face took on a faraway look. "It's a pretty place. Maybe next summer we can go for a visit."

"I'd like that," Claire nodded.

Stuart grinned at her, pleased that, for the first time, she hadn't shut him out when he mentioned a future together.

A comfortable silence fell between them as the carriage made its way through the foggy night until finally Claire ran a hand down her satin skirt and asked shyly, "Do I look all right?"

"You look absolutely lovely," Stuart approved, his eyes scanning her satin gown with its huge hoop skirt and low-cut décolletage, "but tomorrow I *am* going to take you shopping for some new clothes—and I want no arguments about it."

"So you *don't* like this dress . . ."

"It's not that at all. I think it's gorgeous, and that amber color is perfect with your hair. But I noticed when you were dressing tonight that it's the only decent ball gown you have. Since we're invited to no less than five parties in the next few weeks, you're going to need several more. You can't keep showing up in the same dress."

"Well, pardon me!" Claire bristled. "I'm sorry I came to you so ill prepared for the life you lead, but where I come from, there's a war going on and new clothes are hard to come by. I apologize if I'm an embarrassment to you."

Stuart frowned, wondering what had brought on this little tirade. "Hey," he soothed, picking up her shaking hand and kissing the back of it softly. "What's the matter?"

"Nothing," she snapped, refusing to meet his eyes.

"I didn't mean to hurt your feelings."

"I know you didn't," she sighed, looking at him again. "I just don't like being reminded of how shabby my wardrobe is. Before the war, I had the most beautiful clothes of any girl in Savannah, and now . . . well, everything is just so different now. I guess I'll never get used to being poor."

Stuart smiled and kissed her hand again, holding it against his cheek for a moment. "You're not poor anymore, Mrs. Wellesley. You married a very rich husband, and I can assure you, with all my money, you'll never need to worry about shabby clothes again."

"Stuart!" Claire gasped, misunderstanding him, "you don't think I married you for money, do you?"

"Of course I don't," he chuckled, drawing her close. "I'm just teasing you. But frankly, I wouldn't care if you had. All that matters is that I got you—for whatever reason."

Claire's expression softened as she gazed into her husband's earnest eyes. "You know," she murmured, "for a Yankee, you're not so bad."

"Why, thank you, ma'am," he responded, laughing. "I think that's just about the nicest thing you've ever said to me."

They rode along for another few blocks in silence until Claire noticed that Stuart kept glancing over at her with a look of concern in his eyes.

"Is something wrong?" she asked.

"Sweetheart," he began, clasping his hands between his knees and blowing out a long, troubled breath, "I want you to have a good time tonight. I want you to have the best damn time any woman ever had at a ball . . ."

"But . . ." Claire coaxed.

"But, there are going to be two hundred people at this affair, and not a single one of them is a Confederate."

A ripple of apprehension skittered down Claire's spine. "What are you saying?" she asked quietly. "Are you afraid someone is going to say something to me because I'm from the South?"

"I would sincerely hope not," Stuart answered, "but feelings about this war run just as high in the North as they do in the South, so, if somebody gets drunk and says something derogatory . . ."

"I should be ready for it?"

"Well, yes. I mean, no. What I'm trying to say is that if it happens, you should ignore it."

"Would someone actually be that rude?"

"I honestly don't know."

"You don't seem to have much faith in your so-called friends."

Stuart sighed and looked at her with remorseful

eyes. "This war has done things to a lot of people, Claire—on both sides. I've seen brothers kill each other over it. Is there a possibility that a normally very nice, genteel man who is part of Boston society might say something rude to a Southern woman? Unfortunately, I'm afraid so."

"Then, why don't you just take me home?" she asked, her eyes pleading. "You could go to the ball without me. I'm sure that would be a relief to everyone. Your friends would get to welcome you home without the strain of having to be cordial to your . . . your Rebel wife." She paused, then added softly, "And it would save you the embarrassment of having to explain to your friends why you married me."

"I don't have to explain anything to anybody," Stuart said fiercely. "I married you because I wanted you, period. That's all the explanation anyone needs."

"Are you saying that no one knows the real reason you married me?"

"What 'real' reason?"

"You know, the *real* reason," she answered, bewildered by his sudden anger. "That I helped save your life and you felt beholden to me."

"Do you still think that's why I married you?" Stuart asked quietly.

Claire shrugged. "Of course. Why else would you have?"

Before she knew what was happening, Stuart pulled her up against the rocklike wall of his chest and gave her a devouring kiss. "How about because I think you're the most beautiful woman I've ever laid eyes on? How about because you have more courage and spirit than anyone I've ever known? How about because I want you for myself for the rest of my life? How about because I love you?"

Claire gasped at these last, unexpected words, staring at him in slack-jawed astonishment. "You love me?" she whispered. "Do you really mean that? You didn't just marry me because you felt you had to?"

Stuart looked at her for a long moment, then shook his head and threw up his hands in defeat. "I give up."

"Give up on what?" Claire asked, genuinely confused.

"Give up on trying to make you believe I love you. My God, Claire, I tell you every way I can. And after what we shared this afternoon, how can you possibly doubt it?"

"But, I thought that was just . . . just passion," she stammered, ducking her head in embarrassment. "I've always heard that men will . . . will copulate with any woman who lets them—that love doesn't have anything to do with it."

Stuart's eyes flared in offense. "Copulate? Is that what you thought we were doing today? *Copulating?* My God, I guess my performance was worse than even *I* thought!"

"That's not what I meant," Claire protested, her face beet-red with embarrassment. "I've just always been told that, for men, love and s . . . sex . . ." She paused a moment, gulping in disbelief that she had actually uttered that word. Why, half the women in Savannah would faint dead away if they heard this conversation. "That for men," she repeated, "the two don't necessarily go together."

"I'm sure that's true for some men," Stuart gritted, still offended that his wife had called his lovemaking "copulation," "but not for this one."

"But you've made love to lots of women. Surely you couldn't have been in love with all of them."

"My God, Claire! How many do you think there have been? You make it sound like you think I've bedded the entire female population of Massachusetts."

"Of course I don't think that," she mumbled, her color heightening even more. "But there must have been a great many."

"What makes you think so?" Stuart demanded, not sure whether he should be flattered or offended by his wife's suppositions.

"Well, because . . . because you're so good at it. This afternoon, you knew exactly what you were doing—and you knew exactly what I was going to feel, and when. Are you going to sit here and tell me that today was your first time too?"

"No," Stuart chuckled, deciding he was flattered. "I'm not going to tell you that."

"And, did you love all the women you've . . . known?"

"No," he admitted, "I just thought I did at the time. But I want you to know that no matter how I felt about the others, I have never had an experience even close to what we shared today."

Claire felt a little thrill of satisfaction at his words. "What made it different?" she asked softly.

"You," he breathed, leaning close to gently kiss her. "You made it different."

"But . . . I didn't do anything."

"Yes, you did. You made me fall in love with you—*really* in love—way back in Savannah. And that, my precious, beautiful wife, is what made it different—and very, very special."

"Oh, Stuart," Claire moaned, her heart breaking, "you deserve much better than me."

Stuart smiled mischievously and shrugged. "You're probably right," he conceded with an exaggerated sigh, "but after this afternoon, I guess I'm stuck with you."

"Yes," Claire laughed shakily, "I guess you are." Then, in a wistful voice, she added, "I hope I can be the woman you deserve, Stuart."

Stuart forced a laugh, determined to keep the mood light, since they were fast approaching the Hilliards' residence, "I don't know if *that's* possible, but I do know this." Despite his attempts at levity, his voice softened and became serious. "You're the one I love."

Claire smiled tremulously, blinking back the tears that threatened.

"Now, come on," he cajoled, chucking her under her chin. "None of that teary stuff. We're here, so let me see you smile, and remember: no matter how badly you want to do it, Confederate war whoops are *not* allowed at this party."

Claire burst out laughing at his idiotic warning and, feeling more lighthearted than she had in years, happily descended from the carriage, ready to face whatever challenges the Hilliards' ball might bring.

ENJOY ALL THE PASSION AND ROMANCE OF...

Heartfire

ROMANCES from ZEBRA

After you have read HEART-FIRE ROMANCES, we're sure you'll agree that HEARTFIRE sets new standards of excellence for historical romantic fiction. Each Zebra HEARTFIRE novel is the ultimate blend of intimate romance and grand adventure and each takes place in the kinds of historical settings you want most...the American Revolution, the Old West, Civil War and more.

SUBSCRIBER $AVE, $AVE, $AVE!!!

As a HEARTFIRE Home Subscriber, you'll save with your HEARTFIRE Subscription. You'll receive 4 brand new Heartfire Romances to preview Free for 10 days each month. If you decide to keep them you'll pay only $3.50 each; a total of $14.00 and you'll save $3.00 each month off the cover price.

Plus, we'll send you these novels as soon as they are published each month. There is never any shipping, handling or other hidden charges; home delivery is always FREE! And there is no obligation to buy even a single book. You may return any of the books within 10 days for full credit and you can cancel your subscription at any time. No questions asked.

Zebra's HEARTFIRE ROMANCES Are The Ultimate
In Historical Romantic Fiction.
Start Enjoying Romance As You Have Never Enjoyed It Before...
With 4 FREE Books From HEARTFIRE

TO GET YOUR
4 FREE BOOKS
MAIL THE COUPON BELOW.

FREE BOOK CERTIFICATE

GET 4 FREE BOOKS

Yes! I want to subscribe to Zebra's HEARTFIRE HOME SUBSCRIPTION SERVICE. Please send me my 4 FREE books. Then each month I'll receive the four newest Heartfire Romances as soon as they are published to preview Free for ten days. If I decide to keep them I'll pay the special discounted price of just $3.50 each; a total of $14.00. This is a savings of $3.00 off the regular publishers price. There are no shipping, handling or other hidden charges. There is no minimum number of books to buy and I may cancel this subscription at any time. In any case the 4 FREE Books are mine to keep regardless.

NAME

ADDRESS

CITY _____ STATE _____ ZIP

TELEPHONE

SIGNATURE

(If under 18 parent or guardian must sign)
Terms and prices subject to change.
Orders subject to acceptance.

ZH1093

Heartfire Romance

GET 4 FREE BOOKS

HEARTFIRE HOME SUBSCRIPTION
SERVICE
120 BRIGHTON ROAD
P.O. BOX 5214
CLIFTON, NEW JERSEY 07015

Chapter Seventeen

The Hilliards' house was located on Chestnut Street, in the prestigious Beacon Hill area of Boston. Although it looked similar to Stuart's townhouse in Louisburg Square, it was older and larger.

Claire looked around with interest as she and Stuart entered the huge foyer with its wainscoted woodwork and lofty ceiling. The house was magnificent, its many crystal chandeliers casting a sparkling light over the beautiful rooms.

"Pretty place, isn't it?" Stuart whispered, as an immaculately liveried servant took their coats.

"I like your house better," Claire confided softly. "It's more intimate."

Stuart frowned, wondering how long it would take Claire to think of the Louisburg Square house as theirs, not his. Her telling phrase reminded him that he still had not told her of the magnificent house he had just bought for her in Marblehead. He hoped that since he had not lived there before their marriage, she'd think of the new house as her home, as well as his.

He was eager to let her know about the house

and had thought about doing so tonight, but the mansion needed some renovating, so he had changed his mind, deciding to delay telling her about it until he could also show it to her.

Besides, he smiled to himself, I already have one gift to give her tonight. Absently he patted his pocket, assuring himself that the magnificent ruby-and-diamond ring he had purchased the day before was still there. He had bought the piece as a belated wedding ring and had intended to give it to Claire before they'd left the house for this evening's festivities. But they had dallied so long in bed that there had been no time to present it to her properly, so he had brought it along with him in case an appropriate, private moment occurred during the evening. But now, as he looked around at the mêlée of people streaming into the Hilliards' ballroom, he made up his mind to wait until they could be truly private. I'll give it to her tonight—after we've made love again, he promised himself.

The thought of slipping the magnificent jewel on Claire's slender finger while cozily ensconced in his big bed made a tremor of excitement shoot through him. And although he felt slightly disloyal toward his hosts, who he knew had gone to enormous work and expense to throw this ball for them, he secretly wished the evening would end quickly so he could again have his bride to himself. All to myself, he thought lustily, a spark of desire leaping into his gray eyes as he pictured how Claire had looked lying beneath him that afternoon.

His amorous thoughts were soon interrupted as Randolph and Margaret Hilliard entered the foyer to greet their guests of honor.

"Stuart!" Randolph boomed, holding out a

226

welcoming hand. "What a pleasure to see you, boy. We were worried about you for a while there, let me tell you."

Stuart shook Randolph Hilliard's hand warmly. "Believe me," he laughed, "the pleasure is all mine."

"And you must be Claire," Margaret Hilliard interjected, walking up and giving her a friendly hug. "Grenita and Mary have told us so much about you, we feel as if we know you already. Welcome to our home."

"Thank you," Claire smiled, genuinely touched by the older woman's obvious sincerity. "It is so kind of you to give Stuart and me such a lovely party."

Just then, Grenita joined them, holding out both hands to Claire and saying, "What a beautiful dress! Oh, Mother, just look at the hue of this satin. Isn't it remarkable? And these little rosettes that hold up the shoulders. Aren't they clever?"

"It's a lovely gown," Mrs. Hilliard agreed. "And that color is wonderful on you, dear."

Claire smiled her thanks, knowing that her three-year-old dress was slightly out of style and feeling grateful that these kind women meant to put her at ease about it.

"You're a very lucky man," Randolph commented, turning a grin on Stuart.

"I know," Stuart nodded happily. "I can assure you, Randolph, no one is more aware of my incredible luck than I."

Claire blushed at her husband's effusive words as Grenita, her warm brown eyes dancing with merriment, gave Stuart a little push and said, "Stop it, Stuart. You're embarrassing your wife."

"Let's go into the ballroom," Margaret suggested. "James is ready to burst, he's so eager to formally announce your marriage. I can't bear to let the poor man suffer any longer waiting for you."

She ushered the small group forward until they reached a set of massive double doors. "You two wait here," she whispered, then moved into the room to seek out James and Mary.

"This is so exciting," Grenita bubbled. "It's been so long since we've had a reason to give a really big party. I just know tonight is going to be memorable."

Stuart reached over and gave Claire's hand a reassuring little squeeze, just as anxious as his father to introduce Claire to his friends.

At a small sign from Margaret, who was now standing with the elder Wellesleys on a small dais at the front of the room, Randolph whispered, "This is it. Let's go." The orchestra struck up a noisy little fanfare, and with a gentle push, Randolph propelled Stuart and Claire forward.

Claire took a deep breath, offering up a quick little prayer that no one would shout an obscenity at her when she entered the room. She needn't have worried. As she looped her arm through his, Stuart took a confident step forward, and as the couple walked into the ballroom, all two hundred guests turned toward them and broke into spontaneous applause.

Stuart paused for a moment, inclining his head graciously in response to the thundering welcome. Then, with a broad smile, he started forward again as the throng of people parted to clear a path.

"Just like the Red Sea," he whispered, his irreverent witticism causing Claire's tense face to relax into an amused smile.

They mounted the dais without mishap and turned to face the huge room. As the crowd quieted, James moved forward to address the waiting guests.

"First of all," he smiled, "let me say that it is a very great pleasure to see so many old friends tonight. Mary and I know that since we last visited Boston, many of you have suffered terrible personal losses as a result of this tragic war that has raged for so long around us. And although we live far from the center of the conflict, our lives have certainly not been untouched by it.

"As many of you know, our son Stuart was seriously wounded while carrying Union dispatches to General Sherman in Georgia. He was taken to a Confederate fort outside Savannah where he recovered from his wounds in a prison hospital, cared for by a very capable and dedicated nurse named Claire Boudreau.

"Despite the obvious political differences between these two young people, they fell in love and, to their great credit, were able to put these differences aside and start a future together. Discovering a love so profound that it can transcend serious outside difficulties is a rare and special experience, and one which I feel bodes very well for a rare and special marriage.

"Therefore, it is with the greatest of pleasure that Mary and I announce the marriage of our son, Stuart James, to Miss Claire Renée Boudreau. We are delighted to have Claire as a member of our family and hope that you will all join us in wishing our son and our new daughter a long and happy marriage."

James took a small step to the side, and

motioning Claire and Stuart forward, said grandly, "Ladies and gentlemen, may I present Mr. and Mrs. Stuart Wellesley."

There was a moment of silence as everyone in the crowd digested James's heartfelt words, then the ballroom exploded again with the sound of thunderous applause.

Flashing the grin that had broken a hundred hearts, Stuart ushered Claire forward to accept the accolade. "Smile," he whispered, raising their joined hands high over their heads in an age-old gesture of victory, "they're in love with you."

"And *I'm* in love with your father," she returned happily.

Stuart broke into a hearty laugh. "Did you hear that, Pa? My bride has a case on you."

"The feeling is entirely mutual," James responded and stepped forward to embrace the laughing couple.

Little did Claire know as she stood enjoying her brief moment of triumph that deep in the crowd stood a small knot of young women who were neither clapping nor smiling.

"She's not nearly as pretty as Grenita said she was," Sally Rutherford announced.

"I agree," Ruth Halpern nodded. "Whatever do you suppose Stuart saw in her?"

"She's probably fast," Sally replied knowingly. "I've heard those southern belles all are."

"I've heard that, too, and who knows what happened when she was supposedly 'nursing' him?"

"Exactly. I bet she's loose with her favors and Stuart is just infatuated with bed sport. In fact, I wouldn't be surprised if she purposely got herself in the family way and Stuart *had* to marry her."

"Do you really think so?" Ruth squealed. "Oh, what a delicious scandal! Does anyone know exactly when they got married, so we can keep track?"

"It doesn't matter when they actually got married," Sally shrugged. "If she's going to have a baby, they'll just lie about it. Since they got married in Savannah, it would be the easiest thing in the world for her to make up any date that suits."

Many disappointed looks passed between the girls at this realization.

"Well, I, for one, don't want anything to do with her," Martha Cogsworth stated. "I don't care what Grenita says about how nice she is, she's a Confederate, and that alone is enough reason to shun her."

"I feel exactly the same way. If she invites me to tea, I won't go."

Melinda Parker, a plump girl with frizzy brown hair who had not yet entered into the conversation, now heaved a huge sigh.

"What's the matter, Melinda?" Ruth questioned.

"I just can't believe Stuart Wellesley is married —and not to any of us," Melinda answered sadly. "Who are we all going to dream about now?"

"We can still dream about Stuart, because this marriage won't last," Sally predicted. "He will eventually come to his senses and send that little Rebel packing, you mark my words. And when he does, we'll still be here, waiting to pick up the pieces of his broken heart. At least, I know *I* will."

"Oh, we *all* will," the other girls vowed, looking toward the dais, where the object of their longing was handing his new wife down to begin mingling

231

with the crowd.

"You're right, Sally," Ruth nodded sagely. "Stuart is sure to come to his senses, eventually . . ."

As Stuart and Claire stepped down from the dais, Claire found herself immediately swept away by the exuberant James. "Come with me, little lady," he invited, hooking her arm securely through his, "there is someone I want you to meet before your husband steals you away for the first dance."

Arm in arm, they headed toward a solitary lady who was standing on the perimeter of the ballroom floor, sipping a glass of champagne. "Claire, I'd like you to meet Mrs. Yvonne Warren. Yvonne, I want you to be the first guest to officially meet my new daughter, Claire."

Mrs. Warren was a tall woman in her late forties with a kindly face and the most beautiful black hair Claire had ever seen. "I am delighted to meet you, Claire," she said warmly, holding out an elegant hand.

"How do you do?" Claire returned, wondering why James had singled out this particular woman for her to meet. A moment later, she had her answer.

"Mrs. Warren had five sons," James said softly, "all of whom, along with her husband, were killed in the war."

"Oh, I'm so sorry," Claire gasped, truly horrified at the crushing loss this lovely woman had suffered.

"Thank you, dear," Yvonne answered. "I want you to know that I, perhaps more than any person in this room, rejoiced when I heard the news of your marriage. I firmly believe that the only way

232

this country will ever again be one is for all of us to put the past behind us and move forward into a new era of love and unity. If we can do that, maybe women in future generations will never have to endure the losses I have."

Claire smiled tremulously, deeply moved.

Turning toward Stuart's father, Yvonne said, "Would you excuse Claire and me for just a moment? There is something I want to say to her privately."

For just the briefest second, James's eyebrows rose; but ever the gentleman, he bowed and said, "Of course. Claire, I'll be over at the refreshment table when you and Mrs. Warren are finished talking."

As he walked away, Yvonne giggled like a schoolgirl. "I bet James is dying to know what I'm about to say to you, but this is for your ears only."

Claire looked at Yvonne expectantly, unable to imagine what the lady might want to tell her that she wouldn't want James Wellesley to hear.

"You could do something wonderful for this group, Claire," Yvonne announced without preamble.

"Oh? And what is that, Mrs. Warren?"

"Have a baby. Just as fast as you possibly can."

"A baby!" Claire gasped, scandalized that a complete stranger would make such a personal suggestion.

"Yes," Yvonne nodded. "Now, I know that you're probably horrified that I would suggest such a thing to you, but Claire, there is no clearer statement of hope that you and Stuart could make than to figuratively rejoin the North and South by having a child."

"But Mrs. Warren," Claire protested, "Stuart

and I didn't get married to make a statement about anything. We got married simply because we . . . fell in love." Claire nearly choked on her words, hating to lie to this well-meaning lady who obviously had such great expectations for her marriage.

"I know, dear, but Stuart and his family are very influential in this city, and therefore, anything he does is closely scrutinized. The two of you have already made a strong statement of solidarity by marrying while the war is still being waged. I'm just suggesting that that statement could be made a hundred times more strongly if you had a child together."

"I'll . . . we'll . . . think about it," Claire stammered.

"Good," Yvonne smiled, bending forward to place a light kiss on Claire's cheek. "I truly hope so."

A few minutes later, Claire walked back to where James waited for her, her cheeks still flaming with embarrassment. "Do you see Stuart?" she asked, craning her neck around the large room.

James smiled and again offered her his arm. "He's still over by the dais, talking to some of his friends. Shall we join him?"

"Yes, please," Claire nodded, and together they walked over to where Stuart stood, surrounded by a large cluster of men.

Stuart detached himself from the group, and leaning close to Claire, said, "You certainly spent a long time with Yvonne Warren. What were you two chatting about so confidentially?"

."I'll tell you later," Claire whispered.

Stuart wiggled his eyebrows at her meaningfully. "That good, huh?"

Claire threw him a shaming glance and plucked a flute of champagne off a passing waiter's tray.

"Don't get drunk, now," Stuart teased. "We still have to dance in front of all of these people."

"I've never been drunk in my life."

"Really? I'll have to remember that. Getting drunk can be lots of fun—in the right place and at the right time, of course."

"Stuart!"

"Well, it can be! Breaks down inhibitions, and that leads to all sorts of other . . . pleasant diversions."

Claire shot him another reproving glance, but before she could think of an appropriate set-down, the orchestra struck a beckoning chord and Randolph Hilliard again mounted the dais.

"Ladies and gentlemen," he called, "may I have your attention again, please?" When the crowd quieted and all heads were turned in his direction, he announced, "It's time for the bride and groom to open the ball. Stuart? Claire? If you would?"

Stuart nodded, escorting Claire into the circle of space which the crowd made for them. The orchestra took up the strains of a waltz and the couple moved into the dance easily, dipping and swaying in a swirl of amber satin.

"You're a wonderful dancer," Claire complimented as they flew across the dance floor.

"My mother taught us," Stuart laughed. "God, how Miles and I hated all those hours stumbling around the parlor."

"But it's a wonderful thing to know."

"Yes, I have to admit, it has come in handy. You dance beautifully yourself. Did your mother teach you, too?"

"No. I took lessons before my comeout."

Stuart chuckled. "I should have known you had a coming out."

"Why do you say that?"

"Oh, I don't know. You're just sort of the coming-out type."

Claire threw him a saucy look. "And what exactly *is* the coming-out type, Major?"

"Hard to explain, Miss Boudreau, but you are definitely it."

As the dance continued, the two of them chatted and laughed, seemingly oblivious to the hundreds of onlookers who stood by, smiling their approval.

There were no smiles, however, among the four jealous girls at the back of the room. "Look how Stuart is smiling at her," Melinda wailed. "I think he really does care for her, after all."

"Nonsense," Sally protested. "He just has to put on a good show in front of all these people."

"Well, I don't care about the rest of you," Ruth announced. "I'm going to make a point to meet her tonight."

"Oh, you traitor," Sally hissed.

"I beg your pardon!" Ruth huffed. "I'm not a traitor. I'm just curious, that's all."

"Me, too," Melinda admitted.

"Oh, all right," Sally snorted. "If you're all going to meet her, then I suppose I will, too. I've been wanting to see her up close, anyway."

The first dance ended, and as other couples strolled out onto the dance floor, the girls moved toward the corner where Stuart and Claire stood conversing with a group of well-wishers.

"Hello, Stuart," Sally trilled, when they were finally close enough to speak.

"Hello, Sally," Stuart smiled, then turned to Claire. "This is Sally Rutherford. Sally is a . . ."

"Very old friend of your husband's," Sally interrupted, turning a catty grin on Claire and extending a limp hand.

Reluctantly, Claire held out her hand in response, her brow furrowing as she noticed Sally staring at her plain, gold wedding band.

"Sally and I know each other through our church," Stuart said with a slight frown.

"Through church and *other* things," Sally added meaningfully. Turning her attention back to Stuart, she cooed, "It's been so long since we've seen you, Stuart. Other than your terrible wound, how have you been?"

"Other than my terrible wound, I've been busy."

"Obviously," Sally smiled, flicking another cool glance at Claire. "I understand that you've been promoted to Major."

"Yes, I was, but I'm out of the army now."

"What?" Sally asked in feigned dismay. "But, Stuart, whatever is the government going to do without you to design those wonderful warships of yours? Why, I heard your designs were more effective in blowing up the Rebels than anyone else's."

Stuart heard Claire's sharply indrawn breath and skewered Sally with an icy look.

"Oh, I'm sorry!" Sally gasped, fluttering her hand over her bosom. "I probably shouldn't have said that, should I? I totally forgot that your wife is a Reb . . . Confederate. Please forgive me . . . ah . . . I'm sorry, what was your name again?"

"Mrs. Wellesley," Claire said smoothly.

Stuart could hardly contain his laughter at Claire's stinging response, but before either of the antagonists could say more, he turned Claire toward the other girls, saying, "And how are you ladies this evening? Allow me to present my wife, Claire."

The small group spent another few minutes in strained conversation before the girls finally drifted away, casting longing looks back at Stuart.

"I'm sorry," he said, the second he and Claire were alone.

"It's not your fault," Claire assured him. "She's obviously jealous, and my being from the South was the only thing she could think of to hold against me."

"Sally's always been a little witch," Stuart said with a disgusted shake of his head, "but I didn't think she'd have the nerve to be rude to your face."

Claire smiled and patted his arm reassuringly. "Don't worry about it. She's just mad because she wants to be *your* little witch."

"Not a chance," Stuart chuckled, running his thumb gently down Claire's cheek. Then, leaning close to her ear, he whispered, "Can we go home yet?"

"Not a chance," she said.

Stuart sighed dramatically. "In that case, would you like to dance again?"

"Actually," Claire whispered, "I would like to freshen up a bit. Can you point the way to the powder room?"

Stuart pointed to a door off the side of the ballroom and with a last smile, Claire threaded her way through the crowd and disappeared through it. She walked down a small hall, following the sound of women's voices, but stopped short when she realized it was Sally Rutherford's voice she was hearing and that the hateful girl was obviously discussing her.

"Did you see that awful wedding ring Stuart

gave her? That alone is proof that he doesn't care about her. No man who cared about his wife would give her such a cheap ring—especially a man with Stuart's money."

"Oh, nonsense," came another voice. "What does a ring have to do with anything?"

"I beg your pardon, Melinda, but it has everything to do with everything," Sally replied. "One time when Stuart took me buggy riding, I asked him if he didn't agree that a marriage could be judged by the value of the jewelry a man gave his wife."

"And did he agree?"

"Well, sort of. He said that he guessed that if a man bought his wife beautiful jewelry, it was probably a definite sign that he loved her."

"But he didn't say that if a man *didn't* buy his wife jewelry that it meant he didn't love her, did he?"

"You can turn it around any way you want to," Sally snapped. "All I know is that Stuart is as rich as Midas, and that ring she's wearing probably didn't cost five dollars. Now, doesn't that tell you something?"

An angry flush crept up Claire's neck and, despite herself, she glanced down at the plain band encircling her finger. So what? she scolded herself. Material things mean nothing.

And yet she had to admit, it *was* a cheap band— the kind a farmer might buy for his mail-order bride. Or the kind a man would buy for a woman he felt obligated to marry, a little voice niggled.

"You know," Sally's voice floated down the hallway again. "I think there's more to Stuart's marriage than any of us realizes."

"What do you mean?"

"I think it's some kind of marriage of convenience."

"Oh, for heaven's sake, Sally. An hour ago you thought Stuart married her because she's going to have a baby. Then you said she's probably loose with her favors and he's infatuated with the bed sport. Now you think it's a marriage of convenience. The next thing you'll tell us is that their marriage was arranged by their parents when they were just children!"

A baby! Claire gasped. Is that what everyone thought? That Stuart had taken advantage of a weak-willed Southern nurse who was "loose with her favors," and then was forced to do the right thing by her? Or did they all believe, as Sally now did, that her marriage was purely a matter of convenience? Whatever their speculations, it was mortifying. No one seemed to believe that Stuart had married her because he had fallen desperately in love with her. But, why should they? Even *she* didn't believe that—regardless of what he'd said in the coach on the way over here tonight. This situation was just as bad as she had feared it would be. None of these snobby Northerners were ever going to believe that a rich, influential Yankee officer would marry a Rebel girl unless there were mitigating circumstances that forced him to do so.

"Let's go back in," Ruth suggested. "Maybe we'll hear something about Stuart and his new wife that will shed some light on the mystery."

"There *is* no mystery," Sally insisted. "It's just as I've been telling you. Somehow, that red-haired wench trapped Stuart into marrying her, and I intend to find out how!"

"Why? So you can try the same tactics?"

"Oh, shut up, Ruth. You just mark my words.

240

One of these days, you will all be attending one of these affairs for me—when *I* become the *second* Mrs. Stuart Wellesley."

With shrieks of laughter, the girls re-entered the hallway, nearly catching Claire as she fled through the door, their hurtful words still ringing in her ears.

"You weren't gone long," Stuart commented, as Claire rushed up to him. Then, as he noticed the stricken expression on her face, his smile faded to a look of concern. "Claire, is something wrong?"

"Wrong? Why would you say that?"

"Well, you look sort of—I don't know, upset. Did something happen while you were in the powder room?" Suddenly, his face darkened. "Was someone rude to you?"

"Of course not," she responded with a nervous little giggle. "Except for Sally Rutherford, everyone has been very cordial."

"You're not upset about her, are you? You have my word, Claire, there has never been anything . . ."

"Stuart," Claire soothed. "You don't need to explain anything. I told you before, Sally is just jealous."

Stuart looked at her for a long moment, but Claire continued to smile, determined not to let him know how the girls' speculations about them had upset her.

"You're sure nothing is wrong?" he asked again.

"You know, you're going to give me a complex. I go off to freshen up and when I get back, you tell me I look terrible."

"Oh, sweetheart, I'm sorry," Stuart said contritely. "I didn't mean . . ."

Claire forced a bright little laugh. "I'm teasing you, Major. Now, stop worrying about me. I'm having a wonderful time, and I want to dance."

Much to her relief, Stuart smiled, and executing an elegant bow, swept her into his arms and onto the dance floor.

The rest of the evening passed uneventfully. Claire did not see Sally Rutherford again, even though she kept a wary eye out for the malicious girl. Stuart never left her side, playing the role of the loving and attentive bridegroom with such ease and panache that Claire could almost believe that his words in the carriage had been true.

The many glasses of champagne being pressed into her hand did much to relax her as she and Stuart circulated among the guests, and except for the annoying twang in people's voices, it was almost as if she was attending any of a hundred parties in Savannah.

It was nearly three in the morning when she and Stuart finally climbed into his elegant coach and headed back to Louisburg Square. Claire laid her head back against the plush upholstery and yawned expansively.

"Tired?" Stuart asked softly.

"Yes, but I really did have a good time." She hiccoughed, then turned toward Stuart with horrified eyes. "Excuse me!"

"You've had too much champagne," he laughed.

"No, I haven't. I'm just sleepy."

Stuart grinned at the sound of her slightly

slurred voice. Curling his arm gently around her shoulders, he pulled her closer, sighing with satisfaction when she immediately nestled her head into the hollow of his shoulder.

"Don't let me go to sleep," she murmured. "I might never get up again."

"Don't worry, sweetheart," he crooned, kissing her soft hair, "I'll work something out—even if I have to leave you here for the rest of the night."

"You wouldn't do that."

"No," he whispered, "you're right. I wouldn't."

And he didn't. When they arrived back at the townhouse, Claire was, indeed, sound asleep against his shoulder. As the carriage rocked to a halt, Stuart gave her a light shake, but her only response was to murmur a sleepy little protest and snuggle closer to him.

Stuart waited until Samuel crawled down from the high driver's seat and opened the door, then he gathered Claire in his arms and lifted her out of the carriage.

"Need any help, Mr. Wellesley?"

"No, I can handle her."

Samuel watched as his employer carried his new wife up the front steps, then, with a knowing grin, grasped the horse's harness and headed for the back of the house. "If the boss thinks he's going to get any loving out of that little lady tonight, he's sorely mistaken," he chuckled, giving the animal's neck an affectionate pat. "She's done for."

Chapter Eighteen

The sun was high in the sky when Claire awoke the next morning. She stretched and yawned, then looked over at where Stuart lay next to her, still asleep. He was on his stomach facing her, one arm curled over his head and the other flung across her stomach.

Claire smiled, unabashedly ogling her husband's masculine perfection. He was naked from the waist up, the stark white of the sheets a vivid contrast to his dark skin. The well-defined muscles of his shoulders were relaxed now, but Claire remembered how hard they had felt under her hand as they'd danced together the night before.

He really is the most handsome man I've ever seen, she thought dreamily, staring with feminine appreciation at his soft, sensuous mouth. A little shiver ran through her as she remembered the heady sensation of that mouth covering hers when he'd made love to her the previous afternoon.

Another, foggier memory suddenly nudged at the edge of her consciousness—that of being laid down on a soft bed and slowly, gently undressed.

Undressed! With a little gasp, Claire clapped a

hand over her chest, her fingers curling into the silky texture of the sheer nightgown she wore. She had no recollection of putting on the nightrail—or of taking off her satin ballgown. In fact, the last thing she remembered was riding in the carriage with Stuart and being so sleepy she couldn't keep her eyes open. She recalled laying her head on his shoulder and warning him not to let her doze off. After that, she remembered nothing.

"I put you to bed."

Claire jumped at the sound of Stuart's deep, rich voice close to her ear, and turned startled eyes on him.

"Good morning," he murmured, and placed a light kiss on her lips.

"Good morning," she returned, feeling suddenly shy. There was something embarrassingly intimate about knowing that this handsome, virile man had removed her clothes and tucked her into his bed. Just thinking about it made a blush creep up her cheeks.

"I'm sorry I fell asleep last night," she mumbled.

"Why?" he asked softly, reaching out and pushing a wayward lock of her hair off her cheek.

"Well, because you had to . . . put me to bed."

"I didn't mind."

"But still . . ."

"I didn't mind."

With a lazy smile, Stuart shifted himself closer to her, wrapping his arm around her waist and pulling her up next to him. "But," he whispered, his voice husky, "if you're really feeling indebted to me, I can think of something you could do to repay the favor."

Claire's eyes widened as he rolled over on his

back, taking her with him.

"Stuart, it's broad daylight!"

"Who cares?" he drawled, trailing his fingers seductively up her back as he reached for her lips.

Claire's eyes drooped languidly as he kissed her, and without hesitation, she opened her mouth to allow his tongue's intimate invasion. The kiss went on for a long time, becoming deeper and more urgent as the moments passed. Stuart continued to stroke her back, letting his hands drift downward until he cupped her bottom, pressing her against him and rotating his hips suggestively.

Claire's eyes fluttered open, her gaze falling on the plain gold band on her left hand. Then she remembered: "No man who cares about his wife would give her such a cheap ring. . . . She's probably just easy with her favors and he's infatuated with the bed sport . . ."

As Sally Rutherford's hateful words came rushing back, Claire tore her mouth off Stuart's. "Don't do that!" she cried, squirming desperately to move away from where his hard shaft pressed against her.

She saw a flash of offense leap into his eyes and quickly amended her words. "I mean, we'd better get up now. I want to take a walk in the little park this morning, and you told me you had to meet someone for lunch. It's already late, so we better hurry, don't you think?"

Stuart blew out a long breath, insulted and hurt by Claire's obvious rejection of his amorous overtures. He knew she was aware of how aroused he was, and yet rather than being stimulated by his excitement, she seemed to want to get away from him. He badly wanted an explanation for her sudden standoffish behavior, but decided to say nothing, not wanting to risk an altercation with her this morning.

He had been incredibly frustrated last night when they had returned from the ball. All evening, he had looked forward to giving her the beautiful ring he'd bought her, but when they'd finally arrived home, she'd been so sound asleep that no amount of coaxing and caressing stirred her. Finally, he had given up and gone to sleep, vowing that tonight would be different.

They had no engagements planned; no party to go to, no guests to receive—and his parents were invited out for the evening. Tonight, they would finally be alone. He planned to take her out for an intimate dinner and come home early. Then, he'd give her his magnificent gift and spend the rest of the night teaching her the pleasures of slow, leisurely lovemaking. He wanted the evening to be perfect, and he was determined not to let anything spoil it.

With that in mind, he decided not to confront her about her sudden coolness toward him and, with a resigned sigh, released her from his light embrace. "You're right," he nodded. "I do have a luncheon appointment today, and it *is* late."

With a relieved little smile, Claire rolled off him, throwing back the covers and bounding out of bed.

Stuart frowned at her retreating back as she dashed behind the dressing screen. What was wrong with her? She'd seemed so eager to make love again, but now she acted almost relieved that he wasn't going to press her this morning. Could it be maidenly reticence about making love in the daylight? After their passionate encounter yesterday afternoon, he'd figured she'd be past that, but maybe he'd misjudged her.

Or maybe it was something else. Maybe someone at the ball *had* said something to her last night that had upset her. He hadn't really believed her when she'd breathlessly assured him that everything was all right after she returned from the powder room. She'd seemed to be having a good time before that, but afterward, she'd become quiet and withdrawn. Several times, as they'd danced, he'd caught her looking around warily, as if expecting someone to confront her about something. She'd also drunk glass after glass of champagne, almost as if she was trying to numb her awareness of where she was and who she was with.

Stuart's lips thinned. If that bitch Sally Rutherford had said something to offend her, he'd break her conniving little neck. With an angry growl, he ripped back the covers and got up, jerking on his underwear, then cursing as he painfully shoved his still-erect manhood into the confining linen. "Why is everything always so damn hard?" he muttered, then chuckled ruefully at his own double entendre.

Claire reappeared from behind the screen, wrapped in a thick robe. "Do you want to wash first, or should I?"

"Go ahead. I'm going down to get some coffee."

She nodded and hurried off toward the bathing chamber, biting her lip worriedly at his obvious ill humor.

Bracing the heels of her hand against the washbasin, she again stared down at her wedding ring. "No man who cared about his wife would give her such a cheap ring . . ," Sally had said.

Why did those words bother her so? She had never cared much for material things. Her family had been comfortable before the war, and she'd always had everything she wanted, but when the war had come and clothing and jewelry and perfumes were no longer available, it hadn't really bothered her. It was an inconvenience, to be sure, but she had never felt that she was *suffering*.

Why did her modest wedding ring suddenly make such a difference? It wasn't as if she'd expected anything extravagant. She'd known Stuart didn't love her when she married him. He had simply wanted to save her from her grisly fate, the same way she'd saved him from his. That was all that had prompted his proposal.

And she hadn't loved him then, either. She'd simply accepted his proposal as a way to save herself—and to save her father from the pain her death would cause him.

But that was then, and this is now, the familiar little voice niggled. Now, you do love him.

Claire drew in a sharp breath and flung her head back, staring aghast at her reflection in the small mirror hanging above the basin. The little voice was right. Sometime, somehow, in the last few weeks, she had fallen in love with him. When had it happened, and why?

Was it that she'd finally accepted that her beloved David was dead? Or maybe it was even simpler than that: maybe it was just that Stuart was alive and vital . . . and wanted her.

There was no doubt in Claire's mind that regardless of whether her husband truly loved her, he definitely wanted her. Only a few minutes before, when she'd come out from behind the dressing screen, she'd seen the flagrant proof of his continuing desire pressing boldly against the light linen of his underwear.

But was Sally right? Was "bed sport" *all* he wanted?

"No," she murmured aloud, still gazing in the mirror, "it's more than that." They had made love only once, but those few moments of intimacy had sprung from roots planted long before. They had spent a lot of time together during Stuart's convalescence, and even though she had detested him those first days in Savannah, her feelings had gradually changed.

Once she had finally gotten past her initial aversion to him, she had truly enjoyed the time they spent together, even when they had hotly debated the issues surrounding the war.

But when had enjoyment turned into love? She didn't know—couldn't even begin to guess which day, which week, or even which month it had happened. The only thing she was sure of was that it had. She couldn't deny it any longer; she was in love with her husband.

Hopeless tears sprang to Claire's eyes. She didn't want to love Stuart Wellesley. He was a Yankee, an enemy of her people—and she was sure he didn't really love her in return, despite his avowals yesterday in the coach.

Why don't you just let yourself believe him? she chided herself. He said he loved you. Why are you fighting it?

But she couldn't believe it. Not with Sally's words pounding in her brain like a litany.

Thoughtfully, she picked up her hairbrush and ran it through her thick auburn tresses. Now that she finally realized she loved Stuart, what was she going to do about it?

251

"Nothing," she said aloud. "Absolutely nothing." She set the hairbrush down and again stared at her reflection. "If you tell him you love him, it will only complicate matters. Who knows what will happen once the war is finally over and he knows Sherman's pardon can't be reversed? He may decide then that he doesn't want you, after all—that he wants a more suitable Yankee wife, someone he has more in common with. Someone like Sally."

The thought of Stuart preferring one of those catty, snobby girls she'd met the previous night made tears prick the back of Claire's eyes, but she prided herself on being a realist, and in her heart of hearts, she knew it was a possibility. Stuart was, by everyone's admission, the premier catch in Boston, and Claire was worldly wise enough to understand that those spoiled, self-centered girls wouldn't easily give up the man of their dreams—certainly not to a poor Confederate woman whom they'd already astutely guessed Stuart had married for suspect reasons.

Slowly, Claire pulled on a warm woolen dress, mulling over her situation. When she was finally clothed, she still had no real answers to her quandary, but with typical resilience, she pinned her hat at a jaunty angle and murmured, "Forget the stupid ring and enjoy him while you can. For the moment, at least, he's yours."

It was a rare, crystal-clear day in Boston, and as Claire left the house for her stroll in the park, she breathed deeply of the fresh, cold air. Looking up at the cloudless sky, she smiled appreciatively, then tripped down the steps and crossed the narrow cobblestone street.

The oval-shaped park was small, but every inch of space had been utilized to the fullest. Trees were planted at set intervals, and although at this time of year their branches were bare, Claire could tell from their positioning that at the height of summer, their dense leaves would offer a welcome canopy of cool shade.

She sauntered along, looking down at the meticulously placed flowerbeds and wondering what plants would bloom there in the spring. Something to look forward to, she thought happily, like a gift you wait to open.

On the far side of the park was a small bench, and it was here that Claire headed, seating herself and studying with interest a Florentine-style marble statue of Christopher Columbus that stood nearby.

Despite the biting weather, a sense of tranquility enveloped her, and with a contented sigh, she relaxed and let her mind drift. Several minutes passed before she was snapped back to reality by the sound of a key turning in the park's locked gate. Looking up, she saw a pretty, petite woman in her mid-thirties walking toward her. Claire rose to her feet as the woman approached, smiling tentatively.

"Good morning!" she called cheerfully. "I bet you're Mrs. Wellesley, aren't you?"

"Why, yes, I am," Claire answered, surprised that the woman knew who she was.

The woman extended her hand. "I'm Louisa May Alcott. I live next door to you, in Number Ten."

"Oh, yes," Claire smiled, "my husband told me about you. You're a writer, aren't you?"

"Well, I try," Miss Alcott chuckled. "I hope I'm not disturbing you."

"Not at all. It's such a beautiful day that I decided to come out and enjoy the weather. Would you like to sit down for a moment?"

"I'd love to. I've been working on my new book this morning, and I decided to take a break. When I looked out my window and saw you sitting here, I thought it would be a perfect opportunity to meet you. I'd heard that Major Wellesley had married and returned from the war, but I haven't had a chance to come calling yet."

"We've only been back in Boston for a short time."

Miss Alcott nodded. "And you're from Georgia?"

"Why, yes," Claire smiled, her eyes again betraying her surprise at the woman's extensive knowledge about her.

"I bet you're wondering how I know all this. I'm really not a nosy person, but when you live in a neighborhood as small as Louisburg Square, I'm afraid that everyone knows just about everything about everyone else."

Claire nodded, hoping that Miss Alcott hadn't heard the gossip about her marriage. "Do you live here with your family?" she inquired politely.

"Just my father. I'm afraid he's a little . . . eccentric, and since my sisters are married, it fell to me to care for him."

"Fathers tend to be that way, don't they?"

Louisa rolled her eyes. "Mine more than most, I'm afraid."

"How many sisters do you have?" Claire asked, liking the vivacious woman very much.

"Three. In fact, that's what I'm writing my new book about."

"Your sisters?"

"Well, actually, I'm writing about four fictional sisters, but I'm basing the story on my childhood."

"How fascinating!" Claire enthused. "I'll look forward to reading it. Have you given it a title?"

"No, not yet," Louisa sighed. "I never can think of titles. I have plenty of time, though, since I've actually just started this book. There hasn't been much time to write during the past few years, what with caring for my father and nursing at the hospital."

"You're a nurse?" Claire gasped. "So am I!"

"Really? Where have you worked?"

"I served as a volunteer at Confederate hospitals in both Atlanta and Savannah."

"My, we do have a lot in common, Mrs. Wellesley. I have been nursing at the Union hospital in Washington."

Claire smiled with delight, feeling a definite affinity for the friendly lady. All nurses shared a common goal to bring comfort to the sick and dying, and regardless of political differences, that goal forged a bond between them.

"How did you happen to meet Major Wellesley?" Louisa asked pleasantly. "Was he one of your patients?"

"Yes. He was wounded outside Savannah, and I was assigned to care for him."

"Well, I can assure you, you have dashed many young debutantes' hopes by marrying the gallant major. He was considered quite the prize here in Boston, you know."

"So I've gathered," Claire sighed. "When I met him in Savannah, I had no idea how many young ladies were setting their caps for him. He was merely a wounded soldier whom I was called upon to nurse."

"I understand exactly what you're saying. No matter how illustrious a man may be among his contemporaries, when men are wounded or sick, one is much like another. Sickness is a great equalizer."

For a moment, the two women sat in silence, both thinking about the tragic loss of life they'd witnessed in the past few years.

"Well," Louisa said suddenly, rising to her feet, "I'd better get back. It was a pleasure to meet you, Mrs. Wellesley."

Claire rose. "Please call me Claire. And thank you so much for stopping. I hope we'll see each other again."

"I'm sure we will." Taking Claire's mittened hand in hers, Louisa squeezed it warmly. "Let's plan to have tea one afternoon next week."

"I'd like that," Claire said sincerely.

With a last farewell, Louisa turned and walked away.

Claire sank back down on the bench, a happy little smile playing about the corners of her mouth. "Actually," she murmured, directing her words at the statue of Columbus, "Boston isn't so bad, after all."

Then, giggling at her own foolishness, she rose from the bench, suddenly eager to return to the warmth and welcome of her new home.

Chapter Nineteen

"How was your walk?"

"It was wonderful. I love the little park." Claire smiled hopefully up at Stuart as he helped her off with her coat. She was worried that he might still be angry about her not wanting to make love that morning, but his eyes had lost their stormy expression and when he smiled back at her, the little lines of tension around his mouth were no longer visible.

"Is this yours?" he asked, perusing the beautiful wool coat he held.

"No, it's your mother's."

"Don't you have a coat?"

"Of course I have a coat!" Claire snapped, offended, as always, by his derisive comments about her wardrobe. "But, I . . . I haven't unpacked that trunk yet, so I asked your mother if I might borrow hers."

"That was also her satin cloak you wore to the ball last night, wasn't it?"

"Well, yes," she admitted reluctantly.

"Claire, why do you keep lying to me about your clothes?"

"I'm not lying! I do have a trunk I haven't unpacked yet, and it does have a coat in it."

"And is the coat in that trunk suitable for Boston weather?"

"Probably."

"What do you mean, 'probably'? What's it made of? Wool?"

"No," she muttered, leaning down to remove her boots.

"It's not wool?"

"No, it's not wool!" Straightening, she flung her head back and glared at him. "Where would we Confederates get wool when you Yankees barricaded up our ports and there haven't been any shipments from England in three years? We don't raise sheep in Georgia and you know it, so how would we get wool?"

"Claire, I didn't mean . . ."

"My coat is made of cotton," she railed, her eyes blazing. "Heavy, coarse cotton. Cotton is all we have in Georgia, and now, thanks to General Sherman, we don't even have that. Did you know that calico, *calico*, costs twenty-five dollars a yard? Why, that's more than most men earn in a month, and it takes five times that much to make one dress! Can you imagine how much it would cost to make a wool coat, even if we *could* get the cloth? Thousands, Major. *Thousands!* And no one in the South has any money. You know that. All we have is Confederate bonds, and they aren't worth the paper they're printed on."

She paused and took a deep breath, furious with herself when she felt tears of frustration and embarrassment trace down her cheeks. "My cotton coat is very pretty," she gulped, her voice breaking. "It was good enough for me in Savannah, and it'll be good enough for me here!"

To her complete astonishment, Stuart took a quick step forward and put his arms around her. "Claire," he sighed, hugging her close, "don't cry. My darling, brave, proud little Rebel, don't cry."

His tender words only made Claire cry all the harder. "My coat *is* pretty," she sobbed.

"I'm sure it's gorgeous," he soothed, tipping her head back and kissing her wet cheeks, "but sweetheart, you need a wool coat. My folks are going back to Colorado in a few days, and what are you going to wear after my mother leaves?"

"I'll manage."

"Claire, you don't have to *manage*. I will buy you a new coat—if you'll just put aside your damn Rebel pride and let me."

"Oh, Stuart . . ."

"I know you keep saying your clothes are fine and you don't want any new ones, but for God's sake, it's just one coat. I can't for the life of me figure out why you keep fighting me on this."

"I just don't want you to spend your money on me . . ."

Placing his thumbs on her cheeks, Stuart tipped her head back until she was forced to look at him. "Claire, darling, you're my wife. I *want* to spend my money on you. Besides, as I told you the other night, I have so much money that you and I couldn't possibly spend it all if we did nothing but shop every day for the rest of our lives."

Claire gazed at him, her lips quivering in a tremulous smile. "Are you really *that* rich?"

"Yes," he smiled. "I'm *that* rich. Now, I have to leave for my luncheon appointment, but when I get back, you and I are going to go to a little dressmaker I know and buy you some suitable clothes.''

"But I don't need anything except the coat . . .''

"Don't argue," he ordered, cutting off her words of protest with a loud, smacking kiss. "Just be ready. And when we're done shopping, I'm going to take you out for the finest lobster dinner Boston has to offer.''

"Lobster!" Claire said, wrinkling her nose with distaste. "Aren't they just like crawdads?''

"No," Stuart chuckled, "they're not. And you can't live in Boston without eating lobster. It's a law.''

"It is?''

"Well, maybe not a law, exactly, but everyone in Boston eats lobster. Trust me, you'll love it.''

"I doubt that," she muttered, making a face.

"One taste," he laughed, shrugging into an elegant wool greatcoat and picking up his walking stick, "that's all I ask. Then, if you don't like it, we'll order you Yankee pot roast instead.''

"*Yankee* pot roast?''

"Okay," he sighed dramatically, "pot roast. Forget the Yankee part.''

"What is it?''

"It's beef, Claire. Roast beef cooked in a pot with potatoes and carrots and onions.''

"That sounds good.''

"It is good, but lobster is better." He finished buttoning his coat and reached out to again hug her. "Now, give me a smile and promise me you aren't going to cry anymore.''

Claire nodded and gave him a watery little smile.

"And promise me you'll go shopping with me this afternoon and let me buy you some clothes.''

She opened her mouth as if to argue, but then closed it again and nodded.

"And promise me you'll at least try some lobster."

This time she didn't nod, but instead, squeezed her eyes shut and shook her head.

"Aw, come on, you have to try it!"

"Oh, all right," she giggled, opening her eyes. "I promise I'll try your Yankee crawdads."

"They're not crawdads!" he laughed, bending his head to kiss her.

Claire looped her arms around his neck and responded to his kiss with enthusiasm, making him drop his walking stick and pull her closer. When he finally released her, they were both a little breathless. He smiled at her for a moment, then put his lips near her ear and whispered, "And promise me you won't drink too much champagne and pass out on me tonight."

Claire blushed and buried her head against the soft lapels of his greatcoat. "I promise," she murmured, raising her head and looking up at him with a shy smile.

"That's my girl," he grinned. Reluctantly, he released her and leaned down to pick up his walking stick. "I should be back by three."

"I'll be waiting."

For a long moment, Stuart gazed at her, his eyes soft. Then he chucked her under the chin and gave her one last quick kiss. "And I'll hurry."

Les Jeunes was an exclusive little *couturière*'s establishment where only the very elite of Boston could afford to shop. It was to this address that Stuart directed Samuel as he and Claire stepped into his carriage.

"I think you'll like Mademoiselle Bouvoir," he commented, as they clattered along the cobblestones. "She's easy to work with and has the best selections of sketches and materials of any dressmaker in Boston."

"How do you know so much about ladies' clothing?" Claire teased.

Stuart had the good grace to look embarrassed. "Well," he stammered, "my mother . . ."

"Oh, of course," Claire giggled, "your mother shops there . . . even though she lives in Colorado, right?"

"Actually, yes. When she and my father lived here, Mother bought all her clothes from the present Miss Bouvoir's mother. All these years, she's kept up a relationship with the shop. Miss Bouvoir sends her sketches and material samples twice a year, and Mother chooses what she wants and sends her selections back. Then Miss Bouvoir makes up the dresses and ships the finished clothes back to Colorado."

Claire gaped at him, her eyes round with wonder. "Your family is . . . incredible."

"Naw," Stuart laughed, "not incredible. My mother just likes nice things, and my father, who has more money than Midas, likes my mother. I call that an unbeatable combination, don't you?"

"I guess so," Claire chuckled. "So, you're telling me that you learned all about ladies' clothing from your mother . . ."

"Sure," he shrugged innocently. "Where else?"

Claire threw him a disbelieving smile, but before she could say anything further, they pulled up in front of the tiny shop.

"You know what today is?" Stuart asked,

helping her down the carriage steps.

"It's Thursday," Claire answered.

"And what else?"

"It's the twenty-fourth of February."

"And what else?"

Claire looked at him blankly. "I give up."

"It's Christmas, Mrs. Wellesley, and I'm Santa Claus."

"Stuart, you said just a coat . . ."

"I lied," he said happily. "Now, come on. It's freezing out here."

They entered the shop, and before they'd even closed the door behind them, a set of curtains at the back of the room parted and out stepped a beautiful dark-haired woman of about thirty. As her eyes settled on Stuart, she broke into a dazzling smile. "Monsieur Wellesley," she cooed, her gaze raking him appreciatively, "I heard you had returned from the war. What a pleasure to see you!"

"And you, Miss Bouvoir. Allow me to present my wife, Claire."

The sloe-eyed French woman gave Claire a quick, appraising look. "How do you do?"

Claire inclined her head. "I'm pleased to meet you. You have a lovely shop."

"So," Miss Bouvoir smiled, looking back at Stuart, "the rumors *are* true. You *did* marry a Southern girl."

Stuart cleared his throat, not wanting Claire to think she was the object of shopkeepers' gossip. "Yes, I did."

"You know, of course, monsieur, that you have broken many hearts in Boston."

Including yours, Claire thought testily, fully aware of the outrageously overt signals this

263

woman was sending out to her husband.

"I'm sure the good ladies of Boston will survive without me," he smiled.

"Survive, yes," Miss Bouvoir sighed, "but with broken hearts, I assure you."

Despite her annoyance at the flirtatious Frenchwoman, Claire couldn't help but be amused. Never had she seen Stuart so discomfited. Throwing him a teasing, sidelong glance, she said, "My word, Stuart, I had no idea when I accepted your marriage proposal that it would send an entire city into mourning."

"Not the whole city," Miss Bouvoir corrected with a melodic little laugh, "just half."

Stuart had had enough. "We're here to buy Mrs. Wellesley some warm clothes," he said firmly. "I know it's late in the season, but since there should be at least another six weeks of cold weather, she needs a few things."

"Of course," Miss Bouvoir nodded, quickly dropping the flirty little game she was playing in the face of Stuart's obvious annoyance.

Hardly a woman had entered her shop in the past two weeks who hadn't revealed some tidbit about Stuart Wellesley's startling marriage. The one thing they all agreed upon was that he had married this Southern girl purely out of some misplaced sense of gratitude because she had saved his life. Several women went so far as to conjecture that the marriage was one of convenience only—that the couple did not live together as man and wife—and that as soon as the war ended, Stuart would undoubtedly send the little Confederate back where she'd come from.

But what Françoise Bouvoir was seeing between the couple today certainly put the lie to the gossips' speculations. Stuart hadn't stopped touching the girl since they'd walked into the shop, and she, in turn, accepted his light embraces so easily that Françoise did not believe for a moment that she was a stranger to them. No, there was definitely much more between these two than simple gratitude.

Françoise considered herself an excellent judge of women *and* men, and if her instincts were correct, this couple was very much in love and their relationship was anything but platonic.

"Well, madame, where would you like to start?" she asked, suddenly all business. "Do you need underthings as well as dresses?"

"No," said Claire.

"Yes," said Stuart.

Claire turned toward her husband, opening her mouth to argue, but seeing his dark frown, she quickly turned back to the *couturière* and said, "Yes."

"And what do you prefer? Linen, muslin, batiste?"

"Batiste, all batiste," Stuart stated, his voice brooking no further discussion.

"Batiste it is," Françoise smiled, picking up a small pad and pulling a pencil out of her hair to make the notation. "Seven sets?" she said nonchalantly, not looking up.

"Ten," Stuart answered.

Françoise's eyebrows rose as she heard Claire's indrawn breath, but she was careful to keep her head down.

Claire looked at Stuart, her eyes wide with astonishment. "Ten?" she mouthed silently. "No!"

But he just grinned and nodded his head

decisively. "Ten," he mouthed back. "Yes!"

Dropping her order pad on a table, Françoise turned to Claire. "If you will follow me through the curtains, madame, we will take your measurements."

"I'm really just here for a coat," Claire murmured, then shot another look at Stuart where he now stood idly fingering some bolts of silk.

". . . and six day dresses and four ballgowns," he continued smoothly. "Plus two cloaks, three shawls, at least two of them cashmere, and, of course, bonnets, reticules, and stockings to match. Oh, and five or six nightgowns." Raising his eyebrows at Françoise meaningfully, he added, "Sheer ones, mademoiselle, with lace. In every color except red."

Claire turned crimson as Françoise broke into a delighted little giggle. "As you wish, monsieur. Now, Madame Wellesley, if you will just follow me."

As she headed for the curtains at the back of the store, Claire shot Stuart a furious look. "Whatever are you thinking?" she hissed. "That's more clothes than I've had in the last five years!"

"It's only enough to hold you until the weather breaks. Then we'll get you a real wardrobe for the summer."

"Stuart, this is preposterous . . ."

"Claire," he warned, his voice quiet but serious, "don't embarrass me in front of Miss Bouvoir. Just go. Françoise is waiting, and her time is valuable."

Claire glared at him mutinously, but continued on to the back of the shop. She brushed through the curtains and stepped into a tiny dressing room which contained a small table covered with snippets of cloth and an oval pier glass.

Françoise was waiting for her, tapemeasure in hand and a wide smile on her face. "If you'll turn around, I'll help you out of your gown," she offered.

Obediently, Claire turned, allowing the *couturière* to unhook her dress and slip it off her shoulders. When she was clad only in chemise, corset, and pantalettes, Miss Bouvoir began measuring, making many notations in a little book that hung around her neck by a fine silk cord.

Suddenly, the curtains parted to reveal Stuart, who stood framed in the narrow doorway. "I found several sketches out front that I like," he said, directing his words at Claire. "Take a look at them and see what you think."

With a nod, Claire accepted the drawings, setting them down on the table and studying them with interest.

"I especially like that second one," Stuart commented, his eyes feasting happily on his wife's trim bottom as she bent over the drawings. "I think it would be gorgeous in green velvet."

"It *is* lovely," Claire nodded, smiling at him over her shoulder.

"Good, then we'll have that one for sure," he said, turning his attention to Françoise. "Make a note of it, please—in green velvet."

"Yes, monsieur," Françoise smiled, delighted with Stuart's choice.

The curtains fluttered closed and Stuart disappeared. For a long moment, she just sat and thoughtfully stared after him.

Platonic, indeed, Françoise thought. Why, he looked like he wanted to throw her down on my little table and have her right there, and she didn't bat an eye at having him see her in her drawers. La, what a story this will be to tell everyone! Miss Rutherford will die!

"I like this one also," Claire said suddenly, startling Miss Bouvoir out of her reverie.

"Oh yes, yes, that one is very pretty. I think silk, don't you?"

"I don't know . . ." Claire hedged. "Perhaps something a little more utilitarian. Muslin, maybe?"

Françoise bit her lip. The design was not at all suited to muslin, and she knew that Mrs. Wellesley knew it. Why was the girl so timid about spending her husband's money? Lord knew, he had enough of it to buy the whole shop if he wanted to, so what was the girl worried about? "I don't know if muslin would exactly suit," Françoise said vaguely.

At that moment, the curtains again parted. Stuart took one look at the sketch Claire was holding and snorted, "Muslin? Absolutely not. That dress should be made up in silk. Blue silk."

"I agree," Françoise said, nodding eagerly. "I'll mark it down. I just received a shipment of lovely blue silk from Paris that will make up perfectly."

"Good," Stuart nodded. "Do it. And you," he muttered, looking at Claire through narrowed eyes, "you stop it."

Claire glanced quickly over at Miss Bouvoir, but it did not appear that the dressmaker had heard her husband's quiet command. With a little sigh of relief, she turned back to the sketches.

Françoise, however, had heard every word, and she gleefully catalogued the little altercation, more excited with each passing moment. Why, with the gossip she'd have to share after this afternoon's session with the Wellesleys, she'd be making a new dress for every woman in town. Even if the old cats didn't need one, they'd all come in—just in the hopes that she'd share some morsel she'd forgotten to tell everyone else.

It took over two hours for Stuart to be satisfied that Claire had all she needed, and by the time the Wellesleys were ready to leave the shop, Françoise's head was spinning. Never had she taken a single order this large—not even from the elder Mrs. Wellesley, though it was obvious that that gracious lady had raised her son to have the same fine sense of style she did.

Even though Françoise had dealt with Stuart before, it had always been on a small scale—a birthday gift for this one, a Christmas present for another. Never, ever, had she seen him spend like this!

And they all think he doesn't care about her, she giggled as she watched Stuart help Claire into their carriage. Just wait until they hear about this! Why, they'll all be so upset, they'll have to take to their beds.

With a graceful little pirouette, Françoise turned away from the window, clasping her order pad to her bosom and thanking the saints for seeing Stuart Wellesley safely through the war.

Chapter Twenty

"Two lobster dinners, please," Stuart said, smiling up at the impeccably dressed waiter hovering over him, "and be sure they're the best two you have."

"Of course, Mr. Wellesley," the waiter nodded, "I'll choose them myself."

"And a bottle of your best champagne."

"A magnum, sir?"

Stuart threw Claire a secret little smile. "No, not tonight. A regular-sized bottle will do."

"As you say, sir. And may I add that all of us here at Durgin-Park are very happy that you have returned to us safely."

"Thank you, John," Stuart nodded, chuckling. "I'm very happy I did also."

As the waiter hurried away, Claire leaned over the small table where they were seated and whispered, "Is there anyone in Boston who doesn't know you by name?"

"Oh, there must be a few people somewhere—probably recent immigrants," Stuart answered wryly, then started to laugh when he saw Claire's eyes widen. "I used to eat here often before I joined the army," he explained, "so everyone knows me."

"Everywhere we go, everyone knows you," Claire noted.

"That's just because they've all heard that Stuart Wellesley married the prettiest girl on earth, and when they see you, it's an easy guess who I am."

"You are outrageous!" she giggled, embarrassed by his compliment.

"I'm not at all outrageous," he retorted, trying hard to look offended. "I meant every word I just said."

"Well, thank you," she murmured, then gazed around the restaurant with interest. "This is a very pretty place."

Stuart looked around at the artfully arranged tables, each graced with a white damask tablecloth, single red rose, and softly glowing candle. "Yes, it is, and they have some of the best lobster in the city, not to mention the very best Yan . . . pot roast."

Claire smiled at his near slip. "You really *are* going to make me eat crawdads for dinner, aren't you?"

"They're *not* crawdads! You'll know the difference as soon as you taste them."

"Not really," Claire shrugged, "since I've never tasted a crawdad."

"You haven't? Then, how do you know you don't like them?"

"Because I've seen them! They have eyes and claws and antennae. I can't possibly eat something that's looking at me! That's not the way they serve the lobster here, is it? Please tell me it's not!"

"No," Stuart lied. "Of course it's not." He glanced around surreptitiously, hoping that none of the diners at nearby tables were eating whole lobsters in the shell—like the ones he had just ordered. Breathing a sigh of relief when he saw that no one was, he said casually, "Will you excuse me for a moment?"

"Certainly," Claire nodded.

Rising from the table, he hurried off toward the kitchen, catching their waiter just as he came out carrying a tray of bread and appetizers. "John," Stuart hissed, ducking around a corner so Claire wouldn't see him.

"Yes, Mr. Wellesley?" the waiter responded, his brow puckered with curiosity at his patron's strange behavior.

"I just found out that Mrs. Wellesley has an aversion to lobster served in the shell."

"Oh?"

"Yes. She's . . . not from Boston."

The waiter nodded, knowing full well that the new Mrs. Wellesley was from the South. He had heard Stuart's recent marriage being discussed at many a table over the last few weeks.

"Anyway," Stuart continued, "will you please ask the cook to remove the meat from the shell before it's served? I'll be happy to pay extra for his time."

"That won't be necessary," John smiled. "I'll do it myself."

"Thank you," Stuart said gratefully, pressing a bill into the waiter's hand. "I appreciate it very much." Glancing over at the table where Claire sat gazing out the window, he added, "Please don't let Mrs. Wellesley know about this."

"Absolutely not, sir," John assured him, winking broadly.

With a slightly embarrassed smile, Stuart returned to his table and John headed back into the kitchen, laughing. "When you get that order for two lobsters ready, Joe, let me know. I have to take them out of the shell before they're served."

The cook looked at him like he'd lost his mind. "Whatever for?"

"Because Stuart Wellesley's new wife doesn't like the looks of them when they're still in the shell."

"Oh, for God's sake," the cook chortled. "Does she think it's going to jump at her or something?"

"I don't know, but that's what Mr. Wellesley just told me."

"Isn't she from the South somewhere?"

"Yeah, Georgia, I think."

"Well, that explains it, then. She's just an ignorant Confederate who probably doesn't understand that sucking the meat out of the legs is half the fun. It's no wonder the Rebs are losing the war . . ."

"Now, that doesn't look so bad, does it?"

Claire looked down at the plate of flaky white lobster meat in front of her and shook her head. "No, actually, it doesn't. It just looks like little chunks of fish."

Stuart grinned. "That's all it is, Claire. Little chunks of fish. Now, dip a piece in that little bowl of melted butter and tell me what you think."

Claire did as he bade, then slowly lifted the fork to her mouth, hesitating just as it reached her lips.

"Come on, try it!"

With a grimace, she opened her mouth and popped the piece of lobster into it. She chewed down experimentally, then closed her eyes and emitted a little groan.

"Well?"

"It's wonderful, Stuart. Absolutely divine."

"You see?" he laughed. "I told you you'd love it. Why, I'll make a Bostonian of you yet."

Claire opened her eyes and smiled like a satisfied cat. "It's the best thing I've ever tasted," she said, licking her shiny lips where a little smear of butter remained.

"So, you don't want me to order you pot roast?"

"No! Who wants beef when you can have lobster?"

Stuart smiled happily and dug into his own plate. For several moments they ate in contented silence, then he said, "Do you like your new clothes?"

"Oh, yes," Claire nodded, taking a hearty swallow of champagne. "They're all beautiful, and it was very kind of you to buy so many."

Stuart set down his fork and reached over to take her hand. "I'm not trying to be kind, sweetheart," he said earnestly. "I want to wrap you up in silks and satins and furs and diamonds."

"Why?" Claire whispered.

Stuart threw her a grin that was close to a leer and leaned conspiratorially across the table. "Because it will be so much fun to *unwrap* you."

Claire gasped, scandalized by his bawdy comment. "You shouldn't say such things," she reproved, looking around to see if anyone had overheard him.

"Oh, you mean it's okay to do it as long as I don't say it?"

"Stuart! We're in public, for heaven's sake!"

"Then hurry up and finish that lobster so we can go home and be private."

Claire felt goosebumps rise all over her body,

and quickly, she reached for her wineglass.

"And don't drink all that champagne at once," he added, "because that's all you're getting. Remember what happened last night . . ."

Claire's eyes widened over the rim of her glass, but obediently she set it down and speared another piece of lobster.

"I met Miss Alcott today," she said blandly, trying to think of a topic that would cool down her overheated husband.

"Did you? Was she talking to herself?"

"No," she giggled. "She's a lovely woman. We chatted for several minutes in the park. Did you know she's a nurse?"

Stuart nodded. "She wrote a series of essays a couple of years ago called 'Hospital Sketches' about her experiences in Washington."

"Really? She didn't tell me that."

"She's a very prolific writer, actually. The last I heard, she was starting work on a novel."

"She is," Claire confirmed. "She has three sisters, and she's writing about their childhood."

"That should be some story, considering her crazy father."

"Is her father crazy? She told me he was eccentric, but is he truly insane?"

"No, he just has some wild ideas about life and its meaning. He touts some philosophy called transcendentalism and has spent his whole life traveling around, lecturing about it. He's destituted his family in the process, and now they have to rely on Louisa's writing to support them."

"Oh, the poor lady. What a terrible responsibility for her!"

"Yes," Stuart nodded, "it *is* a lot of responsibility, but at least she's doing something she truly enjoys. If you have to work, that's important."

"I'm glad it's not me," Claire murmured.

A pleased light came into Stuart's eyes. "Why, Mrs. Wellesley! Are you saying you'd rather be married to your Yankee husband than be starving in Savannah?"

"Starving?" Claire exclaimed, her fork clattering to her plate. "Are people in Savannah starving? My father . . ."

"Don't worry, sweetheart," Stuart interrupted, cursing his wayward tongue, "your father is fine."

"But, Stuart . . ."

"He's fine, Claire."

Claire looked at her husband for a long moment, then said quietly, "You're sending him money, aren't you?"

Stuart shrugged. "Nothing I can't easily spare."

Unbidden tears welled in Claire's eyes. "Oh, Stuart, you're such a good man . . ."

Stuart frowned when he noticed how glassy-eyed she suddenly looked. "Don't start crying," he pleaded, looking around. "Everyone in the restaurant will think I'm being mean to you, and it will be all over town tomorrow that I'm abusing my new wife."

Claire laughed shakily, then picked up his hand and held it against her cheek. "Thank you," she whispered. "I owe you a great deal."

"No, you don't," he negated. "You don't owe me a thing. In fact, I owe you something."

"What do you owe me?" she smiled, her voice still quaking.

"This," he said, reaching into his pocket and putting a small square box on the table.

Claire looked down at the box quizzically. "What is it?"

"Open it and see."

Eagerly, she picked up the tiny leather box and flipped open the hinged lid. Inside was the most exquisite diamond-and-ruby ring she'd ever seen. The diamond was at least three carats, cut in an oval shape. Surrounding the huge, glittering stone was a ring of perfectly matched round rubies.

"Oh . . ." Claire breathed, looking up from the ring to stare at Stuart in wonder.

"I thought it was about time you had a proper wedding ring," he said softly.

Claire lifted shaking fingers to her lips, a million thoughts crowding her brain. When had he bought this gorgeous ring . . . and why? Had he heard the gossip about her cheap wedding band and guessed she might be embarrassed about it?

Before she could sort out what his motivation might be in presenting her with such an extravagant gift, he answered her questions for her.

"I'm sorry it's taken me so long to give this to you. I bought it the day after we got to Boston, but I just haven't seemed to find the right moment to give it to you."

Much to his dismay, Claire's only reaction was to smile at him tremulously.

"What's the matter, Claire? Don't you like the ring? I probably should have taken you with me to pick one out, but I wanted it to be a surprise . . ." His voice trailed off lamely. Then, to his horror, he saw tears again spring to her eyes.

"Oh, God," he groaned, his face a mask of disappointment, "you *don't* like it, do you?"

"No, you're wrong," Claire whispered breathlessly, "I think it's the most beautiful ring I've ever seen."

"Then, why are you crying?"

"Because . . . because. . . . Oh, I can't explain it." Reaching down, she plucked the ring from its velvet nest and held it out to him. "Would you put it on, please?"

The tension drained from his face, and with a relieved grin, he took the ring and slid it onto the third finger of her left hand. "This is where I'm supposed to ask you to marry me," he whispered, "but, since we've already done that, I'll ask you a different question."

"What's that?"

"Would you like to go home now?"

"Yes," she nodded, "very much."

Pulling out his wallet, Stuart extracted several bills and threw them on the table. Then he rose and helped Claire into his mother's cloak. Making a pretense of straightening the collar, he leaned close to her ear and murmured, "I hope you don't mind that we didn't have dessert."

"I didn't want dessert," she whispered back.

Impulsively, Stuart caught her lips in a quick kiss, heedless of the many curious eyes that were turned their way.

As the couple made their way out of the restaurant, John, the waiter, drew one of his compatriots aside. "I've heard lots of gossip that Mr. Wellesley married that lady when he didn't really want to," he confided.

"I've heard that, too."

John's smile widened. "Just goes to show you that you shouldn't believe everything you hear."

Stuart and Claire were barely seated in the carriage before he started kissing her.

"Did you really like your lobster?" he whispered, pulling her across his lap till he was cradling her like a baby.

"Yes," she smiled, her words muffled against his lips as he kissed her again.

"And do you really like your ring?" he asked.

"Oh, yes," she sighed, "it's the most beautiful . . ." The rest of her words were lost as he again covered her mouth with his. His kiss went on so long that when he finally lifted his head, she was breathless and he was panting.

"Are we almost home?" she gasped.

"God, I hope so!" he returned, looking out the carriage's side window with an expression of near-desperation on his face.

Just then the carriage came to a halt, but before Samuel could even dismount from the driver's seat, Stuart had flung open the door and stepped out. He turned and lifted Claire out of the coach, wrapping his arm around her waist and hurrying her up the front walk. "That's it for tonight, Sam," he called back over his shoulder.

"I'm sure it is," Sam chuckled to himself.

Stuart peeled off his coat, tossing it on a chair near the door, then turned to assist Claire. Much to his surprise, she was not taking off her cloak but was, instead, simply standing and smiling down at her hand, which she was holding out in front of her. He took a step behind her, admiring the way the ring looked on her long, tapered finger. They stood quietly for a moment, both of them mesmerized by the glittering diamond.

"Let's go upstairs," Stuart whispered, reaching around her to unhook the cloak's silken frog. He swept it off her shoulders and tossed it onto the chair with his coat.

They mounted the long staircase hand-in-hand

and strolled down the hall to their bedroom. Stuart closed the door behind them, then frowned as he saw Claire heading for the privacy screen. "Don't change back there," he murmured. "I want to undress you myself."

Claire turned toward him with wide eyes, but unhesitatingly retraced her steps until she stood before him. "I'm all yours, Major."

"God, I've waited a long time to hear you say that," he groaned, pulling her close for a long, languid kiss. As his excitement began to build, his lips left hers, tracing a scorching path down the smooth column of her throat.

Claire could feel his hands on her back, but didn't realize he had unhooked her bodice until he pulled the dress off her shoulders and buried his face in the full swells of her breasts. She threw her head back, emitting a little groan and smiling at the ceiling. Reaching between them, she eagerly began pushing his shirt buttons through their holes, then tugged the garment free of his trousers. But as she reached for the button on his waistband, he took a quick step backward, staying her progress.

"We've got to slow down a little," he rasped. "I don't want to hurry this, and we're moving way too fast."

"All right," Claire answered, embarrassed by her own enthusiasm. "What would you like me to do?"

Stuart drew a couple of deep, calming breaths, then said, "Sit down on the bed and I'll take off your shoes."

Claire did as he bade, lifting her skirts to her knees as he knelt in front of her.

With trembling hands, Stuart removed her right

shoe, then ran his hand up her trim calf, massaging the tight muscles.

"Mmm, that feels good," she murmured, bracing her arms behind her and leaning back. Her unconscious movement thrust her bare breasts forward, causing Stuart's throat to feel like it was closing. Quickly, he dropped his eyes from the lusty sight and slowly shimmied her stocking down her leg. Pulling the silk off her foot, he bent forward, running his tongue along her sensitive arch.

With a shocked gasp, Claire unlocked her elbows and flopped back on the bed, her legs still dangling over the side. Stuart smiled, pleased with her reaction, and quickly removed her other shoe, repeating his light massage on her other leg. This time, when he removed her stocking, he lifted her foot to his mouth and sucked gently on her toes, then laughed with sheer delight as Claire let out a little scream of pleasure.

Reaching beneath her heavy skirts, he worked his way up to her waist, untying the band of her petticoats and her drawers. "Lift your hips," he directed softly, and when Claire instantly complied, he skimmed her gaping dress and underclothes off her body, throwing them aside. Then he turned his attention back to his wife, pausing a moment to feast on her nearly naked beauty.

"Let's take off your corset," he suggested, grasping her hands and pulling her up into a sitting position. With surprisingly deft fingers, he loosened the corset strings and slowly pulled the confining garment from her.

"Ahh . . ." he sighed, his breath coming out in a rush as he drank in the perfection of Claire's nude, candlelit body. "You are the most beautiful woman I've ever seen."

Claire smiled and bent forward to kiss him, surprised by the tension she felt radiating from his hot body. "You have me at a disadvantage," she whispered.

"I do? How?"

"You're still dressed . . ."

Her provocative words sent wave after wave of desire crashing through him and he rose to his feet, wondering if his shaking legs would support him. Many years later, he would laughingly confide to his brother Nathan that he'd never realized it was possible to disrobe so fast, but an instant later, he was nude also.

Claire's eyes dropped to the center of him, fascinated, as she had been before, by the sight of his powerful erection. "You remind me of some great, dark god," she whispered.

Her unguarded perusal of his masculinity, coupled with her throaty words, were potent aphrodisiacs, and again he dropped to his knees in front of her. "I want to taste you all over," he groaned, dipping his head to lick the back of her knee.

His voice was rough with barely controlled passion, but Claire felt no fear. She wanted him as badly as he wanted her, and with a small sigh of surrender she again lay back, spreading her knees slightly as she offered herself to him.

Stuart's heart slammed against his ribs at her intimate invitation, but he was determined to delay his body's throbbing demands until he was sure she would also reach the summit of love's mountain.

Slowly, seductively, he trailed his mouth up the inside of her thigh, moving inexorably closer to the center of her womanhood. He could feel her legs quivering as his mouth brushed the soft curls at the juncture of her thighs and he paused, waiting to see how she would react to this most intimate of attentions. To his disappointment, Claire stiffened and, not wanting to scare her, he abandoned his erotic quest and rose to his feet, bending over her prone body and nuzzling her tenderly.

"Kiss me," he whispered, as he stretched out beside her. With a glad little cry, Claire buried her hands in his soft, dark hair and lifted her mouth to his.

The kiss was lush and sensuous, a merging of lips and tongues that slowly fed their desire until the air around them fairly crackled with their need for each other. With a subtle movement, Stuart knelt above her, his face dark with passion, but his smile soft as he looked down at his wife.

Claire said nothing, but her answering smile told him everything he wanted to know and with the instinct of true lovers, they entwined their legs and melded into one.

Despite his voracious hunger for her, Stuart paused, letting Claire adjust to his presence. Then, slowly, easily, they began moving together, celebrating love's ancient ritual.

Gradually, Stuart increased his rhythm, his sensitivity for his young wife battling against his body's overwhelming demands for release.

As she had the first time, Claire felt a pressure growing within her, a hot, tingling sensation that made her catch her breath and reach for the same elusive quarry that had eluded her before.

But this time, passion's great reward was to be hers. With a little scream of triumph, she tightened her legs around Stuart's lean, flexing hips and opened her eyes, gazing up at him in awe as wave after wave of ecstasy crashed over her.

Her hot, pulsing body sheathing him so tightly quickly sent Stuart over the edge, and with a lusty groan, he let himself go, releasing his life's essence deep inside her.

Finally, he relaxed, sighing with satisfaction as he lowered himself gently on top of her. They were silent for a long moment as both of them slowly recovered from the awesome experience they had just shared.

"Are you all right?" he whispered when his breathing had slowed enough that he could speak again. "I didn't hurt you, did I?"

Claire smiled at him, her eyes drowsy with satiated languor. "No, you didn't hurt me. In fact," she whispered, "I didn't know it was possible to feel so . . . so . . ."

"I know," he chuckled, gently withdrawing from her and rolling on to his side. "I didn't know it was possible, either."

Claire smiled happily into the darkness for a moment, then turned toward him and said, "You know, I don't understand my friends."

"What about your friends," he asked, slowly brushing a lock of her hair against his throat.

"Remember? I told you they all said making love is . . . isn't pleasant."

"Maybe they're making love with the wrong man."

"Are you better at it than most men?"

"I don't know."

"You must be," she sighed. "If every woman had you, I'm sure no one would complain."

Stuart grinned, inordinately pleased with her

praise. "A lot of it is you, sweetheart."

"Me? How could it be? I didn't know what I was doing."

"Well, for not knowing, you certainly did everything right."

"You're very nice."

"And you're everything I ever wanted."

A little shiver of delight ran through Claire and she turned over on her stomach, propping her chin on her elbows. "May I ask you something?"

"Yes, and I'm sure I'll answer, especially if you keep pressing your breasts against my chest. If you'd done this in Savannah, I not only would have told you where that message was, I would have decoded it for you myself."

Claire giggled and rubbed against him, loving the sensation of his chest hair against her nipples. "Would you have, really?"

"Probably," he answered truthfully. "Now, what did you want to ask me?"

"I just wondered why you bought me this ring?" she said, holding up her hand and again admiring it in the candle's soft glow.

"Because I wanted to," he said simply. "I told you before, I want to wrap you up in diamonds. In fact, I think tomorrow I'll go to the jeweler and buy you earrings to match. Would you like that?"

"Of course I would," she admitted, "but you don't need to buy me gifts, Stuart. In fact, as lovely as my new ring is, I still love my real wedding ring best."

"You do?" he asked. "That cheap little band? I never intended for that to be your wedding ring. It was just the only thing I could find in Savannah."

"Well, nevertheless, it means everything to me."

"Does it really?"

"Yes." And to Claire's surprise, she realized it did. Now that Stuart had given her a ring opulent enough to make even Sally Rutherford drool, she suddenly saw that the price of the gift didn't matter at all. It was the sentiment—not the size.

"So, you don't want me to give you expensive gifts anymore?" he teased.

"You know what?"

"What?"

"What we just shared in this bed is the best gift any bride could hope for—and it didn't cost a thing."

"Oh, Claire," he sighed, "I love you so."

"And I love you."

Her softly spoken words hit him like a cannon-ball in the chest. "Do you honestly mean that?" he asked quietly.

"Yes," she smiled, laying her head on his chest with a contented little sigh. "With all my heart."

A long moment passed. Then, to Claire's astonishment, she heard Stuart chuckle.

"What's so funny?" she asked, lifting her head and staring at him in bewilderment.

"What's funny is that I'm lying here thanking God that a Confederate deserter decided to use me for target practice."

Chapter Twenty-one

They stayed in bed the whole next day, talking, laughing, making love, and then dozing, only to wake up and make love again.

It was mid-afternoon, as they lay drowsing in each other's arms, when Stuart announced, "I'm starving. Are you hungry?"

"Yes," Claire admitted, "but I'm too lazy to get dressed and go downstairs. "Besides, I don't want to face your parents. What must they think of us staying up here all day?"

"Claire," Stuart chuckled, getting out of bed and shrugging on a robe, "my parents have eight children. I seriously doubt that we're doing anything up here that they haven't done before."

"I suppose you're right, but still, I know I'll never be able to look your mother in the eye again."

Sitting down on the edge of the rumpled bed, Stuart reached over and pinched her cheek. "You won't have to worry about it much longer. They're leaving tomorrow."

With a gasp, Claire sat up and tossed her tangled hair out of her face. "They are? Then I'd better get up. It's terribly rude of me to laze about in bed all day on their last day here."

"Just lie back and relax. They'll understand. I'm going to go down and make us some sandwiches. God knows, I need some sustenance, the way you've worn me out in the last few hours."

"Worn you out! What about me? Why, I've used muscles today I didn't even know I had!"

Stuart wiggled his eyebrows at her. "I know. Fun, isn't it?"

"Yes," Claire giggled, "more fun than I'd ever have dreamed."

She paused a moment, then threw him a beckoning look. "Y'all gonna be gone long, Major?"

"Why, no ma'am, Miz Boudreau," he answered in a perfect imitation of a Georgia accent, "I'll be back in just a coupla minutes, so y'all just wait for me, heah?"

"Why should I?" she pouted, thoroughly enjoying their game.

"Because when I get back, I'm gonna show you somethin' new. Somethin' y'all are gonna like a whole lot."

"Ooh," Claire squealed, "you *are* evil, Major."

"And you, Miss Boudreau, are the sauciest little wench I've evah bedded and, as y'all know, I've bedded the whole eastern seaboard and at least half the girls in the Confederacy."

"Oh, get out of here!" Claire cried, dropping her coy mien and hurling a pillow at him. "You really are the most arrogant, most self-centered, most full-of-yourself Yankee I've ever met."

With a shout of laughter, Stuart tore across the room and leaped back on the bed, grabbing her out of her nest of pillows and hugging her tight against him. "I love it when you get jealous."

"I'm not jealous!"

"You are, too, and I love it."

"I am *not*. Besides, jealousy has nothing to do with it. You *are* arrogant and full of yourself and . . ."

"Mad about you," he finished, kissing her lustily.

"I thought you were going to get us something to eat," she complained.

"I am, but I demand a forfeit first."

"Now what? You've had everything."

"Oh, no I haven't," he leered, "and I'll prove that to you after lunch."

Claire felt a little shiver of anticipation ripple through her. "Well, what do you want from me now? A kiss?"

"No."

"No?"

"No."

"Then what?"

"Guess again."

"A hug?"

"No."

"A back rub?"

"No, but that's not a bad idea to keep in mind for later. My back is killing me."

"I'm not surprised," she retorted. "Okay. I give up. What can I do that will make you go get me some food?"

"It's not what you can *do*, it's what you can *say*."

"You want me to *say* something?"

"Right."

Suddenly, it dawned on her what Stuart was really asking. She rose to her knees, slipping her hands inside his bathrobe and pressing little, nibbling kisses against his bare chest.

"I love you," she whispered.

"That's what I wanted to hear," he breathed, grasping her around the ribs and lifting her until they were face-to-face. "And I love you, my little Rebel."

Then with no warning at all, he unceremoniously dumped her back on the bed. "Now, what kind of sandwich do you want?"

They sat in bed and ate turkey sandwiches, cold, sliced baked potatoes with salt and pepper, and apple pie. When every scrap of food was finally gone, Stuart set the tray aside and grinned. "That should hold us for a while."

"Mmm," Claire nodded, "probably till tomorrow morning."

"Naw. If I know you, you'll eat again tonight at the Hendersons' party. You'll probably get drunk, too."

Claire licked her fingers free of the last crumbs of pie. "I will not, and anyway, the Hendersons' party is tomorrow night."

"No, it's not. It's tonight."

"It had better not be," she declared, climbing out of bed and heading over to where a tray of envelopes sat on the bureau. Leafing through the stack, she pulled one out and held it aloft. "Here's the invitation." She lifted the vellum card out of the envelope and quickly scanned it, then turned to Stuart with a look of horror. "It *is* tonight!"

"Told 'ya," he taunted. "You need to start keeping a calendar, madam. You seem to have a problem remembering social engagements."

"Oh, you," she sputtered, picking up a pillow and hitting him with it. "If I can't remember 'social engagements,' it's your fault."

"*My* fault!" he exclaimed, shielding his face with his arms as she readied the pillow for another blow. "What do I have to do with it?"

Again the pillow slammed down on his head. "It's your fault because you never let me get any sleep. I'm too tired to keep things straight."

This time as she flung the pillow over her head to strike another blow, Stuart grabbed her by the hips and pulled her down in bed with him. He ripped the pillow out of her hands, threw it across the room, and started tickling her.

"Stuart, don't!" Claire yelped, screaming with uncontrollable laughter. "Don't tickle me. Please!"

"Are you going to stop blaming me for your bad memory?" he demanded, his fingers digging playfully into her sensitive ribs.

"Yes."

"And you'll start keeping a calendar?"

"Yes!"

"Do you want me to stop tickling you?"

"Yes! Oh God, Stuart, *stop!*"

"What are you going to do if I do?"

"Get up."

"No. Wrong answer."

"Scrub your back while you take a bath."

"Better, but still not right."

"What, then?" she shrieked, curling into a little ball as she tried to escape him.

"I want you to let me *really* have my way with you."

"Fine! I'll agree to anything. Just stop tickling me."

His fingers slowed, and as she looked up at him, breathless and panting, a huge, satisfied smile spread across his face.

"What are you smiling about?"

"I've finally found the way to get you to do anything I want."

"Oh, you're terrible!"

"Yeah," he grinned, "I know." Picking up her limp hand, he wrapped her fingers around his stiff manhood. "And so are you. Look what you've done to me."

Claire hadn't realized that their playful battle had aroused him, and her eyes widened when she felt how hard he was. "Don't you ever get enough, Major?"

"Not of you."

He knelt above her for a moment, his head thrown back in an agony of sensation as she stroked him, then bent to kiss her. "You make me crazy, little girl. You're all I think about. You— and doing this." Beginning a slow rotation of his hips, he rubbed the hot, wet tip of his shaft seductively across her palm.

A throaty moan escaped Claire as little rivers of fire streaked up her arm.

"Let me taste you," he whispered, running his tongue along her parted lips.

Claire's eyes flew open. "Is that what you meant when you said you wanted to really have your way with me?"

"Yes."

"But, isn't that . . . forbidden?"

"Yes," he said again, his voice thick as he drew her full bottom lip between his teeth. "And, in Boston, I think it's even against the law." He shifted his hips so that his erection pressed against her womanhood. "But I don't see any police in here, so I doubt we'll get caught."

Claire shivered, scandalized by the thought of doing something so intimate that it was illegal. "Does it hurt?" she whispered.

"No. It doesn't hurt."

"Then why is it against the law?"

"I have no idea."

"It doesn't make sense."

"Let's not talk anymore . . ."

Slowly, very slowly, Stuart began inching down her body, his tongue leaving a warm, moist trail on her skin. He paused when he reached the juncture of her thighs and nuzzled her, his ragged breath hot against her sensitive flesh.

Instinctively, Claire raised her knees, but at the first touch of his lips, she jerked away. He waited until she relaxed, then he kissed her again. "You promised me you'd let me have my way with you," he reminded her softly.

"But, Stuart . . ." Her voice trailed off into a groan of pleasure as he again pressed his lips to her. "Oh, my God, Stuart!"

His entire body started to shake when he heard her moan his name and, spurred on by her excitement, he began stroking her with his tongue.

Suddenly, she screamed: an ear-splitting, erotic cry that put a quick end to Stuart's provocative play. With one smooth lunge, he thrust into her, muffling her shrieks of pleasure with his mouth as briefly, he wondered if his parents and the household staff downstairs would think he was beating her.

They finished almost instantly, coming together with a climax so shattering that Claire thought she might faint. Stuart collapsed on top of her, and for long moments, they lay in exhausted silence.

"Now I know why that's against the law," she whispered.

"Why?"

"Because nothing should feel that good. A person could become addicted to it—like an opiate."

Stuart chuckled, a low rumbling sound from deep in his chest that vibrated against Claire's breasts. "You're right. That must be the reason."

"But, Stuart?"

Tiredly, he raised his head. "Yes?"

"What about you?"

"What *about* me?"

"Well, that . . . what you just did . . ."

"Yes?"

"It must have felt better to me than it did to you . . ."

Stuart smiled and lowered his head back to the pillow. "It can go the other way, too, sweetheart."

"What do you mean?"

"I mean that what I did to you, you could do to me."

Claire's eyes widened at the provocative thought. "Really . . ." she mused.

"But not now," he laughed. "Now, my wild little temptress, we need to sleep a few hours and then get up and go to that damn party."

"Oh, yes, the party," she sighed.

Stuart raised his head again and looked at her with a tender expression. "Who would ever have thought . . ."

"Thought what?"

"That snooty Miss Boudreau would be such a little wildcat between the sheets."

"You're right," she sighed and snuggled closer to him, "who would ever have thought . . ."

Mary Wellesley smiled at Claire as she came slowly down the stairs. "You look ravishing, dear."

"Thank you," Claire mumbled, hardly able to meet her mother-in-law's gaze.

As they had dressed for the party, Stuart had teased her unmercifully about her uninhibited screams of ecstasy and how everyone in Louisburg Square must have heard her.

"You're making that up!" she'd accused, blushing to the roots of her hair. "No one heard me. I wasn't *that* loud."

"Like hell you weren't," he chortled. "Why, I'm sure every servant on the block is gossiping about how the new Mrs. Wellesley screams out her pleasure."

"Oh, Stuart, do you really think so?" Swiveling around on the little stool in front of her dressing table, she threw him a look of genuine distress.

To his chagrin, Stuart realized that she was truly embarrassed, and with a silent curse, he hurried across the room and dropped a kiss on her bare shoulder.

"So what if they are?" he chuckled. "The men will be jealous of me for having such a spicy little wife, and the women will envy you for having a husband who's so studly that he makes you scream with delight."

"But, still . . ." Claire moaned, "to think that

people would talk about us—especially about something so private."

"Sweetheart," Stuart said earnestly, dropping to his knees next to her. "That's something you're just going to have to get used to. People are always going to talk about us—and the more personal the rumors, the more talk there will be."

"But why? Why would anyone care what we do?"

"Simple," he shrugged. "You're beautiful and I'm rich. There's not a gossip in the world who can resist that combination."

Stuart's nonchalance had temporarily placated Claire, but now, as she stood facing his mother, she again felt hot color creep up her cheeks. What must this serene, dignified lady *think* of her?

She needn't have worried. Mary Wellesley was a worldly woman who had enjoyed a passionate love affair and marriage of her own. And although she had looked up at the ceiling in wonder when she'd heard Claire's cries, she'd soon realized what was causing them and had smiled with satisfaction, happy that her son and his new wife had obviously patched up their differences.

"Is Stuart ready for the party yet?" she asked pleasantly.

"Almost. He's tying his cravat."

"Good. He always has trouble with that, so it will be a little while before he comes down. I'd like to talk to you alone for a moment—woman-to-woman."

"Certainly," Claire answered, trying hard not to let her voice betray her trepidation. Undoubtedly, Stuart's mother was going to chastise her for her unladylike behavior.

298

"Let's go into the small sitting room, where we can be private."

With a nod, Claire followed Mary into the elegant little room and perched nervously on the edge of a blue velvet settee.

With a rustle of silk, Mary walked over to a breakfront and poured a drop of sherry into two crystal glasses, then returned to the settee and offered one to Claire.

Trembling, she accepted the glass, trying valiantly to force a smile.

Mary frowned, and setting down her glass, picked up one of Claire's icy hands. "Let's get this awkwardness out of the way right now," she suggested. "Yes, I heard you and Stuart upstairs this afternoon and, yes, I know what you two have been doing all day."

Claire ducked her head, knowing she'd never been more embarrassed in her life.

"But, Claire," Mary chuckled, giving her hand a gentle shake and prompting her to again raise her eyes. "I couldn't be more delighted that you and Stuart have found such happiness with each other. It is something I have been hoping for ever since I first met you, and I'm thrilled I can go back to Colorado knowing that everything is as it should be between you and my son."

Claire felt like a tremendous burden had just been lifted off her shoulders, and her frozen smile relaxed.

"Stu told his father a bit about the circumstances of your marriage," Mary continued, "and I must confess, at first we were a little concerned."

"I understand," Claire whispered. "The circumstances surrounding our marriage were a bit . . . unusual.''

"To be sure," Mary chuckled. "But, now, having seen the two of you together these past weeks, James and I know that Stuart married you for all the right reasons.''

"What do you mean?''

"I mean it's obvious he loves you very much. I've always been close to Stu, and I've seen him with any number of girls—both when he was a boy in Colorado, and then as a man in Boston. As you must have noticed, he is tremendously appealing to women, and he's had many opportunities to marry. As a matter of fact," she chuckled, "I really don't know how he escaped all the girls who have pursued him. Maybe that's why he went off to war.''

Claire couldn't help but smile at Mary's comment.

"Anyway, whether Stuart was in love with you when he married you is something probably only he knows for sure. But there is no doubt in my mind that he is deeply in love with you now.

"But," Mary held up a warning finger, "despite this love, you two still have many hurdles to face. This tragic war has been devastating to everyone in this country, and even when it's over, there are still going to be bitter resentments on both sides.''

Claire nodded.

"Still," Mary smiled, "I have no doubt that whatever problems you and Stuart might face, the love and passion you share will see you through it.''

"I hope so, Mrs. Wellesley," Claire said sincerely. "I truly do. And I promise you, I will do my best to be a good wife to Stuart.''

Mary gave Claire's hand a reassuring little squeeze. "Do you love my son?"

"Yes," Claire nodded. "He wouldn't let me *not* love him."

"Ah, yes, I know how that is. His father was exactly the same way. I was absolutely determined not to fall in love with James, but there's something about the Wellesley men—once they decide you're the woman they want, you might as well give in, because you're fighting a losing battle."

"And you have seven sons," Claire laughed.

"I know," Mary groaned ruefully, "and only two of them are married. Just think of it. Somewhere out in the world are five unsuspecting little girls, innocently playing with their dolls and having no idea what's in store for them once one of those devils of mine turns his eyes on them. The poor darlings!"

They laughed until tears came to their eyes, and when they finally sobered, Mary reached over and impulsively hugged Claire. "Be good to Stuart, dear. Laugh with him, make love with him, give him a house full of children, and the two of you will be happy for the rest of your lives."

"I'll try," Claire whispered, tears of gratitude and affection welling in her eyes. "I promise you I'll try."

"I know you will." With a final little pat on the arm, Mary rose from the settee. "Now, we'd better go find our husbands or we're going to be so late to the Hendersons' party that the rest of the guests will already have gone home."

Claire nodded and rose also. "Mrs. Wellesley?" she called softly as Mary headed for the door.

"Yes?"

"Thank you. Thank you for everything."

With a warm smile, Mary nodded, then turned and gracefully glided out of the room.

"Come on, Claire, just one kiss."

"No! You'll muss me up, and it took me an hour to do my hair."

"I'll be careful."

"Stuart, there isn't time for this. Didn't you say that the Hendersons live only five minutes away?"

"Yeah, and we've already wasted one of them talking." Moving closer to Claire on the coach's wide seat, Stuart reached inside her satin cloak and fondled her breast through the sheer silk of her dress.

"Stuart," she reproved, slapping his hand away, "stop it. You're going to wrinkle my gown, and everyone at the party will know what we've been doing."

"There's a simple way to prevent that," he answered huskily, slipping his hand into her low-cut bodice and releasing one of the plump round globes.

"Stuart!" she gasped, squirming away from his tantalizing caress, "are you crazy? We're going to be there any second."

"Not for at least another three minutes," he assured her. Picking up her hand, he placed it over the front of his trousers, pressing it against the hard bulge of his manhood.

"God, Claire," he moaned, drawing her bared breast into his mouth, "you taste so good."

Stuart's hot mouth on her breast, coupled with

the sensation of his erection surging to life under her hand, suddenly made Claire not care if they ever reached the Hendersons'.

"Do we have time to do this?" she gasped, arching her back to help him free her other breast from her bodice.

"We do if we go around the square a couple of times."

With a look that nearly set his hair on fire, Claire began to unfasten the front of his trousers. "Tell the driver."

Tearing his mouth away from the nipple he was toying with, Stuart picked up his walking stick and rapped sharply on the roof of the carriage. The driver immediately hauled back on the reins, pulling the carriage to a stop. "Sir?" he called.

"We're in the middle of a . . . discussion," Stuart called back, his hoarse voice giving the lie to his words. "Please delay our arrival by fifteen minutes."

"Yes, sir," the driver responded. He clucked to the horses, pulling away from the curb. "I can just imagine what they're 'discussing,'" he chuckled, then turned the carriage down a quiet side street leading away from their destination.

"Now, where were we?" Stuart asked, turning his attention back to his wife.

"You were here," she breathed, drawing his head back to her breasts, "and I was here." Reaching inside his gaping trousers, she cupped him intimately, beginning a slow massage.

To her surprise, Stuart plucked her hand off his lap. "Wait a minute." Lifting his hips off the seat, he squirmed out of his trousers and underwear, releasing his impassioned manhood. "That's

303

better," he groaned, curling her fingers back around him.

"Do you like this?" Claire crooned, stroking him along the sensitive underside of his swelling erection.

"Oh, God . . . yes." He shifted slightly, hooking his arm around the back of her neck and giving her a searing kiss. His tongue plunged erotically in and out of her mouth, simulating the consummation they were irrevocably heading for. When finally he lifted his lips, Claire dropped her eyes to his lap.

"See if you like this even better," she whispered. Slipping off her pantalettes, she turned to face him, then slowly lowered her head and drew him into her mouth.

As her lips encircled him, Stuart nearly came off the seat, and with a moan he buried his fingers in her hair, unconscious of the fact that he was destroying her perfect coiffure.

Claire heard hairpins hitting the carriage floor and knew that her hard work was ruined, but she couldn't have cared less. Nothing was more important than this moment and the pleasure she was giving her husband. Her eyes closed languidly as her tongue swirled up and down his hard, thick length until, from far away, she heard him calling her name. She looked up, her vision foggy.

"Come here," he rasped, "before you get us both arrested."

With a wicked giggle, Claire lifted her voluminous skirts, twisting around until she was straddling his lap, facing him. Then, with a smile that could have set a forest ablaze, she impaled herself on his throbbing shaft.

"Now, if a policeman comes, he won't even realize what we're doing," she whispered.

"Sure he won't," Stuart moaned, thinking that this new, hedonistic side of his wife was more exciting than anything he ever could have imagined. He plunged his hands beneath the multitudinous layers of her petticoats until he found her bare legs, then ran them up the insides of her thighs until his thumbs met at her hot, wet core. For a long moment, he teased her sensitive little bud, reveling in the sensation of stroking both her and himself as she propelled herself up and down.

The sheer eroticism of their frenzied coupling soon brought Stuart to the brink and he gripped Claire's hips, increasing her rhythm until they exploded together with a shout of lusty satisfaction.

When their orgasmic spasms finally ebbed, Claire collapsed against him. "I can't go to this party," she whispered, her voice barely audible above Stuart's labored breathing. "We have to go home now."

"We can't go home," he chuckled. "We're the guests of honor."

Claire shook her head. "I don't care. I can't go. My hair is ruined, and I just want to . . ."

"Stay just like this forever?"

He felt her nod against him. With a tender smile, he drew her head back from where it lolled against his chest and softly kissed her. "So would I," he confessed, "but, like it or not, we have to pull ourselves together and get to the party."

With a long sigh, Claire raised herself to her knees, breaking their intimate contact and collapsing tiredly on the carriage seat next to him. "But, my hair . . ."

"I'll help you fix it," he soothed, reaching down to pull on his discarded clothes. "It'll be fine. It's just a few pins."

Claire threw him a disbelieving look and raised a tentative hand to check the damage their lovemaking had wrought. To her relief, she found he was right. Her hair hadn't come down nearly as badly as she'd first thought. She smiled, realizing that even if her coiffure had been completely destroyed, the past few minutes of rapture would have been well worth it.

Leaning forward, Stuart swept her pantalettes off the carriage floor. "You might want to put these on," he teased, dangling them from one finger. "Or, maybe not. There's always the chance that we'll want to do this again—on a staircase or behind a door or something—before the party is over. You probably don't want to bother with them."

Claire snatched her underwear out of his hand. "You're terrible," she gasped. "You never get enough!"

"Oho, look who's talking, my hot little seductress. Where did a demure southern belle like you learn to do the things you just did to me?"

"Where do you think?" she asked archly. "You told me about it this afternoon. And, anyway, you started this."

"Yes," Stuart chuckled, "but you finished it. And, I might add, in the sexiest fashion I've ever experienced in my life."

Claire shot him a sideward glance, trying to hide her pleased little smile. With a toss of her head, she pulled on her pantalettes and tucked her bare breasts back into her bodice. "If you thought I was being too bold, Major, I just won't do it again."

"You won't?" Pulling her against him, he plunged his tongue between her parted lips.

"Well," she amended, "at least not till we get home."

Stuart burst out laughing and held her close for a long moment. "God, I love you," he murmured, his voice suddenly serious as his lips hovered above hers. "You are the most fabulous creature I've ever encountered, and I still can't believe you're mine."

"But I am," Claire smiled, lifting her head just enough to graze his lips. "I'm *all* yours."

For a moment, Stuart closed his eyes, thanking God for the gift of this woman. "I love you, Claire, my beautiful wife," he whispered. "I'll love you till the day I die."

Chapter Twenty-two

"I'm coming," Claire called, hurrying down the staircase as the knock at the front door became more insistent. She flung open the portal, shocked to see Grenita Forten standing on the other side, looking flushed and disheveled.

"Claire, I'm so glad you're home! Is Stuart here?"

"No, he's up at the shipyard in Essex. He won't be back till tomorrow. Grenita, what is it? Is something wrong?"

Grenita fairly flew into the foyer, whipping her scarf off her head and twirling around in a crazy little pirouette. "My dear, I have the most incredible news," she trilled, throwing her arms around the astonished Claire. "It's over. The war is over! General Lee surrendered to General Grant today."

"Oh, my God," Claire moaned, her face blanching. "Lee surrendered?"

Grenita's eyes widened with horror as she realized what a gross faux pas she'd just committed. "Oh, Claire, I'm so sorry," she blurted. "I shouldn't have told you like that. For a moment there, I forgot that you're . . ."

"A Confederate," Claire nodded, sinking down heavily in a chair. "It's all right, Grenita. I understand." She dropped her head into her hands. "We lost. It was all for nothing. Nothing!"

"Maybe I should go," Grenita said miserably, wishing the earth would open up and swallow her.

"No," Claire insisted, looking up through tear-drenched eyes. "Please don't. Come in and we'll have some tea."

"Oh, my dear, you don't have to entertain . . ."

"Nonsense," Claire interrupted, rising from the chair and forcing a wan smile. "I'm fine . . . really I am."

"Claire, I'm terribly sorry."

"It's all right," Claire whispered. "At least the killing is finished. Now, maybe the country can begin to heal itself—if there's anything left of the South to heal."

The women entered the parlor and seated themselves on the velvet settee. "How did you happen to hear the news?" Claire asked.

"I was at the telegraph office when the wire came in," Grenita explained, "and I was so excited to tell Stuart, what with all his efforts to help Savannah in the last few months, that I didn't even think . . ."

"Wait a minute," Claire interrupted. "What efforts to help Savannah?"

Grenita swallowed and hurriedly looked away. "Don't you know? Hasn't Stuart told you?"

"Told me what?"

"Well, about . . . about what he's been doing."

"Grenita, what *are* you talking about? What has Stuart been doing?"

"I can't imagine that you don't know," Grenita mumbled. "Everyone in town knows . . ."

"Knows *what?*"

Grenita stared down at the gloves she held, wringing them nervously between her hands. "Maybe he doesn't want you to know, for some reason."

"Grenita!" Claire barked, her temper frayed by the game of Cat and Mouse they were playing. "I want you to tell me what this is all about. *Right now!*"

Grenita looked up at her with stricken eyes, desperately wishing she'd never set foot in the Wellesley house this morning. In a voice so low that Claire had to lean forward to hear her, she murmured, "Stuart spearheaded a citywide campaign to offer assistance to the people in Savannah. Apparently, after General Sherman's troops moved out, Savannah was depleted of vital supplies, and the citizens of Boston have been sending food and clothes and other necessary items to assist them. Stuart is using his own ships to deliver the goods . . ."

Her voice trailed off and she looked up at the gaping Claire in bewilderment. "You really didn't know, did you?"

"No," Claire said quietly. "Stuart has never said a word about any of this."

"I wonder why?" Grenita mused. "It's such an honorable thing to do that I can't imagine why he'd hide it from you."

"I can't, either."

Suddenly, their conversation was cut short by the deafening din of hundreds of church bells. "What in the world is that?" Claire gasped, hurrying over to the window.

"I'm sure it's the official announcement of the Union victory."

"What?" Claire yelled, barely able to hear over the noise.

"Victory," Grenita shouted back. "The bells are ringing in celebration."

Claire clapped her hands over her ears and squeezed her eyes shut. "I'm not going to be able to stand this," she moaned.

With a look of sympathy, Grenita walked over and gave her a quick hug. "I'm going to go now, dearest. Please forgive me if I've upset you."

Claire nodded and hugged her back. "Stuart will be home tomorrow afternoon if you want to stop by. Th . . . thank you for bringing us the news."

After Grenita left, Claire sat down on the settee and cried for a solid hour.

The bells rang until dusk, and when they finally stopped, the silence was overwhelming. Claire had spent a miserable day trying to shut out the discordant clanging and go about her routine as if nothing had changed. But everything had changed, and deep down, she knew it.

For the past few months, her marriage had been nothing short of idyllic. The gusty days of March had flown by in a happy haze of laughter, conversation, and lovemaking as her relationship with her husband had grown more and more intimate.

And when the bluster of March gave way to the balmy days of April, the Wellesleys were still a favorite topic of gossip among Boston's elite—not because of the questionable circumstances surrounding their marriage, but rather because of their obvious adoration for each other.

Even Sally Rutherford had given up throwing herself at Stuart, telling her friends that he was so blatantly besotted with his Rebel wife that it made her sick to her stomach to see them together.

As the days passed and Claire fell more and more deeply in love with her handsome husband, she almost forgot about the war that still raged. She received regular letters from her father, assuring her that he was well and that Savannah had come through Sherman's occupation nearly unscathed. His letters did much to ease her worries, and somehow, the war seemed to fade into the background of her new life.

But today, all that had changed. The great conflict was over. With one stroke of Robert E. Lee's pen, there was no longer any reason for Union officials to care if she had spied for the Confederacy—for the Confederacy was no more.

A thousand questions pounded at Claire's brain as the day wore on. What would Stuart's attitude toward her be, now that he was suddenly relieved of his self-imposed obligation to serve as her protector? Would he still want her as his wife, or would he seek to unburden himself of her in favor of a more socially acceptable girl?

By eight o'clock that evening, Claire was exhausted, and suffering from an excruciating headache. She picked disinterestedly at her solitary dinner, then pushed her plate away and wearily climbed the staircase, deciding to go to bed. Stuart wouldn't be home until the next afternoon, and she hoped that a good night's sleep would help alleviate her headache—and her fears.

She had been asleep for several hours when she was suddenly awakened by a man's arms encircling her body. With a sharp scream of terror, she began fighting, beating against the intruder's massive chest as she tried to free herself from his grasp. It was several moments before his low, deep voice finally penetrated her panic.

"Claire, baby, it's okay! It's just me. It's all right, sweetheart."

"Stuart?" she gasped, her fist still clenched to deal him another blow. "Is that you?"

"Yes, darling. I'm sorry, I didn't mean to frighten you."

Claire collapsed against his chest with a sob. "Oh, thank God. I thought someone had broken in."

Stuart slipped down into the depths of the soft bed, pulling her with him. "I must say, madam, it does my heart good to know that if someone did break in, you wouldn't give over without one hell of a fight."

"Oh!" she huffed, angry now that she was no longer afraid. "What a thing to say! What are you doing home, anyway? I thought you weren't coming back till tomorrow."

"I wasn't," he whispered, raising himself on an elbow and lighting a candle, "but after I heard about the surrender, I thought you might be upset, so I decided to come home early."

As the last remnants of sleep fled, all the agonies of the past day again seized Claire and, with a strangled cry, she buried her head against his chest, clinging to him as if she were drowning. "I can't believe it's over," she sobbed. "All that fighting, all that pain and death . . . all for nothing."

Stuart winced as she unconsciously dug her nails into his shoulders. *"Shh,"* he soothed, "it wasn't for nothing, Claire. It was inevitable that it would happen, but now that it's finally over . . ."

"Now that it's finally over, you won't want me anymore," she choked.

A long silence ensued as Stuart tried to digest her unexpected words. Gently he disentangled her arms from around his neck. "Claire, look at me," he commanded softly.

With a gulp, she pushed her hair out of her face and slowly sat up, knowing that the moment she had feared all day was upon her.

Stuart's expression was stony as he stared at her. "What are you talking about?"

Unable to meet his eyes, Claire looked down at the quilted comforter, plucking at a loose thread. "Oh, Stuart, I'll understand. Really I will."

"Understand what?"

Claire sighed, wishing he wouldn't make her say it out loud. "I know you felt obligated to marry me since I'd saved your life in Savannah, but now that the war is over and there's no further need to protect me, I'll understand if you want to get an annulment and marry someone else."

"An annulment!" he thundered, angry and hurt by her lack of faith in him. "Are you out of your mind? We're about a hundred encounters past an annulment, lady."

"Well, a . . . a divorce, then."

At her tortured words, Stuart's anger melted away and he blew out a long, tired breath. "Is that what you want?"

Claire's shoulders began to shake, but still she

didn't look up. "What I want is for you to be happy."

"And you think a divorce would make me happy?"

"Maybe . . ."

"Why do you think that?"

She finally lifted her eyes, her expression agonized. "Because I know there are many girls in Boston far better suited to be your wife than I am."

"Who? Sally Rutherford?"

"Well, yes, she's certainly one."

"I don't want Sally Rutherford. I don't even *like* her. You'll have to think of someone else."

"Well, Ruth Halpern, then."

"No. She has a bad temper, and besides, she looks like a horse. Who else?"

Claire tossed her hair over her shoulder and glared at him indignantly. "I'm not going to sit here and try to choose a wife for you, Stuart."

"Why not? You don't seem to agree with my choice."

"What choice?"

"You. If I remember correctly, I chose you."

"But you didn't, really."

"Yes, I did, really!" he said fiercely. "And I have no intention of getting a divorce. So, if you want to be rid of me, lady, *you* are going to have to divorce *me*. But I warn you, I'll fight you every inch of the way."

The stoic expression Claire was trying so desperately to maintain suddenly crumpled, and with a little cry, she launched herself into her husband's arms. "Do you really mean that?" she asked, her voice breathless with hope. "You really do want to stay married to me—even now that you don't have to?"

"Claire, Claire," Stuart crooned, burying his lips in her hair and pulling her down into the pillows. "I never *had* to. *Never*. You should know me well enough by now to know that if I hadn't wanted to marry you, I'd have found some other way to save you from hanging. Sweetheart, *why* won't you believe that I married you because I wanted to? I think I started falling in love with you the day you threw that soup in my face. You were so proud, so brave, so loyal to your beliefs. God, I admired you. Even when you stole my message, I still respected your courage. And if you hadn't married me when you did, I'd have stayed in Savannah and hounded you until either I wore you down, or you got fed up and killed me."

Claire gazed at him with wide eyes. "So, you really didn't marry me just to be . . . kind?"

"You give me too much credit," he chuckled, running a finger down her cheek. "I'm not kind at all. I'm selfish to the core, and I always get what I want. And I wanted you. I keep telling you that . . . you just refuse to believe it."

"Oh, Stuart," Claire sighed, laying her head on his shoulder and weaving her fingers into the hair on his chest, "you make me so happy."

"You make me happy, too," he whispered, drawing her hand down across his tightly ribbed abdomen and cupping her fingers around his half-aroused manhood. "And I can think of a way we can make each other even happier."

"Wait," she said, pulling her hand away. "There's something else I want to ask you about."

"What now?" he groaned, putting her hand back. "I haven't seen you in almost a week. Can't we talk later?"

"No," she said, again removing her hand and

317

tucking it firmly beneath her. "We'll be too sleepy later, and I have to ask you this."

"Okay," he sighed, "but make it quick, okay?"

"I want to know why you never told me you were sending aid to Savannah."

His eyes flared in surprise. "How did you hear about that?"

"Grenita told me. She said everyone in Boston knew about it—except me. Why didn't you tell me?"

"I was afraid you'd tell me not to."

"Why would I do that?"

"Because you're always so territorial about the South. I was afraid that if you knew I was sending supplies to Savannah, you'd tell me you and your countrymen didn't want my stinking Yankee help. And since I knew I was going to send aid, regardless of how much you objected, I just figured it was easier to do it without your knowledge, rather than fight with you about it."

"Have I been that obnoxious about being Confederate?" Claire asked quietly.

"Not obnoxious," Stuart corrected. "Stubborn."

Claire looked at him for a moment. Then, with a seductive smile, she rose to her knees and threw back the quilt, revealing his fully erect manhood. "Well, Major, all that's over now," she drawled, dipping her head and teasing him intimately with her tongue. "Now that I know you married me because you truly desired me for your wife, I'd better concentrate on keeping your desire from straying."

"Not a chance," Stuart groaned, burying his hands in her hair as her tongue swirled up and down his rigid length. "Not a chance in the world."

Chapter Twenty-three

Claire knew there was something wrong as soon as Stuart walked into the room. There were lines of tension around his mouth, and his eyes held a look of profound sadness.

"Stuart, what is it?" she questioned, laying down her sewing and rising.

"Oh, Claire," he breathed, folding her into his embrace and burying his face in her hair. "My sweet, precious darling, I'm so sorry."

"My God, Stuart," she cried, throwing her head back and looking at him fearfully. "What is it?"

"It's your father," he croaked, his voice breaking. "He had a heart attack, sweetheart. There was . . . there was nothing they could do."

"Oh, my God!" Claire cried. "He's dead? Papa is dead?"

Miserably, Stuart nodded.

The color drained from Claire's face and she fell against him, half swooning. "No," she moaned. "It can't be. He can't be dead."

Stuart picked her up and carried her over to the settee, sitting down with her on his lap and rocking her as she continued her heartbreaking lament.

For a long time Claire didn't cry, even after her mumbled, incoherent words of grief had trailed off into stunned silence. She just sat, leaning heavily against Stuart's chest and staring out the window at the beautiful June afternoon.

Her lack of emotion was frightening, and after a few minutes, Stuart tipped her chin back and looked at her with concern. "Go ahead and cry, sweetheart," he encouraged. "You need to let it out."

It was as if his words unleashed a dam, and suddenly Claire emitted a keening wail—a cry of loss so pitiful that tears also sprang to Stuart's eyes.

They sat together as Claire cried out her grief until, finally, her sobs subsided to choked hic-coughs. "I have to go to Savannah immediately," she murmured.

"All the arrangements are made," Stuart assured her quietly. "We leave in the morning."

"Are you going with me?"

"Of course. Did you think I wouldn't?"

"I just know how busy you are," she stammered. "I mean, you don't have to, if you don't have time. I can go alone."

"Claire, I'm going."

Claire looked at him for a moment, then a little smile touched the corners of her mouth. "Thank you," she murmured. "I was hoping you would."

"Come on," he whispered, again scooping her up in his arms and heading for the staircase. "Let's get you to bed."

*   *   *

320

The train pulled into the Savannah station in the midst of a soft spring rain.

"Sit there for a minute," Stuart directed, pointing to a bench near the station wall. "I'll get our bags and hire a hack."

Claire obediently sat down, taking in all the familiar sights and sounds of her hometown. For months she had dreamed of coming home, but never had it occurred to her that her first trip back would be for such a tragic reason.

Tears again welled in her eyes and she blinked rapidly, trying to force them back. "Quit crying," she told herself fiercely. "It won't bring him back." She bit her lip and took several deep breaths, then opened her eyes as the threatening tears receded.

Stuart returned, accompanied by a grizzled old black man who eagerly picked up their luggage and headed off down the platform. They climbed into a rickety wagon and headed down Oglethorpe Street. Claire looked around curiously, relieved to see that the city still looked as it had when she left.

"I guess Sherman really *didn't* do much damage," she commented.

The old man driving the wagon turned and looked at them curiously. "Hasn't you been here since Sherman came, missus?" he questioned. Then, without waiting for an answer, he continued, "'Spect not, since y'all sounds like you're from the North."

"We live in Boston," Stuart answered.

"Boston, eh?" the old man nodded. "Knew you was from somewhere up there. Always can tell a Yankee by the voice."

Stuart threw a glance at Claire, then quickly

321

turned away, trying hard to hide his amusement at the look of startled offense on her face.

"Like I was sayin', Sherman didn't do much o' nothin' round here 'cause the ladies in town, they just invited him right into their homes and treated him like kinfolk. I guess even old Bill couldn't bring hisself to burn folks out after they give him Christmas dinner!" The old man wheezed with laughter at his own witticism. "His men, though, they done got up to a whole lot of mischief in the old cemetery. You'll see when we pass it."

The wagon jounced along for several minutes until the Colonial Park Cemetery loomed up on their right. The ancient driver sawed back on the reins, bringing his equally ancient horse to a stumbling halt. "See what I mean?" he asked, pointing.

"My Lord, how terrible!" Claire gasped, looking out at the once-neat rows of graves. The cemetery now looked as if the headstones had been pulled out of the ground and then pushed back in, willy-nilly. "What happened here?"

"Well, Sherman's boys used the graveyard as pasture for their horses, and every time it lightnin'ed or a cannon went off, them nags would start a runnin' and just plow right into the gravestones. Some of the ladies in town complained when the markers started topplin', and ol' Bill hisself come out to take a look. He was right mad when he seen the mess, and he told them soldiers they had to put 'em all back, but they didn't know where none of 'em belonged, so they just stuck 'em in anywhere they saw fit. Now, nobody knows for sure who's buried where. Probably never will get it back to rights."

"That's disgraceful!" Claire hissed, glaring at

Stuart. "And to think that man was at *my* wedding."

Stuart threw his hands in the air, astonished that she seemed bent on blaming him for the havoc wrought in the cemetery.

"Yeah, it is, missus, that's for sure," their driver agreed, clucking to his horse and moving on down the street, "but compared to what happened to them other towns Bill visited, I guess we got off plumb lucky."

"I think we should all just be grateful that it's over," Stuart said firmly, ending the conversation. "Now, if you don't mind, driver, we'd like to be quiet for a while. We're in mourning, and my wife is very tired."

"Sorry, suh," the old man said contritely. "I didn't mean no harm. I was just passin' the time o'day."

"No harm taken," Stuart assured him.

Claire stood at the doorway of her childhood home, shaking hands with departing guests.

"It was a lovely service," Randa Jo Foster said as she pulled on her black gloves.

"Thank you," Claire smiled, "I think Papa would have appreciated how many people came to pay their respects."

Randa Jo gave Claire a warm hug. "We'll all miss him very much, but it's a comfort to know that he didn't suffer."

Claire nodded and returned her friend's embrace. "I wish Beau could have come with you."

"I do, too," Randa Jo nodded, "but he's still having trouble getting around on only one leg, and he didn't think he could walk to the cemetery.

He's hoping to see you while you're here, though. How long will you be staying?"

"At least another week," Claire answered. "We have a lot of things to take care of before we go back to Boston."

"Would you have time next week for a quiet lunch? I know it's not really proper to go out in public when you're in deep mourning, but since the war, so many of those rules have changed that I'm sure no one would disapprove."

"I'd like that. Let's plan it for next Friday."

Randa Jo nodded and turned to Stuart. "Goodbye, Mr. Wellesley," she said, reluctantly holding out her hand.

Stuart ignored the girl's obvious reticence and brushed a light kiss on her knuckles. "Goodbye, Mrs. Foster. I hope I'll see you again."

"Perhaps," she responded, smiling in a way that told Stuart she didn't share that hope.

After the last guest had finally left, Claire leaned against the front door with a heavy sigh. "What are we going to do with all this furniture?"

"You don't have to do anything," Stuart answered, putting his arm around her shoulder and leading her over to an overstuffed sofa. "I'll take care of everything. You just decide which of your father's possessions you want to keep, and I'll handle the rest."

"But won't it be a lot of work trying to sell all this stuff? No one has any money, so I can't imagine who could buy it. It will take forever."

"I'm not planning to sell it."

"You're not?" Claire asked, looking up at him curiously. "What *are* you planning?"

"Anything you don't want, we'll just give away. Surely there are families who could use it. You said yourself that some people were forced to burn their furniture for firewood."

"Well, yes," Claire sputtered, "but it's worth *something*. I hate to just give it away."

"Sweetheart, we don't need the money. I'd rather donate whatever you don't want to one of the war charities."

"There are some things here I'd really like to keep," Claire said wanly, looking around at the old pieces, "but there's no room in the townhouse, so I guess we should just donate it all."

Stuart smiled, knowing that after so many months of guarding his big secret, the time was finally right to tell her. "Oh, I think we'll be able to find room for whatever you want," he said casually.

"What do you mean? The townhouse is completely furnished, and with much grander furniture than this."

"That's true," he agreed, "but the Marblehead house is empty."

"What Marblehead house?"

"The one I bought for you," he grinned, pulling her into his arms.

"You . . . you bought another house?"

"Yup."

"When?"

"The week after we were married," he breathed, his lips close to her ear.

"That was five months ago!" Claire gasped, pulling away. "Why haven't you told me about it before this?"

"I've been having it decorated, and I didn't want to show it to you until it was ready."

"Why not?"

"Because I knew once I told you about it, you'd

hound me unmercifully to see it."

"Stuart Wellesley!" Claire cried, jumping to her feet and planting her fists indignantly on her hips. "I don't believe you bought a house and had it decorated without once consulting me!"

"Well, I did," he smiled, unrepentant. "And you're going to love it. It's huge, with a beautiful garden, and it's so close to the sea that you can smell the salt air. It'll be the perfect place to raise our family."

Claire ignored his comment about a family, but sat back down on the sofa and gazed fondly around the room. "And we can really ship some of Papa's things up there?"

"Every stick in the house, if you want it. I already have a ship docked in the harbor, waiting to be loaded."

"You do?" Claire gasped.

Stuart nodded. "I figured you'd want to keep some of your father's belongings, so I had a ship brought down."

"Oh, Stuart," Claire sighed, putting her arms around him and laying her head on his chest. "You're so good to me. I don't know how I'd have made it through the last few days without you."

Stuart hugged her close, thrilled to hear her say she needed him. "I'll always be here for you, Claire," he promised. "Always."

Claire and Randa Jo Foster sat basking in the spring sunshine, sipping a cup of tea and reminiscing about the carefree days before the war.

When the conversation finally waned and a silence fell between them, Randa Jo summoned her courage and asked the question that had been plaguing her all afternoon. "Are you happy, Claire? I mean, married to a Yankee and all."

Claire smiled and a faraway look crossed her face. "I don't think of Stuart as a Yankee. Not anymore. And yes, I'm happy. Very, very happy."

Randa Jo heaved a relieved little sigh. "I'm so glad to hear you say that. Your father told me you and your husband were getting along fine, but I was afraid that after you found out David was back, things might have changed."

Claire's face paled. "What did you say?"

Randa Jo clapped a hand over her mouth, gaping at Claire in horror. "Oh, my Lord! Don't tell me you didn't know!"

Claire's head started to spin, and desperately, she gripped the edge of the table, fearing she might faint.

"Claire!" Randa Jo shrieked, rising from her chair in alarm. "Claire, are you all right?" Grabbing her reticule, she fumbled for her smelling salts, then raced around the table and waved the small vial under Claire's nose.

The acrid smell of ammonia assailed Claire's nostrils, and weakly, she pushed the odorous bottle away. "Don't do that," she murmured. "I'm all right."

"Oh, my dear, I thought you knew," Randa Jo moaned, sinking back into her chair. "I never would have said anything if I'd known you didn't."

Claire gazed off into space, her eyes vague and unfocused. "He's alive. David is alive . . ."

"I thought surely your father would have told you," Randa Jo said in a voice laced with remorse. "David went to see him as soon as he got home."

Claire stared at her friend in disbelief as this

latest bit of shocking news sank in. "Papa knew David was home? And he let me go on thinking he was dead?"

"I'm sure he must have had a good reason," Randa Jo said lamely, feeling worse with every second.

"Where is David now?"

"Um, I'm not sure I know."

"Don't lie to me, for God's sake! Where is he?"

"He's living with his mother," Randa Jo whispered.

"In their house near Oglethorpe Square?"

She nodded.

Abruptly, Claire stood up, picking up her reticule and shawl. "I have to go now," she announced. "It was good to see you."

"Claire, what are you going to do?"

"I'm going home."

"But, then what?"

"I'm going to send David a message. I have to see him."

"Do you really think you should? Your husband might not like . . ."

"I have to see him," Claire repeated, her voice icy with determination.

"Claire, don't do it," Randa Jo cried. "You're making a terrible mistake."

"Yes, well, mistakes seem to be my specialty," Claire said with a mirthless little smile. "What difference will one more make?"

Chapter Twenty-four

Claire sat on the edge of a hard chair in David Henry's parlor, looking about the familiar room impatiently. Why was he making her wait so long? She'd been here for nearly twenty minutes and still he had not made an appearance.

With a frown, she pulled a crumpled piece of paper out of her pocket, knowing full well that she hadn't misread his cryptic message, but checking it again anyway.

C.—

I will meet you at my house on Saturday, June 18, at 2 P.M.. Come alone so we can talk.

D.

Refolding the scrap of paper, Claire pushed it back into her pocket and glanced at the grandfather's clock in the corner of the room. Two-eighteen.

Five more minutes and I'll leave, she thought irritably, then nearly jumped off the chair as the parlor doors flew open.

Looking up, Claire watched David Henry walk into the room, his gaze raking her up and down with almost insolent thoroughness. His face betrayed little of his feelings, but something about the expression in his eyes made Claire suddenly wish she hadn't come.

He looked older—much older than she remembered, and the changes in his appearance troubled her. His golden hair had faded to a dull ash color, and his beautiful blue eyes no longer sparkled with the vitality of a happy man. Most troubling of all, however, were the hard lines around his mouth—lines that betrayed a bitter cynicism that had never been part of his character.

For a moment, Claire let her mind drift back to the last time she'd seen him. It had been a warm, spring afternoon, and they had shared a picnic lunch. The rest of the day had been spent lying on a blanket in the warm Georgia sunshine, planning their future and sharing warm, innocent kisses. David had woven wildflowers in her hair and told her she was the most beautiful girl in the world.

Claire had never forgotten how he'd looked that day, with the sun glinting off his golden hair and the light of youth and first love dancing in his eyes.

Her gaze flickered back to him now as she searched his thin, haunted face for some trace of that happy young man. To her consternation, she could find none. But, she told herself, despite the outward changes, he was still David—her David . . . the boy she'd loved since childhood. The man she'd thought she'd marry.

"How are you, Claire?" he asked, walking forward and stiffly offering his hand.

Claire looked from his hand to his expressionless eyes and her heart sank. So this was how it was going to be between them. "I'm fine, David," she responded, reaching up to kiss him lightly on the cheek. "And you? You're looking well."

David nodded curtly and gestured to a long sofa. With a smile, Claire seated herself, then drew in a surprised breath as he pointedly sat down in a chair opposite.

"You wanted to see me?" he asked without preamble.

"Well, yes," she answered hesitantly.

"Why?"

"Why? Because we're friends."

"We're not friends, Claire. We stopped being friends the day you married the Yankee."

Claire looked at him in bewilderment. "How can you say we're not friends? David, for two years I thought you were dead. Then, three days ago, Randa Jo Foster casually tells me you're alive. Do you know how shocked I was? How overjoyed? And you ask why I wanted to see you? My God, David, do you have any idea how long I grieved for you?"

"I know exactly how long you grieved for me," he spat, his handsome face twisted into a grimace of contempt. "Until the day you found a rich, influential Yankee officer to take care of you."

"How dare you?" Claire cried, shooting to her feet. "What right do you have to talk to me like this?"

"I have every right! You made me the laughing-stock of Savannah."

"That's not true!"

"Not true?" David railed. "My God, Claire, do you have any idea what I went through in that Yankee prison? We were beaten, starved, treated worse than the lowest animal. There were days when I just wanted to die. But I told myself I had to keep on living because when the war finally ended I could come home to you. And then it did end, and I did come home, and what's the first thing I hear? That you've taken off for Boston with some Yankee bastard. How could you do that to me, Claire? *How?*"

"I didn't do anything to you!" Claire cried, her eyes welling with tears. "I thought you were dead. Don't you understand that?"

"Why did you think I was dead? Did you get a letter from the War Department saying I was?"

Claire looked down, unable to answer.

"Well, *did you?*"

"No!"

"Then why did you think that?"

"Because Stuart told me you were!"

"Oh, I see," he sneered. "*Stuart* told you. And, of course, you believed *Stuart.*"

"I had no reason not to believe him," Claire defended. "I hadn't heard from you in two years. Besides, before we got married, Stuart checked with all the Union prison officials to see if you were on any of their lists—and you weren't. Do you honestly think I'd have married him if I'd thought you were still alive?"

"I don't know," David shrugged. "But I do know this—prisoner lists were always incomplete, and a high-ranking Union officer would damn well know that!"

"Well, Stuart didn't," Claire insisted, shaking her head. "I know he really believed you were dead."

"Then he's a fool."

Claire swiped at the tears in her eyes and raised

her chin regally. "He's also my husband, and I will not allow you to talk about him like this."

"Are you saying you love him?"

"That's none of your business."

"Oh, so you don't. What is it, then, Claire? His money? I hear he's richer than Georgia clay."

"Who told you that?"

"Your father," David muttered bitterly. "In fact, he regaled me with stories of what a great leader the major is, how brave the major is, how brilliant the major is. He just went on and on and on until I wanted to vomit!"

Claire shook her head in confusion. "I don't understand. My father barely knew Stuart when we got married."

"That may be, but they obviously got to be great friends afterward."

"Did Papa tell you that, too? That he and Stuart were 'great friends'?"

"Yes! And he also said that you were happy and in love, and that I was under no circumstances to cause any problems in your marriage."

"I don't believe Papa would talk to you like that."

"Oh, he was nice enough about it," David muttered. "He said he felt terrible about how everything had worked out, but that what was done was done, and that I should forget you and move on with my life."

"Is that why you never contacted me?" Claire asked, her voice small.

"That . . . and other things," David responded evasively. "Besides, I was told that Stuart Wellesley is so powerful in Boston that if I crossed him, he could fix it so I'd spend the rest of my life behind bars."

"Stuart's not like that," Claire said hotly.

"No? Well, if he's such a prince, then why didn't he tell you I was alive?"

"I keep trying to tell you, he didn't know!"

"Maybe not when you got married, but he sure as hell has known since April."

"No, he hasn't! He'd have told me. He's far too honorable to keep something of such great importance from me."

"Oh, Claire, for God's sake, wake up!" David barked. "Your father let him know I was back the minute I got home."

"I don't believe you," Claire cried, a sudden icy finger of apprehension tracing down her spine.

"Believe what you want. I saw the wire myself."

"Wait a minute," Claire said, shaking her head as she tried to make sense of what David was saying. "My father showed you a wire he sent to Stuart?"

"Yes. Archibald said that you were Stuart's wife and that it was up to him to decide if you should be told of my return, so he sent him a wire."

"I can't believe this," Claire moaned, feeling as if the very threads of her life were unraveling.

"Wellesley never said anything to you?"

She shook her head, sinking heavily back down on the sofa.

"I thought not," David said triumphantly. "So, now what do you think of your 'honorable' Stuart?"

"I can't think," Claire admitted, rubbing at an ache that suddenly throbbed between her eyes. "I'm too confused."

David stood at the opposite end of the room, looking at the woman he had wanted for so long. Before the war, she'd been the prettiest girl in

Savannah, and although she was now past that first, fresh bloom of womanhood, her new maturity was just as appealing. Despite her high-necked, long-sleeved black mourning dress, her upswept hair, refined facial features, and full, lush breasts gave her a look of worldliness that David found incredibly exciting. He felt himself harden, just thinking how she would look naked.

Of course, things could never be the same between them, now that she had been touched by a Yankee's hands, and even if she were free, he wouldn't consider marrying her, but perhaps her coming here today was a sign that they could enjoy a new, more provocative relationship. He'd enjoy that, especially knowing that with each thrust, he'd be cuckolding the Yankee bastard who'd had the nerve to try to take her away.

"Claire," he said, his voice suddenly soft and beguiling, "why did you come here today?"

Claire looked up at him, her face drawn with doubt and confusion. "I just wanted to see you and let you know that I wasn't betraying you when I married Stuart. I really *did* think you were dead."

"I believe you," David said, sitting down next to her and picking up one of her hands. "And now that I understand that, I want you to know that things between us don't really have to end—at least, not while you're still here in Savannah."

"What do you mean?" she asked vaguely.

"Can't you guess?" he whispered, sidling closer and pressing his lips to the back of the hand he held.

Claire's eyes widened with the dawning of alarm. "David, what are you suggesting?"

With a seductive smile, he murmured, "Oh, I think you know. We're not innocent children anymore, Claire, and this may be our last chance to be together—really together. Let's take advantage of it."

"What?" Claire cried, wrenching her hand out of his grip. "My God, David, are you proposition-ing me?"

"Of course not," he said smoothly. "I'm just suggesting that we should make the most of the time we have. You know if the war hadn't come, we'd have been married, and even though that can never be, we can still share the happiness that should have been ours—at least for a short while."

Claire was livid. How *dared* he treat her like some cheap trollop? Did he honestly think that she had come here today looking for an assignation? When had he become so arrogant, so conceited? Had the war changed him that much, or had he always been this way and she been too young and naive to notice?

For a long moment, she stared at him, trying once more to see some trace of her dashing young cavalier beneath the hard-eyed, cynical mask of the man who sat leering at her.

Claire had no intention of renewing her rela-tionship with David, but she desperately wanted to believe that she was misinterpreting his offensive suggestions. Silently apologizing for the trap she was setting, she leaned toward him and mur-mured, "You know, David, there's a possibility that we could be together for a lot longer than just this short trip. I'm sure Papa told you that I married Stuart under duress. Now that the war is over, there might be some way for me to rid myself of him." She glanced at him out of the corner of her eye to see how he was reacting to what she was so obviously implying, but his face betrayed nothing.

"If I could somehow manage to do that," she plunged on, determined to give him one last chance to redeem himself, "we could be married, just as we'd always planned."

A shuttered expression fell over his blue eyes and Claire felt as if something deep inside her was dying. "That won't happen," he said flatly. "You'd have to get a divorce."

"I know, but I'd be willing to endure that disgrace if it meant we could be married."

David shifted away from her, releasing her hand and standing up. "I'm sorry, Claire, but it's impossible."

"Why?" she asked, her voice suddenly tense.

"It just wouldn't work, that's all."

"*Why?*"

David finally turned back toward her, his expression incredulous. "How can you even *think* that I would marry you now?"

"Now? What do you mean, 'now'?"

"Now that you've been married to a Yankee."

"Why does that make a difference?"

"Why?" he exploded. "Are you crazy? Do you really think I'd lower myself to marry a woman who'd been used over and over by some piece of Bluebelly scum? Why, the mere thought makes me sick."

Claire's eyes widened with disbelief at David's crude words, and with a strangled cry, she jumped to her feet. "Why did you agree to see me today?"

"I wanted to give you the chance to explain your perfidy and ask my forgiveness," he said truthfully. "And now that you've convinced me that you really were duped into marrying Wellesley, I'd be willing to consider a discreet liaison with you. But honestly, Claire, I never dreamed you'd be so naive as to think I'd still consider you as a candidate for my wife. I thought you'd understand that after being sullied by a Yankee, the most you could expect from me would be a more . . . casual relationship."

"I do understand," Claire whispered, picking up her reticule and hurriedly walking into the foyer. She heard David following her and paused at the front door, turning around to take one last look at him. "David," she said, her voice soft, "there's something you need to understand, too."

"Oh?" he responded, crooking an eyebrow at her, "and what's that?"

"The Yankees aren't your enemies any longer. You are your only enemy now."

His brow furrowed with bewilderment at her quiet words, and with a sad shake of her head, Claire left the house. Silently, she climbed into her rented carriage, her head bowed low as she grieved over the death of the handsome, laughing boy she had loved.

Chapter Twenty-five

"How was your luncheon?" Stuart asked, greeting Claire as she walked into the house.

"I didn't go to a luncheon," she answered tonelessly.

"Oh? I thought your note said you were having lunch . . ."

"I lied."

Stuart's smile faded. "You lied about lunch? Why? If you weren't at a luncheon, where have you been?"

"Visiting a friend."

Something about Claire's flat, dead tone made the hair stand up on the back of Stuart's neck. "What friend is that?" he asked casually, having a terrible premonition of who she was going to name.

"David Henry," she answered, brushing by him and heading for the staircase. "My former fiancé. You know, the one you assured me was dead?"

Stuart closed his eyes, realizing that his greatest fear was being manifested. Claire had found out.

Deep down, he'd known she would. From the minute her father'd died and they'd had to return to Savannah, he'd known it was only a matter of time. But still he hadn't been able to bring himself to tell her that David was still alive. Instead, he'd foolishly hoped that they could somehow get back to Boston without her finding out. He'd held his breath every time she left the house, fearing that she might run into the man or that some well-meaning friend would mention his name. Obviously, someone finally had.

"Claire," he said, his voice hoarse with sudden, gut-wrenching fear, "please let me explain."

He started up the stairs after her, but came to an abrupt halt as she whirled around, glaring down at him with blazing eyes. "How long have you known, Stuart?"

"A while," he admitted.

"How long?"

"Since April."

With a curt, dismissive nod, she headed up the stairs again. Stuart stared after her for a moment, trying to think of something, *anything*, he could say that would diffuse her terrible, silent anger. "Claire," he called, taking the rest of the stairs two at a time and sprinting down the hall. "Can we talk about this?"

Claire threw him a withering look over her shoulder and continued on her way.

"Claire!" Stuart shouted, his voice betraying a note of desperation. "Damn it, quit running away from me! We have to talk."

She rounded the corner into her bedroom, intending to lock the door on him, but before she could even close it, he was beside her.

"I don't want you here," she said coldly, walking over to the window and staring blindly out at the beautiful summer afternoon.

340

"I'm sure you don't, but the fact is, I am here and we're going to talk this out."

"Why?" she shrugged, her back still to him. "I wouldn't believe anything you said anyway."

"Claire . . ."

Suddenly she turned, a look of such rage on her face that Stuart took a startled step backward. "You're a liar!" she shrieked, her steely composure finally cracking. "You told me he was dead! You're nothing but a dirty Yankee liar!"

Stuart's eyes flared with offense and outrage. "I thought he was dead, God damn it!"

"Oh, yes," Claire shrieked. "Maybe at first. But when you found out he was alive, you didn't tell me."

Stuart blew out a long breath. "I know," he said simply.

"Why?"

"Why? I would think that would be obvious."

"Well, it's not, so why don't you tell me?"

"Okay," he barked, raking his hands through his hair in renewed agitation. "You want me to say it, I'll say it. I didn't tell you because I thought you'd leave me and go back to him!"

"How could you have been so selfish?" Claire cried. "How could you have let me go on thinking David was dead when you knew he wasn't?"

"Can't you understand?" Stuart countered hoarsely, quickly traversing the floor and grasping her by the shoulders. "I didn't want to lose you!"

"That's unconscionable!" she sobbed, wrenching away from him.

"It's the truth!" he shouted. "You wanted the truth, I'm giving it to you."

"Truth?" she sneered. "What do you know

about truth? You lied to me about David, you lied to me about my being hanged if I didn't marry you. What else have you lied to me about, Major?"

"Nothing."

"No? How about all those times in bed when you told me no woman had ever made you as happy as I did. Were those lies, too?"

"No! How can you even think that?"

"I don't know what to think. I don't know what to believe. And after what I found out about you today, I don't know how I can believe anything you say ever again." Wearily, she sank down on the bed and covered her face with her hands.

Stuart threw his head back and stared at the ceiling in agonized frustration. How could he make her understand? How?

Willing himself to remain calm, he walked over to the bed. "Claire, listen to me."

"No. I don't want to listen to you. Just go away."

"I'm not going away, and I want you to look at me while I tell you this."

Reluctantly she raised her eyes.

"What I did might have been wrong," Stuart admitted, his gaze never wavering from hers, "but everything I did, I did because I loved you and I didn't want to lose you."

Claire shook her head sadly. "I'm sorry, Stuart, but I find that the most difficult to believe of all."

"You honestly doubt that I love you?" he gasped. "How could you, after what we've shared together?"

"I don't know *what* to think, after the way you've betrayed me," she shot back. "But I've told you before, I think you confuse love with desire."

"And I've told *you* before that I'm not some

green boy who doesn't know the difference!" he thundered. "Of course I feel desire for you. I'm not ashamed of it. But I also love you."

"Then maybe it's just trust you don't understand, but unfortunately, Major, it takes both love *and* trust to build a good marriage."

"Don't call me 'Major,'" he raged. "I hate it when you call me that, and you know it."

Claire ignored him, and when she continued, her voice was deadly quiet. "As I was saying, good marriages are built on trust, whereas ours has a foundation of lies, deceit, and subterfuge. Not a very stable base to build on, is it?"

Stuart's eyes narrowed. "What are you really saying, Claire?" he snarled. "Did you and David meet today and decide to pick up where you left off before the war? Is that what this is all about? Now that the war is over and you don't need protection anymore, you're going to get rid of your hated Yankee husband and go back to your handsome Rebel lover?"

Claire's eyes glittered like green ice as she turned on him. "You, more than anyone in the world, know that David was never my lover. And, no, we're not 'picking up where we left off.' We wouldn't even if I wanted to. And do you want to know why?"

"Why?"

"Because of you. Because David told me today that I was no longer a fit candidate to be his wife since I'd been 'sullied' by a dirty Yankee."

A dark, ominous fury swelled in Stuart. "Sullied?" he gritted. "That bastard said that being married to me had 'sullied' you? By God, I'll kill him myself!" With a cry of rage, he lunged for the door.

"Stop it!" Claire shouted, tearing across the room and grabbing him by the arm. "You're acting like a lunatic. It doesn't matter what David said. There's nothing left there. I don't want him any more than he wants me."

"But you don't want me, either, do you?" he asked quietly, his anger suddenly dissipating as he looked down at her hand on his arm.

Claire released her grip and walked back to the bed. Sitting down, she looked up miserably at him. "How can I be happy, married to a man I can't trust? A man whom I can't be sure I can believe, even when he tells me he loves me?"

A great silence fell between them and several endless minutes passed before Stuart finally spoke. "Then we might as well call it quits. If you truly don't believe I love you, there's nothing left to try to save."

"How *can* I believe you? You've lied to me about so much."

"Maybe so, but never about that."

Claire shook her head. "I'm too tired to discuss this anymore. Please go away, Stuart. I just want to be left alone."

"Fine," he nodded, "if that's what you want, I'll leave you alone." And turning on his heel, he strode out of the room.

For the next two days they barely spoke. Claire stayed in her room, taking her meals there and coming out only when she was sure Stuart wasn't in the house.

Stuart left her to herself, busying himself with sorting out the details of her father's estate and sleeping in a small spare bedroom at the other end of the house.

On the morning of the third day, he finally faced the fact that she was not going to break the impasse between them. He ate a solitary breakfast, then climbed the stairs and marched down the hall to their bedroom, his jaw clenched with frustration and pent-up anger.

Approaching the door, he knocked.

"Who is it?" Claire called, knowing full well who it was.

"It's me," he answered flatly. "I need to discuss a few things with you."

"I don't want to see you."

"Claire, open the door. I have to talk to you."

"There's nothing to talk about."

"God damn it, Claire, open the door! There are some things we need to settle regarding your father's estate."

Reluctantly, Claire opened the door, and despite herself, a warm flush washed over her as she stared at her husband. He was so tall, so handsome . . . despite the fact that he looked tired and drawn.

"What do you need to know?" she asked, careful to keep her voice impersonal.

"May I come in?"

"No," she answered hurriedly, glancing over her shoulder at the rumpled bed. The telltale signs of distress were obvious in the scattered pillows and trailing bedclothes, and she didn't want him to know that she was sleeping as poorly as he obviously was. "Let's go downstairs to the parlor."

As she stepped through the doorway, Stuart unconsciously placed his hand on the small of her back, but quickly removed it as she ducked away from the contact. For a moment he stared down at the offending hand, then silently followed his wife down the stairs.

"I made some coffee," he offered, as they walked into the parlor. "I don't know how good it is, but the pot's in the kitchen, if you'd like some."

"Thank you, no," Claire said, sitting down on a small chair. "What is it we need to discuss?"

Stuart was too upset to sit down. Instead, he paced the length and breadth of the room, outlining in short, staccato phrases what he had accomplished during the past few days. Finally, he paused before her, counting off on his fingers those items that required her personal attention.

". . . and as soon as you take care of that, we can return to Boston."

Claire had missed much of his rapid-fire recitation, too exhausted and overwrought to comprehend all the issues he was addressing, but these last words hit her like a blow. "What do you mean, we can return to Boston?" she gasped. "I have no intention of going back."

Stuart's lips thinned. "Well, I'm afraid you're going to have to. You have to be a resident in the same state as I am in order to petition for divorce."

For the first time since they'd entered the room, Claire looked up at him. "Divorce? I thought maybe a separation would be easier."

"No. If you want to end this marriage, we'll end it. I'm not going to spend the rest of my life married to a woman I don't live with."

"But a divorce is so difficult . . ."

"There won't be a problem. You can sue on the basis of duress . . . and I won't fight you on it."

Claire dropped her eyes, unable to look at his hard, set face. "It probably would be best just to get it over with."

"Absolutely," he agreed, his teeth clenched so tightly that a hard knot of tension appeared in his cheek. "But there's one thing I have to know before we can proceed."

"What is that?" she asked, again lifting her eyes to his.

"Is there any chance you're pregnant?"

"No," she mumbled, mortified to feel her face suffusing with hot color.

Stuart quickly turned away, not wanting her to see the disappointment he was afraid he couldn't hide. It had been his most fervent hope that she might be carrying his baby, since it was the only thing he could think of that would halt this headlong flight toward their marriage's doom. But her answer had been too immediate, too confident, and he knew she was telling the truth.

For the past six months, he had eagerly anticipated the joyous moment when Claire would tell him he was going to be a father, but as each month passed and no such news was forthcoming, he had begun to fear that something might be wrong with her—or him. They had made love so often and with such passionate intensity that it just didn't seem normal for her not to conceive.

Historically, his family was so prolific that it was almost embarrassing. His father was one of ten children, and had sired eight of his own. His older brother Miles had been married less than two years, but already he and his wife Alicia had a sixth-month-old son and another baby on the way. Why had he and Claire not had the same luck? Things might have been so different if only they had a child to bind them.

Knowing that this last vestige of hope was gone, Stuart emitted a long, disheartened sigh. "All right, then. Since the possibility of a child isn't going to be an impediment to ending our marriage, I guess there's no reason for you not to proceed with the divorce as soon as we get back to Massachusetts."

"I don't *want* to go back to Massachusetts!" Claire hissed. "A divorce can take years. What am I supposed to do? Where am I supposed to live? My home is here."

"For the time being, you can live in the Louisburg Square house," Stuart assured her.

"I don't want to live with you!"

Stuart winced at her cold words. "You won't have to. I'll live somewhere else."

"But that's not right, either," she argued, her voice shaking with frustration and guilt. "The townhouse is your home. You should live there."

"I'll never live there again," he said with quiet finality.

"But, why? It's a beautiful house, and you've lived there for . . ."

"I don't care about that," he interrupted, his voice rising. "As soon as this is over I'm going to sell it. You can stay there till then." He drew a deep, shuddering breath, wondering how much longer he could maintain his stoic facade. "If you think you can finish up with your father's affairs by next Wednesday, I'll book us on the morning train."

"I'm sure I can," she murmured, "but what about all this?" With a vague gesture, she indicated the room in which they sat.

"What about it?"

"Weren't you planning to sell this house and . . . and . . . ship the furniture north?"

"Considering how things are between us, I'm

certainly not going to do that now," he snapped.

"But what about your ship?"

"My ship?" he shouted, finally giving rein to his temper. "You're worried about my damn ship? Well, don't be. I loaded it up with cargo and sent it back to Boston."

"You did?" she whispered, somehow finding this piece of information more devastatingly final than anything else they'd discussed.

"Yes. I couldn't see any reason to let it sit in the harbor any longer, could you?"

"No," Claire answered softly, her gaze again swinging away from him. "I guess not."

Seeing her defeated expression, Stuart's anger melted away, and for a long time he gazed at her, silently pleading for her to look up at him and put an end to this misery. But she didn't, and after several endless seconds, he finally turned away. "I'm going out, and I don't know when I'll be back. Let me know if there's anything I can do to help you."

"There's nothing you can do."

He paused a moment and his shoulders began to shake with a mirthless chuckle. "I know that," he muttered. "God, don't I know that."

Chapter Twenty-six

Claire had never liked train travel, but the three-day trip from Savannah back to Boston was almost unbearable.

They were standing on the Savannah station platform, waiting to board, when Stuart suddenly handed her one of the two tickets he was holding. "Here," he said quietly, "you'll need this when the conductor comes around."

Taking the ticket from him, Claire gazed at it, perplexed. "Why do I need my own ticket?"

"Because I booked us compartments in different cars."

Whipping her head around, she gaped at him, aghast. "You expect me to travel unescorted all the way back to Boston?"

"You won't be 'unescorted.' I'll be right in the next car. If you need anything, all you have to do is send me a message via the porter."

"What about meals?"

"You can have them in your room."

"For three days?"

"Yeah, for three days."

"But . . ."

"Look, lady," he interrupted, his gray eyes stormy. "You want a separation? Well, this is what it's all about, so you'd better get used to it."

"Fine!" Claire hissed, glaring at him. "Just don't come knocking at my door looking for a dinner partner, because I don't want to see you."

His sarcastic retort was cut off by a deafening shriek of the train whistle and the conductor's voice bellowing. "'Board! All aboard!"

With a last furious look, Claire picked up her skirts and marched down the platform, thrusting her ticket at the surprised conductor, who nevertheless politely directed her to the appropriate car.

The next three days were an agony. Claire barely left her compartment, not wanting to risk running into Stuart in the dining car or one of the public lounges. She ate and slept very little, the constant swaying motion of the locomotive making her head pound and her stomach lurch sickeningly.

Finally, after what seemed like three weeks instead of three days, the journey ended. It was very late when they pulled into the Boston station and Claire was feeling an enormous sense of unease as she stepped down onto the dark platform and looked around fearfully for Stuart. Her fears were soon put to rest, however, as he promptly appeared at her side, cupping his hand around her elbow and propelling her toward the depot door.

Despite her relief at knowing he hadn't abandoned her to find her own way home, Claire was still angry with him, and with a little wrenching movement, sought to free herself of his grasp.

"Don't be a fool," he muttered, tightening his hold on her arm. "This isn't the time for you to assert your independence. It's nearly midnight, we're in a dangerous part of town, and whether you want to believe it or not, there are men out there who, if they caught you alone, would have even more nefarious intentions toward you than you think I do.''

With a silent nod, Claire quit trying to pull away and docilely allowed Stuart to guide her through the station.

Why was *he* so angry? she wondered, as they hurried through the deserted building. Every day since their conversation in the parlor his anger had seemed to grow, his attitude toward her changing from one of regret to out-and-out hostility.

You'd think he was the one who'd been lied to and betrayed, she thought indignantly, as they stood on the curb and waited for a hack. *I'm* the one who deserves to be angry!

But justified or not, as their last days in Savannah had passed, Stuart had become increasingly moody and withdrawn, treating Claire with barely concealed dislike and avoiding her as much as possible.

Even now, as they climbed into the rented carriage for the ride to Louisburg Square, he squeezed himself into a corner, as if loath to have her skirts touch him.

As they silently traveled through the dark, deserted streets, the strain and exhaustion of the last several days suddenly overwhelmed her, and despite her resolve to stay awake, Claire felt her head start to nod. Twice she caught herself, jerking upright as she willed herself to stay awake, but almost immediately, her eyelids drooped again.

Stuart glanced at her out of the corner of his eye,

watching her slowly lose her battle to stay conscious, until finally she slumped toward him. "For Christ's sake," he muttered irritably, reaching out to catch her before she toppled off the seat. Shifting closer, he wrapped his arm around her and guided her lolling head down to his shoulder. His nose filled with her scent, and for a moment he closed his eyes, allowing himself to revel in her nearness.

With a little sigh of contentment, Claire nestled closer to him, throwing an arm across his lap and nuzzling her face into the hollow of his neck.

Stuart swallowed hard, cursing his wayward body as he felt a familiar tightening in his loins. With a great effort of will, he fought back his flaring desire, forcing himself to think about the lonely emptiness his future held until the unwanted erection finally receded.

When they finally made the last turn onto Louisburg Square, he turned to his sleeping wife and gave her a little shake. "Claire," he whispered, "Claire, wake up. We're home."

Her only response was a little mewl of protest.

"Claire," he said louder, taking her by the shoulders and trying to push her off of him. "You have to wake up now."

"Are we there?" she murmured thickly, her eyes fluttering open, then immediately closing again.

"Yes, we are, so wake up."

"I can't," she smiled sleepily. "Carry me."

Stuart drew in a sharp breath, astonished by her request. For the briefest moment, he harbored the hope that maybe she wasn't really asleep—that perhaps their forced separation on the train had been enough to make her realize she didn't want their marriage to end and that this was her way of initiating a reconciliation.

"Do you really want me to carry you?" he whispered, dipping his head so that his lips hovered a breath above hers.

"Um-hmm," she murmured, sensing the closeness of his mouth even in her sleep and reaching up to kiss him.

The sensation of her warm, soft lips against his was more than Stuart could resist, and with a low groan, he gathered her to him, kissing her with all the yearning and love he'd been trying so hard to hide.

Their kiss went on and on as the carriage rolled over the noisy cobblestones in the square. Claire parted her lips, sighing dreamily into Stuart's mouth as his warm, moist tongue invaded the sweetness of hers.

He was just beginning to caress her breast through the tight bodice of her traveling suit when suddenly the carriage lurched to a stop. The abrupt motion caused Claire's eyes to fly open, and a fraction of a second later, full awareness struck her. "What are you doing?" she gasped, slapping his hand away angrily.

"Kissing you," he murmured, his voice husky and breathless.

Sensing his desire, Claire glanced down, her gaze falling on the hard masculine bulge that pressed against his trousers. "Oh, you dirty lecher," she shrieked. "How *dare* you take advantage of me when I was sleeping!"

"I wasn't taking . . ."

The sharp crack of her palm against his cheek cut him off in mid-sentence. His hand flew up to his stinging cheek and he glared at her, his eyes nearly black with fury. "God damn it, Claire, I've had just about enough!"

"Number Twelve, sir," interrupted a man's voice from outside the carriage door. "We're here."

"And not a moment too soon," Claire hissed, flinging the door open and jumping out.

Stuart followed her, stepping down angrily and thrusting a large bill into the astonished driver's hand. "Put the luggage on the stoop," he directed crossly. "I'll take it in later."

"Yes, sir," the driver nodded, his eyes darting nervously back and forth between the seething couple. "I'll be out of your way in just a second."

Claire stood at the door, her back to him as he groped in his pocket for the keys. When they were finally inside and the door was closed firmly behind them, he turned on her, his face dark with rage. "Just who do you think you are, slapping my face?"

"Just who do you think *you* are, fondling me in a carriage as if I were some common strumpet?"

"I can remember a time when you enjoyed being fondled in a carriage," he reminded her snidely. "I can even remember a time when you initiated it."

"That was a long time ago," she shot back, her voice cold, "and a lot has changed since then. Now, I will thank you to leave this house. I want to go to bed."

"Fine. Go to bed. But I'm not leaving tonight."

Claire whirled around, her foot on the first step of the staircase. "What do you mean? Surely you're not planning to stay here."

"That's exactly what I'm planning."

"Well, I won't have it. I want you out."

"Don't threaten me, lady," Stuart warned, taking an aggressive step toward her. "This is still my house, and if you push me too hard, you may find that you're the one who's 'out.'"

"Oh," Claire breathed, clasping her hand against her bosom, "you really are despicable."

"That may be," he shrugged, "but right now, I'm also tired and fed-up. It's one-thirty in the morning, and I'm not about to start roaming the streets of Boston, looking for a place to stay."

"But I don't want you here," she said desperately.

"Too bad. I'm staying."

"Oh, all right! But, you'll have to sleep in the study. I won't have you upstairs with me."

In two strides, Stuart had closed the distance between them. "What's the matter, Claire?" he snarled, his face so close to hers that she could feel his breath on her cheek. "Afraid you might be tempted?"

"Of course not!" she exclaimed, taking a backward step up to the next stair. "I just know that I won't sleep a wink if you're anywhere near my room."

"I will remind you again, Mrs. Wellesley, that this is still *my* house, and that room," he paused and pointed upward, "is still *my* room."

"Not while I'm in residence, it isn't."

"Oh? And just how do you think you will keep me out?"

"I shall simply lock the door," she announced, lifting her chin defiantly.

Her haughty mien caused something to snap deep inside Stuart, and with a bellow of outrage, he grabbed her hand, hauling her up the staircase

357

behind him. Racing down the hall toward their bedroom, he came to an abrupt halt in front of the closed door. He turned to her, his breathing labored, his eyes flashing. "I'm going to show you exactly how much good your precious lock would do if I wanted you." And lifting a booted foot, he dealt the carved door a mighty blow, splintering the beautiful wood and nearly tearing the frame off the wall. The door flew open, banging off the opposite wall before coming to a shuddering halt.

Claire's jaw dropped open as her eyes skimmed over the wreckage. Finally her gaze came to rest on his crimson face and she stared at him almost fearfully.

"Your chamber, Mrs. Wellesley," he announced, ushering her inside with a sweeping gesture. "Now, go to bed."

"For heaven's sake, Stuart . . ."

"No!" he shouted, holding up a warning finger. "Don't say another word. Just get into that bed and go to sleep." Turning, he strode out of the room and stomped back down the stairs.

He was gone when she woke the next morning, and the only sign that she hadn't dreamed the whole ugly scene between them was the sight of the shattered bedroom door hanging crazily by one hinge.

With a weary sigh, Claire threw back the covers and rose, pulling on her wrapper and trudging slowly down the stairs to the dining room.

As she entered the room, her eyes were drawn to an envelope that sat propped against a silver candlestick on the huge dining table. With trembling fingers, she picked it up and opened it, her eyes welling with tears as she read the curt message.

Have gone to Marblehead. Please forgive me for last night. Will not bother you again.

Stuart

P.S. For both our sakes, file divorce petition immediately.

Claire reread the note three times, then crumpled up the paper and threw it into the fireplace. With an anguished cry, she flew up the staircase and threw herself down on the bed.

She didn't get up for two days.

Chapter Twenty-seven

Claire had never known such loneliness as she experienced during the next few months. The invitations that flooded in shortly after their return from Savannah soon waned as Boston's elite discovered that Mr. Wellesley was residing somewhere other than at Louisburg Square with Mrs. Wellesley.

Claire did not see Stuart, nor did she hear from him, though on several occasions she did overhear the servants and their friends gossiping about having seen him at this or that social function.

Only Grenita Forten remained her constant friend, stopping by every Wednesday to share a cup of tea with her. Their afternoons together were always pleasant, since Grenita made a great effort to keep the conversation light and impersonal. She never mentioned Stuart, never even alluded to the fact that she knew him—until one bleak afternoon in November.

Grenita was invited for two o'clock, and as was her custom, she arrived promptly on the stroke of the hour. Claire ran lightly down the stairs and pulled open the front door, surprised to find the usually staid widow grinning at her like a giddy schoolgirl. "Grenita," Claire smiled, her expression curious, "don't you look happy today!"

"Oh, I am, my dear," Grenita giggled, stepping into the house and throwing her arms around her astonished friend. "I have the most exciting news. I'm getting married again!"

With a little cry of delight, Claire hugged her. "How wonderful! So, Will Chatsfield finally declared himself, did he?"

"Yes," Grenita nodded happily. "You know, I was beginning to wonder if he ever would, but finally, last night, he asked me to marry him."

Claire laughed and hung Grenita's coat on a brass çoat rack near the front door. Taking her friend's hand, she said, "Let's go into the parlor. I want to hear everything."

The women settled themselves in comfortable chairs, then spent a pleasant hour sipping tea and eating little cakes as Grenita excitedly recounted the story of Will Chatsfield's proposal.

"So, are you going to have a big wedding?" Claire asked.

"Oh, no, just a few close friends. You know, Will's first wife died in childbirth, and since this is a second marriage for both of us, we're keeping it very small."

"Have you set a date yet?"

Grenita nodded. "December eighteenth, at five in the afternoon. You'll come, won't you, Claire?"

"I would love to," Claire answered slowly, "you know I would. But I don't think it's a good idea, considering my situation."

Grenita's face fell. "Oh, please; it would mean so much to me to have you there. There are only going to be a few people. Please say you'll consider it."

"Is Stuart invited?" Claire asked quietly.

"Now, Claire," Grenita answered evasively, "would I invite you if Stuart were going to be there?"

Claire shook her head and smiled. "No, I suppose not. Okay, let me think about it for a couple of days. I really would love to come . . ."

"Then it's settled. I'm putting you down on my list."

"There are going to be enough people that you need a list?" Claire asked warily.

"Don't worry," she giggled. "It's a short list."

Another few minutes passed as the women sipped their tea and chatted about inconsequential things. When a lull finally fell between them, Grenita put down her plate and said casually, "Speaking of Stuart, did I tell you I saw him the other day?"

Claire's teacup clattered to her saucer. "We weren't speaking of Stuart, Grenita, and you know it. But since you're brought it up, no, you didn't tell me you'd seen him."

"Well, I did," Grenita continued cheerily. "He was in town for a business meeting or something and I ran into him at Durgin-Park."

"He likes the lobster there," Claire murmured, thinking back to the evening when the two of them had eaten at the fine old restaurant, then come home and made love all night.

"So," she said, trying desperately to keep her voice casual, "how did he look?"

"Terrible," Grenita said frankly.

Claire's eyes widened with alarm. "What do you mean, 'terrible'? Is he ill?"

"No, he's not ill. At least, not with anything that can be cured with mustard plasters or castor oil. But he's working too hard, drinking too much, and eating and sleeping too little—and it shows."

"I'm sorry to hear that."

Grenita frowned at the impersonal note in her friend's voice. "Claire, have you spoken to him at all?"

Claire shook her head. "Not since last summer."

"Last summer! Why, that's terrible. Don't you think you owe it to yourselves to try to talk your problems out?"

"There's nothing to talk about."

"Claire!" Grenita exclaimed, "how can you say that? The man loves you, and this divorce is killing him."

"Oh, Grenita, you're such a romantic. Stuart doesn't love me. He never did. You just don't understand the situation between us."

"No, I guess I don't," Grenita snapped, the uncharacteristic anger in her voice startling Claire. "Why don't you explain it to me?"

"There's nothing to explain," Claire sighed. "We got married for . . . unusual reasons, and I think both of us knew that once the war ended, our marriage would, too. We really aren't suited to each other, and it's better for both of us just to end this thing and get on with our lives."

"Oh, yes, and you're both doing that so well," Grenita interjected sarcastically. "You live in this house like a mole, and Stuart runs from party to party, smiling and dancing and trying to pretend nothing is wrong. Why, he's still never admitted to anyone that there's a problem between you."

"He hasn't?" Claire gasped. "How could he keep it a secret? Certainly people must ask where I am. What does he tell them?"

Grenita shrugged. "For a long time, he used the excuse that you were mourning your father's death. Now, he just says that you're under the weather or you had a prior engagement."

"Prior engagement!" Claire snorted. "Do people actually believe that?"

"Of course not," Grenita chuckled, "but everyone's far too well bred to call him a liar to his face. Besides, his refusal to admit that anything is wrong just adds grist to the gossip mill."

"This is an impossible situation," Claire moaned, tears glistening in her eyes. "I just wish the whole thing would be over! It'll be so much easier for both of us when the divorce is final and I can go back to Savannah."

"And when will that be?" Grenita asked quietly.

"Not till next June," Claire answered, shaking her head. "It takes a whole year to secure the final decree—even when there's no contest by either party. And since my suit is based on marriage under duress, there are so many things that have to be proved. It's all so painful and embarrassing, Grenita, I don't know if I can stand it another six months."

"Wouldn't it have been easier to seek an annulment?" Grenita asked gently. "I've heard that many marriages that took place under extreme circumstances during the war are being dissolved that way."

Claire looked down at her lap, unable to meet her friend's eyes. "An annulment wasn't possible for us," she mumbled.

"Why not?"

"Because," she gulped, her face turning crimson, "if certain things happen after the marriage takes place, an annulment can no longer be sought.''

Grenita looked baffled for a moment; then, as the realization of what Claire was alluding to finally hit her, she quickly turned away, a secret little smile quirking the corners of her mouth.

Although she had never known the exact reason for the estrangement between Stuart and Claire, she had long suspected that something terrible had happened while they were in Savannah—something serious enough that they had decided to divorce over it. But despite that decision and Claire's protestations that the marriage had not been based on romance, Grenita was still convinced that they loved each other. One only had to look at the sad, haunted expressions they both wore to know that.

And now that Claire had confessed that they had, at least at one time, cared enough about each other to share the most intimate of relationships, Grenita was sure she was doing the right thing by orchestrating a reunion between them at her wedding.

"I have to go now, dearest," she said airily, standing up. "As you can imagine, I have a million things to do between now and the eighteenth."

"I'm sure you do," Claire smiled, looping her arm through her friend's as they strolled out to the foyer. "I'm so happy for you, Grenita. No one deserves this more than you."

"Thank you," Grenita said, genuinely touched. "I'm very happy also. And you will make me even happier if you'll attend the ceremony."

"I'll think about it," Claire promised. "I really will."

"A few close friends," Claire thought with dismay, as she seated herself on a hard chair at the back of the Hilliards' parlor. "There must be at least fifty people here."

She glanced around surreptitiously, trying to determine if anyone had noticed her quiet entrance. Thank the Lord I was a little late, she thought, relieved that most of the guests were facing forward as they waited for the bridegroom to make his entrance. Now if I can just figure a way out of here before the ceremony is over, maybe no one will even realize I was here.

She bit her lip, trying hard not to be angry with Grenita for misleading her about the number of people attending her wedding. Had her friend lied to her on purpose, knowing that if Claire knew the actual size of the expected crowd she wouldn't come, or was it just that to Grenita, fifty people *was* merely a few close friends?

"It doesn't matter," Claire told herself firmly. "You're here now, so just sit back and relax."

A small door at the front of the room opened, admitting Will Chatsfield and his best man— Stuart Wellesley.

Claire nearly fainted.

Quickly, she took several deep breaths, hoping it would calm her spinning head. You *can't* pass out, she thought desperately. If you do, everyone will know that the sight of your own husband made you swoon. She closed her eyes, grabbing onto the sides of her chair as she fought the wave of nausea that suddenly threatened.

A man whom she wasn't aware of ever having seen before leaned over and whispered, "Are you all right, Mrs. Wellesley?"

"Yes," she nodded. "It's just a little close in here."

"Would you like me to escort you out for a breath of air?" he asked solicitously.

"No! I mean, thank you, but I'll be fine. I'm just a little warm."

The man looked at her skeptically, but nodded and leaned back in his chair.

The nausea and lightheadedness passed, but for a long moment, Claire continued to sit with her head down, afraid to raise her eyes. Finally, her curiosity got the better of her and she flicked her gaze upward.

Her heart leaped into her throat as she allowed herself a long look at her husband. She had forgotten how tall he was; how dark his hair, how straight his back. She had forgotten how handsome he was.

His eyes nonchalantly scanned the crowd, lighting on someone whom Claire couldn't see. He graced the object of his perusal with a dazzling smile and Claire could almost hear the collective sighs of the women in the audience. She closed her eyes, thinking back on the hundreds of times he had turned that same smile on her—over the breakfast table, from the opposite seat in his coach, nestled beside her in his big bed.

She swallowed hard, fighting the ever-threatening tears, then stole another look at him. But this time, when she glanced up, he was looking back at her, the expression on his face so startled and disbelieving that several people turned around to see what he was gaping at.

Claire immediately looked away, not wanting to see the anger she knew she would find in his gray eyes. She stared at her lap, threading her gloves between her fingers until finally, the back doors of the parlor opened and the bride made her appearance.

The ceremony ground on endlessly as Claire wallowed in a haze of embarrassed misery. She didn't want to look at Stuart again, but somehow, she couldn't seem to control herself. No matter how hard she tried to focus on the bride and groom, her eyes continually drifted back to where he stood. And every time she looked at him, he was staring back at her: his gaze cool, his mouth set in that hard line that she'd come to know so well during their last days in Savannah.

Finally the music started up again and the radiant bride and groom made the way back up the short aisle. As soon as they had passed her, Claire excused herself to the people next to her and clumsily climbed over their feet in an attempt to make her getaway.

She almost succeeded. Speeding out of the parlor, she flew across the foyer and flung open the front door, causing the Hilliards' stiff-backed butler to stare at her in astonishment.

She was just stepping out onto the stoop when her headlong flight was abruptly halted by a strong hand clamping around her arm. "Merry Christmas, Mrs. Wellesley. Where are you going in such a hurry?"

With a startled gasp, she whirled around to face her husband, her breath catching in her throat as she looked up into his angry face. "I was . . . just leaving," she stammered, nearly speechless with nerves and excitement. It had been such a long time since she'd been this close to him, and he looked so handsome with the winter wind riffling

369

his ebony hair. For a moment, all she wanted to do was throw herself into his arms.

"I think not," he said quietly, tightening his hold on her arm, in case she was thinking about bolting. "It would be an atrocious breach of manners to leave before toasting the bride and groom."

"I don't feel well," she blurted. "I have to go."

Stuart stared at her for a moment, then a small, knowing smile tipped the corners of his mouth. "You didn't know I was going to be here tonight, did you?"

"No, and if I had, I wouldn't have come."

"I'm sure you wouldn't have," he retorted, a look of pain crossing his eyes before he could hide it. "Well, madam, I didn't know you were going to be here, either, but since we've obviously both been duped, we better try to brazen this out."

"What are you talking about?" Claire cried. "I'm not going to stay here and pretend that everything is fine between us."

"Yes, you are."

"No, I'm not!"

"For God's sake, lower your voice," he hissed, tucking her arm firmly through his and walking down the steps away from the house. "Do you want that damn butler to hear every word we say so he can repeat it to every other servant in Boston?"

"I don't care!"

Stuart stared at her for a moment, his face dark and forbidding. "I'm sure you don't," he gritted. "You're going back to Savannah in June, but I have to live here the rest of my life, so I'd appreciate a little cooperation."

So he knew the divorce would be final in June. He obviously had been keeping track of her meetings with her attorney. "All right," she nodded, "I'll cooperate. But just so you know, I think it's absolutely absurd that you're trying to perpetuate this myth about our happy marriage. Do you really think people don't know the truth?"

"I'm sure they do," he admitted, "but I refuse to give them the opportunity of playing the sympathetic and supportive friends when deep down, I know they're all saying, 'I told you so.'"

"Why would they say that?" Claire asked, pausing in their march around the yard to look up at him curiously.

"Because they all did."

"Did what? Why do you always talk in riddles?"

"And why do you always answer a question with a question?"

"Oh, stop it!" she snapped, yanking her arm out of his warm grasp. "Just tell me what you're talking about."

"What I'm talking about is the fact that all the old social cows in Boston are just dying to be sympathetic and understanding to me about our marital problems so that later, they can remind me that they warned me about you."

Claire's mouth dropped open in surprise. "Your friends *warned* you about me?"

"I'd hardly call them my friends, but yes, the old biddies in that house back there took great pains to warn me that as soon as the war was over, you'd leave me and go back to Savannah. And, even though you're proving them right, I don't care to listen to them say 'I told you so.' Now do you understand?"

Claire nodded, disturbed that her actions had caused him such embarrassment over the last few months. Actually, despite her lonely existence, she was probably the lucky one. Hidden away in the house on Louisburg Square, she didn't have to brave the gossip the way he did.

"I'm sorry," she muttered. "I wasn't trying to embarrass you by leaving. In fact, I was leaving so you *wouldn't* be embarrassed."

"Leaving is not the way to save face, Claire. Everyone in there saw you, and if you suddenly disappear, it'll just make the gossip worse."

"But Stuart . . ."

"Look," he sighed, "I don't know who cooked up this little reunion. All I know is that when Grenita and Will asked me to stand up for them at their wedding, I agreed, with the stipulation that you would not be invited."

Claire was surprised at how much his words hurt, even though she had made the same stipulation. "I guess Grenita lied to us both, then," she said coolly, "because I told her the same thing—that I wouldn't attend if you were going to be here."

To her astonishment, Stuart suddenly started to laugh.

"What's funny about this?" Claire demanded.

"What's funny," he said, shaking his head, "is that not wanting to see each other is the first thing we've agreed on in six months, and yet, here we are."

"Yes," she said quietly, "here we are. So, what are we going to do now?"

"Well, I'm going to go back in that house and eat cake and drink champagne and do my damnedest to make those old cats think I have the happiest marriage on the eastern seaboard. And, if you ever cared anything for me, you'll come with me."

"All right," Claire agreed. "I guess I owe you that much."

To her surprise, Stuart suddenly reached for her left hand, lifting it and gazing down at her ruby-and-diamond ring. "At least you're still wearing your wedding ring," he muttered, relieved that he wasn't going to have to come up with a plausible reason why she would not be wearing it.

"Not the one that counts," she retorted. "I took that off a long time ago."

Stuart squinted at her hand in the darkness, confirming that, indeed, she was no longer wearing the inexpensive little gold band he'd given her in Savannah. Slowly, he released her hand, averting his gaze so she wouldn't see the pain in his eyes.

But she did see it, and for a moment, she didn't think she could go back inside with him, didn't think she could stand to spend the evening with him in light of what they were doing to each other. "Stuart," she said quietly, "how long do I need to stay?"

"A couple of dances would be nice," he frowned, interpreting her question to mean that she didn't want to be near him—even for the space of one evening. "Would that be so hard for you to bear?"

No! Claire's mind screamed. It wouldn't be hard at all. It would be the easiest thing in the world, and that's what scares me!

"I suppose not," she sighed, praying he wouldn't hear her pounding heart, "but a couple of dances and a slice of cake is it. After that, I'm going home."

"Agreed," he nodded, again taking her arm and heading back to the house. "I'm no more interested in prolonging this evening than you are."

His caustic words made Claire want to cry, but instead, she drew upon all her resources and threw him a sugary smile. "Good. At least we know exactly where we stand with each other."

"Oh, there's no worry there," he snorted. "I've known exactly where I stood with you for a long, long time."

Chapter Twenty-eight

It was the most bittersweet evening of Claire's life.

As she and Stuart walked back into the Hilliards' house, he took her hand, but Claire immediately pulled away, causing him to scowl at her. "Damn it, take my hand!" he hissed. "There's no sense in doing this if you're going to act like you can't stand to touch me."

With a contrite nod, Claire looped her arm through his.

"And for Christ's sake, smile," he added.

"When did you start swearing so much?" she whispered, pasting a wide smile on her face as they strolled through the foyer.

"I'm not sure, but I think it was about the same time I met you."

Claire nodded and smiled to several people who called out greetings. "Well, try to control yourself in my presence. I find it very offensive."

"Merry Christmas, John. Merry Christmas, Julia." After calling out the greeting to a couple Claire had never met, Stuart again dropped his voice back to a heated undertone. "Quit doing things that make me swear, and I'll quit swearing."

They had reached the parlor doors, and as Stuart started to step through them, Claire paused, tugging lightly on his sleeve until he turned toward her. "Let's stop insulting each other," she suggested. "If we have to spend the next hour together, then let's try to make it as pleasant as possible."

Stuart's tense face relaxed, and he smiled down at her. "I think that's a wonderful idea. And, Claire?"

"Yes?"

"Thank you for doing this."

Claire nodded and looked away, not wanting him to see how much his warmly voiced words were affecting her. It would be so easy to let herself believe that things were all right between them. So easy to pretend that this evening was more than just a sham for the benefit of Boston's society matrons. Be careful, a little voice warned. Remember all the tears he's caused you.

They walked into the parlor and joined the long line waiting to congratulate the newly married couple. Casually, Claire's eyes swept the room as she tried to ascertain what the other guests' reactions were to seeing them together, but she was surprised to find that everyone was ignoring them.

"No one is paying any attention to us," she murmured.

"That's what you think," Stuart returned. "There isn't anybody in this room who isn't watching our every move."

Claire looked at him in bewilderment, but before she could say anything further, she noticed Sally Rutherford and her mother, Mildred, bearing down on them.

"Get ready," Stuart advised softly, "it's starting."

"Good evening, Mrs. Rutherford, Sally," he nodded as the duo approached. "Lovely wedding, wasn't it?"

"Very lovely," Mildred agreed, then immediately turned her attention on Claire. "What a surprise to see you, Mrs. Wellesley. None of us expected you to be here."

Stuart felt Claire stiffen. "As I'm sure you know, Mrs. Rutherford," he interjected quickly, "my wife has been in mourning for her father, but we agreed that since she and Grenita are such close friends, it would be appropriate for her to attend this evening."

His emphasis on the word "we" was not lost on any of the women, including Claire, who thanked him by lightly squeezing his arm.

"Stuart," Sally cooed, "when are you going to have a party at your new house in Marblehead? We're all just dying to see it."

"As soon as it's finished," Claire jumped in. "It needed renovating when Stuart first purchased it, and they have taken much longer to complete the improvements than either of us anticipated."

Sally's eyes widened with startled surprise. "Really? Why, I didn't know you were even involved. We all thought you were living in the Louisburg Square house."

"She is," Stuart said smoothly. "The Marblehead house is barely habitable at this point, what with plaster and sawdust everywhere. I've been staying there to supervise the work, but I wouldn't think of subjecting Claire to such unpleasant living conditions."

Mildred Rutherford's eyes narrowed as she stared pointedly at the smiling Claire. She didn't for one minute believe this cock-and-bull story the couple was promoting, and she was dying to catch them in their elaborate lie. There had to be some way to crumble Claire's veneer. She thought for a minute, then nearly laughed out loud as she pounced upon what she was sure would be a chink in the girl's armor.

"Well, Claire," she sighed, "I must say, I truly admire you. It's a rare woman who wouldn't be concerned about the state of her marriage, knowing her husband was attending social engagement after social engagement while she sat home alone. Why, for the first several years I was married, I didn't let my Henry out of my sight, for fear that another woman might snatch him away when I wasn't looking . . ."

Claire feigned a look of shock. "Why, Mrs. Rutherford," she drawled, exaggerating a southern belle simper, "it never occurred to me to worry about such a thing, but then, I've always believed that truly good marriages are based on a foundation of absolute trust. It's a subject Stuart and I have discussed at length." Turning, she looked up at Stuart with an adoring expression. "Haven't we, darling?"

"Yes," Stuart nodded, throwing her a wry glance, "at length."

"Well, of course, trust is imperative in any close relationship," Mildred said, not quite understanding what Claire was driving at.

"I'm glad you agree," Claire nodded. "And I'm sorry that the first few years of your marriage were so uneasy. It must have been terrible for you to live with that kind of doubt."

"I beg your pardon. I never doubted my husband!"

"But didn't worrying about his possible infidelities cause you enormous worry?" Claire asked, her voice fairly dripping with concern.

"I was never worried about Henry!"

"Oh, I'm sorry," Claire said quickly, her expression innocently contrite. "I must have misunderstood when you said you were afraid to let your husband out of your sight for fear he'd run off with another woman."

"I did not say that!" Mildred shrieked, her voice so strident that several people turned to look at her curiously.

"Please don't upset yourself," Claire pleaded, reaching forward and patting the woman's arm reassuringly. "I'm sure it's my mistake. I thought you said . . ."

"Mother," Sally interrupted suddenly, "there are the Goulds. We need to say hello to them."

Mildred didn't even seem to be aware that Sally had spoken, as she continued to stand and stare in outraged fury at Claire.

"Mother!" Sally said insistently, trying to gain Mildred's attention without making a scene in front of the gathering crowd of onlookers. "We have to talk to the Goulds. *Right now!*"

Swinging her gaze over to Stuart, Sally said, "Will you excuse us, please?" Then, without waiting for an answer, she grabbed her mother's arm, propelling her forcefully to the other side of the room.

"Have a pleasant evening, y'all," Claire called after them, waving gaily, "and Merry Christmas!"

After the women's hasty departure, she looked up at Stuart, suddenly not sure about how he would react to her outrageous confrontation with one of Boston society's premier matrons. But to her intense relief, he started to laugh, a choked sound that betrayed the fact that he had been holding it in for some time.

"I'm sorry," she whispered, her own lips twitching with amusement, "I know I shouldn't have said those things to her, but I just couldn't seem to help myself."

"You are the wickedest woman I've ever met," Stuart said, his voice strangled as he tried to hide his nearly uncontrollable mirth.

"I just hope she won't take her anger out on you later."

"She wouldn't dare. Not in front of all these people."

"I don't mean later tonight. I mean *later* . . . after I'm gone."

Her reminder that their momentary camaraderie was just that made Stuart feel as if he'd been dashed with icewater. His grin vanished and with a dispirited sigh he said, "Don't worry about it. I'll handle it when the time comes."

An awkward silence fell between them, remaining until they finally reached the head of the receiving line.

"Best wishes, Grenita," Claire murmured, forcing a strained smile as she hugged her friend. "It was a beautiful ceremony."

"Oh, my dear, I'm so happy to see you two together," Grenita whispered. "I just knew that once you saw each other again . . ."

Claire stepped back, cutting off Grenita's words with a shake of her head. "Don't get your hopes up," she said softly, "we're not reconciling."

"But," Grenita stammered, her face falling, "I

saw the two of you laughing together just a moment ago."

"I know, but it's just an act for the benefit of the other guests. I promised Stuart that since we were both here and forced to spend the evening together, I'd not embarrass him in front of his friends."

"Oh, Claire," Grenita moaned, "I'm so sorry if I put you in an awkward position. Will and I both thought that if the two of you just had a chance to talk . . ."

"I know your intentions were good," Claire smiled, "but much too much has happened between us for a simple talk to right things. As soon as we can discreetly manage it, I'm going to leave. I just want you to know that so you're not upset if I suddenly disappear."

Grenita looked as if she might cry. "Will you at least stay long enough to have something to eat?" she pleaded.

"Of course. And I wouldn't miss the bridal toast for the world."

"Did you know Stuart is delivering it?" Grenita whispered miserably.

Claire closed her eyes for a moment, then opened them again and forced a wan smile. "Of course he would. He's the best man."

"Is that going to bother you?"

"No," Claire lied. "Absolutely not. Stuart is a gifted speaker, and I'm sure his toast will be very eloquent and heartfelt. There probably won't be a dry eye in the room."

At that moment, Stuart stepped up beside her, having finished a rather lengthy conversation with Will. "Best wishes, Grenita," he smiled. "I know you and Will are going to be very happy."

"I'm sure we will be, too," Grenita murmured. "And . . . thank you both so much for coming. Having you here means a great deal to us."

"It's our pleasure," Stuart assured her, valiantly attempting to put the poor, guilt-ridden woman at ease. "Now, my dear," he said, turning to Claire, "we better move along. There are a lot of people behind us waiting to offer felicitations. We'll see you a little later, Grenita."

Grenita nodded, her heart breaking as she watched the beautiful, sad couple move off to a corner of the parlor where they stood and silently sipped champagne.

Claire thought dinner would never end. Because Stuart was part of the wedding party, they were seated at the head table, facing the rest of the guests. Knowing that every eye was upon them, Stuart made a concerted effort to lavish her with husbandly attention, even going so far as to offer her tidbits off his plate.

When the dishes were finally cleared away, the bride and groom rose to cut their wedding cake. After feeding each other the traditional first piece, they returned to the table while white-jacketed waiters efficiently poured out glasses of champagne for all the celebrants.

After the last guest had been served, Stuart rose and lifted his glass, cuing the other guests to do the same. When all fifty glasses were raised, he took a deep breath and said, "We are gathered here tonight for a very special celebration. It is particularly so for me, since, as most of you know, Grenita and I have been friends for most of our lives. I shared her happiness at her first marriage,

382

and grieved with her when she so cruelly lost her husband at the battle of Gettysburg. It was my fondest wish that she would find happiness again, and I am most thankful to Will Chatsfield for granting me that wish.

"Now," he continued, turning toward the bridal couple, "I have several wishes that I hope will be granted to you two. I wish you health, prosperity, and long life. I wish you the blessings of children and grandchildren. But, most of all, I wish you a lifetime of endless love—and the faith and trust in one another that is the one true key to making love endure. To Grenita and Will!"

As the crowd echoed the couple's names, Claire set her glass down and raised her napkin to hide her shaking lips. Faith and trust and enduring love . . . how could they have gone so wrong?

Out in the crowd, Mildred Rutherford leaned over to Sally and hissed, "Do you suppose Stuart was directing those words about trust to me?"

"No," Sally negated, her eyes glued to Claire. "He was directing them to his wife."

Mildred's eyes widened as she focused in on the visibly shaken Claire. "You're right," she gasped. "Why, look at her. She looks like she's going to cry."

"Wonderful, isn't it?" Sally smiled snidely. "They can say all they want to about how happy they are, but take my word for it, Mother, something is very, very wrong between Mr. and Mrs. Wellesley. It's my guess that by this time next year, they won't be married anymore."

"And you'll be right there to comfort poor Stuart, won't you?" Mildred chuckled.

"Absolutely," Sally nodded, her eyes dancing as she picked up her champagne glass and took another sip. "You can count on it."

Stuart sat back down next to Claire, looking at her out of the corner of his eye to see if she had gleaned what he had so desperately tried to tell her in his toast, but she was casually dabbing at her lips with her napkin and gave no sign that she had understood his hidden message.

He sighed, toying with the piece of cake that had been set in front of him. Grenita and Will got up and headed for the ballroom to lead off the first waltz. They were quickly followed by most of the guests. "Would you like to dance?" Stuart asked, as the dining room emptied.

Claire shrugged, not trusting herself to speak. "I suppose so."

"We don't have to, if you'd rather just sit here."

"No," she said abruptly, realizing that the last thing she wanted to do was remain in the empty room with him. "Let's dance."

They rose and followed the rest of the party into the ballroom.

A wave of sadness washed over Claire as she stepped into the huge room and remembered that the last time she'd been there had been at her own wedding celebration.

The memories made her throat feel tight as she choked back a knot of unshed tears, and for a long moment, she hovered near the door, unable to go any further.

"Don't think about it," Stuart said softly, seeming to read her mind. Giving her hand a little squeeze, he gently pulled her into the room. They stood near the door, waiting until Grenita and Will finished their nuptial waltz. Then, as the small orchestra struck up another piece, they stepped out onto the floor, picking up the tempo of the music with a natural grace.

"I always thought you danced better than any girl I've ever known," Stuart said quietly.

Claire smiled and moved a fraction of an inch closer, breathing deeply of his familiar spicy cologne.

The waltz ended and another soon started. This time, Stuart didn't even ask her if she wanted to dance again. He merely pulled her back into his arms and spun her effortlessly around the floor.

When the second dance ended, he led her over to the ballroom doors.

"Where are we going?" she asked.

"That's two," he shrugged.

"Two what?"

"Two dances. You said outside you'd stay long enough to have a slice of cake and dance a couple of dances. Well, we've had cake and we've danced twice. I figured you'd want to leave now."

"Oh," she stammered, dismay obvious in her voice. "Well, of course I'm anxious to leave, but first, I have to say goodnight to Grenita and Will."

"I could say your farewells for you," Stuart assured her, his pulse racing at her obvious reluctance to go.

"No!" Claire said quickly. "I mean, I wouldn't feel right about that. I'll go back in and say goodbye."

"All right," Stuart nodded agreeably.

Claire took several steps back into the ballroom, then turned and looked at him curiously. "Aren't you coming?"

"Me? I don't want to say goodnight. I'm not leaving yet."

"Well, yes, but won't it look strange if I go back in there alone?"

"It might at that," Stuart agreed, walking over to where she stood and again hooking her arm through his. "I'll escort you."

Together they strolled along the perimeter of the highly polished floor as Claire's eyes scanned the crowd for Grenita and Will. "Oh, they're dancing again," she said, pointing vaguely in the direction of where the newlyweds were waltzing.

"Guess we'll just have to wait until this piece is over."

"Yes, I guess we will."

They stood in silence for a moment, then Stuart said casually, "I don't suppose you'd like to dance once more while we wait."

"Why not?" Claire shrugged, her heart pounding. Again they merged with the crowd.

The evening flew by in a haze of waltzes, champagne, and conversation. Every time either of them mentioned Claire's leaving, the other found an excuse to prevent it. Either they couldn't spot Grenita and Will, or there were too many people blocking their way to get to them, or the couple was involved in speaking with someone else. Even they were amazed at how creative they became in preventing Claire's departure.

As the evening waned, the candlelight became dimmer and the dances became slower. Grenita and Will had long since departed, and many of the older guests had left as well.

It was well after midnight when the orchestra's violinist stood up and announced, "This will be the last dance, ladies and gentlemen, so enjoy it." Tucking his instrument under his chin, he lifted his bow, and a slow, haunting melody flowed over the small group still assembled.

Without a word, Stuart drew Claire close. It was

late, they were tired, and both of them knew this might be the last time they ever danced together. Slowly, they moved about the floor, swaying to the music and holding each other close. By the end of the long dance, they were so wrapped up in one another that they barely noticed when the music stopped. It wasn't until the other couples started applauding the violinist's virtuoso performance that they finally stepped apart, both overwhelmed by the intimacy they had just shared.

"I'll call my carriage round and get your cloak," Stuart said quietly, and walked off toward the door. Claire watched him go, her heart thudding heavily in her chest with a dull ache she knew would never completely go away.

With dragging feet, she went into the foyer where Stuart was just collecting her cloak from the Hilliards' butler. He saw her coming toward him and with a strained smile, swirled the beautiful wrap around her shoulders. "Is this one of the cloaks I bought for you last winter?" he asked.

Claire nodded, knowing that if she opened her mouth, she'd start sobbing.

"It looks nice on you."

She didn't respond.

They climbed into his coach, sitting opposite each other, and headed for Louisburg Square. A heavy silence enshrouded them until finally, Claire asked dully, "Are you going back to Marblehead tonight?"

"No. It's too late. I've joined a club here in town, and I can sleep there."

Dismally, she nodded, and again, silence fell.

As they pulled up in front of the townhouse, Claire turned toward him, her eyes brimming with tears. "I'm glad I went tonight, Stuart. It was . . .

good to see you."

"Claire, for God's sake . . ."

She held up her hand, knowing that if he said a single beckoning word, she'd break down. "Please don't say anything," she begged. "Just listen to me for a minute."

He sat back, nodding slowly. "I'm listening."

"What I want to say is this," she mumbled, her voice choked with tears. "Since this is probably the last time we'll see each other, I want you to know that I'm sorry about, well, about the way everything turned out between us. I do appreciate all you did for me to save me from my own foolishness in Savannah, and I hope . . . I hope that someday you'll find someone who can truly make you happy." She broke off, a sob catching in her throat.

"Claire, please, let me come in, and we'll . . ."

"No. I have to go now, Stuart." Frantically, she made a grab for the door handle, but paused as his hand covered hers.

"Can I kiss you goodnight?" he whispered.

"No," she croaked, her voice breaking as tears streaked down her cheeks. With a lunge, she flung open the carriage door, nearly falling in her rush to get out. She slammed the door, then turned to take one last look at him through the glass-paned window.

"Goodbye, Stuart."

Before he could answer, she whirled away and flew up the sidewalk, throwing open the door to the townhouse and disappearing inside.

Stuart watched her enter the house, then leaned back in the seat, his shoulders slumping with defeat.

"Goodbye, Claire."

Chapter Twenty-nine

The day had finally arrived.

Claire stood and looked out the parlor window, gripping a tattered piece of paper as she watched two burly men loading her trunks into a large wagon. She really was leaving today. The heartbreak of the past year was finally over.

Smoothing the wrinkled note she held, she gazed down at the message from her attorney, reading it for the thousandth time.

Dear Mrs. Wellesley,

Your petition for divorce has been granted, and the papers are ready for your signature.

Please be in my office at three o'clock on Monday, June 19, to finalize the documents.

If there is a problem with this date or time, please advise.

Sebastian Caldwell

With a sigh, Claire looked out the window again at the perfect summer morning. It seemed ironic that it should be such a beautiful day. Somehow, it would have been more appropriate if it had been storming. "No, storms wouldn't be right, either," she murmured to herself. "The storms are past. But it should be gray. Dull and gray—and cold."

With a bittersweet smile, she turned away from the window just as one of the men who had been loading her luggage walked through the open front door of the house.

"Everything you gave us is loaded, Mrs. Wellesley," he announced. "Is there anything else?"

"No," Claire replied with a shake of her head. "That's all of it."

"Then we'll be leaving for the station now. You said the five-thirty southbound train, right?"

"Yes."

"Okay, then, your trunks will be waiting for you when you get there."

"Thank you, sir, for all your help." Walking over to where her reticule lay on a small table, Claire picked it up and looked at the man expectantly. "How much do I owe you?"

"Nothing, ma'am. It's already been taken care of."

"Taken care of?" Claire asked. "By whom?"

"Why, your husband, I think. Tall, well-dressed, dark-haired man?"

Claire nodded.

"That's the one, then. He came into my place a couple days ago and paid for the job in advance."

Claire shook her head, amazed by Stuart's ability to figure out her every move. "Do you know how my husband knew I had engaged you?"

"Sorry, I don't. I just know he came in and paid me and my partner for a whole day of our time, so if there's anything else you need done around here, we'd be happy to help."

"No," Claire said, setting down her bag. "There's nothing else."

"Well, then, thanks for the business." With a bob of his head, the man walked back out into the sunshine. "That's it, Ned," he called to his partner. "Let's go."

Claire stood in the doorway and watched as the wagon lumbered off down the street. Then, she slowly closed the door and wandered back into the parlor, gazing around wanly at the sheet-covered furniture.

So, Stuart had paid the movers. He had even thought of that. It was the same experience she'd had over and over the previous week when she'd gone round to settle her accounts with various merchants. Her dressmaker, her grocer, even her attorney had informed her that she owed them nothing—that her bill had been paid in full by Mr. Wellesley.

Most startling of all had been the short note she'd received from the Bank of Boston, informing her that fifty thousand dollars had been deposited into an account in her name at her bank in Savannah. *Fifty thousand dollars!*

The note also advised her that all taxes and liens on her childhood home had been paid, and that an escrow account had been set up to cover future levies.

Claire had promptly sat down and written a letter to Stuart, telling him that as much as she appreciated his generosity, she couldn't possibly accept such an enormous settlement from him.

She had received no reply.

Glancing at a small stone clock that sat on the fireplace mantel, she roused herself from her lethargy and started up the stairs, intending to change into a traveling suit. She was barely halfway up the staircase, however, when she heard a knock at the front door. Reversing herself, she walked back down the stairs and opened the front door, smiling when she saw Louisa Alcott standing on the stoop.

"Am I catching you at a bad time, Claire?"

"Of course not," Claire lied. "Come right in."

A hesitant little smile played around the corners of Louisa's mouth. "I'll only keep you a minute," she said nervously. "I saw the men loading your trunks this morning. Are you taking a trip?"

"Not exactly. I'm going back to Savannah."

Louisa nodded. "I thought as much. And, since you've told me that, there's something I feel I have to tell you."

Claire ushered her friend toward the parlor, her curiosity rampant. "Please excuse the state of the house," she apologized, whipping a dust cover off the settee and tossing it on a chair.

"Certainly," Louisa answered distractedly. "I understand." Sitting down, she drew a deep breath. "I know you're busy, so I'll get right to the point. Do you remember that first day when we met in the park and I told you that in a small neighborhood like Louisburg Square, everyone seems to know everyone else's business?"

Claire nodded warily.

"Well, your situation is no different. For some time now, most of us on the street have known that you and Mr. Wellesley are . . . are . . ."

"Estranged," Claire finished.

"Yes," Louisa nodded, ducking her head in embarrassment, "estranged. I don't know what the situation is between you, and it's none of my business, but for months now, I have been thinking about a conversation I had with your husband one day."

"You had a conversation with Stuart? About me?"

"Well, not exactly." Louisa emitted a shuddering sigh, wringing her hands together until her fingers turned white. "I feel terrible about repeating something that was said to me in confidence, but I can't help but think that what he and I talked about that day might be important for you to know. I've vacillated for months about whether I should say anything, but when I saw your trunks this morning, I decided I had to speak my piece."

"Good heavens, Louisa," Claire cried. "Whatever did Stuart say to put you in such a state?"

"It was very strange, actually. I was taking my morning constitutional and he approached me, asking me if I would answer a hypothetical question for him. I must admit, I was very curious, so I agreed."

"Yes? Yes?" Claire encouraged, wishing the kindly woman would get to the point.

"Just a minute, now," Louisa mused. "Let me see if I can remember exactly how he posed the question." She paused, staring out the front window so long that Claire wanted to scream.

"Oh, yes," she said finally. "I remember. He said, 'If you were writing a book and the protagonist in your story knew a secret . . . a secret that if divulged to his wife would possibly end their marriage, could you still write the character as a man of honor if he didn't tell her?'"

Claire blanched and raised a shaking hand to her mouth. "And what did you tell him?" she whispered.

"Well, first of all, I asked him if the secret directly involved the character's wife, and he said 'Yes.' Then, I asked him if the wife's life would be seriously altered if she knew this secret, and he said, 'Yes, but probably not for the better.'"

Despite her shock at Louisa's startling revelation, Claire couldn't help but smile. It was so typical of Stuart that his arrogance would assert itself even in the face of a serious moral dilemma.

"Finally," Louisa continued, "I asked him if the protagonist's life would be altered by divulging the secret to his wife, and he said, 'More than just altered. His life would probably be completely ruined. You see, he is deeply in love with his wife, and telling her the truth will probably cause him to lose her.'"

"So, what did you decide?" Claire prompted, pulling a handkerchief out of the pocket of the dust apron she was wearing and dabbing at her eyes. "Did you tell him that you could still write the character as a man of honor?"

"Yes, I did," Louisa nodded. "I told him that if his divulging the secret would end the protagonist's marriage, thus ruining his happiness, while also causing his wife to be thrown into a situation where she wouldn't be happy, either, then I felt the character might show more honor by keeping the information to himself."

"And how did Stuart react?"

"Well, this is what's so strange—he argued with me. He said that he didn't see how the man could retain his honor when his motivations for keeping the secret were basically selfish, but I pointed out that if the truth of a situation does nothing but hurt everyone involved, then perhaps the truth is better left unsaid."

"Did he agree?"

"I'm not sure," Louisa shrugged. "He seemed . . . relieved, but I don't think he really agreed with my reasoning. Does any of this make any sense to you, Claire, or have I just wasted your time telling you this story?"

"No," Claire negated, leaning forward and giving Louisa a warm hug, "you haven't wasted my time. In fact, you may have just told me the most important story of my life. Tell me one more thing, though. When was this conversation?"

"Oh," Louisa sighed, "let me think. I seem to remember that there were flowers blooming, so I would guess it was probably early May."

"May," Claire murmured, "and he found out in late April."

"Pardon me?" Louisa said politely.

"Oh, nothing."

Louisa rose, smiling at Claire hopefully. "Will any of what I've told you make you change your mind about leaving Boston?"

Claire shook her head. "No, I'm afraid it's too late to change my mind about that, but I do appreciate your telling me this. It is a great comfort."

"Mr. Wellesley's hypothetical characters were actually the two of you, weren't they?"

"Yes," Claire admitted.

"I thought so."

The two women walked to the front door, embracing as they said goodbye.

"Claire, could I say one more thing?" Louisa

asked when they finally stepped away from each other.

"Certainly."

"I want you to know that I've never known a man more in love with his wife than Mr. Wellesley is with you."

Claire looked startled. "You gathered that just from that one conversation?"

"Oh, no. I've talked to your husband many times, and whenever your name came up in the conversation, he would sort of light up. I just thought you should know that."

"Thank you, Louisa," Claire said, smiling tremulously. "Thank you for everything. I'm going to miss you."

"I'll miss you, too, but if you'll send me your address, I promise I'll write, and when my book about the four sisters is published, I'll send you a copy."

"I'd like that."

With one last smile, Louisa started down the steps, then turned back, saying, "By the way, I finally thought of a title for it. I'm going to call it *Little Women.*"

Claire walked slowly back into the house, flopping down on the settee as she pondered all that Louisa had told her.

If only I'd known about this earlier, she thought dismally, maybe things would have been different. Maybe we could have worked things out . . .

But it was much too late to consider that, especially in light of how much her relationship with Stuart had changed in the last six months.

After Grenita's wedding, Stuart had seemed to undergo a reversal in his attitude toward her, almost as if, after their heart-wrenching farewell that night, he had accepted the fact that their marriage was truly over. Gone was the angry, icy silence that had predominated the first few months of their estrangement. Instead, he now occasionally sent her notes—short, impersonal messages letting her know that he had completed some minor business transaction on behalf of her father's estate, or advising her on how to reach him if he was going out of town and something came up that she couldn't handle.

He had even sent her a small gift at Christmas and another on her birthday in April. The gifts, although tasteful and carefully selected, were inexpensive enough that she did not feel compelled to return them. Rather, in both cases, she had sent a brief thank-you note, written in the same language she might have used with a casual friend.

Although Claire was relieved that Stuart no longer seemed to harbor any bitterness toward her, his new, self-imposed role of financial adviser was more heartbreaking to bear than his anger had been. Somehow it relegated her to the status of a "client." And his notes to her, no matter how thoughtful and concerned, were so businesslike that there was no doubt in her mind that he had truly ceased to care for her on any sort of personal level.

Claire had spent many hours trying to analyze why Stuart's change of heart should hurt so badly. She should be grateful. Grateful that they were no longer at swords' points, grateful that he was willing to put his vast business knowledge to work on her behalf, grateful that he had not abandoned her to the carpetbaggers who could so easily have stolen everything she still owned in Savannah.

Why did his new attitude make her so sad? The answer was so appalling that in all the months that had passed since Grenita's wedding, she had refused to give voice to it—even to herself. Until today.

Now, as she sat on the familiar velvet settee, contemplating the quiet, empty house around her and the quiet, empty life that lay ahead of her, there didn't seem to be a good reason to deny it any longer. The furniture was covered, the train ticket purchased, the trunks sent to the station, and the final appointment with her attorney confirmed. It was far too late to change the tide of events, so she could finally allow herself to admit the truth: she still loved him.

Loved him, despite all the things he'd told her that weren't true and all the things he hadn't told her that were. Somehow, none of what had ripped apart the fabric of their marriage seemed very important anymore.

"Fine time to figure it out," she murmured, "now that it's too late to do anything about it."

"Whenever your name came into a conversation, he would sort of light up," Louisa had said.

"But that was over a year ago," she told herself firmly, as Louisa's haunting words floated through her mind, "and, unfortunately, that light went out a long time ago."

With a sigh, she glanced up at the mantel clock, then quickly rose, forcing her melancholy thoughts to the back of her mind as she realized how late it was getting.

"Change your clothes, sign the papers, and get

on the train," she said loudly, as she walked through the foyer. "Don't think about the past, don't think about the future, don't think about what might have been. Just change your clothes, sign the papers, and get on the train."

Steadfastly, she marched up the stairs.

Chapter Thirty

It was nearly two-thirty by the time Claire was dressed and ready to leave for Mr. Caldwell's office. The cab she had engaged had already been parked outside the townhouse for more than fifteen minutes when she finally came racing down the stairs, haphazardly pinning a hat into her auburn curls.

When she heard the knock at the door, she nearly screamed with frustration. "Now who?" she gritted, clenching her teeth. "I've had more visitors today than I have in the last two months."

She yanked open the door, intending to tell whatever well-intentioned friend might be standing on the other side that she simply didn't have time for a visit. However, her words died in her throat when she was met by a small, gnarled man, holding the largest bouquet of roses she'd ever seen.

"Yes?" she asked hesitantly, convinced that he must be at the wrong address. "May I help you?"

"You Mrs. Wellesley?"

"Yes, but I think there must be some mistake. Those couldn't be for me."

"Well, they are. I wasn't supposed to deliver 'em till after four o'clock, but my wife took sick and I want to get home. I hope you don't mind if they're a little early. When you think about it, it'll just give you a few more hours to enjoy 'em."

"You're right," she nodded dumbly. "Who are they from?"

"There's a card," the man answered, thrusting the bouquet into her arms. "Must be someone who thinks a lot of you, though. I had to rob nearly every florist in Boston to get my hands on this many roses all at once."

"Well, thank you," Claire stammered, reaching over to a table by the door to pick up her reticule. She pushed the mountain of flowers down with her chin as she fumbled to find a tip for the man, but finally gave up the fight and laid the bouquet down.

"If you'll wait just a minute . . ."

"That's not necessary, ma'am," the old man wheezed, amused by her struggles. "The gentleman that bought 'em, he already gave me somethin' extra for deliverin' 'em. I'd be obliged if you wouldn't tell him they were early, though. He was pretty specific about when they were supposed to get here. But, you see, my wife, she's real sick, and . . ."

"Yes," Claire interrupted, desperate to be rid of the old man so she could open the card. "I'm sure he would understand. Thank you so much for bringing them."

Shoving the door closed, she whirled around, bending over and inhaling deeply of the flowers' heady aroma as she fished around frantically for the card. She finally found it and with shaking hands, lifted it out of the dense foliage, her heart slamming against her ribs as she stared at her name penned in Stuart's bold scrawl.

For a long moment, she just held the envelope, almost afraid to open it and read the message. "Don't be a ninny," she told herself sternly. "It's going to say 'Goodbye,' that's all."

Finally, she turned it over and broke the seal, slowly lifting out the cream-colored vellum card. Printed on it were nine words. No salutation, no signature. Just nine words. The nine most beautiful words she had ever read:

I will love you till the day I die.

With a shriek of joy, she clutched the card to her chest and whirled around in little circles. When she finally slowed her crazy dance, she grabbed the bouquet and tore out of the house, running down the sidewalk.

"It's all right, lady," the driver of her rented carriage called. "We've got plenty of time to get downtown by three."

"I don't want to go downtown," Claire shouted, skidding to a halt before the astonished man and grinning at him like a madwoman. "I want to go to Marblehead. Can you take me to Marblehead?"

"Marblehead!" the man gasped. "Now, wait a minute, lady. Are you sure you're feeling all right?"

"I'm feeling wonderful!" she giggled, "but I have to get to Marblehead. Can you take me there, or not?"

"Well, sure, I suppose so, but it's going to cost you."

"I don't care what it costs. Whatever your fee is, I'll pay it. Just take me to Marblehead, and get me there quick!"

"Yes, ma'am," he grinned, thinking her completely demented but not caring, as long as she had the price of the fare.

Eagerly, she climbed into the carriage, then frowned at the driver when she realized he wasn't moving. "Well, come on, let's go!"

"Don't you think you should close your front door first?"

"My front door?" she repeated, looking at him in bewilderment.

"Yeah," he said, pointing at the gaping door of the townhouse. "Your front door. Don't you think you should close it?"

"Oh, yes, I suppose so," she snorted, hefting herself off the carriage seat.

"Never mind," he laughed, "I'll close it for you." Sprinting up the walk, he slammed the front door, pausing long enough to make sure it was locked, then returned to the cab.

"All right, lady, hold on to your hat, 'cause here we go." Giving the horses a smart slap with the reins, they lurched off at a bone-jarring gait.

The wild dash up the coast took less than two hours, and for most of that time, Claire sat hugging her roses and smiling with the sheer pleasure of being alive and on her way to meet her love. It wasn't until they were nearing the outskirts of the little seaside town of Marblehead that she began to have misgivings.

The florist had said that Stuart had given strict

instructions not to deliver the roses until after four o'clock. That meant he hadn't wanted her to receive them until *after* she had signed the final divorce papers. But why? The card said that he would love her till the day he died. Didn't that mean he wanted to reconcile?

Laying the roses down on the seat beside her, she rummaged in her reticule until she found the card. She pulled it out, staring at it as if trying to read some hidden meaning into the simple words.

I will love you till the day I die.

Drawing a shaky breath, she pressed the card against her heart, praying that she was doing the right thing.

Please, she prayed, make him be glad to see me. Please!

By the time the cab turned on to Washington Street, Claire was nearly beside herself with doubt. This is a mistake, she thought desperately. I shouldn't have come here unannounced. What if he isn't glad to see me? What if he turns me away?

She nearly jumped out of her skin when the carriage came to a sudden halt and she heard the driver's voice, bawling, "Okay, lady, here we are."

Claire slowly climbed out of the cab, praying that her wobbly legs would hold her up. "How much do I owe you?" she asked.

"You going back?"

"I . . . I don't know. I might be."

"Well, then, why don't I wait until you decide? Tell you what. Give me five bucks to cover the trip up here and I'll wait ten minutes. If you don't come out by then, I'll assume you're staying and I'll leave. How's that?"

Claire nodded and handed him five dollars.

Then, clutching her roses in a death grip, she turned and took her first look at the house Stuart had bought for her. The sight that met her made her gasp in disbelief.

It wasn't a house . . . it was a mansion. The dwelling was shaped like an immense, three-story-tall box, constructed as a classic example of Georgian architecture. Even in the shadowy twilight, Claire could tell that there must be at least eight bedrooms, and from the height of the building, each floor must boast twenty-foot ceilings. The front door was protected by a portico flanked by four pillars, and atop the shallow roof stood a six-sided cupola, with glass on all sides to ensure a spectacular view of the ocean beyond.

As Claire stood gaping at the magnificent house, someone inside lit a lamp. "Thank the Lord," she muttered, staring at the golden glow beaming through the window, "at least someone is home."

With hesitant footsteps, she slowly approached, treading noiselessly up the short walk until she stood before the massive front door. Swallowing hard and murmuring a quick, fervent prayer, she lifted her hand and knocked.

The door immediately swung open, revealing Stuart, dressed in a beautiful gray serge suit, his hat and walking stick in one hand.

For an endless moment, he just stared at her, his eyes flicking from her face to the crushed roses and back again. "Did you sign the papers?" he asked quietly.

"No," she smiled, shaking her head.

"Are you going to?"

"No."

"Why not?"

"Because I received roses from a man who said he'd love me till the day he died."

"Oh, my God," Stuart groaned, dropping his hat and pulling her to him. "Claire, my sweet, precious wife. Tell me you're still mine."

"I am," Claire answered, her voice choked with tears and laughter. "I think I always have been."

"I know you have," he muttered thickly, tipping her head back to kiss her. "I've known it forever. It was you who wouldn't believe it."

"Until today," she sighed, throwing her head back as he began feverishly kissing her neck. "I finally understood today."

"Why? Because of the roses? You weren't supposed to get them until tonight."

Goosebumps sprang up all over her body as he ran his tongue down the cords of her throat. "I know. The man brought them early because his wife was sick and he had to get home. But I didn't come just because of the roses."

"What else, then?" he asked, his voice muffled as he continued to kiss her neck.

"Louisa Alcott."

"What about her?"

"She told me about a conversation she had with you . . . oh, Stuart, I can't talk if you keep doing that!"

Reluctantly, Stuart raised his head, his eyes aflame with desire. "Do you really want to talk about this now?" he asked, his voice rough. "Wouldn't you rather go upstairs and talk about it in bed?"

"If we go to bed, we won't talk," Claire protested.

"Sure we will. We've got all night. We'll squeeze in a few minutes of conversation, I promise."

"No, we won't," she laughed, firmly pushing him away. "Besides, it looks like you are going somewhere." She gestured toward a large valise sitting near the door.

"I was," he admitted, "but I don't have to now."

"Why?"

"Because you're here."

"What difference does that make?"

"A big one," he chuckled, "since I was going to Savannah."

"Savannah!" Claire cried, gaping at him in disbelief. "Why in the world were you going to Savannah?"

"To ask you to marry me," he answered simply.

"What?"

"I figured if we started over, things might work out differently this time. So I was going to Savannah to propose to you."

"Oh, Stuart, you are absolutely mad!"

"Just about you," he growled, again pulling her into his arms. "Get rid of those damn roses. I can't kiss you properly with those thorny things between us."

"No! Those 'thorny things,' as you call them, are very important to me."

"I'll buy you a hundred more tomorrow," he promised, trying to take them from her.

"It wouldn't be the same. There could never be another bouquet of roses as beautiful as these."

"I'm glad you like them, but I still want you to put them down so I can kiss you."

Reluctantly, Claire set down her bouquet and

408

turned back into his arms. "One more kiss," she smiled, "then, I want to talk."

Their "one kiss" lasted a good three minutes, and when they finally broke apart, Stuart wasn't sure he was still capable of talking. "I love you, Claire," he breathed, dipping his head to kiss her again.

Claire smiled, reveling in the words she thought never to hear from him again. She allowed him another long kiss, then took a decisive step backward. "Talk," she whispered.

"All right. Come on, we'll go into the drawing room." Taking her hand, he led her across the marble-floored foyer into an immense salon whose walls were covered with hand-painted wallpapers depicting scenes of the classical ruins of Rome and Athens.

"Stuart!" Claire gasped, her head swiveling around as she gaped at the spectacular room, "I've never seen anything like this in my life."

"Could use a little furniture," he noted wryly, ushering her toward a single sofa sitting in the center of the yawning expanse.

She sat down, then looked at Stuart in surprise as he seated himself at the far end of the long sofa. "Why are you sitting way over there?"

"Because if I sit any closer, we won't get any talking done."

"Honestly," she giggled. "I think you must be the horniest man ever born."

Stuart's mouth dropped open in astonishment. "Horny?" he gasped. "Miss Boudreau, I am shocked. Where did you learn a word like that?"

"Oh, I learned a whole lot of words ladies aren't supposed to know, working in a hospital full of

409

horny men. But of all of them, you have to be the horniest.''

"Well, it's not like I don't have good reason," Stuart defended. "I'm young and healthy, and I haven't made love to my wife in over a year."

"Well, no," Claire murmured, looking down. "You haven't made love to me . . ."

Stuart studied her for a long moment, then a slow smile spread across his face. "Or to anybody else," he added quietly.

Claire lifted her eyes, gazing at him hopefully.

"You're the only one I want, Claire," he said softly, moving down the length of the sofa until he was sitting next to her, "and as soon as you tell me what that sweet little Miss Alcott said that made you decide to come back to your big, horny husband, I'll show you just how much."

Claire smiled, sublimely happy to know that during all the long months of their separation, Stuart had remained true to her. "Louisa told me about a conversation she had with you where you asked her a hypothetical question about honor."

"I remember," Stuart said quietly. "I also remember that she was much too generous with the answer she gave me."

"You should have just told me about David," Claire whispered. "I wouldn't have gone back to him. David was my past, Stuart. You are my future. I knew that, even then."

"But I didn't, and I was so damned afraid I'd lose you if you knew. And then, when we went back to Savannah and you found out, I knew I'd lost you anyway. God, Claire, I'm so sorry for everything. Can you ever truly forgive me?"

With a slow, seductive smile, Claire leaned

toward her husband and deftly untied his cravat. "If y'all would quit talkin', Major," she drawled, "I might be willin' to show you how completely I've forgiven you."

Stuart's eyebrows rose at her unexpected overture, and with a groan, he leaned back, pulling her down on top of him. "Can we go upstairs, now?"

"Yes, if you want to," she purred, "or maybe you'd just rather stay here."

To her surprise, he slid out from under her and stood up. "No, not here. For a whole year, I've dreamed of making love to you again. I want to kiss and touch and taste every bit of you, and I want to do it in a big, soft bed, not on a narrow settee."

A little shiver ran down Claire's spine, and with a graceful, fluid motion, she rose also. "I am at your disposal, sir."

To her delight, Stuart swept her up in his arms, rapidly traversing the huge room and heading back into the foyer. As they passed the front door, Claire whispered, "There's something in my bag that I want. Will you put me down for just a minute?"

Stuart reluctantly set her on her feet. "Hurry!"

Throwing him a smile that promised she would, Claire dashed over to the table and picked up her reticule. Plunging her hand inside the small bag, she rummaged around for a moment, then smiled as her fingers closed around the object she was seeking.

Sauntering back to where Stuart stood, she slowly pushed her inexpensive gold wedding ring onto the third finger of her left hand. "There," she sighed, wiggling her fingers as she gazed down at the plain band, "now everything is where it should be."

"Where's your other ring?" he asked.

Claire shrugged. "I told you once before, the other ring is beautiful, but it doesn't count. This is the one that matters."

Stuart looked down into her beautiful face, so overwhelmed with happiness that he could hardly speak. "I love you, Claire Renée Boudreau," he whispered.

"And I love you, Major Stuart James Wellesley of the Fourth Massachusetts. I will love you till the day I die."

Epilogue

"You can come in now, Mr. Wellesley."

Stuart threw down the glass of brandy he was drinking and tore through the small parlor adjacent to his bedroom. "Is it over?" he demanded, his voice rough with worry. "Is she all right?"

"They're both fine," Dr. Hancock smiled, "and you have a beautiful daughter."

"A daughter," Stuart laughed, throwing his head back with delight. "Just exactly what I wanted."

He charged past a large oval mirror, pausing long enough to run his fingers through his tousled hair and tuck in his wrinkled shirt. "I look like hell, don't I?"

"Actually, you look just like every other new father I've ever seen."

Stuart took one last look at his rumpled appearance, then, with a resigned shrug, hurried on his way. Dr. Hancock shook his head and chuckled, wondering why it always seemed that women came through labor looking better than their husbands did.

Quietly, Stuart opened the bedroom door and padded across the thick carpet. "How are you doing, sweetheart?" he murmured, sitting down carefully on the edge of the bed and picking up one of Claire's limp hands.

"I'm fine," she smiled, opening her eyes and pressing his hand to her cheek. "Just a little tired. Look at our pretty little girl."

Stuart gazed down at the tiny bundle nestled in the crook of Claire's arm. Gently, he pulled back the blanket, staring in awe at the pink-and-white perfection of their child. "She's beautiful," he breathed, leaning forward to touch his lips to Claire's. "Thank you for the daughter, my love."

"I hope you're not disappointed that it wasn't a boy."

"Absolutely not. My father had to suffer through seven sons before he got one of these, but I won the prize on the first attempt. Anyway," he added, "we'll have a son next year."

"Oh, Lord," Claire groaned, "today is *not* the day that I want to think about that."

"I understand," Stuart winked. "We'll talk about it again in a couple of months."

"See?" she laughed. "I was right. You *are* the horniest man ever born."

"That may be, but look what it got us." Again, he swung his gaze over to the sleeping baby. "So, have you thought of a name?"

Claire shook her head. "Not really. I was so sure I'd have a boy that I really didn't think much about girls' names. Have you thought of anything?"

"As a matter of fact, I have."

"Really? What?"

"I'd like to name her Savannah," he said softly.

"Oh, Stuart, what a beautiful thought. Savannah Wellesley. I love it."

"I was hoping you would. I thought it was a perfect blending of North and South."

"Sort of like us," Claire murmured.

"Yes," he whispered, leaning down to gently kiss her. "Exactly like us."

They smiled at each other, sharing the beauty of the moment and the gift of their daughter.

At long last, the war was finally over.